TAKE ME TO NIRVANA

THE IS THE SECOND BOOK BY J Y BARRIS

TAKE ME TO NIRVANA

J Y BARRIS

Printed in the United States of America

First Paperback Edition, 2023

ISBN-13: 978-0999277720
ISBN-10: 0999277723

www.jybarris.com

This book is dedicated to every child abuse survivor. I know life hasn't always been kind—sometimes it's felt like nothing but a relentless cascade of lemons. But thank you. Thank you for your courage in turning each bitter moment into something a little more bearable, for still trying to make your life into something beautiful, even when the world seemed to have other plans.

If your childhood trauma still lingers, let Nirvana carry some of your sorrow. I hope, as you turn these pages, you begin to find pieces of peace, and in time, perhaps even healing. You deserve it, more than you know.

To Sam, my love, my light, my life—if only I could share with the world the depth of your heart, the strength of your soul, and the quiet ways you make everything better. You are incredible. Thank you for being my everything. And our son, Maxwell—what a gift he is. Just as he is, he's perfect, don't you think?

And to my grandma, Sau Chu—"elegant pearl." You were the embodiment of selflessness, the kindest soul I've ever known. I miss you every day, and your memory will forever hold a sacred place in my heart.

Preface

WHENEVER I COME across a heartbreaking case of child abuse in the news, I can't help but think of the children involved—how those traumatic experiences have shaped them, how they've carried those scars through their lives. Having grown up in a family where abuse was a reality, this issue has always been deeply personal to me. It's a social problem I feel strongly about, and one that I hope to help end.

With *Take Me To Nirvana*, my mission is simple: to offer hope to those affected by childhood trauma and to raise awareness about the devastating impact of child abuse, especially by their caregivers. My hope is that this book will convey a message of "you are not alone" to anyone who has faced similar struggles, and encourage them to find the courage to heal and move beyond their past.

While *Take Me To Nirvana* centers on themes of childhood abuse and trauma, it's not just a book for survivors. It's a raw, powerful psychological thriller, filled with twists and turns that will keep you on the edge of your seat. As the story unfolds, it gets darker, stranger, and sometimes even more brutal—but don't worry. It ends on a hopeful note.

So, dear reader, keep going. I can't wait to hear what you think.

J Y Barris

PART ONE

1

A ROUND OF applause rippled through the room before dying down, leaving behind a thick silence. Tom stood at the front of the classroom, facing the sea of wide, expectant eyes.

His stomach churned.

He was good at many things—fixing pipes, unclogging drains, working with his hands—but public speaking? That was a different story altogether. The very thought of it made him anxious and his heart race. He felt a wave of nausea creep up on him as he locked eyes with the students. They looked at him with a mixture of curiosity and unspoken judgment, their young faces filled with a kind of piercing intensity that perhaps only children can manage.

Tom had promised to do this, though. He was a man of his word. He *should* be able to handle this. After all, what was the worst that could happen? Well, if nothing else, he could *not* back down. He'd promised Dominique, and that had to count for something.

Still, he couldn't shake the fact that little Simon's father had just finished delivering a presentation on firefighting that was so engaging and full of passion, that Tom almost felt like he should have bowed out gracefully. The man had practically *breathed* charisma, leaving him feeling utterly deflated in comparison. Tom had spent the whole night practicing his speech, trying to sound both knowledgeable and approachable, but right now, it felt more like he was about to flop in front of an audience of critics. If only loudmouth Hunter in the back corner could keep his mouth shut for the next fifteen minutes, maybe, just maybe, this wouldn't be a complete disaster.

"... And last but not least, representing Jamie is our final guest for today's lecture—Mr. Thomas Ager. Mr. Ager, we are ready when you are ..."

Tom stood, plastering on a grin that felt more awkward than sincere. He walked up to the podium. His palms, usually steady, were slick with sweat. He placed them stiffly on the edge of the desk. *Deep breath. Just say something.*

As he opened his mouth to speak, a voice rang out from the back of the room, cutting through the tension like a knife.

"Hey! Don't you fix toilets?"

The laughter that followed was instant and explosive. Tom froze. Every inch of him stiffened as the children erupted into giggles, some of them even slapping their desks in sheer delight. The homeroom teacher, Ms. Wong, quickly intervened, trying to restore order.

"Hush, class! Hunter, would you like to spend the rest of the day in the principal's office?"

"No thanks," Hunter shot back with a mischievous grin.

"Then you know what to do."

"Sorry, sir," Hunter called to Tom, his voice still laced with laughter. "I was just trying to help lighten the mood."

"I don't think Mr. Ager needs help with that," Ms. Wong said firmly. "And I'd appreciate it if we could all behave. Understood?"

"Fine," Hunter muttered, a few more giggles slipping out of him before he settled down.

"Thank you, Ms. Wong," Tom said, trying to steady his voice. "Ahem... hello... everyone. My name is Tom Ager. You can call me Tom if you'd like." It wavered slightly, but he pushed on. "As Hunter so kindly pointed out, I'm a plumber. I work on toilets every day, but that's just a small part of my job. There's a lot more to it than meets the eye. Like most jobs, mine is made easier by tools. And I've brought a few to show you..."

Tom held up a pair of pliers. "This one here looks like a crab's claw. These are tongue-and-groove pliers. I carry a few of these with me. I'll often use two together. For example, if there's a leaking pipe, I'd use one to stabilize it while I unscrew with the other."

But as he spoke, he saw their faces fall, their enthusiasm beginning to fade. Little yawns appeared like clockwork, their eyes glazing over. He barely made it through the first tool before a few of the students were already rubbing their eyes. He couldn't help but feel a pang of self-consciousness. *This is going terribly.* And then, just as he was about to lose hope completely, little Susie, with her big round eyes and curly hair, interrupted his thoughts.

"Tom, what's that?" she asked, pointing at something near his foot.

Tom blinked in surprise and followed her finger. "Oh, this?" he asked, lifting the heavy object with a grunt. He placed it carefully on the side table and watched as the kids' eyes lit up with curiosity.

"It's a spaceship!" someone shouted, and a ripple of excitement ran through the room.

"I've got one of those at home!" another child piped up, nodding vigorously.

"It's not a spaceship, you dummies!" one of the others corrected, but the enthusiasm was undeniable.

Tom chuckled, his nerves easing ever so slightly. "Right, right. This," he said, tapping the object with a smile, "is a septic tank. A miniature one, to be exact. It's usually made of concrete or, like this one, plastic, and it's installed underground. The job of a septic tank is to collect wastewater and let it decompose over time."

A hand shot up in the air, and Tom nodded at Benny. "How big is a real one?" he asked, eyes wide.

Tom thought for a moment. "Well, a typical one is about eight feet long by six feet tall."

"Can it fit a whole person?" Benny asked, his voice filled with wonder.

"Possibly,"

"Can it fit a grown man like you?" a boy in the back asked with a mischievous smirk.

Tom raised an eyebrow. "I suppose I could squeeze in if I really tried. But trust me, you don't want to spend any time inside a septic tank. The smell alone would scare you off."

"Does it collect poop too?" a girl asked, wrinkling her nose.

"Yes," Tom replied. "It collects solid waste as well."

"Eww! That's gross!" one of the students groaned, making a face.

Tom smiled. "And that's why you don't want to play hide-and-seek in there."

Somebody said, "Looks kinda like a sleeping bag though."

"Yeah, I agree," another child piped up.

Tom chuckled, leaning into the moment. "Right. But all jokes aside, if you ever find yourself at home and your toilet isn't flushing properly, it could be a problem with the septic tank. And if that happens, you'll want your parents to call a septic maintenance provider."

"So you can't fix that?" someone asked.

"No," Tom said with a grin. "Plumbers don't handle septic systems. But that's why you have to call someone who does."

The rest of the presentation passed by in a blur of questions, some silly, some surprisingly insightful. The Q&A went on for what felt like hours, but by the time the bell rang, Tom was both exhausted and oddly relieved. The children had been engaged, and for the most part, he'd managed to keep their attention. It wasn't perfect, but it was more than he had hoped for.

As the students filed out, he spotted Dominique in the crowd and made his way over to her. She waited near the door, a faint smile on her face. She was the reason he'd braved this whole ordeal, and her opinion meant everything to him.

"You were great," she said, though her voice held a hint of discomfort. "The kids loved you."

Tom waved it off, brushing away her praise. "Nah. It was nothing special."

"I hope it didn't take you too long to prepare."

"Ten, twenty minutes," he replied casually. "Had to borrow a few props from Sam, but that's it."

"You mean the tank?" Dominique asked with a knowing look.

"Yeah," he chuckled. "Turns out it was the most interesting part of the presentation."

"Well, maybe you should work for him instead," she teased.

Tom shrugged, a wry smile tugging at his lips. "Maybe. How's John doing, by the way?"

"Busy," Dominique replied, though he could sense there was something she wasn't saying.

"Is he at work?"

"No," she said, her voice tinged with frustration. "He's up north, ice fishing with his Harley buddies. It's an annual thing, apparently."

"I'm sure," Tom replied, though he didn't say more.

"Well," she continued, "I could use some time to myself. Chores, the kids, it's a lot. You know how it is."

"Everyone deserves some time off," Tom said with a nod.

"Exactly. I might even treat myself to a manicure later," she added with a small smile. "Anyway, thank you for doing this. I know it's not easy..."

"It was no trouble," he assured her. "I'm glad I could help."

"I'm their mother, but I can't seem to hold down a job to save my life."

"There's no need to beat yourself up over this," he said gently. "Everything went just fine in the end."

Dominique's lips curled into a faint, grateful smile, but the tension in her shoulders remained. "You're too good to me, Tom," she said sincerely. "I'll do my best to make sure John steps up when Lizzie's Career Day comes around."

"If he's busy then too, just call me," Tom offered without hesitation.

But Dominique hesitated, shaking her head slightly. "I probably shouldn't bother you with this again—"

"No-no," Tom interrupted, his tone firm but kind. "I don't mind doing it over for Lizzie. I really don't."

"Honestly, I don't know why you're still so nice to me after everything..." Her voice faltered, a hint of guilt creeping into her words. "I still feel pretty bad about how we ended things."

There was an awkward pause before Tom responded. "It's no big deal, really. I care about your girls. I'll always help if I can."

Her smile widened, but before she could say anything else, Tom's phone buzzed in his pocket. He checked the screen, his expression shifting from warm to apologetic.

"It's work," he muttered. "I've got to take this. I'll see you at the Christmas party?"

"The one at *Gins*?" she asked.

"That's the one," he replied with a nod. "It's another one of those annual things."

"I'll see if I can get a sitter and if John's in the mood."

"Of course... alright, take care," Tom said, making sure she saw his final wave before turning away to answer the call.

"Hello?"

Mr. Nice Guy! Gabe's voice crackled through the line, teasing, almost too loud. *"How'd it go?"*

"The presentation? It was fine."

"So, you survived! I hope she at least thanked you."

Tom's eyes narrowed. "That's none of your business," he muttered, feeling the familiar irritation bubble up.

"Dude! Hers aren't even your kids!" Gabe nearly laughed. He couldn't resist the jab.

"So? I was glad to help."

"Right. After all, she's not the one who dumped you on your birthday and jumped into bed with the delivery guy. Oh, wait—she is!"

Tom's teeth clenched. His voice dropped to a low growl. "Remind me why I haven't fired you yet?"

"Because I'm such a good employee."

"You know, there's such a thing as 'learning when to quit.'"

Gabe just shrugged through the phone. *"I don't know what you mean, but I do know something called 'quit while you're ahead.' Although, in your case, it's more like 'quit while you still have some dignity left.'"*

"Would you get off my back already?" Tom retorted. He stopped walking in the middle of the hallway, the echo of his frustration bouncing off the walls as his face reddened.

"Come on, Tom," Gabe said, the teasing tone still present, but softer. *"You know I'm just messing with you. If you don't hear it from me, you'll hear it from someone else. It's how I show I care."*

Tom rubbed his temple, his patience fraying. "Just get to the point, alright? I don't have all day to stand here in a school hallway talking to you. What's this about?"

Right then, Gabe's tone shifted from playful to businesslike. *"Someone's here for an interview,"* he said casually.

"Really? So soon?" Tom replied, a hint of surprise in his voice. "I only posted the listing this morning."

"Not the plumber position. It's the other job."

"The other job?" He racked his brain, trying to make sense of Gabe's words. Then, like a lightbulb flicking on, he finally understood. "I see. Tell him to wait. I'll be right there."

2

AS TOM PULLED his car up outside the shop, the sight of only Gabe's vehicle parked there in the lot immediately triggered a keen instinct. *A prank,* he thought—without question. He slammed the door of his car, bracing himself against the cold gusts of the blizzard. His boots squelched in the slushy snow, a rhythmic beat to his growing irritation until he reached the shop's threshold. He shoved the door open like a bear pushing through the brush, ready to unleash his temper.

Inside, Gabe sat casually at the front cash register, comfortable, even smug, as if he had all the time in the world.

Tom shot him a glare.

"Took you long enough," Gabe said with his usual sarcasm, but Tom wasn't having it.

"This better not be another one of your stupid pranks," he barked, his voice rough with frustration.

"What do you mean?"

"You said someone came in for an interview. I rushed back, through all of this—" He gestured sharply at the storm outside, "—and why is this floor so wet?"

Gabe just shrugged, his expression one of easy indifference. "Look to your left."

Tom did. At the crack of his office door, he saw her—a young brunette with shoulder-length hair, sitting in the dim light, drenched from head to toe in her sweat suit.

"It's a lady, by the way, and she walked here," Gabe informed him.

"In this weather?" Tom's voice had dropped to a murmur of disbelief.

"I've got no idea. But I'm out of here. Cal's coming in at two. Don't call me unless it's an emergency. I'll be at the studio practicing with the band. All night."

"Who's covering for you?" Tom asked.

"Tim and I switched shifts last week. Didn't I tell you?"

"You probably did," he muttered, rubbing a hand over his face, "But I've had a mountain of stuff on my plate lately. Guess it slipped my mind."

"Yeah, yeah," Gabe teased. "I'm sure. You've got your 'tasks' to deal with, right?"

"Some," he replied, not in the mood for Gabe's mockery.

Gabe flashed him a smirk. "Can't say I'm surprised. But don't bring this place down with you, no matter what you do. I happen to like my job."

"What are you complaining about? Business is going great. I could just use a little help keeping things in order."

"You've got that right. No offense, but you can't organize for shit."

Tom rolled his eyes. "I thought you were leaving?"

Gabe didn't answer, he just turned and walked out with a casual "Peace out" over his shoulder.

Left alone, Tom stood still for a moment, taking in the strange scene before him. He grabbed a dry towel from the supply closet and then approached his office door. With a distinct knock, he waited.

The woman turned her head at the sound, her eyes meeting his. Her gaze was magnetic—huge, deep brown eyes that seemed to pull him in, yet guarded with a quiet intensity. Her features were delicate but strong, a well-defined jawline and high cheekbones, and she wore her expression with a certain unreadable poise. Tom felt a flutter in his chest as his eyes roamed over her face, and for a moment, he was completely transfixed. He cleared his throat, trying to regain some composure before stepping into the room.

"Hi. Thanks for coming in," Tom said, forcing his voice to sound steady as he sat down opposite her.

"Mr. Erik...?"

"Oh, no," he corrected quickly. "Erik Ager was my father. I took over the shop after he passed away two years ago."

"I'm sorry," the woman said softly, her eyes briefly dropping to the floor. "I just assumed when I saw the banner outside."

"No need to apologize. It happens all the time," Tom said with a dismissive wave. "I'm Tom, by the way. I'm sorry for the wait. The weather's really something today." He was about to continue when his eyes fell on her clothes—sopping wet. "I heard you walked here," he said, his tone shifting with curiosity.

She nodded, a faint blush rising in her cheeks as she avoided his gaze.

He offered her the towel. "Here. I thought you might like to dry off."

The woman hesitated before politely refusing, glancing out the window as though she was reluctant to linger. "No need. I don't think this storm will let up any time soon. By the time I get home, I'll be drenched again anyway."

"You must not live far."

"About twenty minutes."

"On foot?" Tom asked, genuinely surprised.

She nodded, swallowing nervously. "I saw the sign in your window. I noticed it the other day."

"It's been up for a while," he said with a half-smile. "But I can't say I've had much luck finding anyone for this position." His eyes swept across the room before landing back on her. "You brought an ID?"

She nodded, reaching into her pocket and handing him her driver's license without a word.

"'Amber Simmons,'" he read out.

"That's me," she replied firmly. "Sorry for not introducing myself earlier. It's just... I've never been to a job interview before."

"That's fine," Tom said, leaning back in his chair. "We're pretty chill here. But just to be clear, you know this is a part-time cleaning position."

"I'm aware, yes."

"The pay is ten dollars an hour, working two hours a day, three days a week. We pay biweekly."

She didn't say anything for a moment, and when she spoke, her voice was quieter. "Biweekly... meaning every two weeks?"

He nodded, watching her closely.

"I see..." She trailed off, her shoulders sagging slightly. "I was afraid of that."

Tom couldn't ignore the downcast look on her face—the subtle flash of disappointment. "Why is this job important to you?" he asked gently, leaning forward. "You don't strike me as someone who would settle for something mundane like this."

She swallowed again. "May I be frank?"

"Of course."

"This is the only option available to me right now, given my situation," she explained. "Yours is the only place hiring besides the coffee shop around the corner. They already turned me down once... so..."

Tom let her words hang in the air briefly. "I see. May I be frank as well?"

She looked up, waiting. "Please."

"Do you have a family to support?" he asked, blunt but kind.

"No," she answered quickly, almost too quickly. "No family. But I really need money. I'll work hard. I swear. I want to work longer hours if possible."

Tom paused, weighing his next words carefully. "I understand. But the problem is, my shop is small. There's really not much to clean or maintain."

Amber's face fell slightly, her gaze dropping to her lap. He watched as the hope in her eyes slowly dimmed, her brows knitting together in a deepening frown as if the weight of an uncertain and daunting future had just been placed upon her. Though Tom knew he wasn't required to step in, something inside him stirred—a deep, undeniable sense of moral responsibility. It was like so many of his "extracurricular tasks"—once his emotions became involved, there was no shaking them off until he found a way forward. In this case, that meant creating a position for her, even if it was one from thin air, which, in the end, was exactly what he did.

"You know what? In addition to cleaning, how would you feel about becoming a field dispatcher? It'll be full-time and pays more."

"A field dispatcher?" Amber blinked.

"Yup," he continued to explain, "You'll take customer calls and dispatch the next available worker from our system. I'll have to put together some training for you, but it should be simple, especially if you're willing to learn."

She looked at him, something in her eyes shifting—perhaps relief, perhaps gratitude. "I'll learn. I promise."

"Great. Then it's settled," Tom said, a grin forming despite himself. "How does starting tomorrow sound?"

Amber's lips parted slightly, and for a brief moment, she did not know what to say. But then, she smiled—a full, bright smile that made Tom's chest tighten for reasons he didn't quite understand.

"It's perfect," she said softly.

"Good," he replied, offering her a small smile in return. "Welcome aboard, Ms. Simmons."

3

OF ALL CUSTOMERS Erik's Plumbing Co. had ever serviced, three stuck out in Tom's mind like a sore thumb. Mrs. Mackin, the cat hoarder; Mr. Eells, the 600-pound food fetishist; and, of course, Mr. Tilly. Tilly was a relic of his father's past, an old acquaintance from high school—though, by Tilly's own telling, they were life-long best friends, a claim that always seemed to shift with the wind if it benefited him. Once, in his prime, Tilly had been a car mechanic, athletic, and a smooth talker with a knack for charming the lonely housewives in town. But these days, he was better known as "Old Flirt Tilly," a fixture at the local dive bars, peddling dirty jokes in exchange for cigarette drags.

"How much longer is this gonna take?" Tilly complained as he leaned against the bathroom doorframe, arms crossed, a frown tugging at his lips.

Tom didn't even look up from the toilet he was working on. "Not much longer," he muttered, tightening the bolt with precision.

"You can't put an old head on young shoulders these days," Tilly continued with mock disappointment. "Your old man would have had this done by now."

Tom bit back a sigh, keeping his face carefully neutral. "Well, too bad my old man isn't here taking charge anymore," he replied, his tone colder than he intended.

Tilly chuckled, his thick fingers tapping the doorframe. "You should've sent Gabe. He's slow like you, but at least he's got a sense of humor. You know, makes the wait a little more... tolerable."

Tom barely suppressed an eye-roll. "I'll keep that in mind for next time." His hands worked methodically, trying to ignore Tilly's incessant prattling. He tried shifting the mood, making small talk as he wrapped up the job. "Sorry about Mr. Haworth's passing. I heard you two were close."

Tilly's face momentarily softened. His tone shifted, becoming almost reflective. "We went way back... At least with him dead, I can finally put to bed the fact that he slept with my wife... well, ex-wife."

Tom blinked, his wrench pausing mid-turn. "Excuse me?" he asked, unsure if he had heard him right.

Tilly leaned in, his eyes gleaming with a mixture of pride and mischief. "You know Mindy Stewart?"

"Yes, but... is that true?"

"You bet," Tilly said, nodding with smug certainty. "To be fair, I hit on his missus first. He went behind my back after I was done messing with her. It was a revenge thing."

"So, you slept with Mrs. Haworth?" Tom's voice came out in a whisper, as if the question itself was too unbelievable to ask.

Tilly chuckled like he was recounting an old, funny story, chest puffing out a little. "You're sharp, boy. How could he blame me, though? The woman was a damn gift. Perkiest pair of tits in town, and everybody knew it. He should've thought twice before marrying a bombshell like her..."

Tom stared, disbelieving. Tilly caught his gaze, then grinned as if savoring the shock on Tom's face. "What? Don't look so stunned. You know your Uncle Tilly. I was the king of all flirts back in the day."

"It's not that. I've just never heard anyone talk about Mrs. Haworth like that."

Tilly's grin widened. "Oh, it's nothing. I've met plenty more like her in my lifetime. Many of them I've laid with, too."

"Really?"

"Yeah, really. Most of 'em were as dumb as bricks and rubbish in the sack, anyway. Well, all but one, maybe..." Tilly paused dramatically, eyes narrowing as he went into a trance, clearly lost in thought. "There was one very, very special lady..."

Tom raised an eyebrow. "Who?" he asked.

Tilly's face grew serious. "This woman was out of this world. She had that whole Audrey Hepburn vibe—smart, proper, and, damn it, unattainable. By far the most fascinating woman I ever had the privilege of getting to know." His voice softened, tinged with a rare sincerity. "I would've married her, you know. If I could have."

Tom, now intrigued, leaned in slightly. "What happened?"

Tilly's eyes darkened as he shifted his body, his hands falling to his sides as if weighed down by the memory. "She disappeared. Last I heard, she's still on the missing persons list at the sheriff's office."

Tom's eyes widened. "Hold on—are you talking about Catherine Shor, the pianist?"

"So you've heard too."

Tom nodded slowly. "Of course. She became a town legend when she went missing. Isn't her husband some famous composer?"

Tilly grinned knowingly. "He was famous, sure. But not exactly a warm person. At least, that's what Catherine always told me."

"Did you two actually go out?"

"Oh, no," Tilly replied quickly, shaking his head, a faint chuckle escaping his lips. "We had flings here and there, but we weren't really an item. There was a time, though, I was seriously thinking about eloping with her."

He got quiet for a moment, his gaze drifting. "In the end, though, she was loyal to her man, even after everything..."

Before Tilly could continue his story, Tom's phone buzzed in his pocket. He checked the screen, noting the time, and immediately felt the pressure of his next job. He couldn't afford to linger.

"I'm all done here," he told Tilly.

Tilly blinked as if snapping back to the present. "Oh yeah? It flushes and everything?"

Tom nodded, wiping his hands on a rag. "It flushes and everything. Yup."

"Thank goodness," Tilly said. "How much do I owe you?"

"One hundred and fifty," Tom replied flatly.

"Ah..." Tilly grumbled. "That's steep."

"It's the rate we've always charged."

"Your old man must have been giving me the friends-and-family discount," Tilly smirked, his eyes glinting mischievously.

Tom shrugged, not wanting to get into the weeds of that particular conversation. "All right... I'll knock thirty bucks off. As a thank you for sharing your story."

Tilly's eyes lit up at the offer. "Stories you like, huh? I've got plenty of those..."

"I don't want to waste time haggling, Mr. Tilly," Tom cut in, holding out his hand firmly. "How about one hundred even? Please, just pay me so I can get out of your hair. I have another appointment."

Tilly hesitated for a moment, but then smiled, reaching for a five-dollar bill and a quarter. "A hundred it is, then. Let's see what I've got in here..." He fumbled through his worn-out pockets, mumbling to himself.

Tom shifted uncomfortably, his gaze lingering on the dirty socks tangled with crumpled receipts and fast food wrappers strewn across the room. A sudden wave of sympathy washed over him, and for a brief moment, he looked away, his heart unexpectedly softening at the sight of the chaotic, neglected space.

Tilly chuckled, counting out change. "I must have misplaced my wallet somewhere."

"Never mind," Tom said, not even looking at him.

"What did you say?"

"I mean, it's okay. Keep your money," Tom said, his tone firm.

Tilly's face twisted in protest. "Oh no. Old soldiers like me don't owe anybody anything."

"You don't. Consider it a holiday gift from me."

"No-no. I don't need you doing me any favors—"

"Consider this a... a small token of gratitude for your service to our country," Tom said, cutting him off before Tilly could argue further.

Tilly's expression wavered for a moment. "Well, if you insist..." He finally relented, nodding as he hurriedly tucked his money away. "Your old man would've been proud of you. He always liked you more than your brother because, well... you're inherently him—a good, generous man."

Tom's face tightened slightly, and he muttered, "If only that second part were true."

"Sure it is! Why else would he have left you the shop? He trusted you to take good care of it. And you have," Tilly insisted, his voice filled with a surprising sense of earnestness.

"If you say so... It doesn't matter anymore anyway," Tom replied, adjusting his coat. "I should get going."

"Okay..." Tilly said slowly, but then he stopped Tom with a hand on his arm. "Oh, wait—just one last thing," he added, his voice suddenly conspiratorial. "You know Billy from the old key shop? He's been out of work, but he's too scared to tell his wife. Damn coward. Anyway, you might want to check with him for your janitor position. He's desperate—probably lowball him and save a few bucks, eh?"

Tom paused for a second. "Thanks for the tip, but we hired someone last week."

Tilly's eyes gleamed, clearly surprised. "Oh? Who?"

"She's from out of state," Tom replied, keeping his answer short.

Tilly leaned forward eagerly. "Is that right? Should've swung by this morning to introduce myself..." he trailed off, sweeping his long, scraggly hair back as if preparing for an encounter.

"She's young. Much younger than you," Tom added bluntly, trying to snap Tilly out of whatever fantasy he was indulging.

Tilly gave a sly grin. "I like them young. The chirpier, the better—less clumsy, you know? Is she slim? Or Asian?"

"She's fine. You wouldn't miss her in a crowd..." Tom said causally, but there was a faint smile tugging at his lips.

"I see. So, you're hot for her, I take it?" Tilly teased him, narrowing his eyes knowingly.

Tom shot back quickly, too defensively. "What? Me? No way." His voice cracked slightly as he stumbled to recover. "We're colleagues," he added, his voice a little too loud.

Tilly wasn't fooled. "So what? You gonna ask her out?"

Tom's face reddened on the spot. "I haven't really thought about it... Besides, I just got out of a relationship."

Tilly raised an eyebrow. "Wasn't that two months ago?"

"How did you—"

"Know? Dominique talks. And let me tell you, she's moved on. She's smitten with that delivery guy, John. Been for a while now."

Tom stared at him, dumbfounded. "I don't know... Dating someone from work can be complicated. She probably has a boyfriend anyway."

"What happened to your confidence?" Tilly shot back, his voice almost urgent. "If you don't ask her out, I'm gonna." He flexed his muscles, clearly proud of himself.

"She's twenty-one."

"So? I'm in my sixties, but I'm still spry. Hell, I'm like a stallion on steroids!"

"Believe me, she's out of your league," Tom insisted, but Tilly wasn't done.

"Well, someone has to go for it, Tommy Boy," he pressed. "Or you can sit around like your old man did— waiting for someone else to snatch her up. Like your mom running off with your uncle, eh? By the time you realized it, it was too late to do anything about it."

Tom's face tightened. "Thanks for the reminder."

"I'm just telling it like it is," Tilly said, a wicked gleam in his eye. "This is a cruel world we're living in. Unless you want to finish last, stop snoozing and make a move."

4

GABE MIGHT NOT have been Tom's most seasoned employee, but there was no doubt he was the most coveted—especially by their female clientele. At only twenty-five, the charming, witty, and undeniably good-looking young man had a talent for winning over the hearts of nearly every woman who crossed his path. It wasn't that Gabe was any less of a player than the next guy—his reputation as a notorious heartbreaker was well-earned—but it was that same silver-tongued charisma that kept pulling women in.

Since Amber had started working at the shop, Gabe had made it his mission to impress her. Today was no exception. As usual, he was at the counter, effortlessly leaning against the edge like he was the star of a show, flashing his sleeve of inked tattoos as if he were unveiling a hidden treasure. Amber, standing nearby, was looking at them with genuine interest. Gabe was in his element, basking in the attention as he talked her ear off, his voice smooth and confident, laced with that signature charm. It wasn't that Tom minded a little banter or camaraderie—*that* he could handle. But Gabe's constant parade of excessive flirtations and playful boasts was beginning to wear on him. He could feel the familiar stir of irritation as he overheard their conversation from the next room.

"Did that hurt?" Amber asked, curious as she leaned in closer, her eyes tracing the intricate designs on Gabe's arm.

"Some of it. Others were a breeze," Gabe replied with a cocky grin, rolling his sleeve back to reveal the full extent of his ink. His voice dropped into a more intimate tone, leaning closer as if sharing a secret. "This one," he was saying, gesturing to a dragon wrapping around his inner arm, "was the worst. Hurt like hell. Man, I cried like a baby. But once it's done, it's forever, right? Totally worth the pain. Every penny spent."

Amber smiled, eyes twinkling as she continued to study the tattoos. "This graffiti-style one is my favorite."

"Mine too!" Gabe said, visibly perking up. "Got it two days after Cal, our lead guitarist, accepted me into his band. I play bass. It's a passion project right now, but who knows? If our manager can get us some solid gigs, I might go full-time."

"'Animosity,'" Amber read aloud, her finger tracing the words inked on his arm.

"That's us," Gabe said, his eyes practically sparkling. "Five guys, one kickass name. You think the world's ready for us?"

Amber shrugged playfully. "I'm sure," she replied.

"You should come down to the pub sometime to watch us play," Gabe urged, his voice taking on an almost irresistible pitch. "Do you like punk rock?"

"Honestly, I haven't listened to much of it," Amber admitted, her smile slightly sheepish.

"It doesn't matter," Gabe said with a wave of his hand, as if her lack of punk knowledge was nothing. "We rock playing live! It's a whole different experience when we're on stage, especially when the crowd's hyped. You wait till three weeks from now... I'm *pumped* for it!"

"What's happening in three weeks?"

"You haven't heard? It's the Christmas party at *Gins*. It's a huge tradition here, every year," he explained excitedly. "They host local artists, people from all walks of life. Drinks are free, too. Always a plus. That place's gonna be packed for sure. So... Am," He leaned in just a little closer, nudging Amber's elbow gently with his. "Are you up for the challenge?"

"What challenge?" she asked cautiously.

"Do you play any instruments? Or maybe sing? I'm betting you've got a killer voice."

Amber's cheeks pinkened slightly. "Oh, no. I can hum along to a tune, but that's about it. I used to play piano, but I wasn't very good."

"That's fine."

"Yeah?"

"Absolutely!" Gabe exclaimed as he looked Amber over with admiration. "As long as you've got the guts to step up on that stage, people will *definitely* clap for you. I, for one, will be in the front row, cheering you on. You can count on that. Seriously." He gave her a wink as if sealing the promise with an unspoken guarantee. His flattering encouragement naturally made Amber smile. Her smile lingered briefly, a fleeting moment of warmth shared between them, one that didn't escape Tom's notice. Like a green-eyed beetle caught in a trap, his forbearance was wearing thin, the urge to interrupt clawing at him. He couldn't sit through another one of Gabe's self-indulgent rants.

"Gabe, seriously," he cut in, his tone more clipped than usual. "Stop harassing Ms. Simmons with all your band crap."

Gabe blinked, momentarily taken aback, but then recovered. "Excuse me?"

"Yeah, you heard me," Tom said, not bothering to sugarcoat it.

Amber, sensing the tension building, quickly stepped in. "Gabe's not harassing me. We were just having a little chat," she reassured Tom, her voice calm but firm.

Gabe, ever the smooth operator, took the opportunity to throw his arm casually around Amber's shoulder, pulling her into a side hug. "See? Told you she's my kind of girl. Right, Am?"

Tom clenched his fists, resisting the urge to pry them apart. "And which kind is that, exactly?"

"Musicians," Gabe replied with a grin, as if it were the most obvious thing in the world.

Amber raised an eyebrow. "I thought Mr. Ager was in your band, too?"

"Hell no! Tom can't play for shit, or sing," Gabe declared loudly, glancing at Tom with a mischievous smile. "No offense, boss."

"Ha-ha, funny," Tom muttered, trying to suppress the snarl building up inside him. "You've got that thing to do tonight, don't you?"

"What thing?" Gabe looked at him blankly, clearly not picking up on Tom's subtle hint.

"You know... that urgent thing."

His eyes widened, and he finally understood. "Oh, that thing, right," he said with a dramatic sigh, stepping back to gather his things, not without one last smirk in Tom's direction.

As Gabe made his exit, Amber walked toward Tom, handing him the weekly report. "Here you go, sir," she said, her tone warm but professional. "I've highlighted all the dates when we could've used an extra hand as you asked."

"Thank you, Ms. Simmons," Tom replied with a smile, trying to be friendly as he accepted the report. "I'll look it over in the morning."

"Sure thing. If there's nothing else, I'll be off, then."

Tom glanced at the clock. "Is it already six?"

Amber nodded.

"Time flies when you're busy, right?"

Feeling awkward about the side talk, she offered Tom a mild smile. "Well, I should go. Have a good evening, sir."

As she turned to leave, though, Tom's voice unexpectedly cut through the silence. "Ms. Simmons."

She stopped, turning back. "Yes, sir?"

"Please, call me Tom," he said softly, more gently than before.

"And me, Amber," she replied, her tone light.

"Right..."

She hesitated, a faint unease crossing her face. "Is something the matter?" she asked.

"No, no," Tom said, quickly brushing it off. "How's the training going?"

"I finished it last week."

"Already? That was fast. There was quite a bit of material."

"I guess Gabe's a good teacher. Nothing he showed me was too difficult to understand."

He nodded. "Good, very good..."

When he fell silent, Amber assumed the conversation had ended and started to turn away. But just as she moved, he couldn't help himself. "Do you like Chinese?"

Amber stopped, her expression a little more guarded now. "Chinese?"

"Yeah. There's a place a few blocks away. They've got a decent menu, I thought..."

Amber interrupted him. "I'm not really hungry," she said curtly.

Her bluntness hit Tom like a splash of cold water. He fought the urge to flinch, his face betraying the sting of her refusal.

She softened the blow with a half-smile. "Maybe some other time?"

"Sure... some other time," he said, trying to recover, though his voice was less steady than he'd hoped.

After Amber left the shop rather hurriedly, Gabe, unable to stay quiet for long, chimed in with his usual smirk. "Man, I didn't know you liked her like *that*, but after witnessing *that*... yeah, you're never getting past the friend zone. You would be lucky even to reach the friend zone."

"She has a boyfriend?" Tom asked, his voice flat, though he already knew the answer.

"I'm not sure about that, but... 'Do you like Chinese?' Ha! Did you steal that pitch from a twelfth-grader?"

"I panicked, okay?" Tom grumbled, rubbing a hand over his face. "What's wrong with *Woks*?"

"Nothing. It's you that's wrong," Gabe shot back with a laugh.

"Do I even want to hear this?"

"I'm just saying—don't go bouncing off the walls like that until you figure out what she likes first," he warned Tom, crossing his arms, his lips curling into an amused grin.

Tom exhaled a heavy sigh. "You say it like it's easy," he muttered, his shoulders slumping slightly.

Gabe snorted, raising an eyebrow. "And you're talking like it's your first time asking out a lady. Come on, man, you're not a rockstar like me, but you've got the whole package."

Tom's gaze flickered toward him. "You think?"

"I don't think. I know," he shot back, his confidence unwavering. "When it comes down to it, every woman wants a nice guy—especially a successful one who doesn't look like he's been sleepwalking through life."

Tom ran a hand through his hair, the frustration morphing into self-doubt. "I don't know... My exes seemed to find me dull, even when I tried to crack a joke. My humor just came off flat, like it never wants to land." He sighed again, voice low.

Gabe's lips curled into a knowing grin. "Tell me about it. But come on, don't let that mess with your head. You're thirty-five, not ancient."

Tom shifted uncomfortably, feeling the weight of those words more than he cared to admit. "I could be old to her."

"Old? To her?" Gabe almost shouted, wanting to shake some sense into him. "There are tons of women out there who prefer the mature, experienced type. Hell, they *crave* that. You, my friend, are ripe for the picking. But— you're stuck, man. You're stuck in the past, constantly trying to be the knight in shining armor for your exes. It's like you've forgotten you have a life of your own."

Tom stiffened, narrowing his eyes. "I'm only there for them when they need me, as a friend."

"Yeah, sure," Gabe replied with a hint of sarcasm. "Keep telling yourself that. You're not fooling anyone."

"What do you want me to do? Not help them?"

"That's a start."

"Humph, I'm not self-centered like you..."

"Self-centered? Well, excuse me for putting my own life first," Gabe retorted, slightly offended by Tom's slip of the tongue. He jabbed a finger toward him, emphasizing his point. "You're not some saint. You help them because, deep down, you think one of them will come running back to you. And that, my friend, is pathetic."

Tom clenched his jaw, the sting of Gabe's words landing with painful precision. He paused briefly before continuing, his voice rough. "Fine. Maybe I'm pathetic. We're too different for any comparison anyway."

Gabe shrugged as if no offense had been taken. "I'll give you that," he said, "but I think we're more alike than you realize. You just won't listen to good advice when it's staring you in the face."

"What are you suggesting now?"

"Need I say more? If you want to make any progress with women, you've got to stop letting your past relationships control you. Forget about your exes, especially *Dominique*," he added, throwing a pointed look. "And remember, 'every new girl is a brand-new adventure.' You've got to look forward, not backward."

Tom grimaced, rubbing the back of his neck. "You're not gonna sing me a song again, are you?"

Gabe chuckled, a low, husky sound. "I don't need to, but thanks for noticing. In any case, let's go," he said, heading for the door. "I'm starving. How about some cheap Chinese food?"

Tom shot him a wary look. "Nah, I'm good. I'm eating alone at my place. You're just looking for someone to pay the bill."

"Seriously? Man, that's just sad. But, hey, I've been talking to Amber more lately, and I think I can help you out. I've got a few pointers on what she likes, what she doesn't. You're welcome."

Tom paused, considering the offer. "No tricky business?"

"I swear," Gabe responded, his grin widening but there was a level of sincerity in his tone. "And while we're at it, I'll help fine-tune your dating skills. Trust me, you could use it."

"This dinner's gonna be interesting."

He let out a loud, triumphant laugh. "See what happens when you hang out with me? You're already improving your sense of humor." He slapped Tom on the back, leading him toward the door. "Let's walk and talk. You know what they say about the ladies: you've got to be spontaneous. Make them think they can't say no."

"I thought I was doing that."

"That's where you were wrong. Sometimes just being spontaneous isn't enough. It takes planning and good timing. A little finesse."

Tom rolled his eyes, but the tiniest spark of hope glimmered in his chest. *Maybe Gabe was onto something, after all.*

5

MBER RAN. IT wasn't just running—it was survival. She pushed herself through the slushy, icy sidewalks, each step feeling like an assault against her bones. Her feet slipped beneath her, but she didn't stop. She couldn't.

Her legs were shaking from exhaustion, the bitter chill biting at her skin. Finally, her body refused to keep moving, and she staggered to a halt, bent over with her hands pressed hard against her knees. Her breath came in harsh, ragged bursts, but then, she lifted her head. And there he was—Michael.

He stood on the doorstep of her trailer, leaning casually against the railing, his silhouette cutting in the dim light. The sight of him made Amber's heart drop like a stone into the pit of her stomach. She *was late*—too late. She knew Michael wasn't the one she needed to fear, though. No. That horror was waiting inside, behind the thick, curtained-off steel walls of a home.

Him.

With a shaky breath, Amber squared her shoulders, forced her feet to move, and trudged toward the door. She kept her eyes on the ground, too afraid to meet Michael's gaze. As she reached the door, Michael's voice sliced through the cold air, his tone too calm, too knowing.

"I wouldn't go in if I were you."

Amber's hand hovered over the doorknob, her heart stuttering. The words clung to her like cobwebs, heavy and stifling.

She glanced at him, but his expression was unreadable, though the subtle motion of his hand brought a chill to her spine—he mimicked a drinking gesture. Amber's stomach churned. She swallowed hard, trying to force her voice steady.

"When did he get home?" she whispered.

"Too early, apparently," Michael replied, his eyes flicking briefly to the trailer, then back to her. He raised an eyebrow, as if weighing whether or not to add something else. "Need a hand?"

Amber shook her head sharply, the last thing she needed was anyone else involved. She felt the heat rise in her face, irritation creeping through her veins.

"Stay out of this, Michael. I will handle him."

She didn't wait for another word. Her hand closed around the doorknob with an almost desperate force. She breathed in deeply, trying to calm the storm inside her, but it was useless. She couldn't calm it now.

The door creaked as it opened, a sound far too loud for the fragile moment. She stepped into the darkness, the quiet broken only by the murmur of a wrestling match on the TV. The room smelled stale—sweat, old beer, and something far worse—something Amber had come to loathe.

Mason was there, sprawled on the couch, a half-empty carton of beer bottles scattered across the floor at his feet. He looked like he'd been waiting for her, his gaze daunting and cold, his posture stiff with barely contained rage. His bloodshot eyes glared at her as she entered, and Amber's pulse quickened.

Here we go.

"Where the hell have you been?" His voice was low, guttural, dripping with accusation.

Amber felt her body tighten, every muscle instinctively pulling inward. She needed a moment, just a moment, to think. To breathe.

But she couldn't afford to stand there in silence. He would only grow angrier. So she did what she always did—she turned and walked toward the bedroom. She couldn't give him the satisfaction of seeing her flinch.

Mason's footfalls were immediate, heavy, and unrelenting behind her. His anger followed her like a shadow, closing in, and then—

BANG!

The bedroom door was kicked open with a force that instantaneously knocked her over to the floor, sending a jolt of terror through her. Amber barely had time to react before Mason was there, towering over her, his breath hot against her face. His hands balled into fists by his sides, but he didn't touch her—*yet.*

"How dare you walk off while I was talking to you?" His voice cracked with fury, each word a venomous lash.

Amber's heart slammed against her ribs, but she wasn't about to back down. Slowly, she rose to her feet. Her body ached, but she made herself stand tall. Her back straightened, despite the overwhelming weight of him in the tight space.

"You don't need to yell," she said, her voice firmer than she felt. She took a slow step back, making sure her words were clear, measured. "I'm right here. And I'm not your servant to command."

His laugh was a low, gravelly sound, a cruel thing that scraped along her nerves. "Don't give me that load of shit! I'll speak in whatever fucking volume I please! What the *hell* can you do about it?"

Amber's stomach twisted with disgust. She muttered, barely a breath, "Nothing."

Mason's lip curled, a savage smirk that didn't touch his eyes. He advanced on her, his massive frame closing the distance between them, filling the room with suffocating heat. "You got that right. So tell me—where the hell were you?"

After weeks of enduring his cruelty, Amber had come to recognize the full extent of his threats. After all, Mason was an insecure, fat scumbag beyond redemption, a belligerent redneck who took pleasure in tormenting women. She knew all too well not to dodge his question further. A lie was her only armor.

She swallowed the bitter taste that rose in her throat and replied with as much calm as she could muster. "I went to Gerry's. I knew you were coming home, so I checked to see if they had steak. Now, if you would just give me some privacy, I'd like to get changed and fix dinner."

Mason didn't speak for a moment, his gaze narrowing as he looked her over. Then, he sneered. "You're telling me you went *nowhere* except to the grocery store? Nowhere else?"

"That's what I said," she answered flatly, her voice steady but low.

Mason's face twisted with rage, his fists clenching, knuckles cracking in the tense silence. *He didn't buy it.* She could see the wheels turning in his head. He was going to tear through her words, rip her apart if she didn't answer right.

"*Look me in the face* when I'm talking to you!" Mason's voice was like thunder, demanding attention. His glare drilled into her.

Amber's eyes met his—cool, unwavering, like a glacier in the face of a storm. "That's right," she said, "I went to Gerry's and came straight back—"

"Then where is the stuff?"

She kept her composure. "They don't have steak."

"So, you went shopping for *nothing* for two fucking hours?" His voice was rising now, thick with disbelief, like he couldn't even begin to fathom the explanation.

Amber's pulse was pounding in her ears, the quiet hum of fear vibrating, but she stood firm. "Well... I—" she began, but the uncertainty in her voice was enough to send Mason into a frenzy.

"Don't you *fucking* utter another word! Who do you take me for? You think you can fool me with that cunt face of yours!" A harsh comment exploded from his mouth. His foot shot out and kicked the dresser so hard the wood groaned beneath the impact. The sound of it was a deafening crack, and the dresser rocked violently, toppling over onto the floor with a resounding crash.

The force of his rage hit Amber like a tidal wave, but before she could react, Mason was already moving toward her. He stalked forward, his body like a predator's—controlled, lethal, a large mass and fury. He reached her in an instant, his hand closing around her arm, pulling her toward him intensely.

Amber hardly had time to think. The world seemed to tilt, spinning around her. "Let me explain," she said, her voice a little breathless, but still attempting to maintain that edge of control. She knew it was probably futile. The moment his rage had exploded, reason had no place here. But she had to try.

Meanwhile, Mason yanked her closer, his face inches from hers, his breath hot and rancid against her skin. He jammed his nose against the crown of her head to give it a decisive whiff. "You've been *lying*, haven't you? You think I can't smell him on you? Huh? You think I don't know you've been sneaking around behind my back to see that piece of shit again?"

His accusation was deadly, and before she could respond, his hand shot out with brutal speed and smacked her across the cheek. The sting was immediate, an explosion of pain that sent her reeling.

She stumbled, just managing to catch herself on the edge of the bed. The force of the slap left her dazed, her skin burning. Before she could gather herself, Mason was there, growling.

"Stay down, you cunt! Did I tell you to get up? Don't forget, if I hadn't saved you that night, you'd still be stuck on that highway in the cold. You could've died, and I wouldn't have cared."

His eyes, dark and stormy with anger, bore down on her, suffocating her with their madness. Her chest heaved, trying to gather air. She wouldn't break. She couldn't break. Not now.

"You're right. I might've been dead if it weren't for you then. But if this is how you're going to treat me, you might as well have left me there."

Her words hit Mason like a slap. He sneered, a low, almost mocking chuckle escaping his lips.

"Ha! I might as well have—"

"You might as well just kill me." Her voice was sharp, cutting through the room like a blade. She held his gaze, her eyes locked on his with an intensity that almost seemed to dare him to challenge her. Her body was tense, coiled like a spring ready to snap, yet there was a quiet defiance in her posture.

She wasn't cowering.

For a moment, he stood there, frozen, his arrogance gleaming in his eyes as he tried to regain control of the situation. "Don't dare me. You don't want to see what I'm capable of. I took pity on you and took you in. You don't even need to lift a fucking finger, and you get money to put food on the table. Do you have any idea how lucky you are?"

"I wanted to get a job, but you wouldn't let me."

"This is my house, my rules!"

"*You are hardly ever home!* I don't know what you expect me to do by myself around here."

"You could have cleaned this place spotless, you could have had dinner prepared before I got home, but no... no, instead, you had to go behind my back and fuck me around, you *fucking*, ungrateful whore!"

He smacked her once again. This time, her nose started to bleed. Outraged, Amber wiped off the blood with the back of her hand and persevered resolutely.

"Where's the proof... Where's your fucking proof!" she yelled. "Don't you accuse me of something I didn't do just because you think you can. You were gone for two weeks, Mason! Two fucking weeks. I was stuck here, alone, in this cage you call a house. So yeah, I went out— just to the shops. That's all. I walked there, I walked back. How is that a crime? How the *fuck* does that justify this— *this*—the punishment you think I deserve?"

Her voice cracked with the undercurrent of her anger, but she quickly steadied it, her eyes burning with the fury of someone who knew she wasn't wrong, someone who was done begging for understanding.

"If you don't believe me, I'll have nothing further to say..."

As she spoke bravely, Mason, on the other hand, had shifted his focus from her words to the image of her sitting there, half-clad, vulnerable. Her resistance, however fragile, had stirred something inside him, something that thrilled at the power he wielded, at the way he could make her tremble even while she stood her ground.

He could tell she was afraid. Amber was doing her best to hide it, but he could smell the fear rolling off her in waves. "Was that all?" he smirked.

"Yes. Nothing more, nothing less," Amber replied firmly and quickly, her eyes defiant despite the slightest tremor in her voice. Her response should've ended the argument, but for Mason, it only deepened the hunger, the unsettling awareness of how badly he wanted to dominate, to strip her of whatever little pride she had left. His anger had morphed into something darker, more primal.

His gaze fell over her, and he couldn't stop himself from seeing her as a thing to claim, a thing to possess. She was his, in his house, under his rules.

Without thinking, he moved quickly, his hands grasping her arm and forcing her to turn over, the suddenness of the action making her gasp. "You don't get to leave this easily," he muttered, his voice almost a whisper, thick with dark intent.

Amber realized hell had come when she heard him wrestling his belt off. Soon, she felt his flabby belly press up against her, and somewhere in there—his protruding thing. His hands came around to fondle her breasts while his mouth, rubbing behind her ear, opened to moan. She knew, by the sheer size and strength of him, this would never be a fair fight. The odds were too stacked against her, and so she remained silent, resigned to endure for her own safety. Her body stiffened beneath him, but she did not struggle.

It didn't take long for him to finish, the sounds of his movements slow and mechanical, as if he were indifferent to what had happened. His breath came in heavy, drunken snores moments after. Amber lay still, her mind racing but her body unmoving. She welcomed the quiet that followed, a fleeting moment of peace in the midst of her chaos. Her heart was thundering, but at least now she had time to collect herself, to push the terror back into the farthest corners of her mind.

She carefully rose from the bed so as not to make a sound. As she stood, she paused for a fraction of a second, her eyes flicking to the side. A quick glance, a careful study of the beast to ensure he was still fast asleep. With an almost imperceptible sigh, she moved toward the dresser.

She opened the bottom drawer with a soft, deliberate motion, her fingers brushing over the rough wood before dipping inside. She dug out the fanny pack she had hidden away, the one she had bought at the strip days ago. Her fingers found the stack of cash almost immediately—her hard-earned money. Her heart beat faster now, not with fear, but with a quiet sense of purpose.

She closed the fanny pack and then set it aside. There was something else inside—an envelope. She hesitated for a brief moment, her thoughts already spinning ahead to what needed to come next.

"All in good time," she whispered under her breath. "All in good time."

6

THURSDAY. TOM STEPPED into the shop, looking unusually stylish in a dark blazer tailored to perfection. His attire, so out of place for a typical workday, added a certain emphasis to the otherwise mundane atmosphere. As closing time neared, he approached Amber, twisting nervously a pamphlet in his hands. Amber had just finished a call, and his question seemed like nothing more than a way to bridge the silence.

"Who called?"

"They didn't speak. Wrong number, I guess," Amber replied, "The third one today."

"That guy's still at it...?" he mumbled.

"Excuse me?"

"There used to be a guy who prank-called here. We never figured out who he was. My dad thought maybe a competitor was trying to tie up our lines. But we never had proof..." Tom explained, his voice trailing off as if he hadn't meant to ramble on. After a brief silence, he shifted, awkwardly trying to change the subject.

"Slow day, huh?"

Amber nodded.

"I heard you like classical music. Gabe mentioned it the other day."

"I do," she said, her gaze softening. "But I haven't had the time to enjoy it lately."

"Really? That's a shame."

"Do you listen?"

"What?"

"Do you listen to classical music?"

"Sometimes..." Tom paused, as if wrestling with a thought, his fingers unconsciously smoothing the pamphlet's edges. "Well... I have two tickets to a concert tonight. It's classical."

"A classical concert?" Amber repeated, genuinely curious.

"Yeah. Some guy named Tchaikovsky," he said, unrolling the pamphlet with a small flourish. "'Enjoy a night of classical delight with the Edvard Philharmonic Orchestra.' They came all the way from Norway. I've heard they're amazing."

A sudden realization flashed across Amber's face. "That's why you're dressed so nice today."

Tom looked down at his blazer, a slight flush creeping onto his cheeks. "You mean this old thing?" he said, adjusting it a little. "I got it for my mom's wedding. She made me get it tailored just before her big day... but, uh, I'm sorry. I'm sidetracking." He cleared his throat, a nervous laugh escaping him. "I was wondering if you'd like to come with me? To the concert, I mean."

Amber blinked, clearly caught off guard. "You want to take me?" she asked. "Wouldn't you rather go with your girlfriend?"

"My girlfriend?" Tom looked baffled for a moment, then his face lit up with understanding. "Oh, you mean Dominique? We're not together anymore. We broke up months ago, but we've stayed friends. I thought you knew?"

Amber shook her head, surprised by the revelation. She smiled faintly, as if the puzzle pieces of their conversations were finally clicking into place.

"Anyway, the concert. It's at eight. We could grab a bite before. What do you think?"

"It sounds wonderful... but I don't have anything proper to wear."

Tom smiled with relief, his shoulders relaxing as he reassured her, "Don't worry about that. What you have on will do just fine."

He had originally planned to take Amber to an upscale restaurant, where elegant courses would be served by polished waitstaff beneath soft, intimate lighting. But, as Amber had insisted, they ended up at *Woks* instead. Settling into a window booth across from each other, she seemed a bit apprehensive at first. He, too, felt a flutter of nerves, as if it were his first date.

Thankfully, the tension soon faded. Tom did most of the talking, focusing mainly on work. Amber, though quiet, listened intently, asking just enough questions to keep the conversation flowing. He quickly sensed she was a private person, graceful and reserved, the type who preferred to observe rather than dominate the conversation. Respecting that, Tom kept things light, steering clear of anything too personal for the time being.

When they arrived at the Music Hall later, Amber borrowed his blazer, adjusting it carefully to match the elegant crowd gathered for the evening. A well-dressed attendant greeted them promptly and escorted them to their seats, moving with the kind of quiet precision you'd expect from such a grand venue.

Tom had only ever read about the Music Hall—its reputation as a masterpiece of architectural history, praised for its detailed craftsmanship and cultural significance. Yet, nothing could have prepared him for the actual sight. The ornate details of the grand auditorium took his breath away—the intricate carvings, the sweeping arches, the lavish red velvet chairs. He sank into his seat, feeling a quiet satisfaction just being there, surrounded by such grandeur.

For a moment, his mind wandered. He pictured himself in Vienna, seated in a similar hall, surrounded by the finest minds of the day, sipping tea under an acoustic, coffered ceiling. A wry smile crossed his face as he imagined himself rubbing elbows with Mozart and the aristocrats of old. *This must be how they spent their afternoons*, he mused, half-jokingly. It was a fleeting thought, but in that moment, he felt as though he had stepped into something timeless.

Just then, the lights in the theater began to fade, until the entire chamber was bathed in a hushed, expectant glow. The heavy velvet curtains parted with a soft rustle, revealing the stage beyond. A deep silence settled over the audience, so profound that the click of the conductor's shoes on the polished floor echoed clearly, each step heavy with anticipation. As he ascended the podium, the room seemed to hold its breath. With a single, fluid movement, the conductor raised his baton. And just like that, the orchestra swelled to life, a wave of sound cascading into the room.

Tom had never truly understood classical music before, but now, with each note rising and falling around him, he was enraptured. The music—ethereal, triumphant, and tenderly poignant—pulled at something inside him. It was a sound so rich, so layered, that he felt like he could lose himself in it. Amber, however, seemed distant in her own way. Her expression was serene, almost unreadable, as if she was immersed in her own private world. Her gaze was fixed unwaveringly on the grand piano at the center of the stage, its ivory keys catching the dim light like a beacon. Her face gave nothing away—no signs of awe or excitement, nor any trace of disinterest. She was still, her lips parted slightly as if in deep contemplation.

Occasionally, her eyes fluttered closed, and her fingers, resting lightly on her lap, twitched in rhythm with the pianist's delicate movements—gentle taps, a silent accompaniment to the performance. Tom found himself drawn to Amber, observing her with a curiosity he couldn't quite explain. Her calm demeanor spoke volumes—*perhaps this was no new experience for her.* He wondered if music, this music, held special memories for Amber. Maybe this was something she had known for years, something that ran deeper for her than he had expected.

The concert unfolded over the next hour and a half, sweeping through every possible emotion with grace and precision. When the final note rang out, a perfect, lingering silence followed before the audience erupted into applause, a wave of exhilaration crashing over the room. The orchestra stood in unison, bowing humbly as the crowd cheered with admiration.

Yet, when Tom glanced over at Amber, his applause faltered. She remained seated, her back straight and unmoving. The contrast between the standing ovation and her stillness was almost jarring. It wasn't until he leaned closer that he saw it—two faint tracks of tears had stained her crimson cheeks.

He reached for her gently, his voice quiet, unsure if he should break the reverence of the moment. "Are you all right?"

Amber blinked as if momentarily startled by the question before offering a small, reassuring smile. "Yeah, I'm fine," she replied, her voice steady, though there was a slight tremor in it. She took the handkerchief he offered and dabbed it delicately beneath her eyes, as though trying to erase any trace of vulnerability.

"Shall we go?" Tom asked, his tone soft, full of understanding.

Amber nodded, her smile deepening, though her eyes lingered for a moment longer on the stage before she reached out and placed her hand in his. With a gentle pull, he helped her rise from her seat.

Back in the car, Tom kept quiet, his hands lightly gripping the steering wheel as he stole a glance at Amber. The night had settled around them like a heavy blanket, the only sound the hum of the engine and the occasional breath of air passing through the cracked window. He didn't rush her to speak. She would, when she was ready.

After a long pause, Amber's voice broke the silence. "Thank you for inviting me to the concert. I'm sorry if I embarrassed you. This must have been the worst date you've ever been on."

Tom's lips curled into a smile. "Hm... no, actually, it wasn't the worst," he mused. "One time, I went on a blind date with someone I met online. Turned out he was a 65-year-old man from the city. I should've picked up on the clues—his makeup was a bit of a hint—but he waited until after dinner to tell me he was a professional drag queen. Like it was this big reveal." He chuckled, shaking his head at the absurdity. "Definitely a strange way to end the night, I'll tell you that much."

As his laughter faded, a warmth in his voice seeped in. "But despite the confusion, he was one of the most genuine, sophisticated people I've ever met. We ended up having this amazing conversation about ice fishing. Honestly, I had no idea what it was about at first, but by the end of the night, I felt like I could teach a class on it."

Amber smiled in quiet amazement, her gaze drifting toward the window as the soft curve of her lips lingered. "Those tickets must have cost you a fortune," she said with a hint of curiosity.

Tom shrugged. "Nah, it wasn't a big deal. I had a great time. I hope you did, too. I couldn't have brought a more worthy person with me. Truly."

Amber's gaze met his and softened. For a moment, she seemed to consider his words.

He continued, "I take it that wasn't your first time?"

"My first time...?"

"At a classical concert. It definitely was mine." He laughed, the sound a little self-deprecating. "I don't know what I expected, but tonight was... impressive. I mean, the performance was impeccable! Not that I'm any kind of music critic. I'm a complete newbie to this."

Amber's expression shifted, and she gave him a small, knowing smile. "My parents used to perform with orchestras. When I was little, the theater was my second home."

Tom blinked, very much shocked. "They're both professional musicians?"

She nodded. "My father gave me piano lessons until he got overwhelmed with work. After that, my mother took over. The first piece on tonight's program was the first composition I ever learned from him."

Tom sat back, his mind reeling for a moment. "Wow... I didn't know. Guess I should have picked up an instrument or two growing up..."

"Why?"

He shifted in his seat, a little self-conscious. "To be honest, I've always envied people like you. You, your parents, Gabe... people who can connect with music so deeply. There's this mysterious confidence, this vibe artists seem to have. I've always wanted that. I think I'd be a better person if I had it."

Amber gave him a look that seemed almost pitying. "I've never really thought about myself that way. To me, it's more of a burden."

Tom turned toward her. "Why's that?"

Amber shifted slightly, her eyes momentarily distant. "To be sensitive like that—it makes you more vulnerable. When you feel deeply, it makes everything feel sharper. It's like you're always on the edge of something, waiting for the hurt." She glanced at him, almost nervously. "I've always seen crying as a sign of weakness."

Tom's eyes widened, and he shook his head firmly, the words slipping out with unexpected force. "Now, I don't think that at all." He turned toward her fully, his gaze intense. "I think it's actually one of the bravest things a person can do—to be so open with their emotions. To allow yourself to feel, without holding anything back."

She gave him a small, skeptical smile. "You're only telling me that because you don't hate me."

"Hate?" he echoed, incredulously. "Of course not. Who could hate you?"

Amber shrugged, her eyes clouding briefly with something sad, some sadness he couldn't quite read. "I don't know... Sometimes, people don't need a reason to hate. Do they?"

As the meaning of her words sank in, Tom wasn't sure what to say. He took a breath, almost hesitant to ask, "I wonder... would it be wrong of me to ask about your arms?" His eyes searched hers, his voice tentative. He knew it was a delicate question, one that might be crossing a boundary, but he couldn't help himself.

Amber stiffened for a second before her expression relented into something more resigned. "You mean my scars."

"Yeah. I noticed them when you were taking off the jacket."

She went silent for a beat and then told him, "I was in a terrible car accident once."

Tom's heart clenched. "A car accident? Those are burn marks?"

She nodded, her voice a little tight. "Yeah. It happened eight years ago. I... I'd rather not go into the details, if that's okay."

Tom gave her a quick, reassuring nod, not wanting to push her further. "Of course. I understand."

Amber's fingers tightened around the sleeve of her shirt, her eyes momentarily drifting down to her lap. Tom's brow furrowed as he looked at her, his voice gentle but firm. "If you ever think you need to hide them, I'd tell you not to bother."

"Why?" she asked.

"Because I don't think that changes anything. You are still you. They certainly change nothing about your attractiveness."

Amber looked at him, taken aback by his blunt sincerity. "You don't?"

"Absolutely not!" he replied, his voice filled with conviction. "You survived, Amber! That alone is something worth celebrating. If I were you, I would wear them proudly. They're a part of your story."

Amber's eyes glistened for a moment, her lips curving into a small, genuine smile. Tom hadn't expected it, but the warmth in her gaze felt like a quiet victory—one that made his heart beat a little faster.

"You're one of a kind, Tom," she said sincerely. "A very good kind."

Tom felt the compliment settle into him, warming him from the inside. He scratched his neck awkwardly. "Nah, I'm just a regular guy."

"Then I wish there were more regular people like you. This world would be a much nicer place."

He smiled in return and let it be. As their conversation tapered off, they fell into a comfortable silence, the kind that stretched between them like an unspoken understanding. The night was winding down, and Tom turned the car toward Amber's home.

Just as they neared the entrance to the trailer park, Amber's voice sliced through the quiet, commanding yet gentle.

"Stop here, please," she said.

Tom braked instinctively, confused. "I thought you said Lot 104? It's just up there, a little further."

"I know," she replied, her voice quiet but resolute. "I prefer to walk from here."

He glanced over at her, trying to read her expression, but her gaze was fixed ahead, her posture tense in a way that left him with a lingering sense of uncertainty. It was as if there was something she wasn't saying, something she needed to keep between them for now.

"Okay... sure," he murmured, the words slipping out reluctantly.

With a soft exhale, he reached for the door handle, offering her a small, respectful smile as she unbuckled her seatbelt. Amber didn't look back as she stepped out, her movements precise but guarded. She closed the door behind her with a soft click that resonated in the quietness of the night.

But then, she came around to his side and leaned down as he opened his window. Without warning, she pressed a kiss to his cheek, light and quick. Her lips held there for just a heartbeat, a touch of warmth in the cool evening air.

"Thank you for the wonderful evening," she said softly. "I want you to know that it meant a lot to me."

Tom's smile grew, though he kept his response simple. "Yeah? Well, I'm glad. We should do this again sometime."

"I'll see to it."

They shared a silent exchange of glances, and then Amber stepped back, retreating into the shadow of the trailer park as Tom drove off and disappeared shortly from her view.

7

AMBER FLIPPED THE light switch on and instantly froze, startled to find Michael lounging in the living room. She let out a quick breath, instinctively clutching her chest. "You scared me," she said, her heart still pounding. "Have you been standing there in the dark this whole time?"

"I might as well *be* the dark," he muttered, his voice dripping with sarcasm. "I'm practically invisible. Always a secret."

Amber rolled her eyes, choosing to ignore the bitterness in his tone. She stepped past him, making her way toward the bedroom.

Michael's voice followed her, cutting through the silence. "You look like you had a good time," he observed. "Your cheeks are red, and that smile you wore on your way home—tells me this one's special."

Amber paused at the doorway, turning to face him. "Have you been spying on me?"

"Only through the curtains—"

"Don't," she cut him off harshly. "As I've said before, this isn't home. I'm leaving this shithole as soon as I can."

"If you really wanted to leave, you would've left by now."

Amber's fingers tightened on the doorframe. "You want me to live on the streets? You think that's fun?"

Right then, a sardonic laugh escaped Michael's lips. "Scary, wouldn't that be?"

Amber's eyes hardened. "The beast is hardly here. I'll be fine for a while. I'm not doing anything to jeopardize my plan."

"Sounds like you have it all figured out. But you don't need to try so hard to avoid the topic. I was just curious about the guy."

"Tom is just a friend," she insisted, her voice firm.

"Ha! 'Friend.' Is that all?" Michael scoffed. "That beast you mentioned was just a 'friend' at first, too. Look where you ended up with him."

Amber snapped, her patience slipping. "Fine," she confessed, "I like him. I like Tom a lot. Happy now? But I don't owe you an explanation. I've had a long day. The last thing I want is to argue with you about it. I just want to shower and go to sleep."

Without another word, Michael turned and headed for the door. Then, something in Amber stirred. Instinct told her she should let him go, just as it had so many times before. But despite that, she found herself stopping him.

"Do you have a problem with me?" she asked out loud.

Michael halted, glancing back at her. His gaze hardened. "Nope. No problem," he replied.

"Don't you want me to be happy?"

"I haven't said anything."

"But I know what you're thinking. Dr. Rimer said I should focus on moving on. Only look forward. She—"

"She also told you to sever all ties with me, right? But here we are again," he interrupted, his eyes sharp as he looked Amber over.

Amber stiffened, feeling an old ache rise in her chest. "Why are you so upset?"

"Upset?" Michael laughed bitterly. "How could I be upset? God forbid anyone get in the way of your perfect new life—whether I'm in it or not."

"This isn't a negotiation," she bit back, trying to keep her voice steady.

"I wasn't negotiating. When you left Heartstone, I thought it was over between us. A part of me died that day you left, but hey, I wasn't complaining. I let you go. I was supportive as hell."

"Then what changed? What is all this?"

"What is this?" Michael echoed, his voice hard. "Ask yourself that, why don't you? Because, sooner or later, you'll have to face your dilemma."

"What dilemma?"

"Are you or are you not finished with me?"

Amber felt the pressure of his question rush through her like a wave. She didn't want to engage in this battle, this endless loop of bullshit argument with no winner whatsoever. "I can't do this anymore," she said bluntly. "I'm not even supposed to be talking to you."

"Well, then don't. You never have to again," Michael replied coldly, his voice almost mechanical. "Consider this your release, or whatever you want to call it. Just go live your life. I'll show myself out."

Amber's heart twisted. Before she could stop herself, she found herself hurrying to step into his path, her voice quiet, pleading, "Please... stay. I want you to stay."

Michael stood frozen. "Why? After everything you've said?"

"Because I... I still think about you," she blurted out, her face flushing with the honesty of her words.

Michael stared at her for a long moment. "When?"

"Earlier... at the concert."

"Concert...?" he mused, an almost amused look crossing his face. "Tchaikovsky."

Amber nodded shamefully. She buried her face in her hands, unable to stop the tears from falling.

A small, smug grin tugged at Michael's lips. He reached out, pulling her close, wrapping her in his arms. His touch was gentle, yet possessive, as he rubbed her back, slowly coaxing her into calm.

"I don't know what's gotten into me tonight," she murmured.

"You don't, but I do," Michael said, his tone confident. "You're overwhelmed."

"I try, Michael. Every single day, I try. I don't know how long I can keep this up."

"I'm not surprised. You were there for so long. Heartstone is all you know."

"All I want is to be like everybody else. Normal," she emphasized, the word almost foreign to her.

Michael's chuckle was dry, edged with bitterness. "That line of thought's never going to fly," he said.

"Why not?" Amber pulled back slightly, looking up at him.

"Do you come from a normal family? What was your childhood like? Have you forgotten all the nights you spent locked away, alone, fearing the worst?"

Her eyes flickered, the old pain resurfacing. She wiped at her tears, trying to force the memories away. "It's hopeless. I get it," she whispered, her voice trembling. "I don't want to hear about it anymore."

"Do you get it, though? Really? I don't think you do."

She turned away, frustrated. "I don't care. Just don't bring up my childhood again."

Michael's voice dropped to a low hum, trying to ease her. "Alright, alright. You know we can always reverse. Take a break, go back... You've had your taste of adventure. It certainly would be easier to give up and go back."

"How is that easier?"

"Well, considering how everything went—"

Amber shook her head firmly, tears still fresh on her cheeks. "I can't go back, Michael. I won't."

"No one would laugh at you," he said, almost tenderly. "Some of them might even be happy to see you."

"What are you saying? I've sacrificed so much just to get here. You know that."

"I hear you."

She sniffled. "I need to adapt better, faster, and be more... normal."

Michael didn't respond right away, instead, his eyes seemed to pierce through her. "I think you've got bigger things to worry about than normality."

She stared at him. "I told you. I'll leave as soon as I'm more able."

"I wasn't talking about that," he said ominously.

Amber's stomach dropped. "You weren't talking about Mason?"

"No," Michael said, shaking his head.

"Jo..." The thought hit her like a punch to the gut.

Michael's voice grew harsh and every bit menacing. "Do you think she'll let you go just like that? After that little stunt you pulled? After you left her wondering what the hell was wrong? You think she'll forget about you?"

Amber's breath caught in her throat as she catastrophized the idea. "She's coming for me, isn't she?"

"And when she does... where will you run? Where else can you hide?"

"I... I haven't thought that far."

"What if it's tomorrow, huh? What if she shows up here while you are asleep? She would do anything. You *know* she would. How are you ever going to escape her?"

"I... I could..." Suddenly, Amber's legs felt weak, and she stumbled back, collapsing onto the floor. Michael quickly moved to her side, his arms wrapping around her tightly. Once again, she was timely reminded of why she needed him. She buried her face in his chest, letting his presence soothe the panic gnawing at her insides. For a moment, all that mattered to her was the warmth of his embrace.

He held her close in his arms, where she habitually nestled, allowing her to fall dependent on his care. She kept her eye closed to focus on the beating of his heart that soothed her like no other—that gradually lulled her into a trance free from all her immediate worries.

"Take me away, Michael. Take me away forever," she proposed. "Take me somewhere pleasant. Somewhere, I'll not feel pain or sadness. Take me to that place you spoke of—nirvana, where nothing hurts..."

Michael's eyes were dark with intent. He looked at her—not with pity, but with something complex. He contemplated a moment and then exhaled. "I would take you there gladly, if I could. But unfortunately, reality... it's one long, solitary struggle."

Amber looked at him with a certain desperation. Her lips trembled slightly as she spoke again. "Then let me die," she said, almost with anger, as if surrendering to the thought. "I'd rather be free from all of this."

"You would, wouldn't you?" Michael smirked, his tone sardonic. "Don't speak so hastily. I can always check on you more often. If that's what you want, I'll make sure you're never alone in your misery."

"You would do that for me?" she asked, a faint hope threading through her voice.

"Of course," Michael replied, his expression softening. His hands reached out, cupping her face gently. His thumb brushed the curve of her cheek before he pressed a kiss to her forehead—soft, tender, like a promise. "Anything, just to make sure you're okay... Even if that means I have to stay hidden away, kept a secret, just to be near you. I'll do whatever it takes."

Amber swallowed hard. Once more, her eyes welled with tears she couldn't hold back. She clutched his shirt, pulling him closer, as if afraid he might vanish if she let go. "Please," she whispered to him, "don't ever leave me."

8

"*A*LL DRINKS ON *the house!*" The bartender's voice rang out, cutting through the laughter and chatter of the crowded pub. The carousing crowd erupted in applause and cheers, the energy of the evening surging to new heights. It was the annual Christmas party at *Gins*, and since six o'clock, the place had been filled with gleeful revelers eager to make the most of the festive night.

The pub owner, a tall man with broad shoulders and a booming voice, climbed up onto the bar counter. He raised his glass, catching the attention of everyone in the room. "A toast," he called, his eyes brimming with pride.

"To my son, Danny, who is soon to be married. May his life be filled with the same joy and love that I've known. This is a moment I've dreamed of since the day he was born. Danny, you make me proud every day. Congratulations, son."

The crowd cheered, clapping enthusiastically as Danny, the guest of honor, beamed at his father. Without hesitation, he dipped his fiancée, Penelope, and kissed her deeply on the lips. The room exploded in applause, whistling and hollering.

"Speech! Speech! Speech..."

Danny's three best friends led the chant, their voices loud and jovial, egging him on. Danny grinned, flashing a playful smirk, and grabbed the microphone as if he were accepting an Oscar. "Thank you, everyone, for being here tonight," he began, his voice thick with emotion. "I wouldn't be standing here without two very special people. The first is my dad. Everyone who has worked for him knows that this pub has been his blood and bone since its birth. So, for him to hand it over to me? That's the greatest gift I could ever receive. Thanks, Pop, for retiring early and giving me this as the icing on the wedding cake. Cheers, everyone!"

"Cheers!" the crowd shouted in unison, raising their glasses high.

A voice from the back shouted, "Who's the second fellow?"

Danny paused, looking around at the crowd with a mischievous glint in his eye. "I was just getting to that." He cleared his throat theatrically. "The second man I want to thank is my longtime friend, Tom Ager. Tom, where are you? Don't be shy. Step up!"

Tom reluctantly stepped into the center of the room. The eyes of everyone in the pub turned toward him, and his nerves kicked in.

"There he is!" Danny announced, grinning. "Handsome, isn't he? You may all know Tom as 'that plumber guy,' but let me tell you—this man and I go way back. We grew up together, rode the same bus, spent hours after school just hanging out. Our parents were friends for years. Some of my best memories are with this guy right here." Danny took a beat, his tone growing sincere. "So, Tom, I just want to say thanks. Thanks for being there for me, man."

Tom raised his glass, nodding in appreciation, but his throat felt tight. "You're welcome," he said with a tight smile, but before he could sip his drink, Danny jumped in again.

"Hold it, hold it," he interrupted, a grin spreading across his face. "I wasn't done yet. What I really want to thank Tom for is... blowing his chance with Penelope." He air-quoted the word "blowing" for extra effect.

The crowd laughed knowingly, and Tom's stomach sank. He couldn't stop it now. Danny continued, "I mean, we shared a lot of good times—his mom's chicken pot pie, our first beer, and, of course, the deepest secrets. And according to the rumor mill"—he paused dramatically— "there was that one incident in high school, the one where a student, um, had a little accident during a class presentation..."

Tom's face flushed a deep red. He had known this was coming, but hearing it aloud was an entirely different matter.

Danny grinned wider. "Well, folks, that wasn't a rumor. That was all Tom. Apparently, lactose intolerance and a first date with Italian food do not mix. His stomach didn't thank him, his pants didn't thank him, but I sure did, especially for the lasagna he gamely scarfed down. If it weren't for that little 'blowout,' I wouldn't be marrying this amazing woman right now." He raised his glass to Penelope, who smiled, shaking her head. "If you want to hear more about that legendary date, I'm sure Tom would be happy to share the details, blow by blow."

The room broke out in laughter, eyes darting around to catch Tom's reaction. Whispers rippled through the crowd as more and more people turned to him with knowing looks. Tom's jaw tightened, bracing himself for the storm.

Penelope, sensing his discomfort, stood up. She cut through the crowd of snickers and defended him, her voice firm but quiet. "Enough, Danny. Stop dredging up that story."

She turned to the others, addressing them calmly. "Just for the record, everyone, I was the one who prepared that lunch. Tom was too polite to refuse my offer, and I didn't know about his condition until much later, after we'd both moved on."

Danny quipped without missing a moment, "Oh, it's really sweet of him to self-sabotage so I could win the prize." He chuckled to himself, but no one joined in this time.

Penelope shot him a look of warning. "Dan..."

Tom exhaled slowly. "It's alright, Penny," he reassured her, lifting his glass. "I don't mind being the butt of the joke for a night. But let's raise a glass to Danny and Penelope, two incredible people I'm lucky to know. Here's to your future happiness. Cheers."

The group chorused a half-hearted "Cheers" before the conversation quickly moved on.

As Danny and his two friends approached Tom for a quick chat soon afterward, the atmosphere became suffocating. Tom felt small, outnumbered, and increasingly alienated in his own skin.

"... You know I was just kidding around, right?" Danny patted him on the shoulder, his tone casual, as though that could make it all okay.

"Sure," Tom replied, keeping his voice flat, refusing to engage with the insult any longer.

"How've you been, Tom?" Penelope asked, turning to him. "Last I heard, you were dating Ms. Ellis."

Tom's expression softened slightly. "That's right. We've broken up."

"That redheaded spinster with two little kids?" one of Danny's friends chimed in, "I saw her the other day with some guy. She looked pretty cozy."

Penelope tilted her head, considering. "I've got a friend, Scarlett, from yoga. She's recently single, and I think you two would get along great. I could ask her if she wants to hang out sometime. She could really meet a decent guy like you for a change."

Tom shook his head, his smile warm but firm. "I appreciate it, and I'm sure she's lovely, but I'm not looking for anyone right now."

Danny, ever the instigator, chimed in again. "Yeah, darling. Our boy Tom's a big boy. He doesn't need your help to hook up. He's got that all under control, don't worry."

Tom shot Danny a sideways glance, but didn't rise to the bait. Instead, he played along. "I can handle myself just fine, thanks."

"Well, hey, Tom," Danny continued with a smirk, "when's your big day? Or are you still cruising down bachelor lane, too scared to park?"

"I'll get there when I get there," Tom replied. "I'm not in any rush."

Danny grinned. "You might want to hurry. Otherwise, you'll end up with the leftovers. Or maybe you're eyeing a cougar?"

"Dan..."

Ignoring his fiancée's nudge, he added, "Hey, come to think of it, how about Mrs. Pedersen? Tyler's eighty-year-old grandma. Isn't she always hunting for a new boy toy?"

Tyler, always eager to add fuel to the fire, nodded. "I think so," he chimed in, leaning into the joke.

"He *thinks* so. Isn't she, like, a clean freak?" Danny pushed, his eyes gleaming with mischief.

"She never goes anywhere without first changing into a fresh pair of panties," Tyler said, laughing, clearly enjoying the discomfort he was causing.

"No fucking way!" their other friend gasped, incredulity mixing with humor.

"Honest to God. I heard it from my mom—her daughter's own mouth," Tyler confirmed with a wicked grin.

"Ha! No kidding! Are you listening to this, Tom? Mrs. Pedersen's a real trooper. Taking care of her own diapers and shit. Maybe Tyler can pass on your number, so she can give you a call in her spare time when she's not wiping down her mahjong tiles—"

"DANNY!" Penelope suddenly bellowed, her voice piercing like a whip. She stared at her soon-to-be husband with a fiery intensity, her lips pressed into a thin line.

Danny froze, the mocking grin on his face faltering just slightly. His two friends were snorting with laughter, but Penelope's glare made it clear the joke had crossed a line.

Tom had, too, reached his breaking point. He was done. This had gone on long enough. He scanned the room, seeking an escape from this bombardment of insults. His eyes landed on Amber, standing near Gabe and the bandmates by the stage. Instantly, his face softened. He wanted to rush over to her, but first, he needed to get the last word in.

"Okay," he said to the guys, his voice cutting through their laughter.

Danny blinked, momentarily thrown off. "What?"

"I'll take it," Tom replied, his tone deadpan. "Go ahead and pass my number on to Mrs. Pedersen. She sounds like a real catch."

Danny's grin wavered. "Heh... you're joking."

"Nope," Tom continued, his voice cool and controlled. "Just make sure she calls me so I can tell her all about *her* and how I managed to learn so much about a woman of her age in such a short time. I bet we'll have a lot to talk about."

The faces of Danny and his friends quickly shifted from amusement to irritation, the air growing thick with the sudden turn of the conversation. Tom could see the soreness settle into their eyes, their humor deflated like a balloon losing air.

"Now, if you'll excuse me," Tom added, "I've got other company waiting." He turned without waiting for a response, leaving the trio dumbfounded in his wake.

As he walked away, a sense of relief washed over him. He was rather proud of himself, to quit playing their games. His gaze focused on Amber, her presence a beacon of normalcy in the chaotic pub. A genuine smile finally broke across his face as he made his way toward her, feeling the stress of the evening lift off his shoulders.

"Hey, boss!" Gabe greeted, noticing Tom's approach. "You're looking *flamboyant* tonight."

Tom arched an eyebrow, looking down at his own attire—a festive tie with a button shirt—and gave a wry smile. "When did you guys get here?"

"We rushed over right after closing up," Gabe said, his voice a little too casual, like he was trying to sidestep some past misstep.

Tom's eyes narrowed in playful suspicion. "Did you close it, close it?" he asked.

"Come on, man. You gotta let that one go," Gabe shot back, shrugging as if it was no big deal.

A confused look flashed across Amber's face. Gabe gave an exaggerated sigh and leaned in closer, dropping his voice in mock confession. "Alright, fine. There was this one time I kinda... sorta... forgot to lock the gate."

Tom added with a smirk, "And the door."

Gabe waved him off, brushing the moment aside. "Okay, okay, and the door. But don't get all technical on me now. Let's focus on the one key fact here: everything turned out fine. No toilet lids went missing. No scratches on the property. Everything's peachy."

Amber let out a soft giggle. "Sounds like it was a shockingly happy ending."

Gabe grinned, slapping Tom on the back. "Totally."

Tom, still mildly amused, shifted the subject. "So, when's your band playing?"

"We're fifth in line," Gabe said, holding up his fingers. "Right after Chubby Isaac with the sax and before Ms. Amber here."

"Amber's performing?" Tom asked, his eyes widening, impressed.

Amber's face lit up with a smile that was warm but tinged with something—nervousness. She hesitated, then shrugged. "I don't know. I haven't really decided."

"Oh, come on, Am," Gabe insisted, leaning forward with enthusiasm, his voice brimming with excitement. "It'll be fun! You've got to help me convince her, Tom. You should've seen her earlier on my buddy's keyboard. She's outstanding!"

"I'm not that good—"

"I'm with Gabe on this one," Tom cut in, his tone light but serious.

Amber blinked in surprise, looking from one to the other. "You are?"

Tom nodded confidently, his voice softening with a touch of encouragement. "Why not? What's the worst that could happen? You'll either have fun or regret never giving it a shot. But, trust me, you'll regret *not* doing it more."

"Exactly!" Gabe chimed in, practically bouncing on his feet. "It'll be a breeze. And when you're done, we'll get you properly drunk. Right, Tom? Tom?"

The two of them turned toward the entrance, noticing that Tom had gone quiet. His gaze was fixed on someone standing in the doorway. Dominique. Wrapped in a blanket, she looked urgent. Something was wrong.

"Excuse me a moment, guys," Tom murmured, his voice low, almost apologetic. "I'll be right back."

Before either Gabe or Amber could respond, he was already moving toward Dominique.

They stepped outside so that they could talk in private. Once they were out the door, Dominique wasted no time.

"I was in the girls' room, playing, when I noticed John's phone on the nightstand," she said, her hands trembling slightly as her fingers tightened around the blanket. "I couldn't help myself and glanced at it... and when the screen lit up, I saw a naked picture of his ex."

"Oh my... Did the girls—"

"No, they didn't see it. At least, I hope not. I tried to act like everything was fine, but I... you know I'm terrible at pretending."

"Maybe it was an old photo? One he forgot to delete?" Tom suggested, though even he could hear how weak it sounded.

Dominique shook her head, her eyes darkening. "I checked. It was sent to him yesterday."

"Did he explain?" Tom asked, though he had no idea what explanation could make this better. "Maybe there's some kind of misunderstanding?"

"How could there be?" she questioned, her voice upset. "It's clear what it is. He was looking at it."

"I mean, he could've meant to talk to you about it, but got distracted."

"Well... so I didn't give him a chance to explain. I was so mad, I threw his phone at him in front of his friends. Then I grabbed my keys and left."

"I see."

"It sounds bad," Dominique continued. "It is bad. We've been together since October, and he's already cheated on me twice. Do you remember what happened the last time?"

She vented, her upset spilling out in a cascade of hurt, her eyes brimming with unshed tears. Tom listened quietly, offering the occasional word of reassurance, trying to soothe her.

"Don't jump to conclusions too fast," he said softly. "The last time turned out to be nothing. Maybe this time it'll be the same. Don't let it eat you up."

"But how can I be sure?" she asked, voice edged with desperation. "How can I not worry when this keeps happening?"

Tom stepped closer, his hand instinctively reaching out to comfort her, placing it gently on her shoulder. "You won't know for sure until you know. But trust me, the truth will come out. It always does."

Dominique looked away, staring out toward the distant city lights. Her shoulders sagged, as if the long night had finally caught up to her. After a long pause, she finally sat down on the large arched window ledge, resting her back against the cold glass, exhaling slowly.

Tom removed his jacket and draped it over her shoulders, the gesture soft, almost protective. She gave him a small, tired smile, but the warmth was fleeting.

"Come, sit with me," she said, her voice quiet. So he joined her, settling beside her on the cool stone.

For a long while, Dominique poured her heart out. "I'm just... tired, Tom. Tired of playing this game called 'love.' I know what I am—a thirty-four-year-old divorced woman with two kids and no real future. Not the catch I used to be."

"Don't say that," Tom said, his voice firm. "You're not some 'catch'—you're you."

"But that's just it," she sighed, her words heavy with exhaustion. "I'm not fun anymore. And on top of all that, my ex is filing for full custody of the girls." She met his gaze with raw frustration. "Can you believe that? After all we've been through?"

"I didn't know," Tom said, his eyes full of empathy.

"He called, and we had a big fight over it. He said he didn't want to have to deal with me anymore. He's marrying that woman he cheated on me with," she continued, shaking her head in disbelief. "Isn't it ironic? The man who hurt me the most is now getting what he wants."

"I'm sorry."

She laughed bitterly. "I'm sorry, too. But more for us, I think."

She looked at Tom then, her eyes searching his, and suddenly the world felt much smaller. "Why does this keep happening to me? Why do I always pick the wrong guys?"

Tom's heart ached for her ever so slightly. "Maybe because you haven't found the right one yet," he said quietly, almost as if thinking out loud.

Dominique shook her head once more, but there was a flicker of something in her eyes. "If only every man could be like you."

"Is that a compliment?" he teased lightly.

"Of course it is," she said, her tone turning serious, almost intimate. She reached out, her fingers lightly grazing his jaw, sending a jolt through his heart. "Why can't they all be as sweet, as kind, as thoughtful as you?"

Tom felt the heat rise to his cheeks. *Don't get lost in this,* he warned himself, but it was too late.

Her eyes were locked on his, and in that moment, everything else faded. The world outside vanished as she leaned in, her lips close enough that he could feel her breath against his skin. He couldn't pull away, not now, not with her so close, not when everything inside him screamed to kiss her.

But his hesitation surfaced. "Are you sure you want to do this?" he asked, his voice barely a whisper.

Dominique froze, pulling back, a hint of hurt crossing her face. "What do you mean?"

"I just—what about John? What would he think?" he blurted, the words slipping out before he could stop them.

She stiffened, standing up abruptly, her face hardening. "I don't know what he thinks," she said coldly.

"I'm sorry," Tom said, feeling his words land heavily between them. "I don't want to complicate things."

She didn't say anything, just grabbed her phone, glancing at it with a frown. "It's John. I should go."

"Yeah... right... okay."

She gave him one last look, a mixture of frustration and something else—something he couldn't place—before turning to leave. "Can I at least get a goodbye hug? Or is that too much to ask?"

Tom hesitated for only a moment before pulling her into an embrace. It felt like a goodbye. A finality that he couldn't explain. And as they stood there, holding each other, he wanted to say something—anything—that would make her stay. But he didn't.

She pulled away, quickly returning his jacket. "Thanks, Tom," she whispered, not looking back as she hurried out, her footsteps fading into the night.

9

TOM STEPPED BACK into the pub, his heart heavy, the kind of burden that sat low in his chest and didn't want to let go. As he moved through the haze of clinking glasses and louder voices, he realized that he'd just missed Gabe's band—*Animosity*—by mere minutes.

The room pulsed with energy, but Tom barely noticed, his mind still lingering on the conversation he'd had with Dominique. He was still sorting through his thoughts, still wondering if he'd said the wrong thing, if he should've tried harder to understand her.

The presenter's voice broke through his internal noise, cutting the air with a teasing tone:

"... That was some deafening rock 'n' roll. And now, a quick word for all you event planners out there: 'If you want to book *Animosity* for your future events, please direct your request to Avery Taylor, their manager.' Okay, tempting, I must say, but maybe not for your grandparents' ninetieth birthday. Otherwise, do it at your own risk..."

A surge of laughter spread through the crowd, the kind of laughter that made the room felt alive. The host chuckled to himself and then, with a quick flick of the wrist, readied the audience for the next act.

"... Moving on. Our next performer is perhaps a little more subtle. Give it up for twenty-one-year-old Wisconsin-bred, Ms. Amber Simmons!"

The crowd's initial applause was light, uncertain, but when Amber stepped from behind the curtain, the atmosphere changed—shifted, almost imperceptibly, but unmistakable. The babble of the pub faded, and for a few suspended seconds, it felt like everyone was holding their breath.

She walked toward the stage with the kind of quiet grace that made it impossible not to watch. Amber wore simple light-washed jeans and a white blouse—nothing ostentatious, yet everything about her presence exuded an undeniable pull, a magnetic aura that no one could ignore. There was an intangible confidence in the way she moved, as if the very space around her was designed to bend toward her. It wasn't just about beauty—it was something deeper, something that reached inside and tugged.

"She's pretty. Doesn't she work for you, Tom?" a woman whispered near him, her voice faint, almost lost among the shifting bodies. But Tom didn't catch the words. He couldn't. His eyes were locked on Amber, and he felt a strange mixture of awe and excitement. And not just him—everyone in the room seemed to be drawn to her, their eyes hungry with curiosity and admiration.

As she reached the keyboard, the intensity of the moment deepened. She took her seat on the stool, the beam of light above her cutting through the low hum of the room like a spotlight on a stage, framing her in an ethereal glow. For a moment, she simply sat, taking in the sea of faces that had now quieted, all of them hanging on her next move. There was something unsettlingly quiet about her presence, as if she held an unspoken power in her stillness.

She adjusted the microphone, the soft clink of metal against the stand sending a ripple through the audience.

"Hello, everyone. Good evening," she said, her voice a gentle yet piercing invitation. The men—young and old, the refined and the rough—responded instantly, some calling out, others whistling, their eager approval rising like a tide.

Amber's smile was subtle, warm, but with an edge—a smile that could melt anyone who thought they were immune. She let it linger just long enough before turning back to the mic.

"I'm here tonight to perform a song I wrote when I was fifteen," she continued, her voice carrying just the right amount of vulnerability, "called *I Wish You Well.*"

The crowd, already enchanted, fell into a deeper hush as she placed her hands on the piano. Her fingers brushed across the keys with a tenderness that made the air seem to shift. Each note seemed to be chosen with care, meaningful yet free, weaving a melody that was soft but full of scale. It was Mozartian, in the way it floated effortlessly, yet beneath it lay something heavier—an ache, a longing. Amber played as though the music was pulling itself from the depths of her soul, and her voice followed, emerging with a quiet force that felt as if it had been waiting for this moment to be heard.

You are the light, the sun to my meadow,
You are the dark, the sorrow I follow.
You gave me a name, as unique as your form,
I was a dahlia, withering in the storm.

Goodbye to innocence, goodbye to youth,
I'm no longer naïve, no longer the same.
If I called out, would you hear me?
Would you remember the day I dared face you?

Now I'm wary of what's to come,
I long for rain, but it never comes.
There's no use in talking, no use in tears—
Love can't heal what time steals away.

I was a dahlia, bending in the wind,
Longing for a storm to end.
Go now, my dear, I wish you well,
For better or worse, I'll say farewell...

Her voice wasn't just a voice—it was a language all its own. Raw, tender, and soaked in an emotion that only music could carry. The room was frozen, spellbound. There was no audience now, no pub, no noise. There was only Amber and her song. The words weren't just heard; they were felt in the marrow of every person present. Even the women who might've found her competition before now sat in stunned silence, disarmed by the depth and beauty of her performance.

When she finished, the last note lingered, suspended in time. Then, as if the world exhaled at once, the crowd erupted in applause, not the casual applause one gave to a decent performance, but the kind of applause reserved for someone who had offered a piece of themselves. There was reverence in the air. The respect was palpable, a tangible thing that pulsed through the room like a heartbeat.

As soon as Amber stepped off the stage, Gabe swooped in, claiming her attention before anyone else could. Lucky enough to score a table during the evening's peak rush, he'd already ordered a couple of shots for the freshly minted star, just as he'd promised.

"... What do you mean you've never drunk before?" Gabe's voice was loud and laced with surprise, as if this were some kind of challenge he couldn't quite grasp. "I've never met a twenty-one-year-old who hasn't had their first drink," he continued, raising an eyebrow. "Not even on your birthday?"

Tom, overhearing, couldn't resist but add his voice to the mix. "Maybe Amber doesn't like alcohol," he said, joining them at their table. "Has it ever occurred to you that some people just don't like to drink?"

"How can you not like something when you've never even tried it?" Gabe challenged.

"Like *you* are the one to talk," Tom shot back. "You don't even drink anymore."

"Hey, leave my sobriety alone," Gabe smirked. "And just because I'm trying to quit doesn't mean I don't enjoy the occasional bellywash."

Amber, intrigued by the conversation, asked, "Why are you quitting?"

Gabe shrugged, a wry smile on his face. "Just don't want it to become a bad habit. I'd rather die from choking on tobacco than alcohol poisoning, if that makes sense? It's tough though... quitting, I mean. Bad genes, you know? Unlike Mr. Ager here, who doesn't drink or smoke. He's a card-carrying goody two shoes if you ever saw one."

"Just because I didn't pick up those disgusting habits doesn't mean I don't know how to have fun," Tom replied, crossing his arms defensively.

"Right. So, what do you do for fun, then?" Gabe pressed, clearly enjoying himself.

"Puzzles," Amber interjected with a mild tease, "Crossword puzzles, to be exact. I've seen you do them at your desk."

Tom hesitated, then shrugged. "Well, that's not really what I do for fun. I only do them when I have nothing better to do."

Gabe leaned back, his grin widening. "Come on, Tom. Didn't you take a flower arrangement class last month? Admit it, you've got a thing for flowers."

"I do *not* have a thing for flowers," Tom insisted, though his cheeks flushed slightly.

"Then why spend a whole day learning how to display them so perfectly?" Gabe teased. "And that tie? Seriously? You planning to start selling floral ties for Valentine's Day?"

Amber let out a quiet snigger. Tom glanced over at her and wasn't about to let the last shred of his pride go up in smoke—not in front of Amber, at least.

"This is a poinsettia, also known as the Christmas Flower," Tom informed Gabe, pointing at his tie. "And it's Christmas. That's why I'm wearing a festive tie."

"I can't argue that."

"Artists have written about poinsettias in many Christmas songs over the years. You don't even know that, and you call yourself a musician?" Tom snapped.

"Oh, absolutely. The *manly* Christmas songs and *manly* flowers," Gabe shot back, dragging out the word "manly" with a grin.

Amber, her laughter still bubbling just beneath the surface, couldn't help but be curious. "You really took a flower class?"

Tom's resolve cracked just a little. "I took it because Dominique needed a partner. Nothing more to it."

"Dominique—of course." Gabe was on a roll now. "A partner, partner, or just a flower buddy?"

"What's the difference?"

"Only you can answer that... ha-ha-ha!" Gabe cackled at his own half-witted joke. Once more, Tom glanced over at Amber, who was also chuckling, and realized with a sinking feeling that his attempt to save face had completely failed.

"Whatever," he sighed, throwing his hands up. "Would you stop being such a twerp? I've had enough embarrassment for one night."

"Why? Did something happen with Dominique? She didn't dump you again, did she?"

"I don't want to get into that. But we're done for good."

"For real?" Gabe questioned, his tone doubtful. "Good for you. Unless she breaks up with that delivery guy and comes crawling back in a month."

"I don't think so," Tom said.

"We'll see about that," Gabe replied with a wink.

Just then, a waiter appeared with a tray of six shot glasses filled with tequila.

"Now, who's going to drink all this?" Tom asked, eyeing the glasses with concern.

"Am-ber?" Gabe suggested, looking over at her with a playful grin.

"Don't be mean," Tom warned, narrowing his eyes at Gabe.

"Relax, I'm just messing with her," Gabe said, a teasing smile tugging at his lips. "I didn't scare you, did I, Am?"

"No," Amber responded with a smirk, her tone light but firm. "I'll do it."

"Really?" Both men asked, clearly surprised by her casual response.

Amber shrugged. "Why not? How bad can it be?"

"I love this girl!" Gabe declared with a dramatic fist pump.

"Hold up," Tom interjected, suddenly more concerned. "This is hard liquor. Why don't we each take two for this round? That way Amber gets to have a taste, and if she likes it, we can always get more later."

"I like that idea," Amber agreed, her eyes sparkling with both gratitude and anticipation.

"Gabe?"

"I'm cool with that," Gabe said with a nod, leaning in toward Amber. "But let's make it fun. We'll chug them on three. No chickening out, Tom."

"Who said I would?" Tom shot back.

"Ha! Just making sure. You in, Am?"

"Let's do this!" Amber said with enthusiasm, her voice full of confidence as she raised her glass.

While they downed their shots, Tilly, who had been sitting at a nearby table, kept his gaze fixed on Amber with unsettling intensity. After a moment, he stumbled over to their table, his steps unsteady.

"Good evening, Mr. Tilly," Tom greeted him.

"I'll be damned," Tilly slurred, squinting at Amber. "So, she's your new hire. How convenient."

Tom's brow furrowed. "Do you know Amber?"

Amber's eyes narrowed slightly, but she remained quiet.

"Amber... Is that the name she goes by now?" Tilly chuckled darkly, his eyes roaming her with a mixture of familiarity and something more unnerving. "I saw you up on that stage. At first, I thought I was seeing things, but now that I've seen you up close, I'm certain it is you."

Amber stiffened. "I think you have the wrong person," she said, her voice cool and collected despite the rising tension.

"Nah, I'm not that old yet. Nirvana Shor... You look just like your mother. Beautiful. Talented. Just like her."

Tom's hand shot out before Tilly could touch Amber's cheek. "Watch it, Mr. Tilly. I think you've had too much to drink," he warned.

Tilly's gaze lingered on Amber for a moment longer. "Suppose I'll be seeing a lot more of you." He gave a drunken half-laugh and staggered away toward the bar, muttering to himself.

The guys were left slightly stunned.

"What was that about?" Gabe asked.

"No idea," Tom said, still trying to shake off the strange encounter.

"What was the name he mentioned again? Nevada something?"

"Nirvana Shor," Amber replied softly, her eyes distant.

"Wow, what a name," Gabe said, scratching his head. "Sounds like something he made up on the spot to get your attention. That guy's a total skirt-chaser. Always has been."

Tom nodded, agreeing with Gabe. "Yeah, the guy is old and drunk. Plus, military men can sometimes act entitled."

"Tilly never served in the military," Gabe clarified, "He hurt his back during the draft. They didn't want him."

"So he lied to me for a discount... again. That son of a gun," Tom muttered, the realization hitting him.

But Gabe wasn't really paying attention to Tom's gripes. He turned his attention to Amber, his tone light but sincere. "You good, Am? Want me to go pound his ass for you?" he offered, half-joking but fully ready to act if needed.

Amber gave a soft, reassuring smile. "I'm fine," she said. "Just a little shaken and confused, that's all."

Gabe, wanting to lighten the mood, looked at her and grinned. "Well then, looks like we need another round of tequila." He flagged down the waiter. "Excuse me!"

Just then, a different waiter appeared at their table, holding a message.

"Ms. Simmons?" she asked.

Amber looked up. "Yes?"

"You have a phone call waiting at the bar," the waiter said, her expression neutral.

"A phone call?" Amber repeated.

"Yup."

"Who from?"

The waiter shrugged. "That's all I know."

"Right... Excuse me, guys, I'll be right back."

Right after Amber stepped away, Gabe slid his chair closer to Tom, his tone shifting to something more serious. "So, are you still into Amber?" he asked bluntly. "Because if not, I'm thinking about asking her out myself."

Tom shot him a defensive glance. "What makes you think she'd say yes?"

Gabe held up his hands in mock surrender. "Whoa, easy there, Tiger. No need to jump straight to insults."

Tom rolled his eyes. "I didn't mean it like that," he muttered, rubbing his temples. "I'm just... still figuring it out."

"She's not a science project, Tom," Gabe scoffed, clearly impatient with his agonizing pace. "You're overthinking it. Just... do something already."

"Can you lay off?" Tom snapped. "And stay away from Amber."

"Not big on competition, huh? Alright, I get it," Gabe said and leaned back, but his expression remained serious. "But, you better move fast, man. Like, real fast."

"Why's that?"

"Are you really this dense? Haven't you noticed all the creepy eyes directed at our table tonight? They certainly aren't gawking at you or me. If we weren't sitting here, who knows how many thirsty dudes would be swarming her by now. You've got a head start because she knows you, but that won't last forever. Someone else is gonna make their move, and it'll be too late."

Tom fidgeted, feeling a knot form in his stomach. "You're exaggerating."

"I am not. Did you see Avery? He practically chased her down to hand her his card after she nailed that performance. If he didn't show up with his girlfriend, Amber would've been at his table."

"Even if that's true, they'd just be talking business."

Gabe shook his head, exasperated. "No, Tom. Avery's a good manager, but he's also a known sleaze. Do you want Amber to fall victim to his slimy hands? Let him take her home? Because if he manages to get her in his car, let me tell you—he ain't taking her home, if you catch my drift."

Tom's stomach churned, unease settling in. His thoughts were a whirlwind of frustration and self-doubt. He knew Gabe was right—time was ticking.

With a nervous sigh, he pushed away from the table and stood up, his mind racing. But despite the sudden burst of urgency, he was still really nervous. When it came to anything spontaneous, Tom felt like an untrained diver plunging into the deep end—no prep, no practice. He might score a point or two, but the odds were high he'd sink without a trace, with no chance to resurface and try again.

I'm overthinking this, he thought to himself. His nerves tightened in his chest as he walked through the crowd, heart thudding in his ears. The closer he got to the phone booth, the more his anxiety ballooned.

Soon, he found Amber standing there, looking startled and lost, her eyes wide with worry. In that moment, Tom's fear of rejection melted away, replaced by a wave of concern for her. He took a deep breath and approached her softly. "Hey..." His voice was gentle. "Everything okay?"

Amber turned to face him, and he could see the uncertainty written on her face. It was like a silent alarm went off inside him.

"What happened?" he asked.

Amber paused, staring at the phone booth for a beat before finally meeting his gaze. "Oh... Tom," she replied slowly.

"Who called?"

"I don't know. They hung up as soon as I answered."

"Are you okay?"

"Yeah..." She hesitated before asking, "Actually, can I ask you for a favor?"

"What is it?"

"Can you take me home?"

"Of course. You mean now?"

She nodded sharply, the seriousness in her eyes clear. Almost pale at the thought of any delay, Amber's expression left no room for argument. Tom, sensing her distress, quickly guided her through the back door and toward his car. They didn't waste any time; they were out of there and speeding down the road.

The drive was silent. Neither of them spoke, as Tom didn't want to disturb her thoughts of unmistakable importance. He could feel the stress emanating from her, and he knew there was something more to her abrupt departure than she had let on.

As they neared the trailer park, Amber's demeanor shifted. Before they reached her home, she quietly asked, "Can you drop me off here?"

Tom hesitated, glancing at her. "Are you sure?"

"Yes, please," she said firmly.

Tom pulled over at the curb, unlocking the door for her. "Thank you," she whispered.

"Don't mention it," he replied, but the words hung in the air awkwardly.

Amber paused in the seat, her body rigid as if weighing something in her mind. Tom could see the turmoil brewing beneath her calm exterior. Sensing it was now or never, he spoke again, more gently this time. "Would you like to talk about it?"

Amber didn't answer right away. She avoided his gaze, her hands clenched tightly in her lap. After a long pause, Tom tried again. "Is it something to do with your family? Or Mr. Tilly? He can be really... rude and pushy."

"That's not it," Amber answered quietly, but the words didn't hold much conviction.

Tom looked at her carefully, concern deepening in his eyes. "Amber, you look like you're in trouble."

Her eyes flickered toward him. "So what if I am?" She asked, the vulnerability in her voice unsettling.

Tom took a breath, choosing his words carefully. "If something's going on, I want to help. Whatever it is."

Amber shook her head, a rueful smile crossing her face. "You have such a good heart, Tom. But I'm afraid this is beyond anyone's comprehension."

"I know I can be a bit thick sometimes," he said with a small chuckle, "but I can be pretty intuitive too, or so the others tell me."

Amber's smile faded. "This... has nothing to do with you. Truly. Some things I just have to handle myself. It's something I need to learn to deal with. And this is one of those things."

Tom sighed, sounding regretful. "I get it. I think I understand."

She gave him a sad look, as if silently apologizing for not being able to explain. "I should go," she said. "Thanks for the ride."

She opened the door and stepped out.

"Just a second... Amber."

She leaned down, looking at him through the window. "Yes?"

"I just want to say... Merry Christmas," he said softly. "I meant to tell you at the end of the night, but it looks like this is it."

She smiled, faint but genuine. "Merry Christmas to you too, Tom. Now go back and have fun. Tell Gabe I said sorry—we rushed out of there so fast, I didn't get a chance to tell him goodbye."

"I'm sure he'll survive," Tom said, managing a smile, "but I'll let him know."

Amber nodded. She lingered for a moment, watching Tom drive off, before turning toward the gusting wind, a chill creeping into her bones.

The storm ahead wasn't just the one in the sky—it was the one waiting for her at home, where a far darker danger loomed, and she wasn't sure how much longer she could avoid it.

10

THE MOMENT AMBER stepped into the trailer, a chair came flying at her with a deafening crash. It missed her by inches, the back of the seat scraping her cheek as it whipped past. The sound of wood splintering against the wooden floor echoed through the cramped space, and for a split second, all she could do was stare in stunned silence.

This was it. She had just crossed the threshold into hell.

She stepped back, eyes darting toward Mason, who stood in the kitchen, his body rigid with rage. His fists clenched like he was about to tear something apart. Amber could see the veins in his neck bulging, the muscles in his jaw twitching as he stared back at her, dark eyes burning with something wild.

"Where the *fuck* were you?" His voice broke out like thunder. There was no greeting, no trace of familiarity—just fury.

A wave of panic threatened to rise in Amber's chest, but she pushed it down. She had learned long ago how to mask it, to stay calm when it felt impossible. The silence stretched between them like a taut wire, and she swallowed hard, forcing the words out.

"You said you wouldn't be home till Monday—" Her voice trembled slightly, but she held her gaze, trying to appear unshaken.

"That's not the point," he spat, cutting her off with a violent snap. "I'm asking where you *were*."

Amber's stomach churned, but she didn't back down. She refused to be intimidated by him. "I told you, I went out. I needed a break."

Mason's nostrils flared. He glared at her like she had just committed the gravest sin. He downed the last of his beer and hurled the empty bottle against the kitchen counter. Amber flinched at the sound, her heart skipping a beat as it shattered into a jagged mess of glass. She instinctively took another step back, but the movement only seemed to fuel Mason's rage. He staggered toward her, his body swaying with drunken menace.

Without hesitation, he grabbed the broken bottleneck, the sharp glass gleaming in his hand like a weapon. In one swift motion, he forced her back against the wall, pressing the serrated edges against her cheek, the cold bite of glass sending a shiver down her spine. His breath was hot and ragged as he growled, "You want to see what I'm capable of? Is this how you want to play?"

Amber froze. He was close now, too close, but she forced herself to stand tall, even though every instinct screamed at her to run. She couldn't. Not this time.

"Do I look like I give a *shit* about you needing a break?" Mason snarled. "You think you can just walk out whenever you feel like it? You think you can come and go as you please?"

Amber's heart hammered, but she swallowed her fear. "I'm only human, Mason. I get bored. I get restless," she said, her voice surprisingly steady. "I thought you of all people would understand that."

The words seemed to hit Mason like a slap. His face twisted, eyes narrowing into slits as he let out a derisive laugh, the sound cold and guttural. He shoved her away, making her stumble back.

"Understand? You think you can get away with this crap because you're 'only human?'" He laughed again, but there was nothing funny about it. The laughter was merciless, bitter, like a prelude to something far worse.

He tossed the broken bottleneck, and then, in a furious whirl, he yanked her around by the strain of her arm and pushed her onto the couch. When she tried to rise, he shoved her back down with a brutal force, his one beastly forearm pinning her in place, leaving her gasping beneath him.

"You see right here? This is my strength versus yours, so I suggest you quit playing games with me."

"You're the one playing games," Amber snapped back. "You knew I was at the pub."

Mason's face lingered in confusion, but the anger never left his eyes. "Pub? What pub? Larry didn't say a damn thing about any fucking pub. What the hell are you trying to pull?"

Amber's pulse quickened. The doubt in his voice sent a ripple of concern through her. *What was going on here?*

"If you weren't the one who called looking for me, then—" she hesitated, her mind racing.

Mason's eyes narrowed, his lips curling into a snarl. "Then you better wake the fuck up, because I sure as hell did. Our next-door neighbor called me. You know what's worse than being lied to? It's finding out the truth from someone else."

Amber met his gaze with cold defiance. "I'm not lying," she insisted. "I went down to the strip to see what all the fuss was about. It's Christmas, for God's sake—"

Before she could finish talking, Mason's hand shot out, slapping her across the face to shut her up. "I told you not to cross me," he hissed, his grip tightening like a vise.

"Larry told me everything, you fucking cunt. He said you've been working down at the plumber's shop. What are you trying to do, huh? Run away?"

"If I was trying to run, I would have done so already."

"Don't you start with that smartass mouth of yours. It's not going to save you this time."

In an instant, Mason yanked a wad of cash from his pocket, the rubber band snapping as he brandished it in front of her. His eyes gleamed with malice as he waved the money in her face, relishing the control he had over her. "Care to explain this?" he sneered, his voice dripping with contempt.

"Where did you get that?" she demanded, trying to keep the tremor out of her voice.

"Where did I get it? Pff! I'm the king of this house! Everything in here is mine. You can consider that overdue rent."

"That's my money... Give it back!" Amber yelled. As her fingers closed around the cash, desperation flooding her veins, she pulled with all her might—determined, frantic. But the tighter she gripped, the more infuriated Mason became.

Mason yanked her by the hair, his fingers burrowing into the strands like iron claws, and yanked her upright. Amber gasped, her scalp screaming in protest, but before she could steady herself, his boot drove hard into her stomach. The air whooshed out of her lungs in an involuntary grunt, and her body buckled, folding to the floor with an almost mechanical inevitability.

She tried to pull herself together, but Mason was already one step ahead. He sprang into the air, his knee slamming into her with a sickening thud, as if he were a prizefighter delivering the final blow. Amber's body absorbed the impact, and she crumpled beneath him, her vision swimming with spots of light.

He stood over her, his heavy boot coming down again and again with ruthless precision. Each kick was a statement, each strike a command for her to stay down. He wasn't just beating her—he was trying to break her spirit, to make sure she couldn't rise again.

Amber curled into herself, her arms wrapping tightly around her head. She wasn't sure how much longer she could take it—her body was a battlefield, battered and bruised, but she refused to scream. She refused to give him the satisfaction.

For a moment, Mason stopped to undo his belt, and she could hear the rasp of his breathing, heavy and uneven. She summoned every ounce of strength she had left and rolled onto her stomach. Her arms trembling as she pushed herself up, every movement slow and deliberate, as though her limbs had forgotten how to work.

But it didn't matter. The door was so close—just a few more feet. She could make it.

Her breath came in shallow gasps, but she didn't dare look back. She could feel his presence behind her, like a storm building on the horizon. A shadow loomed over her, and she heard his voice, low and mocking, as his boots scraped across the floor.

"Where do you think you are going, you fucking cunt! You are not going anywhere. I'm going to rip you up and beat you to pieces with this..."

Amber's fingers curled into the wooden floor, the edges of her nails digging into the grain as she fought to inch forward. Her muscles cried, each movement a painful reminder of the beating she had taken. Mason could feel her struggle—he always could. And that was part of the game. He loved the way she fought, the way she never quite gave in, as if there was something inside her he hadn't quite crushed yet.

The belt buckle clinked in his hands as he tightened it. The sound echoed through the quiet room as he whipped her—oh, how he whipped her—like he would have done to a disobedient slave who had betrayed their master. His arm swung quicker and harder until she gradually slackened and ceased to go on any further.

"Get up! I said get the hell up!" His voice was a whip-crack of command, but Amber didn't stir. She couldn't. Her body was numb, each breath a struggle, her back a searing mass of pain. Every inch of her felt like it was splintering apart.

In a daze, her gaze drifted—slow, sluggish—toward the doorway. A pair of long, slender legs stood there, impossibly still, like they belonged to a figure carved from ice. Amber's eyes followed them upward. Soon, her focus locked onto the gaunt figure that filled the frame of the door.

Michael.

Her heart stuttered, then clenched. He was standing there, his posture a twisted mockery of nonchalance—his thin body drawn like a piece of brittle paper, his face a mask of utter indifference. His eyes—flat, cold, and detached—held no trace of recognition or care.

Amber's lips parted in a whisper, but the words never fully left her mouth. *Help me.* She didn't even know if he could hear her; her voice was a fragile breath, lost in the static of pain and confusion.

But Michael didn't move. Didn't speak. His eyes simply locked onto hers, unblinking, unwavering—a mirror of apathy reflecting nothing but cold emptiness back at her.

"No one is going to help you," the beast mocked her, hurtling to remove his pants. "You think you are the princess of Persia? You are nobody—nothing—ptui!"

Frustrated and desperate, Amber screamed—her voice a primal thing that tore from her chest like a wild animal in agony. She screamed as if her very life depended on it, hoping—praying—that someone, *anyone*, might hear and come to her aid. But the room swallowed her cry whole, leaving only a heavy, suffocating silence in its wake.

No one was coming. She was alone.

She knew, with sickening clarity, that if she didn't act now—right now—the next time the beast laid his hands on her, it might be the last chance she'd ever have to escape. The consequences of inaction were too dire to contemplate.

"You'd better not fight me, or I'll fucking strangle you," he warned her.

She could feel the quickening beat of her heart—fear and adrenaline coiling tight inside her. Her hand trembled slightly as she gripped the pocketknife tucked inside her sock. With a sharp inhale, she pulled it free in one swift motion. "YAAAH!" The cry broke out from her lung like something feral breaking free. Her fingers curled tighter around the handle, her wrist flicking with a savage precision. There was no hesitation—no second-guessing.

She moved, fast and violent. In a heartbeat, the blade found its mark, plunging into the exposed flesh of his thigh. And she felt it—the sickening satisfaction of the steel biting through muscle and bone.

The force of her strike sent the beast stumbling backward, his body jerking with the pain. He had no time to defend himself—just the shock of the wound and the sting of the blade sinking in deeper.

Amber didn't pull the knife out immediately. She left it there for a moment, letting him feel the full extent of the injury, his skin stretched taut around the steel. His eyes went wide with disbelief, then narrowed in agony. Finally, her hand yanked the knife free. The beast crumpled to the floor, his legs giving way as if they were no longer capable of holding him up. His hands shot to his leg, but there was no stopping the bleeding. His face contorted in a grimace that was half anger, half fear.

"Blood... there's so much blood... Have you gone nuts? You've cut me real bad!" he cried.

"Not bad enough," Amber retorted, standing up. "You are lucky that I missed."

"Missed...? You... you—"

She crouched down beside Mason, her voice a whisper now, only for him. "Give me your car keys," she commanded.

"Like hell I will!"

Upon his refusal, she positioned her thumb over his wound. Without thoughts of mercy, she pressed down, driving it deep into his flesh, watching with a steady gaze as his flesh yielded to her pressure, until her thumb was no longer visible.

He let out an anguished wail, a jarring sound that scraped at the edges of her resolve, but she didn't flinch. His body shook violently in reaction, and she felt the pulse of his blood beneath her thumb, the heat of it seeping into her skin. In seconds, his complexion shifted from ghostly pale to an unhealthy, sickly white, and his body gave way, collapsing like a dead whale, sprawling awkwardly across the living room floor with an unsettling thud.

"Coward," she muttered.

The silence stretched, thick and oppressive, before Michael's voice sliced through it, keen and unexpected. "If he's a coward, what does that make you?"

Amber had almost forgotten Michael's strange presence in the room, his figure lingering in the shadows like a haunting memory. The sound of his voice drew her attention fully, but before she could respond, the wind outside howled, fierce and sudden. It rattled the trailer, sending tremors through the walls. The door of the cage slammed open with a deafening crack, as if the very air around them had come alive with an eerie force.

Amber whipped around, eyes scanning the room, but all she saw was a gust of snow swirling in through the open doorway. Michael was gone. There was no trace of him—no shadow, no echo of his footsteps.

She didn't waste time searching for him. She moved swiftly, her instincts driving her forward. She snatched the crumpled bills from Mason's pocket, fingers trembling as she pulled out the last of her money. The keys were next, slipping easily from his limp grasp. Finally, she retrieved her fanny pack from the trash, the familiar weight of it a small comfort in the chaos of the moment.

It wasn't the departure she had anticipated—not the kind of leaving she'd been bracing herself for. But as she stood there, alone with the snowstorm outside and Mason's motionless body at her feet, she knew one thing for sure. She had to leave. And tonight, no matter how long or difficult the road ahead, she would.

A long night awaited her.

11

"I CAN'T BELIEVE you chickened out," Gabe said with a laugh, inspecting the pearl earrings nestled delicately in their velvet-lined box. "These would've made her day, man. If you had given them to her, I bet she'd be smiling right now."

"Give it," said Tom, snatching the box from Gabe's hands. I didn't chicken out. Like I said, the moment wasn't right."

Gabe's eyes narrowed skeptically, but he let it go. "Still, people like getting gifts, whether it's Christmas or not."

"I didn't think of it like that at the time." Tom's voice trailed off as he stared at the box in his hands, then set it aside. "Anyway, thanks for coming in on short notice. I tried calling Cal, but he wouldn't answer."

"Of course not. Calling him at that ungodly hour?" Gabe let out a loud, exaggerated yawn. "What time did you even call him?"

"9 a.m."

"You didn't! The guy was hammered last night. Calling him at nine would be like waking a bear from hibernation." Gabe paused and then added, "But hey, you did me a solid. Ms. Babington probably would've locked me in her apartment for a week if I hadn't told her I had to come into work."

"Was it that bad?" Tom said, asking just to ask.

Gabe grinned with a smirk that could rival a Cheshire cat's. "The sex? It was good, not that I haven't had better."

"Then what are you griping about? Her personality?"

"If she has one, I haven't seen it yet. The woman was clingy, and I like my space," he said with a shrug, standing up straighter. "I like to let my arm rest sometimes, you know?"

Tom rolled his eyes. "Like I've never heard that before. I don't know which is worse: your commitment issues or her falling for it."

"Hey!" Gabe shot him a pointed look. "I may be groggy as hell right now, but my ears are still sharp."

Tom chuckled, shaking his head. "Why? How long did you end up *not* drinking last night?"

"Long enough..." Gabe's words were vague, and there was a slight hesitation before he spoke again. "After you guys left, I got invited to do a few twelve-ounce curls. Here and there."

"What? What happened to getting sober?"

"Appreciate the dad talk, Tom," Gabe muttered, his tone guarding. "But what happened to minding your own beeswax?"

Tom shot him a look but did not comment further, too familiar with Gabe's defensiveness.

"I'm here now, am I not? And awake. That's what matters," Gabe added with a smirk, a glint in his eye. "Besides, I can't wait to hear how many times Amber's dodged your calls."

Tom's face darkened at the reminder. "Five," he said softly, a deep frown creasing his forehead. "Including the one you walked in on."

Gabe paused, the teasing dying on his lips when he saw the shift in Tom's mood. He softened his tone. "She hasn't called back once? Not even a voicemail?"

"I've checked everything," Tom muttered. "Cell phone, desk phone, even the house phone. She's skipped work before, but never this long without one call or text."

"That's not like her," Gabe admitted, scratching his chin thoughtfully. "Maybe she's just sleeping it off. Or... I don't know."

Tom's jaw clenched as he ran a hand through his hair. "I'm thinking of stopping by her place. If you can stay and watch the shop..."

"Bold move," Gabe said, lifting an eyebrow. "Chicks dig that. Shows you care, or whatever. I'm sure she's fine. Probably had too much to drink last night. She might've just overslept. Happens to the best of us."

"I hope so," Tom said. He wasn't sure what was going on with Amber, but something didn't sit right with him.

They exited Tom's office and were met by a woman walking through the front door. She was striking in a way that was impossible to ignore—buzzed hair, butch clothing, and an aura of fierceness that seemed to fill the room as soon as she entered. She looked around, her gaze locking onto Tom. "Nina! Nina!" she shouted, voice high-pitched and urgent, her body language brimming with agitation.

Gabe's instinct kicked in, and he stepped forward. "May I help you?" he asked, trying to calm her down.

"I need to speak to your manager," she said, her tone commanding.

Tom overheard the conversation and immediately came forward, his own tone shifting into professional mode. "I'm the owner," he said, meeting her gaze with an even stare.

"You Erik?" she asked.

"No, I'm his son. Tom. What can we do for you, Miss...?"

"Shor. Jo Shor." She paused, glancing at them both with an intensity that suggested she wasn't here to waste time. "I'm looking for my sister, Nirvana. I believe she works here."

Tom and Gabe exchanged a quick glance, both surprised by the mention of the name. *Nirvana?* Tom's mind immediately went to Amber, but he said nothing. Jo continued, her voice unwavering, "You may know her as Amber Simmons. Here, I have a photo of her."

Tom took the photo and studied the image of a much younger Amber. He handed it back to Jo after a moment, his face tense. "Amber's out sick today," he said, trying to keep his voice neutral.

"She's out sick?" Jo repeated, her brow furrowing in suspicion. "She hasn't shown up for work when she's supposed to, has she?"

Tom hesitated, not sure how to respond.

"I don't understand," Gabe interrupted, scratching his head. "How come she has two names?"

Jo let out a heavy sigh, her shoulders slumping for a brief moment. It was as though a heavy burden had settled on her, and now she was ready to spill a truth long kept. "Let me put it simply. Nirvana... who you know as Amber... she's not the person she says she is. She's been using a fake ID to conceal her true identity."

"Why would she do that?" Gabe asked.

"Beats me," Jo said with a bitter edge to her voice. "I've been trying to track her down for weeks. We lost contact after she left the hospital. I hate to tell you this, but I'm afraid she's in a really vulnerable position."

"Vulnerable?"

Jo nodded grimly, her eyes burning with urgency. "Do you know where she is?" she asked, her tone shifting to something more desperate.

Tom absorbed every word Jo said. The more he thought about Amber's disappearance, the clearer it became: the only way to get to the bottom of this was to track her down.

"Let's get some answers," Tom said. Without waiting for an answer, he left Gabe in charge of the shop and straight off led Jo to the trailer park. This time, he pulled up to Lot 104, parking directly outside.

Jo didn't wait for him to make the first move. With a swift, decisive motion, she was out of her own car, heading toward the door without a second thought. Her steps were brisk, purposeful. Tom followed, matching her pace but taking a deep breath as he approached the rundown trailer. He could hear his heart in his ears—loud, rhythmic, an undercurrent to the steady crunch of gravel beneath their boots.

They reached the door, and Tom raised his fist, knocking—three solid raps. He could feel Jo's presence beside him, her shoulders squared, her jaw set. It wasn't just about finding Amber anymore. It was about demanding answers.

They waited in tense silence. Then, a moment later, the door swung open with a harsh screech, and there he was—Mason, half-dressed. His face was clouded with anger, as though being disturbed from whatever he was doing was a personal insult.

"WHAT?" His voice bellowed, raw with annoyance, like he was already fed up before the conversation even started.

Tom blinked, taken aback by the aggression in Mason's tone. His body instinctively took a half step back, but he quickly recovered. "Hello," he said. "Is, uh... is Amber home?"

Mason looked at him with contempt, his eyes narrowed as though he was sizing them up. "Who the hell are you?"

Tom swallowed. He wasn't prepared for this level of hostility. "My name's Tom Ager. This is—"

Mason's gaze flickered to Jo, and the sneer on his face grew sharper. "You're not one of her other boyfriends, are you?"

Tom's eyes widened at the inappropriate accusation. "What? No." He shot a quick look at Jo, who stood there stiff, like a wall of quiet fury. "I'm Amber's boss. She works for me."

Mason's face twisted into recognition. "I knew I'd seen you before," he muttered, his eyes running over Tom with a sudden, dismissive glint. "You're that plumber guy. How dare you show your face at my property?"

Before Tom could answer, Jo cut in. "Excuse me," she said, her eyes locking on Mason's, unwavering. "Is Amber here?"

Mason looked at her like she was an inconvenience. "And who the hell are you?"

Jo didn't falter. She held her ground. "I'm Amber's sister."

For a brief moment, there was a flash of shock in Mason's eyes, followed by a rush of irritation. "I thought she didn't have any family." He spat the words like they were foreign to him. His face flushed with rage, and he gripped the doorframe harder, his muscles tensing. "That bitch lied to me again, goddamn it. She stole my car last night and—" His voice rose, wild with indignation. "She stabbed me with a fucking knife! Now I'm stuck here, missing work because of her."

Tom blinked in disbelief, his gaze automatically falling to the thick bandage wrapped around Mason's thigh. He could see the discoloration of the skin beneath it, the clear evidence of an injury that didn't look like it had been caused by some casual accident.

"She did this to you?" Tom asked, very much shocked, his finger pointing vaguely at Mason's leg.

"Damn right she did," Mason growled, his voice tinged with something close to pride. "She stabbed me good. Left me lying there like trash, out cold. And then she just fucking took off. Gone. Probably off to screw someone else." He shook his head in frustration. "She's a fucking freeloading whore. I should've known better."

The venom in Mason's words felt like it could reach out and strangle them both. Jo's eyes flared with anger. She stepped forward, a slight but intentional motion that made Mason stiffen. Her voice dropped low, but every word cut through the air like ice. "You'd better watch your mouth," she warned, her glare so fierce it could've drawn blood. "I'm sure what happened to your leg was an accident, but you wouldn't want another accident in less than twenty-four hours."

Mason's expression shifted briefly. His eyes flashed with something—fury, yes, but also a tinge of caution. He took a half step back, but his scowl didn't soften.

"You think you can intimidate me?" he sneered. "Get lost. Both of you. I don't know where she is, and frankly, I don't care. She's gone. And if you don't leave, I'll call the cops."

Before either of them could react, Mason had already slammed the door shut.

The visit had been a bust, crushing, particularly for Jo. Tom could see the exhaustion etched in her features, the quiet frustration of yet another dead end. It was clear she was pushing herself too hard. She needed a break—she needed something other than this right now.

"Come on," he said softly. "Let's take a break. I know a café just down the street. You look like you could use a moment."

Jo nodded, a faint sigh escaping her lips. She didn't argue. She didn't have the strength to. It wasn't long before they settled into a quiet corner.

The waiter arrived with a hesitant smile, but Jo, lost in her thoughts, didn't even seem to notice him standing there. Tom exchanged a brief glance with the waiter before stepping in. "Two glasses of water, please," he said, his tone polite but firm, knowing Jo wouldn't register the request.

As soon as the waiter was out of earshot, Jo's voice broke the silence, so soft Tom almost missed it. "Did Nirvana ever mention me?"

Tom blinked, caught off guard by the question. "Well... no. Not really." He scratched the back of his neck, looking for the right words. "Then again, she's not much of a talker."

Jo's lips twitched in a small, bitter smile. "I know the type. The ones who keep everything bottled up inside. Unless you're someone she can absolutely trust, she wouldn't share anything. Not a thing."

Tom's curiosity piqued. He leaned in slightly. "Earlier, you said she was vulnerable. Why? What do you mean?"

Jo fixed her gaze on him, searching his face for something before speaking again. "Let me put it blunt. My sister's not well. She's getting better, though. A hell of a lot better. That's why the hospital discharged her. They told me the news a few weeks ago, said she was ready to leave. But when the day came..." She paused, her jaw tightening. "She ran away. I'd driven to pick her up, and when I got distracted for a second, she'd already run off with the car I arrived in. It took me days to even figure out where to start looking."

Tom opened his mouth, hesitated, then said cautiously, "I don't want to sound intrusive, but—"

"That's okay," Jo interrupted quickly, almost too eagerly. "I expect you to have questions. Go ahead."

"Thank you. How did you find out she was using a fake name?" Tom asked, genuinely intrigued.

"From the head nurse. She told me after doing a bit of digging. Turns out, one of the ward mates managed to sell Nirvana a fake ID. She confessed right away."

"What kind of a hospital are we talking about here?"

"Ever heard of Heartstone? It's a psychiatric asylum. They keep all the crazies there."

"She went there?"

Jo raised an eyebrow. "She never told you?" she asked. "Not even a hint?"

Tom shook his head, still grappling with the truth. "I suppose it's not something you just bring up. And honestly, she seemed so... normal. I never would've guessed."

"That's my sister for you," Jo said with a shrug. "She's a master of disguise when she wants to be. You ever hear her talk about the scars on her arms?"

"The burn marks," Tom said slowly, recalling the conversation from earlier.

Jo's eyes darkened. "Is that what she told you? No. Those marks? They were from an attack. From our family dog." Her voice was hard, almost scolding, as if to correct a long-standing misconception.

Tom blinked in surprise. "That actually makes more sense. I didn't question it when she said they were from a car accident."

"Accident?" Jo scoffed. "No. There was no accident. Those were intentional wounds. Nirvana has a hard time talking about our mother. She was abusive—horribly so. I'm the only family Nirvana has left. Everyone else's either gone or gone to hell. So I'm it. I'm the one who's left to pick up the pieces."

Tom sat back, taken aback by the burden of her words. "I... I didn't know."

Jo's gaze softened. "I hope you don't take her lying to you personally. She doesn't know how to trust anyone. She's been let down so many times, she doesn't know who's worth believing anymore."

Tom opened his mouth to respond, but his phone buzzed on the table, cutting the moment short. He glanced at the screen. The name "Amber" flashed in bold letters. He did a double take and looked up at Jo sitting across from him, whose eyes much brightened, her gaze darting back and forth between him and the call.

"She can't know I'm here. If she does, she'll run again. I guarantee it," Jo said quietly but firmly. Her fingers curled slightly into a fist on the edge of the table. She leaned forward, her eyes locked onto his with an intensity that was almost pleading. "Please—answer on speaker. We have to keep her calm."

Tom hesitated. Every instinct of his screamed to be cautious, but Jo's urgent expression left little room for doubt. He inhaled deeply, forcing his nerves to still, before he swiped the screen and put the call on speaker with practiced composure.

"Hello?"

"Hi. Tom." Amber's voice, soft and sweet as always, carried an undertone of something else. Guilt, maybe. *"I'm really sorry I wasn't there this morning. I should have called."*

"It's fine. No harm done. How are you? Everything okay?"

"Yeah. I'm just... not feeling too great. I probably shouldn't have tried to tough it out last night. All those shots..."

"That wasn't your fault," Tom said quickly. "Gabe suggested it. He's the one to blame."

"I hope I didn't cause too much trouble."

"No trouble at all. I had Gabe come in to cover your shift, so..." Tom's voice trailed off as he glanced at Jo, who was watching him intently. As the conversation unfolded, her body remained unnervingly still. Her breath was shallow, her focus razor-sharp as she hung on every word. She leaned in slightly, listening for any clue, any slip that could give her the information she needed. So far, she got nothing.

Her fingers twitched, betraying the quiet anxiety that danced behind her stoic exterior. She reached into her pocket and pulled out a pen. Her movements were smooth, but there was a roughness in her grip, as if the pen itself was an extension of her frustration. She scribbled quickly on the napkin and slid the note across the table with a subtle push, her gaze lingering just long enough to ensure Tom saw the message.

"FIND OUT WHERE SHE IS"

Tom's eyes flicked to the note, and he nodded almost imperceptibly, his own anxiety mounting. He needed to tread carefully.

Waiting for the right pause in the conversation, he casually slipped in the question. "So, where are you right now? I'm sorry to ask, but I stopped by your place to look for you earlier."

A tense pause followed. *"You came over? Did someone answer the door?"*

"A man did," Tom replied. "I didn't catch his name, but he seemed... upset. He mentioned something about you stealing his car."

Amber fell silent. A long, uncomfortable silence.

"Amber?" Tom prompted softly.

"I'm here. Sorry," she finally replied, her voice strained. *"He's just... someone I've been staying with. We had a fight last night. It's over. I didn't mean to keep him from you. There just... never seemed like a good time to tell you."*

Tom's gaze turned to Jo, who was now nearly vibrating with anticipation. Her hand was hovering over the napkin, tapping relentlessly. He felt the intensity of her stare, her quiet plea for him to push further.

He let the silence stretch a little longer, then asked gently, "Where are you now, Amber? I just want to make sure you're okay."

"I'm at a motel," she said, her voice quiet but resigned. *"The one on 12th Street... Room 126."*

Before Tom could respond, Jo was already on her feet, chair scraping noisily against the floor. She gave him a curt nod, her expression tight with determination.

"Hang on. I will be right over." He got off the phone soon after.

"I'm going alone," Jo said, insistent. "No offense, but I know her better. She'll freak out if we show up together. I don't have the time or the energy to chase her down again."

Tom stood up too, feeling the abrupt shift in Jo's energy. It was as if a switch had been flipped, and she had transformed before his eyes. Her previously controlled demeanor seemed to unravel in an instant, her movements now direct and purposeful.

He reached into his jacket pocket and pulled out his business card, holding it out to her.

"Here," he said, his voice steady but thick with meaning. "This has my numbers on it. If there's anything—anything—I can do, please don't hesitate to call. I haven't known your sister long, but I consider her a dear friend."

Jo's gaze flicked to the card, but she didn't take it. Instead, she waited just long enough for Tom to feel the awkwardness. It was the kind of awkwardness that pressed in on him, a quiet warning. Then, finally, her lips parted, her words sharper than he anticipated.

"Haven't you learned anything from what I told you about Nirvana?"

Tom's heart stilled for a moment, but he carried on. "Yes, that's why I want to help."

A bitter laugh escaped her, a sound that held no humor, only jagged edges. "You are a strange man, you know that? Most people would have run as fast as possible after realizing they've been dealing with a loony."

"I suppose I still fail to see her that way—"

"Well, then start," Jo told him point-blank. Her eyes hardened, and her posture shifted, a certain severeness radiating from her. "You don't get it. You can't help her, period. Do you seriously think playing a hero can cure her in any way?"

Tom's throat tightened. "No, but—"

"Don't bother explaining," Jo interrupted rudely. "Just do me a favor. Forget about her. She isn't worth your trouble. Believe me."

Her dismissive tone, her cold detachment—it was as if she had already decided Tom's place in all of this and would not tolerate any deviation. She didn't wait for him to speak. Without sparing him so much as another glance, she turned and walked toward the door. Each step she took felt like a door closing, solid and irreversible.

Tom stayed rooted to the spot, his fingers still clutching the business card he had offered her. As he watched her hurry away, his mind scrambled, everything feeling strangely out of place. But it was too late for regret. She was already gone, in the blink of an eye, disappearing as quickly as she had arrived.

PART TWO

12

"SOME SAY HEARTSTONE is a metaphoric prison. Once you check yourself in, you forfeit your name. They give you a number—a cold, impersonal string of digits that defines your existence here. They decide when or *if* you'll ever leave. The only mercy, the only shred of freedom, is that you don't have to shuffle around with shackles on your feet and your hands cuffed behind your back.

Everything in this place is about one thing: keeping 'positive.' Keeping your head down, pretending you're not breaking apart on the inside. At least, that's the prevailing belief—*if* you're lucky enough to stay in the 'better' ward. The one with decent food and less brutality. If you're unlucky enough to be assigned elsewhere, though—beyond that steel gate behind the nurses' station—the environment changes. The air grows colder, heavier. The treatment is less than humane.

In those parts of Heartstone, they lock you away in your little cell. You can cry, you can scream, but there's no one coming to help you. Not the doctors. Not the nurses. They tell you that if you behave—*and only if you behave*—they might release you. Maybe. Like a dog that's been broken and trained to fit back into society. But you'll never be quite the same after they've had their way with you. Survival becomes your only option, and survival here means one thing: keep your hands off your throat. You have to constantly remind yourself not to end it.

At night, you can't sleep. You *try* to sleep, but it's impossible. The howling from the next cell reverberates through the walls, through your bones. It's relentless. And it doesn't just come from one side of you. It echoes from the left. Then from the right. And sometimes it feels like the entire building is screaming along with them. It's a horror show that doesn't end. The night stretches on, endless and suffocating..."

"Quit bluffing, Sid. You're scaring them," Meg's voice cut through the heavy air like a dull knife. She glanced at the two new girls—both wide-eyed and pale, their mouths slightly open as they clung to every word Sidney said. She wasn't just speaking for them; a part of her was tired of hearing Sidney rehash her *daunting* experience in the isolation ward like it was some badge of honor.

"They asked," Sidney reasoned, her eyes flashing. "I'm being honest with them. They need to know what they're in for."

Meg let out a small, exasperated sigh. "It's getting old, Sid. If I had a dime for every time I heard you tell that story, I could bribe the guards into letting us all go free."

Just then, Callie, always Meg's loyal sidekick, didn't hesitate to add her comment to the mix. "Yeah, Sid, you're full of shit," she said, her tone dripping with mockery.

Sidney's eyes narrowed at the two of them, her jaw tightening. "Hey! I'm just telling it like it is. Don't call me a liar unless you've been through what I've been through," she growled.

Meg scoffed, shaking her head as she uncrossed her arms and placed them on her hips. "You were there five months ago, Sid," she shot back, her gaze hardening. "*For one day*. One. Day." She rolled her eyes, as if the entire conversation were beneath her.

Callie shot Sidney a disapproving look, her lips curled into a sneer. Without missing a beat, she uncrossed her arms in sync with Meg, the two of them forming a united front against Sidney's bravado. "Yeah, don't get cocky. You're just as miserable as the rest of us," she added.

The air in the room thickened. What had started as a minor spat—just a few petty exchanges here and there—was quickly escalating. But the real trouble only came when Jean, the antagonizing queen bitch, decided to join the fray.

"No one here believes you, Smith," Jean sneered, her lips curling into an almost predatory smile. She leaned against the wall casually, calculating. "What did the head nurse call you this morning again?" She paused, tilting her head with fake curiosity, the cruel glint in her eye barely veiled. "Oh, that's right. A compulsive liar."

Sidney's heart sunk. The words stung, but she refused to let them show. She stared Jean down, her fingers tightening into fists at her sides. "Fuck you, Malloy."

Jean's grin widened, her eyes glinting with dark amusement. "Ha! Come on then, Smith. Come get some. I *dare* you," she mocked, her posture shifting into something more combative, challenging.

Sidney stepped forward, the muscles in her legs coiled like a spring, ready to snap. "At least I'm not a fucking nymphomaniac like you," she shot back.

"Oh, that really hurts. That *really* hurts my feelings," Jean crooned sarcastically, a laugh bubbling up as she crossed her arms and leaned back, looking like she was enjoying the show. "Why don't you have a go at my tits, huh? I'm all for sharing. Oh, wait, wait—*you can't*, can you? What kind of fucking idiot is afraid of nipples?"

"Amy, you told!" Sidney hissed, her voice a strained whisper of frustration. The accusation hit like a punch in the face. Her face flushed with both anger and humiliation

Amy's eyes widened in panic. "I did not," she denied quickly, throwing her hands up in an almost defensive gesture. "I didn't say anything. I swear. You have to believe me."

The rest of the room erupted into cruel laughter at Jean's demeaning taunt, the sound of it spreading like poison. Sidney stood there, silent for a moment. She couldn't quite look anyone in the eye. Her words, once so certain, fell away into a murmur. "My mom raped me as a child, okay?" she defended. "You girls don't know anything. So back off."

Jean was not finished. "Yesterday, it was your teacher. Today, it's your mother? Who's it going to be tomorrow, huh? The hospital chief? What's the point of you if you can't even get your own story straight? Why don't you do us all a favor and kick the bucket already?"

Her words were pointed like daggers, relentless as ever. And just when it seemed like Sidney might break, something shifted in the air.

"Leave her alone, Jean," Nirvana's voice rang out, cold and calm, breaking the tension. She rose from her seat slowly, her eyes locked on Jean's with quiet authority. The laughter died, and the room fell silent. It was like time stopped for a second. Even Jean seemed to hesitate. Her smirk faltered, but only for a moment.

"Sure, Nirvana. Anything you say, Nirvana," she replied sarcastically.

"Sidney isn't wrong," Nirvana continued, her gaze steady, unblinking. "The isolation ward isn't a place you want to linger in—*ever*."

"I believe Nirvana," Amy said quietly, like she was trying to convince herself just as much as anyone else. "I overheard the nurses talking once. They said there was a girl who stayed there for an entire month. She refused to eat at first—just stared at the food like it was poison. And then... she started eating the flesh of her—"

"I wasn't talking to you, Amy. I was talking to Nirvana," Jean cut in before Amy could finish her sentence, her tone harsh like a slap. She turned toward Nirvana and continued, "So, tell me, Ms. Dare-to-do-it-all. What was it like living there? You spent three whole years on the other side, didn't you? One of them. Got any ghost stories to share?"

Nirvana was used to Jean's cruel needling, the way she sought out the most painful truths and twisted them into something for her own amusement. But this time, Nirvana wasn't going to let her bait her. Not this time.

For a moment, the room seemed to hold its breath. The hoarse crackle of the intercom shattered the silence like a gunshot.

"... 6165. Report to the nurses' station..."

Nirvana's head jerked toward the speaker, the call ringing in her ears, familiar but somehow jarring.

"... 6165 to the nurses' station..."

The voice echoed again, a little more insistent this time. But Nirvana didn't move. Not yet. With slow deliberation, she turned her gaze back to Jean. "I'll tell you what it was like," she said. "There were five suicides while I was there. Three of them hung themselves. The other two... they bit off their own tongues. One of them was my cellmate." She let the words settle, watching the effect they had on the room. "I watched her carve into her wrists for two days before she finally ended it."

The room was still, utterly still. Everyone shifted uncomfortably, their eyes darting between Nirvana and the floor. Jean, however, seemed unfazed.

"You're joking," Jean said coldly, a slight sneer tugging at the corner of her mouth.

"No," Nirvana replied flatly, her gaze unwavering.

Jean's lips twisted into a bitter smile. "And you did nothing?" she shot back, her voice thick with twisted excitement. "You just *watched*?"

Nirvana nodded slowly. The room was unnervingly quiet now. Everyone was watching them—waiting.

Jean opened her mouth to speak, but the intercom blared again, louder this time.

"Nirvana Shor! Report to the nurses' station NOW!"

The sudden intensity of the announcement pulled Nirvana out of the dead heat, its command like a jolt through her spine. It was impossible to ignore. Though reluctant, she gave way to quiet, inevitable obedience.

Without another word, she turned toward the door. "Good luck with your parole officers!" Jean called out after her, mocking, as she walked away. The words echoed in her mind with uncomfortable accuracy. It wasn't *parole officers* per se, but the bureaucratic dance she had to go through in this place—the endless assessments, the panels of so-called "experts," the decisions made by people who had no idea what it felt like to be confined—was eerily similar.

To Nirvana and her gang, the idea that someone had to approve her exit from this godforsaken hellhole, to declare her "sane enough" for the outside world, was absurd. It felt like a mockery—*these* people holding dominion over the rest of them, as if their word meant more than the pain and the struggle lived day in and day out. But it was the *golden rule* here at Heartstone, passed down through generations, enforced with unwavering rigidity. Every inmate had to prove they were worthy, and only if they reached that point—*if* they reached it—would they be considered for release.

Her steps were measured, each footfall resounding in the sterile hallways. She walked toward the nurse's station, her mind already focused on the conversation ahead.

"What was that about?" the nurse asked.

"Nothing special," Nirvana replied, her voice even. "Just a minor quarrel."

The nurse raised an eyebrow, not buying it for a second, but she let it slide. "Next time you're called, come immediately." Her warning was firm, but Nirvana didn't let it rattle her.

"Ready?" the nurse asked, though the question seemed more rhetorical than anything.

If "ready" meant mentally rehearsing every word she had to say, then yes, Nirvana was ready. More than ready. She had avoided conflict for months, played the part of the compliant patient, kept herself out of the spotlight. This day—the final analysis—had been looming for so long, and despite the months of careful preparation, the butterflies in her stomach still fluttered restlessly.

The walk to the staff building felt long, every step a mix of tension and anticipation. She waited outside Dr. Rimer's office, her heart beating a little faster than usual. When the door finally opened, Nirvana stepped in, forcing herself to calm her nerves. Dr. Rimer sat at her desk, her eyes keen behind those thick glasses, the epitome of cool professionalism.

Dr. Rimer had been her therapist for six years now—longer than any of her previous ones had lasted. Those first few years had been a mess: mania, psychosis, constant battles with authority, and none of them had known how to reach her. It had taken Dr. Rimer a long time to get her to where she was now, and though they didn't always see eye to eye, Nirvana respected her. The doctor was competent—brilliant even—and a little less hard-edged than most, but still, there was a steel inside her that made Nirvana wary.

Nirvana shifted in her seat, trying to keep her voice steady. "... They've been fine. No more staring at the ceiling for hours for sure."

Dr. Rimer took note, her pen moving steadily across the page. "Are you still on medication for insomnia?"

"No. I've been off them for a week now."

"Good," the doctor nodded. "But if you need it again, don't hesitate to ask."

"I'll keep that in mind." Nirvana's fingers twitched nervously in her lap, but she held herself together.

"Night terror?"

"No, nothing like that. Although, I hear the newer girls... I hear them sometimes. Their screams take me back to when I was in that same place."

Dr. Rimer paused, her eyes narrowing with curiosity. "How are you getting along with them?"

"Fine, I guess. We haven't really spoken much. Some of them came to Amy's birthday party at the visitor center."

"Amy's birthday?" Dr. Rimer asked, jotting down another note. "Tell me about that."

"Mrs. Bachman came to visit with her little Chihuahua. A real piece of work, that dog. Yaps and growls at everyone, only tolerates Amy. I stayed close to it, kept my distance from the others while they tried to pet it."

The doctor noted her words carefully. "Did the dog's barking bother you?"

"I was startled at first. But..." Nirvana's voice trailed off, her hands folded neatly in her lap, "No. Unlike before, I didn't feel the need to cover my ears or scream at it."

"That's progress," Dr. Rimer acknowledged with a slight nod. "Did being around the dog bring back any memories of the incident?"

Nirvana's gaze flickered for a moment, but she kept her expression neutral. "No. At least... not that I'm aware of."

Dr. Rimer didn't press further but continued with her questions. Nirvana glanced around the room, her unease growing, the silence between them thick with unspoken expectations. Finally, unable to hold back any longer, she blurted out her question.

"Aren't the board supposed to be here?"

Dr. Rimer's eyes flicked up from her notepad, assessing. "Why do you think that?"

"Well, they've been here for every other assessment. I just assumed..."

"That's why you're more nervous than usual today, isn't it?" she said with a perceptive tilt of her head. "Listen, either I'm checking off these boxes, or they are. Does that settle your worry? Shall we continue the analysis, or would you prefer to reschedule?"

"Oh no, please, do continue," Nirvana assured her.

"I will, but only if you can promise to be present and honest with everything you share."

"I have been, honest." She took a deep breath. "I'm sorry."

"No need to apologize." Dr. Rimer's tone softened, but only slightly. "Now, let's continue. Tell me about Michael."

The name landed like a brick in Nirvana's chest. She swallowed hard, her body tensing in that familiar, unavoidable way. She had known this question was coming; it was only a matter of time.

"Do you still keep in touch with him?" Dr. Rimer probed, her gaze unwavering.

"No. Haven't since I stopped most of my meds about three months ago." Nirvana's voice was flat, betraying nothing of the storm inside her.

"Have you had the urge to see him?"

"He's in my thoughts sometimes, but no, I haven't felt the need to see him."

"And him?" Dr. Rimer asked, her tone growing more insistent. "Does he come around to see you?"

For a moment, Nirvana hesitated, unsure of how to answer, her mind racing. She had expected this question but hadn't prepared for it. Her silence didn't go unnoticed.

"Does Michael still visit?" Dr. Rimer repeated, her voice gentle but firm. "I need you to be honest with me, Nirvana. Does he?"

"It depends."

"On what?"

Nirvana took a breath, choosing her words carefully. "Can I ask you a hypothetical question first?"

Dr. Rimer's eyes sharpened, and she set down her pen. "Go ahead."

"Let's say you've lived your entire life in a place like this—a shelter, a prison, whatever you want to call it—and it's all you've ever known. Would you stay and live a lie just to be safe, or would you run for it?"

Dr. Rimer paused, her expression unreadable. "Why would you want to run for it?"

"Pardon me?"

"I said, why would you want to run for it? Is there a goal, a purpose in that?"

"I... I'm not sure. I guess there might be."

"Which is?"

Nirvana gathered her thoughts and replied, "Maybe it's for a shot at something better. A better life. Just like that frog in the well who finally wonders what's outside."

Dr. Rimer nodded thoughtfully. "I think you've just answered your own question."

Nirvana blinked, a glint of understanding crossing her mind. The doctor's words weren't just about the hypothetical. They were about her, about *now*.

"What's your hope today, Nirvana?" Dr. Rimer asked, her tone quieter, more personal.

"My hope?"

"Uh-huh. Do you want to get out of here?"

"Yes... I think," Nirvana said slowly. "I'm back and forth."

Dr. Rimer leaned forward slightly. "I see that. But if I were you, I'd stop looking behind me. Focus on what's ahead."

"That's easy for you to say."

"Why? Do you think I don't have my own struggles just because I'm a doctor? That I don't face disasters? If you keep dwelling on them, that's what holds you back. You've got to focus on adapting to this new life you're about to start. This road won't be easy for you, considering you've been here for—"

"Eight years, two months, and counting," Nirvana interrupted.

"That's right. I think you're ready."

A spark of hope twinkled inside Nirvana at those very words. "Really?"

Dr. Rimer nodded, her face softening for the first time. "Really. Just think back to your first months here—fighting with nurses, screaming down the hall with no self-control. You've come a long way. You should be proud of how far you've come."

Nirvana felt a warmth in her stomach, a small but undeniable pride.

"So... when do I get to leave?" she asked.

Dr. Rimer's expression hardened again. "The specifics aren't up to me. Once I file the paperwork, it'll go to the chief, then the administration. But based on what I've seen, I'd say within a month."

A month. Nirvana let that sink in, a mixture of excitement and fear flooding her system.

"But," Dr. Rimer added, "until then, I suggest you mind your behavior. No more bickering with the nurses, no more 'minor quarrels' with anyone. Stay out of trouble."

Nirvana's face tightened. "I didn't bicker with them," she protested, though her tone was defensive.

"It's their word against yours."

"And I suppose their word counts and mine doesn't."

"This is exactly the attitude that'll keep you here longer," Dr. Rimer warned.

Nirvana clenched her fists, but before she could let her anger spill, she bit her lip, forcing herself to stay calm.

Dr. Rimer softened slightly. "Just remember, everything you do here gets recorded, whether you and I like it or not. The last thing you want is to sabotage yourself over something petty."

"I get it," Nirvana said curtly. "Are we finished here? *May* I go?"

Dr. Rimer gave her a sharp look, but nodded. "As long as we're clear. You may be dismissed."

13

"HAVE YOU GIRLS seen Mia?" Nirvana asked the gang sprawled across the common room, a black-and-white movie playing on the giant projector screen, its haunting music filling the background.

"Nope," Sidney mumbled, her eyes never leaving the screen. Her fingers absentmindedly twirled a strand of hair.

"Me neither. Probably snuck off to hoard more shit somewhere," Meg said casually, shrugging. Her lips quirked in a smirk, but it was enough to provoke an eruption of laughter from Callie, who found the casual cruelty hilarious.

Meg leaned forward eagerly, her eyes bright. "How'd it go with Rimer?" she asked Nirvana.

"Fine," Nirvana replied, her tone flat. "Same old depressing session."

"Did she at least make it worth your while?"

"I guess so."

"No shit!" Meg raised an eyebrow, leaning back. "When?"

"Maybe next month. She doesn't have all the details yet."

"Ah. Don't get your hopes up then," Meg said, her voice low, almost solemn.

"What's that supposed to mean?" Nirvana asked, surprised by Meg's sudden lack of confidence.

"She told Vicky G. the same thing last month," Meg continued, her eyes cold now. "We all know how that turned out."

Callie burst in with an almost malicious glee, unable to hold back. "They locked her up... Ha! Hahahaha!" She wiped tears from her eyes, reveling in the gossip. "I heard she tried to punch the door open so hard her knuckles needed stitches. What a fucking idiot. They're thinking of moving her permanently to the isolation ward if she doesn't get her shit together soon."

"The isolation ward? Seriously?" Meg's voice dropped, a shadow crossing her face. She cast a glance at Nirvana, her eyes darkening with doubt. "See what I mean? One minute, they're offering you a glimmer of hope; the next, they take everything away."

Sidney, overhearing the conversation, scoffed. "I'm sure Nirvana is different. They wouldn't do that to her."

"Says who?" Meg shot back, her tone biting. "If any of the nurses have a decent memory, Nirvana won't be getting off their 'difficult patient' list ever. Trust me, it follows her."

"Their opinion means jack," Sidney cut in. "Let them hate her all they want. Those minions can stew in their own bitterness. But Rimer? She's always had Nirvana's back."

Meg snorted. "Yeah, sure. She's the only one who hasn't been treated like dirt by her. The rest of us? She forgets that *we're* the ones who make sure everything stays afloat. Without us? She doesn't get paid. She doesn't get *shit*."

Nirvana opened her mouth to argue, but stopped herself. Before the conversation could spiral any further, Glenda, the ward's oldest resident, shuffled toward them, her frail hands clutching a headless teddy bear to her sagging bosom. The sight was unsettling in its own right— Glenda's trembling hands making it seem as though the bear was an extension of her very soul.

"Nirvana!" Glenda's voice cracked with urgency, her eyes wide with some nameless distress. "Can I borrow your teddy? Somebody did a number on mine. I want to teach whoever it was a lesson... a serious lesson."

"Uh... Sure. Go ahead." Nirvana's words were slow, unsure.

"Really? Thank you! Oh, thank you!" Glenda's face brightened as though Nirvana had just handed her the moon, and she quickly scurried away, her feet barely touching the floor as she disappeared into the shadows of a hallway.

"What teddy?" Meg asked.

"Don't know," Nirvana replied, confused.

"You're the only one who has the patience for that ancient weirdo."

"I think we're all considered weirdos here," Nirvana said.

"That's true... Hey, have you tried the dungeon?" Meg proposed.

"The dungeon?"

"Mia. Aren't you looking for her? She's probably down there making a mound of her 'precious' finds, figuring out a way to hide them better so she won't get caught again. The head nurse busted her just last week. She hasn't been here much since."

Sidney smirked. "Or wait for the next med call. You're guaranteed to see her then."

"I think I can use a walk," Nirvana said.

"Okay, I would walk you there, but I'm faint-hearted. My mom died in a car crash in a tunnel when I was just an infant. I barely remember it, but... yeah. I'll leave the big, scary walking to you."

"Just go, Nirvana," Meg added with a look of annoyance. "You know she'll just keep blabbing if you don't. And for the love of sanity, come back in one piece, okay? I'm this close to losing my ability to have a reasonable conversation with someone at supper."

Nirvana flashed a quick grin, though the tension in her shoulders didn't completely relax. "I'll do my best," she said, giving Meg a half-wave as she turned to leave.

She made her way toward the abandoned tunnel—the one everyone called the "dungeon." Years ago, it had become a grim landmark after an inmate's body had been discovered, tucked away in its depths. The rumors were ghastly, painting a portrait of a young girl lured to her death by malevolent guards. The administration had covered it up quickly, leaving only the whispers of her brutal fate, her name a ghost among the living.

As time passed, the dungeon had become more than just a place—it was a story. A cautionary tale, a haunted passage where a girl's death still lingered, her spirit claimed by the cold walls. Few ventured in alone, but Mia was different. Mia always had a fascination with things that haunted—she was drawn to them, as if they were the only truth left in the world.

"Mia? Are you there?" Nirvana called softly, pausing when she found herself blocked by a pile of cardboard boxes.

"Nirvana?" a voice answered from the other side. "Is it time for my piano lesson?"

"I came to talk. Can I come through?"

Without warning, a small hole appeared at the bottom corner of the boxes. Mia's face popped out, her wide eyes gleaming. "Over here," she whispered, the urgency clear in her voice. "Hurry, before someone sees you."

Nirvana ducked through the narrow space, her shoulders brushing against the jagged edges. Once on the other side, Mia quickly covered the hole with sacks of empty bottles and tin cans, the faint rustling noise filling the otherwise quiet space.

"Aren't you worried they'll find you here again?" Nirvana asked as she sat down beside her.

"They wouldn't look here so soon. Besides, this is one rare area that is out of their 24-hour surveillance," Mia said, her eyes distant, her words carrying an air of certainty. She curled her knees to her chest, her gaze drifted upward, her eyes locking on the shadowed ceiling. "Do you see what I see?" she asked, her voice soft, almost dreamlike.

Nirvana followed her gaze, seeing nothing but the brick arch above them. "I see a long stretch of brick, arching to form a vault. What do you see?"

Mia's eyes narrowed, her focus intense. "That—the noose hanging from the beam."

"A noose?" Nirvana blinked. "Where?"

"It's everywhere… They speak to me."

Nirvana nodded slowly, recognizing the shifting from reality into delusion. "What are they saying?"

"They were nagging me all day," Mia continued, her eyes darting around as if the voices were still there, haunting her. "But when you came, they stopped. Before... they wanted me to look down. From up there. To see what would happen..."

Nirvana swallowed hard, reminding her, "You are not alone, Mia."

Mia sighed, attempting to release the tension within herself. "I think the closer truth is that we all are—too alone. I can barely separate my illusory thoughts from reality these days. Sometimes, I wonder if it's easier just to let them guide me, wherever they want. At the same time, I keep asking, when will the all-powerful God finally release me from this lonely, desolate place...?"

Nirvana knew better than to interrupt, so she simply nodded, letting Mia's words linger for a moment, heavy with unspoken pain. "Have you told Rimer about any of this?" she asked, her voice gentle but lined with concern.

"What can she do except increase my dosage of antidepressants? Like that's really what I need." Mia replied, almost to herself, as though the tunnel had turned into a confessional. "You must have heard they locked up Vicky G. I still can't believe it. Just last week, she was talking about leaving Heartstone, about driving up north to dip her feet in Lake Superior. She had all these plans. But now, it's all just a pipe dream."

Nirvana leaned in and touched Mia's arm gently, trying to draw her back into the here and now. "You are not Vicky G., Mia. What happened to her won't happen to you."

"Yeah? But we're all the same to them, aren't we? They won't let us out, not really."

"I don't know. But I want to believe that they will. Eventually."

Mia shifted, her lips curling into something like a smile, but it wasn't full of joy. "You've been here for so long. Yet you're still here."

Right then, a glimmer of something bright flashed across Nirvana's face. "Well, if it's any consolation, I get to leave next month."

Mia turned her head sharply, eyes searching Nirvana's face with an intensity that bordered on disbelief. "Did they really... wow."

"Rimer told me this morning."

"That sounds... great," Mia said, her voice a hollow echo. She smiled—more out of politeness than anything else. "I'm happy for you. Really, I am."

Nirvana studied her, her concern deepening. "Are you okay?"

Mia blinked slowly, like she was waking from a dream. "Of course," she said, "Let's just hope they're not bluffing."

"I don't think they are. She even warned me to keep to my best behavior."

"Like you haven't been already."

"Right. Guess I should have come back at her and see how she takes it," Nirvana said, a faint attempt at humor that didn't quite warm her expression. "Are you sure you're okay?"

Mia met her gaze with a serious look, but her voice softened, filled with something that tugged at Nirvana's heart. "Nirvana."

"Yeah?"

"You don't have to worry. I'll miss you, for sure. But if you don't leave when you can, when will you? Only... if you do leave, I don't know who to turn to when I need a shoulder."

Nirvana's face tightened with guilt, but she tried to smile. "You'll still have the others."

"Who are we kidding? You know I only talk to you."

She exhaled, her heart aching a little. "Right. I'm sorry."

Mia, in turn, smiled, the kind of smile that said she appreciated the apology even though it wasn't quite enough. "Where would we go?" she asked curiously, despite the heaviness of the subject.

Nirvana's eyes glowed with a hint of excitement. "We could go to that summer fair you've always raved about. We could eat ice cream and smear it on each other's faces—"

Mia let out a breathless laugh.

Feeling encouraged, Nirvana grinned and continued, "We could toss bean bags, eat grilled corncobs, and stuff our faces with cotton candy."

"Oooh... and cheese curds!" Mia's face lit up, the nostalgia pulling her in. "I know this stall that sells the best of the best. My brother and I used to go three times a day, trying all their different savory flavors. We'd get there early, dressed as cowboys, and stay until sundown, checking out the farm animals. Those were the days, Nirvana. The days to beat."

Nirvana's heart ached even more now, the memories so vibrant in Mia's voice. "I'd need you to lead me the way."

Mia's smile softened, almost wistful. "Lead you where?"

"To that cheese curd stand," Nirvana said with a smirk. "I don't want to miss out on the best of the best."

As Mia giggled, Nirvana's smile faded, and the moment shifted. She cleared her throat, feeling the importance of the next words she had to say. "Speaking of your brother... I need a favor."

Mia's expression changed. "What is it?"

Nirvana took a deep breath. "I need him to get me a fake ID."

Mia's face tightened. "A fake driver's license?"

Nirvana nodded.

Mia leaned back slightly. "Can you drive?"

"Does it matter?"

"I'm not sure. But I remember hearing him talk about it when he used to do business out of our garage. There's a price difference, but either way, it's pretty expensive."

"How much?"

Mia's eyes flicked up to the ceiling as she did the mental math. "A couple hundred bucks, I think. But if he's not undercutting his competition, it could go for thousands."

Nirvana blinked. "I only have about five hundred saved up."

"Five hundred!" Mia stared at her in shock. "Where did you get that much?"

"Part-time being a janitor at the library. They needed people then, so I volunteered."

"The library here? And the head nurse let you?"

"A few of their staff quit at once. They were desperate, I guess."

Mia didn't answer right away. She simply gazed at Nirvana. "Are you sure about this?" she asked.

Nirvana nodded firmly.

After a pause, sensing the seriousness of the moment, Mia finally said, "That should be enough for the ID. If not, I'll figure something out. When my brother comes next week, I'll tell him."

Nirvana let out a breath of relief. "Thanks, Mia."

Shortly after making the arrangement, Nirvana gave Mia the space she had asked for. She then turned back the way she came. But just as she was out of the tunnel, she saw Jean, leaning casually against the entrance, cigarette in hand.

Nirvana's mood soured instantly.

"It's good she's hoarding trash now instead of cutting herself all the time," Jean called out loud enough to make sure Nirvana heard. "That was getting old."

Nirvana stiffened but didn't stop walking. Jean's voice followed her like an annoying fly. "Nothing to say to defend your bestie, huh? Whatever happened to that fiery girl I used to know? The one who used to wreck the nurses' schedules, drive them mad, defy their rules? What happened to her?"

Nirvana spun around, her patience snapping. "You won't get to me. Not today. And you better stay away from Mia."

Jean sneered. "Or else what? You can't protect her forever. You're just leaving her behind when you go."

Nirvana's fists clenched at her sides, her jaw tightening with a sudden surge of anger. "Don't bring her into this. You're just upset because I get to leave and you don't."

"Upset?" Jean's lips curled into a mock smile. "I thought you were going to say jealous. Aren't we all jealous of the great, talented Nirvana Shor from Grand Prairie?"

Nirvana's hands were shaking ever so slightly, but she decided to relent her irritation. Jean wasn't worth the energy. Not anymore.

However, Jean's voice cut through the air once again, probing. "So, what are you gonna do with your fake ID? Looks like you've got your whole future figured out."

"That's none of your business," Nirvana bit out, guarded.

"Oh? And who's to say I won't tell? One little blemish on your record, you can kiss your freedom goodbye."

"You wouldn't dare."

Jean shrugged. "Why not? No threat's ever been enough to stop me from doing what I want—"

"Because I swear I would fucking kill you this time!" Nirvana interjected harshly, her eyes mad as she charged and grabbed Jean by the neck, barely restrained from punching her in the face. Jean was taken aback by her erratic menace, at least at first, and then her appalled face gradually contorted into a hoot of laughter.

"I swear to God, I would," Nirvana insisted. "You think I'm joking?"

"No... not at all. I just wasn't sure you still got that fire in you." Jean's smirk disappeared, replaced by an almost genuine laugh. "I thought they'd tamed you. I like this version of you better. She's meaner and feistier but also much more capable in a good sense."

Nirvana was still furious, but the tension drained from her shoulders just enough for her to keep her cool. "What do you want, Malloy? Tell me now before I do something both of us regret."

"All right, chill." After Nirvana released her grip, Jean reached inside her jacket and removed a joint from her cigarette pack, offering it to Nirvana. "This is the real deal," she bragged, "Jose, our night guard, smuggled it in for me for a cheap hand job. Humph, men. Take it. It will relax you."

Nirvana hesitated to accept it, but not for long, and let Jean light it up for her. Upon her first drag, Jean continued purposefully, "I need you to do something for me."

"I figured."

"I need you to deliver a letter to my son."

Nirvana blinked, unsure she'd heard right. "Your son? I didn't know you were—"

"Married? Hell no. I'm only twenty-one years old. I was fourteen when I got here, right after I gave birth to Elijah. I like to call him my 'little miracle,' although, I presume, he's not so little anymore. He's the only thing that keeps me going these days."

"What about your parents?"

"I never knew my dad. As for my mom, she's dead," Jean said bitterly, her expression hardening as if getting triggered by a particular memory that was both painful and precious. "I still remember the moment the nurse handed me Elijah. I had never held anything so soft and dainty in my arms before, but then next, they took him... Do you have any children of your own?"

Nirvana shook her head.

"Well, if you ever get them, hold on tight and never let anyone take them from you. You can't trust anyone in this world, especially not those closest to you... I'm assuming you will be heading home once you are released—this should be along your path. If you promise to do this for me, your secret's safe with me."

Nirvana studied Jean, sensing the layers of suffering behind her cold exterior. "Why not ask someone else? Why me? Or give it to the nurses to mail it?"

Jean's eyes narrowed, her tone defensive. "Don't you think I have already considered my options? I need you to give the letter to Elijah yourself and involve no one. Can you do that or not?"

Nirvana considered it for a moment. She wanted to say no, but the truth was, she didn't have much of a choice. "Okay. I'll deliver it for you."

Right then, a flicker of relief flashed across Jean's face. "You mean it?"

"Sure. But I might not be able to do it right away."

Jean beamed, almost like a child who had just gotten a precious gift. But the smile faded just as quickly, replaced by a serious, calculating expression. "As long as you do it, that's all that matters. I'll give you the envelope when your day's near. But first, we need the address."

"You don't know where your son lives?"

"I had a good guess, but I needed to be sure. So, I had someone check on it for me a while back."

Nirvana leaned in, suspicion creeping into her voice. "By someone, you mean someone in here?"

Jean lowered her voice, as though speaking of something secretive and dangerous. "She's a senior inmate, locked up in isolation. Frizzy hair, quirky as shit. They barely let her out. They're terrified she still poses a threat. It's ridiculous, if you ask me."

Nirvana didn't even need to think. "You're talking about Doris Parker."

"You know her?" Jean's lips curled into a small smile. "I've met her. Once, at the library, by chance. Apparently, we both come from the same small town. She's got a hell of a memory. I swear, she described my neighborhood in perfect detail—streets, houses, the layout. When she offered to get the info for me through her grandson, I didn't hesitate. Paid her right there. Now I just need to figure out how to contact her again."

Nirvana shook her head, her voice cool, almost dismissive. "No."

Jean blinked, confused. "What do you mean, no?"

Nirvana's gaze hardened. "I assume you want my help to get to her. But my answer is no."

Jean's face stiffened, but she wasn't about to give up. "Don't shut me down just yet. Let me lay it out for you." She leaned forward, her eyes gleaming with intensity. "I've been watching the nurses' routine like it's a textbook. Every Friday at 3 a.m., they leave their station unguarded for an hour. That's our window."

Nirvana crossed her arms. She couldn't help but feel intrigued. "What about the security cameras?"

Jean's grin turned sly. "Matt, the guard on the graveyard shift? He's already in my pocket. Took the bribe, no questions asked. Even got me a keycard to the gate and a master key for the cells. As long as we don't mess around, we'll be fine."

Nirvana understood the risk all too well—if they got caught, everything she'd worked for, her shot at freedom, would slip through her fingers. The thought of it churned in her stomach, but there was something about Jean's plan that caught hold of her. Something about it felt tempting. Maybe it was the rebellion in her, buried for so long. Maybe it was just the fact that nothing ever seemed to change around here, and this could be a perfect opportunity to feel something alive.

Jean's voice broke through her thoughts. "Come on. What do you say? Dare to take one last ride into your old nest?"

Nirvana sighed, knowing it was inevitable. "Okay. You sold me."

"Really?" Jean's smile returned. "Because I was going for it either way. But with you helping, it'll be faster."

Nirvana shot her a look of mock annoyance. "I already said yes. Don't make me take it back."

Jean sealed the deal with a playful "zip it" gesture.

The air outside began to chill. Snowflakes drifted from the sky, each one a reminder of the consequences they were about to invite into their lives.

"Anyway, tonight. I'll meet you in the hallway at the exact time. Think of this"—Jean slipped a small glass vial into Nirvana's pocket—"as my little thank you. Found it under Callie's mattress. Seems like the hysterical loon's been saving up."

Nirvana had an inkling of what the glass vial contained, and so she didn't bother examining it. Instead, she took a long drag from her joint, handing the rest back to Jean. "I'm going inside. You coming?"

Jean was caught off guard by the unexpected warmth of the invitation. "Just because we're doing this doesn't mean we need to be friends. I still hate you and your little clique."

"Okay," Nirvana said flatly.

In turn, Jean stood still, expecting some kind of retort, a jab or sarcastic comeback. But when Nirvana did neither, her defensive walls crumbled just a little. "You go on ahead," she said. "I'm staying for a bit longer."

Nirvana gave her a sidelong glance, concerned for Mia. "You're not gonna—"

"Chill. I'm done messing with that crony of yours. She's lost her charm with all the new faces flooding this place every damn hour."

With the little guarantee Jean managed to muster, Nirvana started walking away. A few seconds later, Jean called after her.

"Hey, Nirvana! You know you're lucky, right? You get to be home for Christmas!"

14

THE DEAD OF night dawned. Nirvana lay in her bed, heart pounding in the thick silence. The clock ticked ever closer to three, and with every passing moment, her anticipation swelled. When it finally struck, she rose, moving like a shadow, each step quiet and motivated. She paused at the door where Jean was already waiting, her figure a dark silhouette against the hallway light.

"You have the keys?" Nirvana whispered at her.

Jean nodded, her eyes glinting in the dim light. "Right here in my pocket," she replied. "I need to check their records anyway. No use for the keys if we don't know the cell number Parker's in."

They moved swiftly down the hallway, the faint hum of distant machinery echoing off the cold walls. When they reached the nurses' station, Jean opened a drawer with a creak, pulling out a three-ring binder and flipping through the pages with practiced speed. Her fingers stilled when she found the information she needed.

Nirvana leaned in, her gaze flicking nervously toward the hallway from where they had just come. "Look!" she murmured, her voice tight with sudden dread.

A figure emerged from the darkness—Glenda, her face partially illuminated by the overhead light. She waved at them, and Nirvana's stomach sank. *Crap*. Before Glenda could say anything, Jean's reflexes kicked in. In a flash, she stepped forward, her hand went and wracked Glenda in the head.

Glenda crumpled without a sound, unconscious before she even hit the floor. Nirvana blinked, staggered by the suddenness of it all.

"What are you staring at me for?" Jean said, almost with a hint of amusement. "The old you would've done the same."

"I know. I just wasn't expecting to involve more people."

Jean shrugged, rolling her eyes. "Me either, but it is what it is. Now, hurry up and help me. She's heavier than she looks."

Together, they dragged Glenda's limp body behind the nurses' desk, hiding her from sight. Next, Jean swiped her key card through the reader with a soft beep, the steel gate swinging open in front of them. They moved through it like ghosts, undetected, unseen. The inner doors creaked open as they unbarred them with the same quiet precision. They were in.

The isolation ward stretched out before them—a maze of cells, each one holding a broken mind. Rows upon rows of self-contained units, each as cold and unforgiving as the next. Nirvana's chest tightened as she took in the familiar sight. This place. It was as if she'd never left. The walls were still as sterile, the hallway still as lifeless, the whimpers of the inmates still echoing off the walls. Some sobbed, others muttered incoherently, and some—some of them fought, their rage palpable even from the distance.

There was no time to dwell on the past now. Nirvana moved forward, guided by muscle memory to the cell marked "503." It was empty.

"I don't get this," Jean muttered, frustrated. "I swear this is the correct number. This *has* to be her cell."

Nirvana's brow furrowed. "Unless..."

"Unless what?"

Nirvana's suspicion grew, but she held her tongue. "Unless they moved her recently."

Jean's frown deepened. "But they always record that stuff. They've been so strict about keeping everything up-to-date."

"Unless it's too recent. Come. Follow me."

They moved quickly through the ward, slipping past the cells with the stealth of thieves, until they reached another locked gate. Jean swiped her card once more, and the door clicked open.

The room beyond was unsettlingly quiet, the air thick with the scent of antiseptic and something else—something darker. Six cells stood before them, spaced far apart, as if the ward was trying to isolate its inhabitants even further.

Jean couldn't help but voice her disbelief. "How much more isolated can they make us? Being locked in one of these is like living in hell... inside hell."

Nirvana's lips twitched into a dry smile. "Only if you're aware of what's happening. Most of the time, you're so out of it, you don't even know."

"What do you mean?" Jean probed.

"They put you in one of these cells when you're considered too much of a disturbance. If you can't be controlled, they lock you away here."

"I thought that was the purpose of those cells back there."

"It's a matter of severity," Nirvana explained, her voice distant, as if she had lived this reality a thousand times. "If you think those cells are mad, the people locked in here—well, they must have been awfully destructive in the nurses' mind."

Jean pondered what she said, her brow knitted in curiosity. "Did you ever get locked in one of these?"

Nirvana glanced at her with a look of annoyance, which was enough reaction to rouse Jean's fascination.

"My, oh my... exactly how crazy were you?"

"I'm going to ignore that question."

"Oh please-please, please do tell. Destructive, as in you screamed in their faces non-stop, or destructive, as in you yanked one of the nurses' ears off?"

Nirvana didn't respond, instead choosing to focus on the task at hand. She moved from steel door to steel door, peering through small glass panels, looking for any sign of Parker. And then she stopped.

"I think this is it," she said, her voice low, tense.

Jean hurried over, her heart pounding. She peered through the glass and saw Parker sitting on the floor, her back to them. Without a word, Jean swiped the master key and unlocked the door.

As the door creaked open, Parker's head snapped around, her eyes narrowing, assessing the intruders.

"Doris!" Jean called out to her. "Do you remember me? I'm Jean Malloy. We spoke at the library a few weeks ago."

Parker's expression shifted—first, confusion, then recognition, followed by a flash of anger. In one fluid motion, she leaped to her feet, her fingers clawing at Jean's skull. Jean tried to pull away, but Parker's grip tightened, yanking her back with a force that surprised them.

"Witch! WITCH!" Parker screamed, her face twisted in fury. "You murdered my husband! MURDERER!!!"

The shock of the attack knocked the breath out of them both. Jean struggled to break free, her movements frantic. Nirvana rushed forward, grabbing Parker and shoving her to the ground.

Jean stared, horrified, as Parker lay still.

"Oh my God... what did you just do?" Jean exclaimed, her voice cracking.

"Keep your voice down," Nirvana warned, moving toward Parker. She checked for a pulse, her fingers pressing against the woman's wrist.

"Anything?" Jean asked anxiously.

"Yes, but faint."

"What now?"

Before Nirvana could respond, Parker twitched. Her eyes fluttered open, and she blinked up at them, confused but conscious. The girls stepped back, watching as Parker's mind reassembled itself, slowly but surely.

"Doris?" Jean said again, this time more gently.

Parker smiled, as if the outburst had never happened. "Ms. Malloy. Good to see you again."

Jean exhaled sharply, relieved. "It sure is," she said, wasting no time. "I just need that address for my son. I hope you haven't forgotten our deal?"

Parker's eyes gleamed. "Of course not! My grandson delivers what he's told."

Jean's grin widened. "And?"

"And," Parker continued, her voice suddenly serious, "he's still there. Just like you thought."

"So... my mom's kept him all this time."

"I thought your mother died?" Nirvana questioned, having overheard Jean's murmur. Parker, in turn, riveted her eyes on her.

"Who's that behind you?" she asked Jean.

Jean stepped aside, giving Parker a clear view of Nirvana. The old woman's eyes widened.

"You," she said. "Haven't we met?"

"I don't think so," Nirvana replied.

"Yes, yes we have!" Parker insisted, her voice growing excited. "You're Catherine, aren't you? Catherine Shor? Ginny spoke of you all the time."

Nirvana's heart skipped a beat. "You know my grandmother?"

"Grandmother?" It just occurred to Parker. "Oh yes, Catherine's daughter. You came with your mom when you were barely an infant. What brings you back here?"

Jean quickly answered for Nirvana, her tone teasing. "She's an inmate here. Longest stay in our long-stay ward."

"Are you now?" Parker said, surprised but not too surprised. She chuckled softly, shaking her head. "It's that generational curse I know all too well of. It's in your genes, your blood. You can't escape it no matter what you do. I was you once forty years ago."

"The difference is, she gets to leave in a few weeks."

"Tsk! I've been freed numerous times."

"You have?" Nirvana asked inquisitively.

"You bet! I just always ended up back home."

"Home? You mean here...?"

"It was much easier to run away then. They've sky-rocketed their security measures since the '70s. The one time I was actually let go, I had to lie my sweet ass off. They were so very inclined to make me jump through hoops to impress them. So, enlighten me, young lady, what did you have to make up to get them to give the OK?"

"She probably slept with the panel," Jean mocked, smirking at Nirvana, "Looks like you will wind up back in here after all."

Nirvana stepped back, her eyes hard, casting a disapproving glance at Jean. She didn't say anything further. With a single, tight motion, she turned and left the room, her footsteps tight and quick as she moved down the hallway. She didn't know it, but having her little-known family history, something so deeply personal and buried, exposed in front of Jean was far more unsettling than she'd expected.

Jean followed her, smug and unfazed, the rhythm of her steps a little too confident for Nirvana's liking. Soon, they reached the steel gate behind the nurses' station, only to be met with a small commotion—people gathered around Glenda, who had awoken on the floor. The distraction was just what they needed. Without hesitation, they sidestepped the scene, gliding through the hallway with the stealth of shadows, unnoticed by anyone.

Before parting ways, Jean couldn't help herself. "You know, I didn't mean what I said back there," she called out with a teasing grin, the words slipping off her tongue like a half-hearted apology.

Nirvana's gaze flicked over her, the coldness in her eyes a sharp contrast to Jean's playful demeanor. "Yes, you did," she replied, her tone matter-of-fact. She knew better than to believe that people like Jean could change overnight. Especially someone with such a twisted, unsound mind.

Jean's laughter rang out, high-pitched and too eager. "Oh, I'm sure everyone's going to love hearing about your little secret," she smirked excitedly. "The 'Nirvana's Shame' story is gonna be gold tomorrow."

Nirvana felt a fire stir within her. "Just give me the damn letter when you have it," she told Jean. "In the meantime, leave me alone."

"Oh, I will," Jean purred, her eyes glinting with wicked amusement. "Who knows how far you'll spiral with those cursed genes of yours. You might even snap any second."

Nirvana's fists clenched, the anger pooling like hot coals deep inside her. She could feel the tension in her arms, the impulse to lash out clawing at her. But then she thought of Dr. Rimer's message, her reminders of control. She forced herself to unclench her fists, taking a slow, deep breath.

When she felt calmer, she continued, her voice lowering, dangerous. "You're right. At this rate, I might not even make it to my release day."

Jean's curiosity piqued, but she kept her smirk firmly in place. "What do you mean?"

Nirvana stepped closer, her words hushed but filled with ice. "From now until then, you'd better sleep with one eye open, if I were you."

Jean chuckled, not taking her seriously. "Ha, is this your idea of a threat?"

Nirvana didn't flinch. "It's more than that. You know it will happen. I can't stop it. I can't stop myself. So you never know when I might stab you in the back... *literally*... with my pocketknife."

Jean's smile faltered. Her eyes widened slightly, the gravity of Nirvana's words settling on her. She swallowed hard, the thrill of the situation suddenly evaporating into something far less amusing.

"You are sick, you know that?" Jean shot back, her voice small, no longer mocking.

Nirvana's lips curled into a cold smile. "Likewise. Good night, Malloy. Sleep tight."

15

ONE THING GOOD about being declared mentally rectified was that Nirvana no longer had to endure the suffocating gaze of a fifty-year-old, beady-eyed nurse while she bathed. The oppressive rules, all wrapped in the banner of 'precaution,' had turned what should be a basic human right into a privilege at Heartstone. A private bath—such a simple thing—was now a rare commodity, doled out only to those deemed dignified enough to be their own person again. A twisted irony, really. Only here at Heartstone.

"Paperwork, please," the nurse muttered from behind the laundry counter, barely looking up.

Nirvana slid the permission slip across the counter, her fingers grazing the cool paper. The nurse snatched it without a word.

"What are you here for?"

"Isn't it written on there?" Nirvana asked.

The nurse's eyes flashed with irritation. "You are supposed to answer when asked, not question," she snapped, her tone cold and clipped.

"I'm here to bathe," Nirvana replied flatly.

"Aren't you the privileged one..." The nurse's lips curled into a thin, sour line as she glanced over the slip. Then, as if the name had just crawled into her mind from a dark corner, her eyes widened in realization. "Nirvana Shor?" She adjusted her glasses, scanning Nirvana with a renewed, almost raptorial interest. And then—"Oh Christ..." She blinked, horrifying recognition sinking in. "It's you!"

Nirvana sighed, resisting the urge to roll her eyes. *Here it comes.*

"You're that hellion from Ward A," the nurse spat in disdain. "The one who used to run wild, leaving a mess wherever you went. You made us all see red!"

"Like you said, 'used to,'" Nirvana answered coolly. "I'm different now."

The nurse sniffed, a derisive laugh escaping her lips. "I see you've managed to convince your physician. But still..." Her fingers flicked her short fringe upward, revealing a thin scar near her hairline. "Nothing will ever erase this nasty thing you gave me."

Nirvana's gaze went to the scar, the painful memory surfacing as she remembered the exact moment she'd caused it. A quiet pressure settled in her gut, urging her to offer something—regret, maybe.

"I'm sorry," she said reluctantly. "Obviously, I didn't mean to hurt anyone. I wasn't in the right state of mind."

"Yeah, yeah. You gals never are. You don't need to justify yourself to me. It's all water under the bridge, right?" The nurse waved her hand dismissively, her tone almost mocking. Then she snatched up a clipboard with a registration sheet attached and thudded it down in front of Nirvana. Her eyes flicked back to Nirvana's face, then to the paper, then back to Nirvana's face again with a look that spoke volumes—*You're still beneath me, no matter what.*

"Sign your name above the line," she instructed. "From now on, you'll sign in every time. Grab a towel from the cabinet over there, by that bench. You can choose any open room, and leave this clipboard in the container on the door. Someone will check on you when it's time. You have fifteen minutes."

"I was told thirty," Nirvana countered.

"Well, for *you*, it's fifteen." The nurse's eyes narrowed, smugness twisting her features. She leaned forward slightly, her eyebrows raising in challenge, expecting submission. "Understood?"

Nirvana clenched her jaw. For the sake of peace, and to avoid a pointless argument that would only feed the nurse's petty power trip, she gave a short nod. "Fine," she muttered.

The nurse's lips curled into a satisfied smile. "Very good." She straightened, her posture almost preening. "Unless you want your precious privilege revoked, I'd advise you not to try anything funny."

"Believe me, that's the last thing I have in mind."

After getting dismissed, Nirvana moved swiftly toward a small, private bathroom. The door shut behind her with a soft click, the world outside fading away. Her body sagged against the door momentarily, letting the tension bleed out of her shoulders. She hadn't realized how much the confrontation had bothered her. But now, standing in this small, dimly-lit room, she could let it all go.

The freestanding bathtub, old but comforting in its simplicity, stood before her, an invitation to finally unwind. She twisted the faucet, feeling the cool metal beneath her fingers, the hiss of water filling the tub. She moved quickly, shedding her clothes efficiently, eager for the brief reprieve.

When the tub was full enough, she stepped in, the warm water enveloping her body like a gentle embrace. She sank back against the curve of the tub, her head tilting back over the edge. A soft murmur escaped her lips, the noise blending with the sound of running water. It was everything she had craved: quiet, solace, and just a moment of calm.

Then, like a sparkle in the back of her mind, she remembered the glass vial Jean had handed her last week—the one she'd carefully hidden away. She reached for it, her fingers trembling slightly as she unscrewed the cap. Five small pills rolled into her palm. She stared at them for a long moment, feeling a mix of nostalgia and hesitation.

Her heart thudded, the rush of euphoria from the past flooding her thoughts. She could still remember that high—the way the world blurred into softness, how every breath felt like a caress. It would be so easy to slip back into that comfort.

With a long, steadying breath, she popped all five pills into her mouth. She took a quick gulp of water and then submerged her head beneath the surface, letting the bitterness linger. Just as the acrid flavor began to settle on her tongue, a voice called to her, breaking through the haze.

"Nirvana! What do you think you are doing?"

Her heart stopped.

Daddy... The voice was unmistakable. A low, tremulous ache echoed in her core.

"Nirvana, I said—just what do you think you're doing?" The voice was closer now, a shadow looming above her, filling her vision. Startled, she shot up from the water, gasping for air. Her throat burned as the bitter pills spilled from her mouth. She fumbled, her hands shaking, desperately trying to cover her exposed body.

"What haven't I seen of my girl? You really don't have to do that," said Michael, his tone mocking. He hovered just outside the tub, leaning in as though it were all some sick joke. "Another blatant violation of their precious rules ... tsk, tsk, tsk. What are we going to do with our nervy Ms. Nirvana?"

Nirvana scrambled for composure, her breath ragged. "Oh my god, Michael... What are you doing here? Are you trying to get us both in trouble?" She whispered urgently, but Michael remained unbothered, his eyes gleaming with that knowing, infuriating glint.

"I don't think you need help with that," he said coolly, lifting the empty vial from the floor between them, twirling it between his fingers. "If acknowledging my existence is already bad, this? This has to be beyond the pale."

"That's—*that* isn't what you think," Nirvana said nervously.

Michael's eyes bored into hers, his expression shifting into something darker. "Don't bother explaining to me," he said softly, a cruel smile curling on his lips. "After all, I'm the one credited with your first experience, aren't I?" He turned off the faucet with a casual flick of his wrist before sitting down on the edge of the tub, his fingers trailing through the water in an almost hypnotic motion. His gaze never left her. "I heard talks that they're letting you go. Is that true?"

Nirvana wanted to lie. She wanted to scream at him to leave her alone. But he would find out soon enough. With a heavy sigh, she gave in. "Yes," she answered quietly.

Michael processed it slowly, his eyes narrowing as though he were trying to piece together a puzzle. But before he could speak, she added, "I'm not supposed to see you anymore."

"Yeah, yeah. No seeing. No talking. No thinking about me. I know," he said bitterly.

"Will you just go?" Nirvana's voice cracked as she struggled to regain control, her hands now wringing helplessly at her sides. "Or at least hand me that towel—"

"In a minute," Michael said curtly, not bothering to move. Instead, he reached for a sponge, dipping it in the water with practiced ease. He lathered it with soap and, without waiting for permission, began to rub it along her back.

"Hold still," he commanded, as if the words weren't a demand, but a statement of ownership.

Nirvana's stomach churned, a wave of nausea rising within her as the sponge slid over her skin. "I can scream, you know," she warned, her voice a low, tense hiss. But Michael didn't flinch. He didn't even look up.

"Go right ahead," he said. "Maybe then Dr. Rimer will finally realize you've been lying to her about me." He smiled thinly, a mockery of sympathy in his expression. "That four-eyed leech must have been blind the last time she analyzed you. Because I just don't believe it."

"Don't believe what?" Nirvana shot back, her anger flaring. "That I'm finally free? I've been wasting my life in this hellhole for so long. Don't I deserve to leave?"

"Oh, yes. You do deserve it. A hundred percent," he said with unsettling calm. But the words felt empty, like a broken record playing the same hollow tune.

"Then what's your problem?" Nirvana demanded. "Are you trying to sabotage me? Is that how you make your day?"

"You're missing the point," Michael snapped, suddenly raising his voice, his fingers digging into her chin and forcing her to look at him.

Nirvana, in turn, yanked her chin from his grasp, defiance in her eyes. "What do you want from me? Why don't you just say it and put me out of my misery?"

Michael paused, exhaling sharply before starting again, tossing the sponge aside and abandoning his charade altogether. "Okay, let's talk real," he said bluntly. "There's just one thing I need clarity on: is this really how you want it to end between us? Eight years. Eight fucking years I've been here for you."

Nirvana's heart twisted painfully, but she didn't let him see it. "I appreciated it. I really did. But I have to move on somehow. Someway."

Michael's gaze hardened with her every word. "So, you're saying I'm holding you back?" His voice had turned cold, dangerously so. "Has it ever occurred to you that maybe, just maybe, I'd like to be part of your new journey?"

Nirvana shook her head, her mouth dry as she swallowed hard. "That's not possible."

"So you plan to do this all alone?" Michael scoffed, his voice an accusatory whisper, piercing the air. "Are you *sure* you can do this alone?"

"I've been through worse. If starting over is what it takes, I'm ready to dive in."

"Except I will always be your committed lifeguard. Even if it means I have to watch you from the sidelines. A raise of your hand, and I'll be right there, pulling you from the rough sea."

"I won't need any more of your saving," Nirvana shot back, firmly and conclusively, aiming to shut down every one of Michael's rationales before they could make her question her own competence. "I'll be meeting new people, good people, I'm sure of it."

"I think you are in for a big surprise. The real world isn't as accepting as you think because if it is, you wouldn't have to be here in the first place."

"You should know, I don't care what you think... anymore."

Michael studied her unyielding expression, hidden beneath the guise of definitive self-assurance, and offered a smirk, deciding it was unnecessary to press further. "If that's your intent, fine. I didn't come here to spar. But I'm going to miss this..." He reached out and lightly traced Nirvana's wet cheek with a finger, his touch soft, too soft, and it sent a shiver down her spine. With careful, intentional force, he tilted her chin up, forcing her to meet his eyes. The gesture was gentle, almost intimate—but Nirvana knew better.

"How about one last time for old time's sake?" His voice was low, the words wrapped in a veneer of warmth, but the undertone was something darker, something demanding. It wasn't pleading, not really—not like a request. No, this was a command, a calculated ultimatum, one he expected her to obey.

The familiarity of his control pressed down on Nirvana's chest. The air between them grew thick, and she could feel the room shrinking with every passing second. Her mind screamed to break free, to lash out, but the silence that followed his question seemed to suffocate any chance of defiance. She knew exactly what he was doing—playing on the threads of what remained between them, twisting memories into leverage.

He sat down comfortably on the floor. At his signal, her hand went under the water and proceeded with what he implied her to do. "Take your time," he said, "I want you to enjoy it. Your fingers, feel them..." Even with her eyes shut tight, Nirvana could sense his gawking brazenly at her action with a look of amoral ecstasy. She could hear his lips just part, his mouth open slightly, spilling moans, and his hand move faster. Soon, she felt an old sensation coursing through her body—an overwhelming wave of disgust and shame. Despite this gut-wrenching feeling erupting inside her, she had to settle it until he reached climax by his own masturbation.

No more, she thought, her resolve solidifying.

This is the last time, she swore inwardly. And this time—this time, she meant it.

16

"*NIRVANA SHOR IS here!*"

At the announcement, a woman rushed forward, flinging her arms around Nirvana in a flurry of excitement. The nurse escort smiled at the woman's exuberance, but Nirvana remained still, aloof, her arms hanging loosely at her sides, unruffled by the outpouring of affection. There was no urgency to match the woman's eagerness, no trace of the warmth expected in return.

"I thought I told you not to come," Nirvana said to the woman, her voice laced with a quiet, unspoken disapproval. The nurse, sensing the tension, chose silence and slipped away, leaving the two to handle their business.

The woman hesitated, pulling back, and exhaled deeply, her face a portrait of disappointment. "That was an inhospitable response," she said, no longer the enthusiastic welcome of moments ago. "You haven't returned any of my calls. I nearly thought something bad had happened. I drove all this way... I wanted to see you." Her gaze lingered over Nirvana, who, despite her cool demeanor, couldn't help but notice the slight concern in the woman's eyes. "Have you been eating well? You look thinner than last time."

"I'm fine."

The woman's face fell for a moment, but she quickly recovered. "Would you like to sit down?"

"I won't stay long," Nirvana said coldly, as though she was already halfway out the door.

But the woman, unshaken by Nirvana's frosty reception, pressed forward, determined not to let the conversation stall. "Have you been practicing lately? It's been so long since I heard you play the piano. I've started listening to that classical station on the radio—"

"Why are you here, Jo?" Nirvana interrupted, her question harsh and direct.

Jo's shoulders stiffened for a moment, her smile tightening. "To see you, like I said," she continued, her voice more measured now, though still tinged with anxiety. "I've joined a new church—a Lutheran one this time. One that isn't so judgmental and fixated on converting people's sexual orientation. I even made friends with a reverend."

Nirvana didn't miss a beat. "I'm not interested."

"You don't have to sound so definite," Jo said, ignoring the dismissal. "No one's asking you to be devout right this second. Not that I've forgotten you've been an atheist your whole life."

"So have you," Nirvana reminded her, her tone flat. "Why are you telling me this? Is it supposed to impress me?"

"You want me to change, so I'm showing you the extent of my commitment. I even went and bought this." Jo reached inside her shirt, pulling out a small crucifix hanging on a chain.

The gesture hit Nirvana like a dull thud, only intensifying her irritation. "If you prefer to keep playing games. I'm out of here."

Before Nirvana could turn away, Jo grabbed her arm. "Is it really so awful for you to believe that I've missed you? I love you, for Christ's sake," she pleaded, her hand moving toward Nirvana's cheek, only for Nirvana to deliberately pull back, avoiding the touch.

Jo, though visibly stung, masked her hurt with an unconvincing attempt at indifference. "Just because you're in denial doesn't mean I stop loving you."

"You're the one in denial, Jo," Nirvana countered, yanking her arm free. "Remember our last conversation?"

"I remember it all too well..." Jo's voice dipped, regret briefly darkening her eyes, before it was taken over by frustration. "I see you're still sulking about that."

"You are not listening to me—"

"Hey! I'll listen as soon as you start to make sense," she retorted. Her voice rose, sharp and bitter. "Let's face it—I'm the only one who's been there for you. The only one who's consistently worried and cared about you. And now you want to toss me aside like a used tissue? Maybe we should get a second opinion from your doctor. See whose side she's on."

"I don't oppose that idea," Nirvana said, her remark biting. "Maybe then she'd finally see who really needs help."

"Wow... that was harsh, Nina. Look, I didn't come here to bicker." Jo's face tightened with hurt, but Nirvana pressed on.

"Don't you all say that? At the end of the day, you're all expecting something from me."

Jo's brow furrowed, suspicion crossing her face. "What do you mean?" she asked. "Who else besides me has come to see you?"

"That's not your business."

"Not my business?" she echoed, her frustration boiling over. "I think you've been the only business I've had since we met!" Her voice, louder now, was attracting the attention of others in the room. She didn't care. "Remember those nights when your mom locked you out in the freezing rain? Who stayed with you, who reassured you? Me! Who taught you how to smoke your first cigarette and do all that 'grown-up' stuff? Me! I was your favorite person. The sunshine in your miserable life—"

"My lips are sealed, Jo," Nirvana interrupted quietly but firmly. "I haven't said a word to anyone. Don't you trust me? You used to trust me."

"A lot has changed since then."

"But I'm still the same person."

"Are you kidding?" Jo's tone sharpened. "We used to be inseparable. Now there's this big, nasty rift between us."

"Is that my fault?"

"I never said it was. I blame your shitty upbringing. If it wasn't for that, you wouldn't be so *damn* defensive all the time."

"If it wasn't for my upbringing, we wouldn't have gotten to know each other."

"And you wouldn't be so afraid to love—to love me."

Nirvana's eyes narrowed. The heat of their conversation, once again, dragged her into the past. She was so tired of this back-and-forth, tired of reliving the same painful loop. Jo's words rang in her ears like her mother's, unyielding and stubborn. And it filled Nirvana with an overwhelming sense of hopelessness. With a heavy sigh, she shook her head, a gesture that felt far too heavy for her.

Jo, eyes glistening with unspoken feelings, pushed on resolutely. "I just want to love and be loved in return. Like we used to. That night in your bedroom... it was everything I'd ached for my whole life. Curiosity might have brought us there, but what we've built together has long surpassed that. Our relationship is more than any teenage infatuation or mere physical desire. It's a love that transcends everything else. This love I have for you—"

"I don't love you, Jo. And we are not in a relationship. We are not anything," Nirvana said, her tone steady, unwavering in its finality. "We can only be acquaintances at best."

Jo's face crumpled immediately, shock flickering across it. "Acquaintances? Humph! Acquaintances! HAHA! After everything we've been through? Who do you think you are fucking with!" she fused, her voice a shrill of desperation.

Despite her outburst, Nirvana persisted, gently, as if pleading for something more than just understanding. "It's especially after everything we've been through that I don't want to know you. Listen to me, Jo, please. It's over. We are over."

"NO!"

"No?"

"You heard me," Jo shot back, loud and clear. "If you think I'd cave this easily every time I hit a snag, you've mistaken me for my fucking, cocaine-addict of a mom who abandoned me just because some guy she was dating convinced her to. Nah-uh. I'm not like her. That's not me."

"And I'm the one who has to pay for *her* debt to you. Is that fair to me?"

"How can you be so selfish..."

"I'm being selfish? Where do you get your logic!" Nirvana fired, every bit of her in disbelief. After all, it was her wishful idea to try to reason with Jo through perseverance. Soon, she also got swept into this compounding wave of aggravation, not knowing how to quit it.

Their words clashed violently, sending ripples through the visiting hall. People froze in place, exchanging tense glances, eyes darting between the two. The argument escalated, drowning out everything else, filling every inch of the room with its fury. The tension was palpable, thick enough to cut through, and it felt as though time itself was holding its breath.

A nurse, eyes wide with concern, finally appeared at the doorway. She stepped forward, her presence quiet but commanding, and her calm authority diffused the explosive energy between them, giving the two hotheads a brief moment to simmer down.

Jo, her chest still heaving with rage and frustration, glanced around at the few reproachful stares that followed her from nearby tables. The suffocating heat of the moment pressed down on her, and she knew it was time to leave, but the bitter taste of defeat lingered on her tongue.

"I'm finished here anyway," she muttered to the room. Her gaze, however, softened as she turned back to Nirvana, her anger fading, replaced with something more fragile. "I'll come back in two weeks, Nina. Two weeks. I'm still hopeful. If you have any courtesy left in you, you should be, too."

Nirvana's response was as cold as ice: "Don't bet on it."

Jo swallowed hard. Her lips trembled with a mixture of hurt and lingering pride, but she managed to keep her composure, forcing a smile that felt foreign, brittle, and thin—barely a façade. She spoke slowly, as if measuring the impact of each word before letting them fall. "I can change everything else about myself, Nina, but there's one thing that will never change. That's my love for you." Her voice broke slightly, and she cleared her throat to steady herself. "Don't you see? I'd go to hell and back for you. You mean everything to me. So sleep on it, okay? Give it a few days. I know you'll come around. You always do. Just... don't do something you'll regret."

Her hand moved instinctively to her neck, fingers trembling ever so slightly as she touched the cool metal of the chain that held the crucifix close to her heart. With an intentional motion, she unclasped it, her gaze fixed on Nirvana as she placed the small, worn cross into her palm. The weight of it, the symbol of her devotion, felt heavier than it should have.

"I'm that bird in your hand, Nina," she said assertively, her eyes searching Nirvana's face for some glimmer of understanding, something that would anchor her. "Never forget that."

It was a promise, a plea, an offering—and perhaps, a last attempt to hold on. Nirvana, in turn, stood there, still and unreadable, her fingers curling lightly around the crucifix. Neither moved, neither spoke, the distance between them growing with everything to stop it.

With that, Jo turned to leave.

17

THE GANG GATHERED around as Nirvana approached her last note on the piano. The masterfully played music had moved some of them to tears, whereas others were not so impressed.

"Well," Meg began, breaking the silence with a tone that was more judgment than praise, "I'm not saying I hated it, but Mozart? It's just... not my thing. I prefer songs with real meaning, you know? That depressing song you wrote a while back, though? That one stuck with me. It was pitiful, but somehow, uplifting." Her lips curled into a half-smirk, as if offering a backhanded compliment.

"I second that," Callie chimed in, her arms folded, posture stiff. "I'm with Meg."

Amy sniffled, dabbing at her eyes with a handkerchief. "I think it was beautiful," she said softly, voice thick with emotion. "I've never been to a live concert, but if it sounds anything like that, I understand why people pay so much to experience it."

"Thank you, Amy. But I'm not sure I'm good enough to have my own concert," Nirvana replied humbly with a slight edge of discomfort.

"Stop being so modest," Sidney interjected, waving a hand dismissively. "You're great at what you do. Did I ever tell you I played the trombone in school?"

"Yeah, Sid, we've heard the trombone story," Meg quipped, cutting her off mid-sentence before she could ramble on, then shifted the focus back to Nirvana. "Are you going home to become a musician?"

Nirvana hesitated. "Honestly, I haven't thought that far ahead," she said, glancing at Mia. "What do you think, Mia? Do you think I have what it takes?"

Mia, who had been quietly observing from the corner, took a deep breath and finally spoke. "Of course you do," she said, her voice unwavering in its certainty. Then, her gaze shifted to Nirvana's bandaged fingers. Concern flashed across her face. "What happened? Have you been biting them again?"

Nirvana shrugged. "Yeah, my little vice." She let out a small, bitter laugh. "Believe me, I loathe this place just as much as all of you, but... I guess I'm nervous about leaving at the end of the day."

Mia's face softened with empathy. "Don't be afraid," she said gently. "Leaving is a good thing. But a good pianist must have good fingers. You need to take better care of them."

Nirvana smiled, though it was more out of appreciation for Mia's kindness than conviction. "I will."

"I can't believe Rimer even considered delaying your discharge because of some chewed-up fingers. What was she thinking?" Meg remarked indignantly as if she was the one who was leaving.

"She was just being cautious," Nirvana said, though she suspected it was more than that.

"Cautious? About what? That you might gnaw yourself to death?" Meg huffed, disbelief in her voice. "If you don't leave now, can you imagine what other excuses she will bring up next time just to keep you?"

"There won't be next time," Sidney interrupted with a knowing look. "Nirvana's fine now. She's cured. That gives us all hope." She gave a small, confident nod.

"Amen to that," Amy added softly.

The gang laughed, their moment of camaraderie lightening the air. But their laughter was quickly cut short by the head nurse's patronizing holler from the hallway.

"Nirvana Shor! Where is she? Is she in here?" The nurse stalked into the room, glancing over the group with barely concealed frustration

"You're done saying your goodbyes, right?" she snapped, fixing Nirvana with a glare. "Your ride's here. The engine's running."

"I'll be right out," Nirvana told her.

"You have five minutes to report to the nurses' station. If your bed isn't cleared by three o'clock, anything left will be tossed without a second thought," the nurse warned and then hurried off to her next task.

"Three o'clock, how generous," Meg muttered under her breath as the nurse left. "Am I the only one who finds her squeaky voice unbearable?"

Sidney grinned and added, "Just her voice?"

Laughter rippled through the group once more, but it was quickly replaced by Amy's reminder, "Don't forget to hit the bathroom before you leave. You know it's going to be a long ride."

"Isn't it a four-hour drive back to your hometown?" Meg asked, arching an eyebrow.

"I think so," Nirvana replied, her mind already whirling with nerves. "I don't remember for sure. It was so long ago when I got here. I should get moving anyhow before they start making a real fuss. Goodbye, girls. Goodbye, Mia."

Once the others had moved on, Mia stepped forward to speak to Nirvana privately. She had been holding back a frown the entire time, but eventually, her intense wave of nostalgia won out. "I'm really going to miss our piano lessons," she confessed, her voice tinged with regret.

Nirvana reached out, gently rubbing Mia's hands in a reassuring gesture. "And I'll miss teaching you," she said sincerely. "I left the music sheets and all my notes on your bed. Thought you might like to look through them when you get bored."

Mia's lips trembled as she gave a small, wistful smile. "Everything's going to be different after today, isn't it?"

Nirvana's chest tightened with the same sadness, but she forced herself to smile. "I hope so," she said, her voice softer than she intended. "For the better."

Mia smiled in return, the smallest of smiles, but one filled with understanding. "Right. For the better."

They hugged, the warmth of the embrace something to cling to in the face of the unknown. "I'll write you as soon as I settle down," Nirvana promised.

"Really?" Mia's eyes lit up, hope stirring in them.

"Of course." Nirvana pulled back slightly and held out her pinky. "Pinky swear?"

Mia grinned and linked her pinky with Nirvana's, sealing the promise with a small, meaningful shake. "Take care, Nirvana," Mia whispered as they pulled apart. "May your journey bring you all the good luck in the world."

After parting with Mia, Nirvana retreated to her room briefly, a state of nervous excitement coursing through her. Her eyes flicked to the bag resting by the foot of her mattress. She snatched it up, shoving it hastily under the bed. It had been years since she'd felt this wound-up—not since the incident where she gave the head nurse a bloody nose—but even then, it wasn't quite like this. Not nearly like this. With a deep breath, she walked back into the hallway, her hands empty, her heart racing.

She kept her morale high, maintaining a low profile beneath her zipped-up sweatshirt, the hood pulled low over her forehead. As the nurses were distracted, she quietly slipped past their station, heading toward the sky walkway. Once she crossed over to the visitor center, she exhaled in relief—but the hardest part was still ahead. Now, she had to stay calm and avoid detection. If the security team's radar caught wind of her, God forbid, all bets would be off.

"Good afternoon, miss." A staff member from the lobby approached her with a smile, greeting her as if she were one of the guests.

It was a good sign.

"Good afternoon," Nirvana replied, trying her best to sound composed. "Could you point me to the nearest phone booth?"

The man gestured toward a small corridor. "Right over there."

Nirvana glanced over and saw a row of pay phones mounted along the wall. "Thank you," she said.

"Visiting someone?"

"Uh... yes. Would you excuse me?"

Before the man could react, Nirvana already hopped on one of those phones, slipping a quarter into the machine and dialing Jo's number. She pressed the receiver close to her ear and waited, meanwhile steadying her breathing.

"Hello?" Jo's voice came through the line seconds later. *"Who is this?"*

"It's me," Nirvana said quietly, her voice barely above a whisper, as if speaking too loudly might break the fragile connection between them.

"Nina?" Jo responded concernedly. *"Where are you? I've been waiting for twenty minutes. What's taking so long?"*

"I'm sorry. It took me longer to pack than I expected, but I'm ready now. Just need a little help lugging my stuff out," Nirvana said calmly despite the lie.

"Why do you have so many things? I was expecting just you and your bag. I had to borrow my boss's coupé at the last minute. It's got a tiny trunk."

"It is just me and my bag, mainly... and the keyboard Judy left me a while back."

Jo's laugh was soft but skeptical. *"That unwieldy secondhand junk? Are you sure? I can get you a brand new one once you settle down at my place. Well, our place now."*

Even over the phone, Nirvana could hear the smile in Jo's voice, full of fervor. She refused to let it derail her plan, however, so she swallowed the sudden lump in her throat and continued, "I know, but she insisted I keep it. She was such a sweet old lady."

"*You and your sentiment,*" Jo teased lightly. "*At this rate, we will need a bigger place soon just for storage.*"

"I'm sorry."

"*I'm just kidding. Bring whatever you want, just hurry. Should I come meet you somewhere?*"

Nirvana's eyes darted around the quiet lobby, making sure she wasn't being watched. "Where'd you park the car?" she asked, her voice purposeful.

"*Right up by the curb at the east entrance.*"

"Perfect. Just come in the lobby in ten minutes. I'll meet you there."

"*Got it.*"

"Also, can you leave the car running? I heard it's freezing out there, and I'm only wearing a tee."

"*Fine, but we'll have to be quick,*" Jo said reluctantly. "*Like I said, I've been here a while. Not sure how long I can keep the spot without getting towed.*"

"It will be a get-in-and-get-out, I promise."

"*Okay.*"

"Good. I'll see you in a bit."

Just as Nirvana was about to hang up, Jo's voice stopped her, urgent and filled with something softer beneath the surface. "*Wait! Nina!*" she called out, her words tumbling out in a rush. "*Can I confess something?*"

Nirvana paused, a strange feeling swirling in her gut. "Yeah?"

Jo's voice softened, vulnerable. "*You sound... cheerful. I'm glad. When I waited, and waited, and you still hadn't shown up, I was getting worried.*"

Nirvana's heart fluttered, and she closed her eyes for a moment. "You worry too much."

145

"I know," Jo laughed softly, but it was edged with something real. *"That's only because I can hardly contain myself. The thought of us living together—despite all the mess we've been through—it's... it's exciting. I want us to spend every day together, like we used to. Just us, far away from everything else."*

Nirvana knew exactly what Jo meant, but the words felt like a burden on her, dragging her down. She sighed softly, keeping her tone neutral. "I know what you mean... and I feel the same."

"I knew you'd come around! I knew it!" Jo exclaimed, her excitement bursting through the line. *"You won't believe how happy I am. Wait until you see the apartment. It's not much, but it's home..."*

Nirvana kept quiet and listened to her go on further about their prospective life, a happy picture of them residing in a small, high-rise condo by a lake, all of which sounded lovely, all of which she resented. For she had a thoroughly different idea of living in mind, one that was free from the constraints of her past and, precisely, one that excluded Jo. As a result of such ambition, she was pinning her full faith on the next couple of minutes for everything to work out accordingly.

She couldn't afford for things to go wrong now.

As soon as the call ended, Nirvana quickly headed toward one of the side doors, eager to get outside. But before she could slip away, a receptionist from the front desk, who had been watching her with growing suspicion, stepped in her path, blocking her exit.

"Hold it," the receptionist said rudely, her eyes narrowing as she looked down her haughty nose at Nirvana. "I recognize you. Aren't you a patient here?"

Nosy rats, Nirvana thought, suppressing a contemptuous jeer as she forced herself to stay calm. "Yes," she replied.

"Where are you going?"

She glanced over the receptionist's shoulder. "I was looking for the bathroom, and it looks like I just found it."

"You should go to the ones at your ward. Haven't you been advised not to use the visitors' lavatory?"

"Yes, but they were cleaning them then, and I couldn't wait. Plus, I'm scheduled to leave today."

"You are?" the receptionist asked doubtfully, pulling out her tablet. "What is your name?"

"Ni... uh, Amber. My last name's Simmons... May I go, please? I really can't hold it in any longer."

The receptionist sighed, deciding to spare Nirvana a little leniency. "Fine, but just this once. If you're departing soon, you should be escorted to meet with your guardian. I'll make an exception and call a nurse for you. She should be here when you come out."

"Okay. Thanks for your help..."

Nirvana practically bolted into the ladies' room after that unfortunate encounter, checking carefully to make sure no one else was inside. Once she was alone, she sank to the floor, a wave of despair washing over her. She felt cornered, like a wild animal trying to escape the clutches of its captors. Time was slipping away, pouring through her fingers like loose sand, and there was nothing she could do to stop it. She knew she had to act now. A little trepidation couldn't undo the effort she had taken to get her this far.

She looked across the room and spotted a double-hung window on the back wall. Quickly realizing it was her only way out of the building without compromising her plan, she rushed to slide it open. A quick glance behind her, then she climbed outside, her movements swift and practiced. The moment her feet hit the ground, she felt a fleeting sense of victory. But there was no time to savor it. Male guards patrolled the area, and any moment of standstill could jeopardize everything. She moved fast, turning sharp corners and staying low until the east entrance came into view.

As expected, the car sat just ahead, its engine idling. Nirvana hesitated for the briefest moment, wondering if Jo might be returning soon. The thought lingered in her mind, but it was gone as quickly as it came. She sprinted toward the car, her feet pounding the pavement, and slammed the door shut.

Her gaze snapped to the ignition—empty. Her heart thudded as a wave of panic rushed through her. The steering wheel felt foreign beneath her hands, its presence like a challenge she wasn't sure she could meet. She had never driven before—never even touched the controls. Her fingers gripped the wheel tightly as though willing it to understand her. *Focus*, she told herself.

Her fingers fumbled for the gearshift. She wasn't sure what to expect, but instinct screamed at her to move. She threw it into drive, and in her panic, her foot collided with the gas pedal. The car jerked violently. The screech of tires tore through her ears as she slammed her foot down on the brake, throwing the car back into its place with an ungraceful lurch. Her pulse roared, her hands trembling as they clutched the wheel.

She could feel the panic worsening, a tightness in her chest, but she fought it off with a sharp inhale. *No. Focus.* Her fingers flexed, gripping the wheel again, firmer this time. She needed this. She had no choice. "I can do this... I need to do this..." Her second attempt was more controlled. She eased her foot onto the gas pedal, the car responding more smoothly this time. For a split second, she felt it—the surge of power. The engine hummed beneath her, but it was more than just the mechanical hum of the car. It was the hum of her own inner strength, the spark of something deep within her rising to meet the moment.

Her hands, though still unsteady, guided the car with growing confidence. Every turn of the wheel steadied her nerves, pushing her forward. She accelerated, slowly but with an increasing sense of purpose. The car crept toward the exit, the secure gate that had once held her in place now slipping away. And then, just like that, she was out.

Beyond the hospital.

Beyond the walls that had defined her life for far too long.

The air hit her like a wave, heavy with the scent of freedom. It tasted sweeter than she ever imagined. It was as though the world had opened up to her, lighter, full of possibilities she had never allowed herself to dream of.

She was free.

At last.

18

THE SKY DUSKED, and the bitterly cold day soon transitioned into a raw October night. Three hours since Nirvana left Heartstone, the highway ahead of her looked endless still, with miles of wintry landscapes and bleak backdrops to come. Moreover, she finally encountered her first real problem—the car was running low on fuel.

Sometime later, it sputtered to a halt, its engine winding down as if exhausted from the journey. Nirvana stepped out, bracing the piercing wind in sweats and a pair of old sneakers. She paced back and forth along the curbside, her thoughts a whirlwind of uncertainty. Traffic had proven to be scarce on this particular stretch of road and virtually non-existent at this time. After spending ten minutes in the freezing cold, she decided to get back inside the car when, suddenly, luck struck.

A semi-truck was coming down her way. Seizing the opportunity to hitchhike, Nirvana extended her arm and gestured with a thumb up to get the driver's attention. It worked. She watched the vehicle pull up behind the coupé. A man of considerable size stepped out shortly after, holding a flashlight that flared in her direction.

"I don't recommend wearing all black on an empty road with no streetlights," the man said, approaching her. "If I hadn't spotted you from a distance, I might've run you over by accident. What's going on? Car trouble?"

Nirvana nodded.

The man continued. "What have we here? A Ford Mustang? What's wrong with it?" he asked, circling around to inspect the car.

"I'm not sure... it just stopped suddenly," Nirvana replied, trying to sound as nonchalant as possible, though her nerves were beginning to fray.

"Oh yeah? So it just died on you... There's no key in the ignition. Have you been driving it without one?"

She kept quiet while the man carried on. "Looks like it ran out of fuel. That's the last thing you want in this atrocious weather. I happen to keep a can of gasoline in the back of my cab—"

"That's okay."

"What do you mean? You want it working again, don't you?" When Nirvana hesitated to respond, a flash of realization crossed the man's face, and he added, "I see. Are you from Wisconsin?"

"Why?" Nirvana asked, guarded.

"I don't mean to sound like a wiseacre, but I deliver freight between the two states. I know this highway like the back of my hand, no kidding," the man said, his tone matter-of-fact. "The only folks who use it are truckers like myself—unless you came from that insane asylum out east, which I highly doubt. Now, I've come across lost travelers and runaways before, and you kinda remind me of a girl I picked up once."

"Yes. I am from Wisconsin. Madison, Wisconsin," she affirmed him.

"What are the chances! My grandmother's from Madison. She owns a bakery down there, Martha's Cakes and Breads; maybe you've heard of it? No?" he asked, raising an eyebrow as he waited for her response.

Instead, Nirvana shook her head.

The man went on to pry some more. "How old are you?" he asked, eyeing Nirvana with curiosity.

"Twenty-one," she replied, her voice steady but her guard rising.

"Oh really? I was certain you were a lot older. No disrespect, but you look mature for a twenty-one-year-old. Beautifully mature..." He looked her up and down, his eyes lingering a little too long.

Nirvana tried to distract him by changing the subject. "What is your name, sir?"

"'Sir?' I don't think I've ever been called 'sir' before," the man chuckled, shaking his head. "I guess you college kids are more civil and well-mannered than most. Haven't met many in forty years... I'm rambling. My job keeps me isolated. I don't talk to anyone much." He paused, collecting himself. "Back to your question. Mason. Mason Hill, to be exact. And you are? Miss...?"

"Amber. My name's Amber," Nirvana answered, almost too certainly.

"Amber, like the gemstone?"

"Yes."

"Pretty! Ha. This might be none of my business, but... where'd you swipe the car from?"

"Excuse me?"

"I meant, where did you steal it? I see that it has a Minnesota license plate."

Nirvana was taken aback by the accusation. "Oh... just... from town," she stuttered, avoiding eye contact. "Some woman left it unattended on the side of the road."

"So, they just... left it?"

"Mm-hmm."

"You bad girl!" Mason smirked, his eyes fixating on her with an unsettling intensity. Nirvana felt her skin crawl under his gaze, growing more uncomfortable with each passing second. She decided it was time to get straight to the point.

"Look, Mr. Hill, are you able to help me? I've been stuck here for some time, and it's freezing. I need to get to Grand Prairie."

"Grand Prairie? What coincidence! I am heading that way myself," he told her excitedly.

"Really?"

"Sure thing! In that case, hop on."

Mason began to lead Nirvana toward his truck, his curiosity never waning. "So, you going to school in Grand Prairie or something?" he asked, his voice light but probing.

"No," Nirvana answered briefly.

"Visiting family?"

"No, no family... I was told that it was a good place to start your life over."

Mason chuckled. "Who told you that? There's not much in Grand Prairie, only the prairies. You are a brave little small-town girl, aren't you? A rebel without a cause." He leaned casually against the truck, studying her like she was some kind of puzzle he was trying to figure out, and then suddenly, he exclaimed, "Oh, damn! Damn it!" He looked down at the ground as if just realizing something, his hand running through his hair in frustration.

"Something's wrong?" Nirvana asked.

"Nothing except I must clean up the passenger's seat before I can let you 'hop on.' I'm such a loner on the road. My truck rarely gets the care it deserves. Does that make sense?"

"Sure."

"Can you wait here? I'll call you over. Better yet, you can get your stuff from the trunk ready," he instructed her.

"I didn't bring anything with me..." Nirvana said.

"For real? Now, that's odd. I could've sworn I heard something coming from the back earlier. Thought maybe you had a cat—or a pet ferret, something like that. Anyway, hang tight. I'll be right back."

As soon as Mason hurried off, Nirvana's ears caught a faint, muffled cry coming from the trunk of the small coupé. Promptly, she approached it to investigate. Taking a deep breath, she lifted the trunk lid—and froze in shock. There, huddled inside, was Michael.

He quickly sat up from his awkward position, stretching his cramped neck and arms, trying to relieve the tension. "Well, well, my little piglet," he greeted Nirvana.

Utterly stunned by the unexpected sight, Nirvana instinctively took a step back, her mind racing to process what was happening.

"What's wrong, piglet? You don't look too pleased. Rough day?" he continued with a sarcastic smile, gingerly climbing out of the trunk.

"Don't come any closer!" Nirvana snapped, but Michael ignored her warning and took a step forward.

"Is that a threat? Or are you just repeating what Rimer taught you to say?"

"How did you even get in there? This doesn't add up..."

"Why? Are you really that surprised to see me?" Michael's voice dropped into a low, mocking tone as he took another step closer, his eyes never leaving Nirvana's. He paused, tilting his head slightly, a twisted grin playing at his lips. "Or maybe you're just scared. Has my sudden appearance on your big day thrown you off? Taken the wind right out of your sails?"

He took another step forward, his hand reaching up to adjust his jacket as if he were settling into the moment. His presence was heavy and oppressive. He could see Nirvana retreating frantically, but he did not stop, his feet deliberately closing the distance between them, slowly but surely.

"For years, you've learned to hate and grudge me. You think it's just over like that between us? Not so fast. Not like that. Not when I'm still here. I'm coming, Nirvana. I'm going to get you!! I will huff and puff till I blow your defenses down one by one like what's happened to the three little piglets. One by one, I will tear them apart. I will crush them. Remember that bedtime story about the three little pigs? Wasn't that your childhood favorite? PUUUFF!"

As Michael advanced toward her, his voice thick with increased anger and his fists clenched as though he were about to strike, Nirvana stumbled backward onto the concrete in a clumsy retreat. The sight caused him to burst into a dark, mocking laugh, halting in his tracks to stand over her, savoring the moment and gloating at her misery.

"It's time to wake up and smell reality," he alluded to her, which started her thinking.

"What do you mean?" she asked.

"There's no reason why the wolf and his little piglet can't get along and have a happy ending, is there?" he taunted, his voice dripping with dark amusement as he leaned in closer, eyes gleaming with a twisted satisfaction.

As soon as he took another step forward, Nirvana's voice broke through the air, desperate: "Get back! I said, GET BACK!!" The words seemed to shake the air, but not Michael. She kicked furiously against the pavement, her body sliding back, desperately inching further away from him. Her hands, raw and blistered, scraped along the ground as she pushed herself harder, inching toward the yellow centerline. Her heart pounded like a drum, every movement fueled by pure panic, her breath ragged.

"LOOK OUT!" Michael exclaimed, alerting her of a large vehicle looming over the horizon. Nirvana heard the menacing growl of the engine before she saw the truck hurtling toward her, its headlights cutting through the night like a predator on the prowl. She whipped her head around to catch a glimpse of it racing down the road.

"Come back here, Nirvana! There's no running away from us. There's no ending this unless you end yourself; believe me, it isn't fun getting squashed by a truck," Michael sneered, stepping closer. He held out his hand, fingers splayed wide, a mocking grin stretched across his face as the truck roared ever closer.

"Now, come on! Grab my hand, quick!" His voice dripped with feigned urgency, but his eyes sparkled with sadistic delight. He took another step closer, his hand reaching out as the truck's engine roared louder, the sound of it swallowing up the distance between them.

"Fuck you, Michael. *Fuck* you," Nirvana retorted, and rather than doing a roll and tumble to safety, her body stilled as the world seemed to slip away. She closed her eyes, letting the steady rumbles beneath her feet vibrate through her bones, the cold, hard surface of the road grounding her in that singular, fleeting moment. The rush of everything—her fear, her anger, her frustration—faded into the background, swallowed up by the silence.

The world was gone. It had ceased to exist.

But then, a shift. The stillness shattered. She sensed the blinding beam of headlights sweeping over her face, searing through her eyelids. The world returned in a harsh, unforgiving flash. The sound of the truck's engine roared to life in her ears, its presence overwhelming, like a force of nature bearing down on her.

She froze, caught in that final, suffocating moment between life and death...

Warmth.

19

NIRVANA WAS ON the verge of waking from her stupor when a beam of light pierced the darkness of the room. The sound that accompanied it was awful—a groan from the hinges, as if heaven's door was creaking open. Slowly, she opened her eyes, squinting against the brightness. Gradually, she made out a pair of legs descending the steps.

Clink. Clink. Clink...

In a futile attempt to clear her blurred vision, she whimpered from excruciating pain. But the pain wasn't her greatest concern. What truly unsettled her was the sudden realization that she had been tied to a chair.

This was not heaven.

This was more like hell.

Unable to move, she called out to the darkness to get someone's attention. "Hello? Who's there?"

The figure paused at the bottom of the ladder, their voice soft and contemplative. "Isn't the golden light of dawn divine? I'd give up everything just to be enveloped by its celestial beauty."

Nirvana immediately recognized Jo's voice as the figure stepped into the light. "You don't want to move too much," Jo said gently, her tone full of care. "I swabbed and applied ointment to your back half an hour ago. It should numb the pain soon. I was surprised the rubbing alcohol didn't wake you. You seemed to be having such a frightful dream."

"So—you've found me," Nirvana said flatly.

"Yes, yes I did," Jo responded, her voice tinged with the faintest trace of annoyance. "Amber Simmons... Need I guess where you got that idea from? You really don't make this easy for me, do you? By the way, thank you for taking my boss's car for a joyride and dumping it on the freeway. He fired me soon after finding out I had lost it."

Nirvana surveyed the familiar surroundings. "How did I end up here?" she asked.

"You don't remember? You called me to pick you up at the motel. You said something about feeling lonely, about how you missed me and loved me—all that shit," Jo said bitterly.

"You're lying," Nirvana shot back as her clouded mind slowly cleared, her voice wavering but sharp. "I called Tom... but you showed up at the door instead. You put a towel over my face, and I was out like a light."

"So you are not totally gone." Jo's lips curled into a twisted smile. "A nice bloke, he was, I must say. Gullible, but nice. As for that guy from the trailer..." She shook her head slowly before adding, "He's the one who did this to you, isn't he? The one who beat you?"

"Mason... How did you know about him? Have you been investigating me?" Nirvana's voice trembled slightly, but the sharpness remained, cutting through the tension in the room. She glared at Jo, trying to mask the creeping dread in her chest.

"Ha! Have I?" Jo laughed mirthlessly, her eyes narrowing. She almost seemed offended by the question, as if Nirvana had underestimated her persistence. "I practically turned Heartstone upside down looking for you that afternoon. First, I went to the front desk. People started freaking out when they found out a patient had gone missing. The head nurse got involved, and before I knew it, the hospital's chief was in on it. No one knew where you'd gone until your little friend spilled the beans about the fake ID. Took me another month to track down your trail. Part of it's my fault, I guess—Grand Prairie... I should have figured it out sooner."

"I never wanted you to come look for me," Nirvana countered.

"I also never expected you to lie to me, so I guess we're both thunderstruck," Jo snapped back. She paused briefly, her tone softening as she continued, "I'm not interested in quarreling with you, because if you're not sick of it yet, I am. You've been out cold for two days. I can't imagine you're not starving by now." With that, she reached into her bag and pulled out a package of a mini cheesecake, carefully unwrapping it and topping it with a dollop of whipped cream. The creamy texture shimmered under the dim light. She held it up, her eyes glinting with a strange mix of care and control.

"Tempting, isn't it?" Jo murmured as she leaned in closer, offering the dessert to Nirvana.

Nirvana, in turn, turned her face away, rejecting the sweet gesture. As she did, some of the whipped cream smeared across her cheek, a stark contrast to the pallor of her skin. Jo's eyes darted to the mess, her expression flickering with a brief flash of tenderness, but she quickly masked it with impatience.

"Don't be stubborn," she urged, reaching out to wipe the cream away, her fingers hovering near Nirvana's cheek. But Nirvana recoiled, her resolve as firm as ever.

Jo sighed in frustration. "You're making this harder than it needs to be."

"Tell me why you are doing this," Nirvana demanded.

"That's a silly question. I love you. I care about you," Jo replied, her voice laced with affection as she leaned in to kiss Nirvana on the lips. But Nirvana recoiled a second time, rejecting the kiss. Jo pulled back slightly, her brow furrowing with concern. "What's wrong?" she asked, her tone shifting to something more curious, even a bit hurt.

Nirvana responded angrily. "What's wrong?" she retorted, "I'm not some animal you can just tether to a post whenever you feel like it!"

Jo stood up straight. Her eyes widened with a bitter edge as she glared down at Nirvana. "You want me to untie you... Why should I? So we can play chase again? Oh no, not this time. I can't even leave you alone for a minute without you running off, causing chaos. Look at you—look at the state you're in."

"We've been over this. We're finished. Don't you get it?"

"I never agreed to that."

Nirvana's face hardened, her gaze cold. "Then look who's the stubborn one? My problems are mine to deal with. I never asked for your help, and I'll never need it."

"How unappreciative of you!" Jo bellowed suddenly, her voice rising with anger. "Remember how your mom used to treat you? Remember that night in the backyard? Who showed up to save you?"

Nirvana's gaze remained cold and distant as she responded flatly, "I'm not happy that you did... but thankful that you did." Her words were devoid of emotion, as though she had detached herself from the very memory Jo tried to provoke.

Jo was relentless however. "How could you... If it weren't for me, that dog would have chewed you up and eaten you alive! You think you could've handled it on your own? That you could've run from it? *From her?* I was the one who kept you from getting torn apart that night!"

"You killed her, Jo... You... you killed my mother." Nirvana, unmoved, shot back at Jo with cold clarity. "No matter how much she was tormenting me at the time, I never would have wished for that outcome in a million years."

Just then, a single tear fell from Nirvana's eye, streaking down her cheek. Jo's gaze fixed on it, her face tightening as she watched, feeling a slash across her heart.

She took a step back, her fists clenched at her sides, her body stiff with frustration. "And you hate me for that," she said in disbelief, "I did everything necessary to save you, and you hate me."

"I *don't* hate you," Nirvana said firmly, her voice steady, hoping the message would finally sink in this time, "I just don't want to know you anymore."

As usual, Jo didn't take it well. "So you'd rather save your compassion for a monster than for someone who's willing to go to war and die for you? That crazy woman practically tortured you every single day. Have you forgotten? How many times did you complain to me about her, about her murdering your cat, about her treating you like a dartboard, about her banging your head against the wall, hitting and stomping on you, about all the time you had to live in hell after your dad died—"

"ENOUGH! I didn't go to Heartstone and back just to be dragged into the very things I ran away from—the things that sent me there in the first place."

"I disagree. I think you... you need to check your conscience, badly," Jo spat, her voice trembling with rage. She paced back and forth in the dark room, giving what she had in mind a final consideration, and then, she made a decision. "I never wanted it to come to this, but I don't see any other way to get you to see straight again." She yanked a bandana from her pocket, approaching Nirvana with a determined look. "This should remind you who the real villain is in all of this," she said resolutely.

"No... NO!" Nirvana shouted, struggling against the restraints, but her protests were powerless as Jo continued, placing the bandana over her eyes and knotting it securely behind her head. "You've gone crazy," Nirvana muttered, helplessness creeping over her.

Despite what Jo had just done, she responded unusually calmly to Nirvana, her lips curling into a chilling, self-deceptive smile. "Mrs. Jones used to call me crazy. Remember her? My foster parent number nine, your old neighbor. That deaf old woman never knew what was coming until it hit her face. Once, I locked her up in her room for a day, and from that day, she learned never to turn her back on me again. You, unfortunately, are just like her. You have to learn things the hard way." She spoke with an eerie certainty, as though she truly believed the lesson was inevitable.

"Don't do this, Jo. I know you. You will regret this soon and hate yourself for what you've done. I swear,"

Nirvana pleaded with a mix of desperation and warning, which seemed to have little effect on the cold intention in Jo's eyes.

"You are right. I very much might, but not if that's what needs to be done. Honestly, if your mom were still alive, had I not tossed that gun into the lake after I shot her, I would have done it over again in a heartbeat. I've wept for you, Nina. I've dreamt of the day you'd finally get well, that we could be happy together at last. I even went so far as to decorate our little place with your favorite flowers, but I can't take you there and show it to you—not until you're totally on board with me."

Through the blindfold, Nirvana could vaguely sense Jo moving around, the sound of footsteps growing fainter as she left the room. Moments later, she returned with something in her hand. Before Nirvana could react, a low, ferocious growl echoed through the room, and her heart jumped. The sound was so close, so menacing, that she nearly jumped out of her skin.

"Jo... is... is that...?"

"You bet," Jo responded. "This way, you'll remember exactly what happened—what got us here—loud and clear." She paused and then added in a tone that was almost tender: "It's all for you, Nina. All of it."

"You can't do this to me... Let me go! LET ME GO, JO!!!!!" Nirvana screamed, but it mattered not how much she bawled, for Jo would not hear her further. She noticed her shadow gradually recede into the background and the fading of her footsteps disappear up the ladder.

Clink. Clink. Clink...

In a moment, the room plunged into pitch black as the door slammed shut with a deafening thud. The ravening snarls, however, remained relentless and terrifying, their guttural growls vibrating through the walls. Each sound gnawed at Nirvana's sanity, pushing her closer to the edge. Yet, despite the suffocating darkness and her growing fear, she fought to maintain her composure. With a stern expression, she forced herself to whistle softly into the void, clinging to the faint hope that the simple sound could keep her grounded—keep her spirits up, even for just a moment.

Stay calm, or you might lose it, she thought to herself, the mantra repeating in her mind. That little creature could sniff out fear, and she knew better than to surrender to it—not again. She could feel the terror creeping up her spine, but she steeled herself against it. Closing her eyes, she focused on drowning out the shrill barks, the low growls, and the blood-curdling bays that reverberated through the dark room. Long, steady breaths followed— each one an act of defiance against the rising panic. She could feel the tremors of unease threatening to overtake her, but she fought to suppress them.

In the silence of her focused mind, something shifted. Her sense of reality began to warp, like the air around her thickening, bending at the edges.

"Nirvana...!!"

The voice pierced the dark silence, a sharp echo that resonated through the void.

Mommy...

She couldn't see, but her heart could see everything: the lights spangling in the windows of her childhood home, the warm glow from the kitchen where her mother stood, calling for her with that familiar urgency.

Her nose twitched as the scent of summer weeds and damp earth crept into her senses, pulling her back to the overgrown backyard where she had once sat, lost in thought. The sun-dappled grass beneath her, the chirp of crickets in the air—it was all so vivid, so real, that she almost felt the weight of the world on her shoulders once again.

A deep yearning clung to her.

I should go to her... the thought swirled, each word heavier than the last. I *need to tell her something. Something I've been holding onto for too long. Something she may not want to know. But I have to say it. For what it's worth, I have to say it.*

PART THREE

20

"**Y**OU MIGHT WANT to have someone come take a look at your septic tank," Tom said, pulling his hand out of the toilet bowl.

Tilly handed him a rag. "Is it that bad?"

"Hard to say, but it shouldn't be clogging this quickly, especially since I was just here fixing it. Do you remember the last time you had the tank pumped?"

"I never have. My old cottage didn't have one, so it didn't ever cross my mind."

"Yeah, well, I gather it should be pumped every few years. Like I said, you should have someone come inspect it. If you want, I can give you Sam's card. He's an expert in this sort of thing and can explain it to you much better than I can."

Tilly heard Tom speaking about his blood uncle with such fondness, and couldn't help but comment. "That's okay, I know Sam," he said, then quickly added, "On a side note, I see you've forgiven that wife-stealing old fart pretty easily."

Tom shot him a defensive glance as he packed up his tools. "What are you talking about?"

"Funny you should ask," Tilly smirked. "What do you think your old man would've said if he knew you and his double-crossing brother were on good terms now?"

Tom paused, his hands stilling for a moment. "I wasn't asking for your opinion, and besides, nothing. He would've said nothing. Just like he said nothing the moment she left..."

Tilly caught the last sentence Tom muttered and raised an eyebrow in surprise. "You mean he just let his wife walk out the door with that backstabbing bastard?"

Tom shrugged, his tone flat. "Pretty much... I don't feel like digging up what's been swept under the rug, if you don't mind. As long as he's good to my mom, that's enough for me."

Tilly snorted. "What's the matter? Getting misty-eyed?" He nudged Tom with a wink. "You can't afford to be a pussy in this day and age. If you are, you might as well let someone else run your life. You've got to be your own boss."

"I am my own boss," Tom declared, standing a little straighter.

Tilly stared him up and down. "I'll need to see some backbone to believe it."

"I don't have to prove myself to you."

"Attaboy! Now we're talking," Tilly grinned, clearly pleased with the exchange.

Tom sighed, knowing there was no beating Mr. Tilly's smart mouth. In the blink of an eye, Tilly found his next target. "Speaking of your clan," he said with a mischievous gleam in his eye, "how's that ambitious brother of yours? How's Mark?"

"He's just fine, I presume," Tom replied disinterestedly. "I'm meeting him in an hour. I'll ask him for you."

"I missed him at the Christmas party. Last I heard, he was a big shot, working on some high-profile case down in George County."

"Mark wasn't at the party."

"No?" Tilly gave a low chuckle. "Too busy to mingle with us commoners, huh?" He shook his head as though amused by the thought. "Tell him he's always welcome at Uncle Tilly's. We'll order takeout, flop in front of the TV, and get wasted like we did before," he said proudly, as though it was an offer worth relishing.

Tom glanced at him, a bit flabbergasted. "I didn't know you guys hung out."

Tilly chuckled again, scratching his chin. "Well, just the one time, but hell, that was the best time I've had in a long while. That brother of you is really something."

Tom gave a small nod. "I'll make sure he knows that opportunity's still open."

"Good, Tommy Boy." Tilly's expression shifted as his eyes glimmered with some deeper thought. "That reminds me. I swung by your shop this morning—didn't see anyone sitting at the front counter. Whatever happened to that girl you hired? That Nirvana girl."

"She, uh... quit, I suppose," said Tom, the words trailing off as his mind lingered on the brief, strange phone conversation he'd had with Nirvana that morning.

"Quit? She didn't run away, did she? Humph, like mother, like daughter, I guess," Tilly remarked with a certain confidence as if it were an established truth.

Tom stiffened slightly, his eyes narrowing. "How is she like her mother?" he asked curiously.

Tilly took a long breath, his shoulders sagging as he leaned against the wall, looking off into the distance, clearly preparing to share something that had been weighing on him. "Well, if you must know, I was with Catherine the day before she disappeared."

Tom blinked. "You were?" he questioned. "What did you do to her?"

Tilly held up both hands in mock surrender. "I didn't do anything. When things started to get serious, she just up and left."

"You mean when you suggested eloping with her?"

Tilly's expression shifted into one of shock. "How do you know about that?"

"You told me last time," Tom replied, his voice steady but pointed. "You said she was the one woman you've ever loved."

Tilly smirked, shaking his head as if trying to downplay it. "I doubt I said that," he said, though his eyes held a knowing glint. "But hell, you've got a damn good memory, boy. Anyway, that's what I thought happened after I couldn't get in touch with her the next day."

"So, you don't believe she ran away anymore?"

"Certainly, I'd like to think my proposal had such an impact, but after all these years of trying to make sense of it, I know that just can't be the case."

"Then..." Tom stepped forward, the slight movement bringing an intensity to his gaze. "Where do you think she went? Do you think she's still alive?"

Tilly met his gaze directly, his tone suddenly serious. "If you're asking if I think some horrendous accident took her life... maybe. But if you're asking if I think she committed suicide, then hell no. No way. The Catherine I knew—she was tough as nails. Wouldn't have done something like that, even when guilt was gnawing at her."

Tom's eyebrows shot up. "She felt guilty about something?"

"Oh yeah. Big time. But once she sorted out that guilt, she'd turn right around and do the same thing that got her in trouble in the first place. It was like a cycle, a damn broken record. She's always had an anger problem if I haven't told you."

"You didn't. Was it that bad?"

Tilly's face twisted. "Bad enough. Never took it out on me, though. But I had seen her snap at Nirvana—more times than I care to count. Over the dumbest little things. Sometimes, she'd lock her in the basement, no food, just because the girl stood her ground. If Nirvana ever fought back... hell, I can't even imagine the beatings behind closed doors."

Tom's eyes widened. "If that's true, she's a horrible person."

"Yeah... I hear you." Tilly looked away, deep in thought. "If there's one place I think she might've gone, it's that psychiatric hospital up on the outskirts of Oseding."

"Heartstone... Why do you think that?"

"Because she once mentioned to me about getting herself committed, after one of those punishments she gave Nirvana. It was that twinge of guilt, you see? Some days, I'd imagine she's still alive and well, just going by a different name."

Tom shook his head, the thought of it repulsing him. He added, "I can't believe the father didn't do something to stop her."

"Well, he was always off on tour for some big concert when that shit went down. I don't know how he handled it when he came home and saw his precious child bruised all to hell."

"Did she only take her anger out on Nirvana? What about her other daughter, Jo?"

Tilly blinked, genuinely puzzled. "What other daughter?" He looked at Tom as if he'd asked something completely absurd. "Catherine only has that one girl, as far as I know."

Tom felt a cold shiver run down his spine, a nagging doubt creeping in. "Are you sure?" he pressed, his voice tight. "Maybe she had another affair or another child from a previous marriage she never told you about?"

"Are you saying she lied to me?"

"I'm not saying anything. I just want to know the truth."

Tilly studied him for a moment. His arms crossed in a slightly defensive manner. "I know my Catherine. She might've been a great many things, but a liar she wasn't. And I was her only confidant at the time. Why would she tell me all her misdeeds, huh? You think it was her thing to go around town spilling her dirty laundry? No. You've probably mistaken some other kid for her daughter. What did you say her name was?"

"Jo."

Tilly shrugged, a dispassionate look in his eyes. "Never heard of her. But there was this older boy who came around a few times when I was over at their place. Didn't talk to him much, but I knew he and Nirvana were close."

"I don't think that's relevant."

"I'm just telling you what I know firsthand. Don't go spreading rumors. Get your facts straight."

"I understand," Tom replied, his voice firm and clipped.

Tilly's grin returned, smug and knowing. "Why the sudden interest, boy? You're not usually this nosy. Could it be someone's falling for somebody?"

Tom faltered for a second, caught off guard by the question. "I was just curious."

"Curiosity, huh? That's all it takes." Tilly leaned in slightly, his eyes twinkling. He sighed, then looked off into the distance, his smile growing wistful. "When I saw Nirvana perform that night, it was like watching her mother on stage. Same damn presence. Same power. There's something about women like that, something magnetic. You can't help but be drawn to them. Despite everything Catherine did... I still miss her. She was the one woman I didn't mind doing the mundane stuff with. Sitting on the deck, watching the moon rise... We weren't married, but we were happy in our own way." He paused, almost lost in the memory. "Now that I think about it—I wonder if that old country house in the woods is still there..."

21

DUE TO THE overlong chat with Tilly, Tom was running late to meet his brother for lunch at *Woks*. When he arrived, Mark was already settled into their usual booth, nursing a beer.

"It's unlike you to be late," Mark said with a smirk as Tom slid into the seat opposite him.

"It's also not like you to be on time," Tom shot back, glancing at the menu. Then, turning to the waiter, he added, "Water, please."

"Still sober, huh?" Mark teased, swirling his beer casually.

"What do you mean 'still?' I never was much of a drinker."

"We haven't gotten together in months. A lot can change between then and now."

"Nothing ever changes around here with me or the shop," Tom said matter-of-factly. "How about you? How's the new precinct? How's the team treating you?"

Mark leaned back in his booth, throwing a casual arm across the top. "Whoa, slow down there, big brother. I'm not in a rush today. Took the day off."

"Really?" Tom raised an eyebrow.

"Yeah. Work's good, though, frantic as hell. You wouldn't believe how many cases get filed every day down there. Keeps me busy, that's for sure."

"If work's so busy, how do they afford to let you take leave?"

"I'm entitled to a vacation after slaving away for four and a half months. Besides, nobody tells Detective Marcus what to do." Mark grinned widely.

Since childhood, Mark had always been the wild one—the one who took risks, who went to parties, who got in trouble. He'd been the daredevil, the one with the endless supply of stories that earned him a certain kind of cult following. Tom, on the other hand, had been more grounded. They were opposites in nearly every way, though Tom couldn't deny a sense of pride for his brother's success.

Even so, a part of him still wished Mark would calm down a bit. The cockiness, the arrogance, the constant need to show off—it never really stopped.

"...Remember when I scored 98% on my promotional exam?" Mark jogged Tom's memory, as though he had no doubt it would be hard to forget.

"How could I not remember? You called to tell me as soon as you heard the news—and reminded me again the next morning, and the next."

"You know me, I like to be thorough," Mark said with a wink. Then his expression shifted slightly, his usual bravado flickering for just a second. "I never learned to quit once I set my mind to something. I'm a man who gets things done. Unlike some people I know."

Tom's lips tightened. "Hey, I get things done."

"Yeah, but a little slower," Mark teased. "Let's just hope the people you're helping have enough patience to wait."

"I do things meticulously," Tom defended, his tone firm. "But no matter. I don't tell you how to do your job, so leave mine alone."

"Fair enough..."

The mood shifted as Mark leaned forward, a teasing glint in his eyes. "So, what about your lady? How's Dominique?"

Tom paused, then sighed deeply, his gaze turning toward the window for a moment, as if seeking a distraction. "She's fine, I guess," he said quietly. "We broke up... and she's with someone else now."

Mark blinked, caught off guard. Then, in his usual blunt manner, he asked, "Let me guess. She cheated on you and dumped you?" His voice had an almost clinical edge, the question feeling more like a statement.

The directness stung, especially coming from Mark. Tom had always found his younger brother's sharp tongue to be one of his more irritating qualities. "That's one way to put it," he muttered, his face growing taut.

"I've always had a feeling that she might do that but didn't want to tell you to spare your feelings."

"Oh, great," Tom kidded dryly. "Thanks for looking out for me."

"No problem," Mark replied with a playful wink. "I'm just saying, I have an eye for spotting bad apples, while you... Well, let's just say you're more of the 'hopeless romantic' type. Always too trusting."

Tom knew Mark deep down meant well, but even good-natured banter could get tiring. Mark soon noticed him getting quiet and thus moved on to a more positive note.

"All jests aside, could a new lady be in your life? Maybe a good apple this time?"

Tom shook his head. "Actually, I need your help with something. It's about a colleague of mine. I'm worried about her."

"You know, there's something called 'just ask her,'" Mark replied with a bit of "duh" in his voice, but then, as he kept listening, he became increasingly intrigued by what Tom was telling him.

"...Are you saying she hasn't been showing up to work? When have you last seen her?" he probed.

"We hung out at *Gins* Sunday night," Tom told him. "Today's Wednesday, so it's been three days. She also called in sick Monday morning."

"Maybe she lied to go on a secret job interview and then conveniently 'forgot' to tell you she quit after getting recruited. Some people can be very irresponsible."

"I don't think that's her character."

"How long have you known this girl?"

"A month... There was also this strange woman who came into the shop that same morning desperate to find her. The woman claimed to be her sister."

Mark's brow furrowed. "What do you mean, 'claimed?' You think she lied?"

Tom hesitated, not sure how much to share. "Yeah... I found out later that she wasn't her sister after all."

"Okay... deep breath..." said Mark, putting on his detective hat. "What's your colleague's name?"

"She used to go by Amber Simmons when I hired her. But now I believe her name is Nirvana Shor."

"No one has two legal names. Didn't you check her identification?"

"Of course. Her driver's license said Amber Simmons. I didn't have any reason to doubt it."

Mark shook his head, incredulous. "You didn't run a background check on her? Nothing?"

"It was just a cleaning job," Tom replied, meeting his gaze coolly.

"What about her wages? Her deposit records?"

"I paid her in cash. From the start, she made it clear she didn't have any bank accounts or anything like that."

"And you didn't even ask why?" Mark scoffed.

"I'm not as investigative as you are, okay? I don't start my day with a million questions about every person who walks through my door."

"Right. You just take everything at face value."

Tom was getting annoyed by his brother's patronizing remarks and almost regretted bringing Nirvana up. Mark studied him for a moment before continuing, his tone still cutting but more thoughtful. "You're sure her real name is Nirvana Shor? Come to think of it, that name's ringing a bell..."

"Her mother's name is Catherine Shor. She vanished years ago."

Mark's eyes widened, and his mouth curved into a knowing smile. "Oh, *that* Shor. The crazy lady who ran off into the woods."

"That's not what I heard."

"Everyone around here's got a story about her, some crazier than others. It's up to you which to believe. But let's come back to the point. You were saying there was another woman involved? And she was pretending to be Ms. Shor's sister?"

"Yes, she told me her name was Jo," Tom continued, "she came in that morning anxious to see Nirvana. Apparently she had been trying to find her for weeks. Later, we were at a café when Nirvana called me and said she was at a motel nearby. Before I even hung up the phone, Jo was already up and ready to leave, having obtained Nirvana's location over the speaker. That was the last I heard from either of them."

Mark's eyes narrowed. "A motel? Which one?"

"The one on 12th Street. I went by to check, but the staff couldn't give me anything."

He sighed as if the answer were painfully obvious. "That place is a dump. It's known for its lack of safety measures. If anyone's gonna go missing, that's the spot."

"Are you saying Jo's abducted her?"

"Not yet, but it sounds like there's something sketchy going on. Did you try her numbers?"

"She didn't give me one."

"I meant Ms. Shor's. Did you try *all* her numbers?"

"She only has that one number," Tom said, but before long, an idea sparked. "Wait a minute..."

Without wasting a moment, they returned to the shop, and Tom immediately pulled Nirvana's employment form from the file. The number underlined in the "Emergency Contact" section stood out like a beacon.

Tom picked up the phone and dialed the number, tapping his fingers anxiously on the desk. After three tries and no answer, the line went cold.

"She didn't write down a name for the number. Care to guess whose it can be?" Mark asked.

"Probably her boyfriend's," Tom mused.

"She told you she had a boyfriend?"

At that moment, Gabe entered the room where they were, having overheard the conversation and been itching to say something. "She told him she was living with a guy. That man is a dingus and a half if you ask me."

"You've met him?" Mark asked Gabe.

"I didn't. They did."

"Jo and I stopped by his place briefly to look for Nirvana," Tom informed Mark.

"Did you now? Awesome! So we can skip the introduction and get straight down to business. Let's go bug the guy one more time, huh? What do you say?" Mark suggested.

"I'm not so sure," Tom replied, his voice tinged with uncertainty. "Last time, he wasn't exactly helpful. And what about the shop? I can't just leave it hanging in the middle of the day."

"I'll keep an eye on it for you," Gabe said, his tone light, but with an undercurrent of seriousness. "I was supposed to catch a movie with some buddies, but this? This is way more important."

Tom was still unsure, however. "If the guy didn't open up last time, what makes you think he'll suddenly cooperate now?"

Mark grinned, the cocky detective in him fully resurfaced. "Leave that part to me, Thomas. You just worry about getting us there."

22

"IT'S YOU. WHAT did I say about coming back here?" Mason growled, his voice rough and clipped as he stood in the doorway, a flash of fury in his eyes. His hands, calloused and clenched into fists, hung at his sides, but he didn't move. His gaze shot past Tom, landing on Mark. He narrowed his eyes, sizing the man up.

Mark, unfazed by Mason's fiery glare, took a step forward. "I'm Agent Marcus Ager," he introduced himself, his voice even, authoritative, his badge gleaming as he flashed it in front of Mason. There was no mistaking the steel in his tone. "What's your name?"

Mason hesitated, his nerves momentarily giving way under the pressure of Mark's imposing presence. But then he squared his shoulders, drawing himself up like he was trying to will the fear away. He puffed out his chest, chin raised, a poor imitation of confidence.

"Mason Hill," he replied, his voice a little louder than necessary. "What's this about?" His eyes darted between the two men, challenging, but not without a flutter of uncertainty.

Mark didn't respond right away. Instead, his gaze swept across the room, his posture relaxed. "Mr. Hill, may we come in for a quick chat?" The question wasn't an invitation—it was an order.

Mason's lips curled into a sneer. "Hell no." His voice broke like thunder in the tense silence, and his body tensed in preparation for whatever might come next.

Mark raised an eyebrow and, without missing a beat, pointed to something on the wall behind Mason. "Oh? What's that on your wall?"

Mason's head whipped around, but before he could process the direction Mark was pointing in, the agent made his move. Like a shadow moving too fast to catch, Mark stepped into the trailer, his presence sweeping past Mason's startled form.

"Hey!" Mason barked, spinning on his heels and charging at Mark, his fist flying toward the man's jaw with all the fury of a trapped animal. But Mark was quicker—too quick. He sidestepped, grabbing Mason's arm mid-swing, his grip iron-tight.

"You don't want to hit a police officer, believe me," Mark said, his voice cold and calm, like a teacher giving a warning to a misbehaving child.

Mason's chest heaved with a mix of frustration and embarrassment. He'd missed, and now he felt foolish, humiliated in his own home. But his pride refused to crumble.

"What do you want!" he howled, retreating several steps back into the dimness of the trailer. He didn't want to give in, but every instinct screamed to make them leave.

Mark's eyes flickered briefly over to Tom, then back to Mason. He stepped forward. "Like I said, a chat," he replied, his tone smooth, almost patronizing. "There's no need to get hysterical."

"A chat about what!" Mason spat. He took a small step toward them, but the gravity of the situation kept him rooted in place, like a man teetering on the edge of a cliff, unsure whether to jump or retreat.

"We are investigating a missing person," Mark said, his voice cutting through the air with precision. He stood firm, his gaze unwavering as it locked onto Mason's. "About this woman who's been staying with you—Nirvana Shor."

"I don't know anyone with that name," Mason said, offering a dismissive wave.

Tom stepped in, his voice low but insistent. "She's also known as Amber. Amber Simmons. I was just here looking for her the other day."

Mason stiffened at the name, his posture rigid, but his eyes betrayed him for a split second, just long enough to be noticed. And for a moment, he didn't speak—his lips pressed together as if weighing his options.

"Amber Simmons... Yeah, I know her." His eyes narrowed as he let out a humorless laugh. "That whore."

"Wait a minute," Mark said, his eyes darting around, scanning the room as if he were trying to catch a fleeting sound. "What's that tantalizing moan in the background?" He took a slow, deliberate step toward the kitchen, his gaze flicking across the countertops. Then, his eyes locked onto a computer monitor sitting on the kitchen counter. His expression shifted from confusion to mild amusement, lips curling into a smirk as he leaned in closer to get a better look at what was playing.

"Is that... is that porn?" he asked.

"I wasn't expecting company," Mason shot back to save face. "Last I checked, I'm still allowed to do whatever the hell I please on my own property—"

"You sick, fat, old, cocky son of a bitch!" Mark interjected him cattily, aiming to silence his nasty attitude once and for all. "Is that how you speak to a police officer!"

Mason swallowed hard, the knot of nervousness choking him as it twisted in his throat. For his own sake, he reduced his hostility to nothing, keeping his voice barely audible, like a mouse's squeak. "No," he muttered, almost to himself, before stumbling through an explanation. "I'm just saying... I don't like being disturbed when I'm doing my thing, in my own domain. I'm not hurting nobody." His eyes darted to the floor, hoping it might shield him from the storm brewing in Mark's gaze.

"This repulsive place is hardly a realm even for a butthole like yourself, so I wouldn't brag too much if I were you. Now go turn that disgusting thing off," Mark commanded him, and Mason swiftly acted on it.

"Is 764-346-3333 your phone number?" Mark asked him after he returned.

"I don't think so."

"You don't *think* so?"

"I have a work phone, a pager, and a cell phone," Mason explained. "I don't keep my numbers memorized by heart."

Without a word, Mark pulled out his phone, dialed the number, and listened closely. The silence that followed—no ring, no connection— was the only answer he needed. So he hung up and continued his interrogation. "Has Ms. Shor contacted you since Tom's visit?"

"No. Like I told him, she stabbed me, stole my car, and disappeared. Now I'm out a week's pay because of her."

"She stabbed you?" Mark's eyes narrowed in suspicion.

"She said you had a terrible fight the night before," Tom recalled, his tone casual but edged with much curiosity.

Mason's eyes widened for a fraction of a second—an involuntary quiver of fear—but he quickly masked it. His face flushed, and he suddenly started to sweat profusely as if the room had become suffocating. "She told you that? What else did she say?" he pried, the edge of paranoia cutting through his words, thick with tension.

"Why? Is there something we should know?" Mark probed.

Mason was suddenly wary of his words. "No, no," he said, "It's just—she's the problem, not me. That woman's a fraud. I don't want you guys buying into whatever lies she's telling."

Mark leaned in, his face inches from Mason's, continuing his tactic of intimidation. "We'll figure out what's true and what isn't. You don't need to worry about that. What you should worry about is that lying to a police officer is a criminal offense. So go ahead—tell us what you're withholding."

Mason's jaw clenched, and he looked away, beads of sweat dotting his forehead. "I'm not withholding anything. I swear."

"Okay... then tell us what you meant by 'fraud.'"

Mason hesitated, then released a breath like a man who'd been holding it in too long. "She's a compulsive liar. First of all, she wasn't even using her real name. And second... I didn't even know she had a job until my neighbor told me."

Mark's eyebrow arched slightly. "So she was working. And that's... *bad* because?"

"Look, I drive a truck, alright? When I'm on the road, it's 24/7. Meanwhile, I put a roof over her head. I *take care* of her. She's supposed to stay here, manage things while I'm gone."

"By 'manage things,' you mean doing chores."

"Yeah, mostly... and cook."

"So, you wanted her to act like a couple from the fifties with you."

"Exactly! Like the fifties," Mason exclaimed as if he'd made his case.

But Mark didn't let up. "In 2004, that sounds more like coercion."

Mason's face tightened, and he shot a defensive glance at Mark. "That was the agreement from the start."

Tom, just then, chimed in with much eagerness. "You said you put a roof over her head. How did you two even meet?"

Mason's eyes darkened as he recalled the memory, but he answered quickly, his voice smooth with practiced nonchalance. "Found her on the side of the highway one cold night, next to a car she stole. She was hitchhiking to Grand Prairie, and I was decent enough to give her a ride."

"She told you she stole the car?" Tom asked, shocked.

"Pretty much. Look, officer, I don't know how you're going to catch this serial thief, but I sure hope you do. As far as I can tell, the woman's got no self-respect. She'd use her body any time to get what she wanted. I was too weak to see it coming."

Mark's voice dropped, to the point. "So to be clear, you haven't heard from her since she took off?"

Mason stood up straight, his eyes locking with Mark's. "No, sir. No contact," he answered assertively.

"And you have no idea where she's gone?"

"Well... I don't have proof, but if I were to guess, she probably ran off with some jerk from Wisconsin. She's probably freeloading off of him by now."

"Tell me about 'him,'" Mark demanded.

"I don't know the guy. Never met him. But I've caught her talking to him. Real sneaky-like. His name's Michael something. Can't you do a little tappy-tap on your computer and find out?"

"Did I ask you to tell me how to do my job?"

Mason flinched, instantly regretting the comment. "No, sir... sorry."

"Anything else you think we should know?"

"No. Nothing. If I knew where she was, I'd be out looking for her myself."

The brothers exchanged a glance, their judgment silent but clear. Satisfied they had squeezed out everything they could from this self-serving, pathetic excuse of a man, Mark extended his hand for a handshake.

Mason, eager to appear cooperative, lunged forward, grasping Mark's hand—but as soon as their palms met, Mark's grip tightened, pulling Mason in close with a calculated force. His voice was low, laced with a chilling threat. "Thank you so much for your cooperation, Mr. Hill. But should I *ever... ever* find out you've been dishonest with me, I'll be back. Off-hours, if I have to. Do we have an understanding?"

Mason's heart was racing. His breath came in shallow gasps, and the fear in his eyes was impossible to miss. He could barely muster the strength to whisper a trembling "yes."

Once they were back in the car, Tom turned to Mark and asked, "You think the guy's lying?"

Mark's expression was grim, his gaze distant as he considered the question. "No. He might've overplayed the victim card, trashing Ms. Shor's reputation to make him-self look better, but I believe the facts he gave us are genu-ine."

"Then why the whole Terminator thing at the end?"

Mark's lips curled into a half-smile. "You mean the 'I'll be back' bit? Just in case. And honestly, I saw someone at work do it once, thought it was kind of cool. It seemed to get the point across pretty effectively."

"I see..." Tom said, his tone taking on a touch of knowing amusement as he was suddenly reminded of his brother's fondness for being overly dramatic. "So, now what?"

Mark's eyes softened, a slight weariness settling in his bones. "Now, the boring part. Research. Research. Re-search."

23

"**O**VER HERE!" MARK'S voice pierced through the hush of the library, breathy and urgent, fol-lowed by an almost blaring whistle. A nearby librarian glanced in his direction with a mask of disap-proval in her expression, her fingers rapping on the "KEEP QUIET" sign, a silent reprimand to bring the ruckus to an immediate halt.

Mark shot her an apologetic look, his face a mix of sheepishness and mild amusement, muttering a quick, "Sorry," as he shifted his attention back to Tom.

Tom approached, joining him at the table. "Do you always do your research at a library?"

Mark leaned back in his chair with an air of comfort-able ease, his feet casually propped up on the adjacent chair as if the room belonged to him. "It's nice, right? Peaceful. No one bothering me. No incessant chatter from my colleagues. I can actually think here." He gestured toward the quiet of the room, the only sounds being the soft rustling of pages and the occasional murmur of distant conversations. "This is exactly the environment I need to clear my head. Anyways, how'd it go on the phone?"

Tom shrugged. "Same as before," he said, somewhat disappointed. "No one picks up, and there's no answering machine." He leaned over to glance at the papers spread out across the table. "I see you've been busy."

Mark gestured vaguely at the spread of oxidized, yellowing newsprint, his eyes twinkling with satisfaction. "You bet. I've made some progress on my end."

Tom leaned closer to get a better look. The musty scent of old ink and paper filled the air. "What's all this?" he asked.

Mark's fingers flicked through the old newspapers, the edges crisp and brittle with age. "One of the perks of coming here," he began, a hint of pride in his voice, "is the exclusive access to old local press archives. Everything's stored right here. If you're willing to dig a little, you can unearth all sorts of juicy tidbits. Take Ms. Shor's mother, for example." His eyes glinted with a mischievous sort of enthusiasm. "Catherine Shor? You wouldn't believe how many times her name's popped up in the press. I've pulled a few of the more... *interesting* reports." He dropped one of the papers in front of Tom, pointing at a headline with a smirk. "There's even an entire .com devoted to the rumors surrounding her disappearance. A real gold mine if you're into the *drama*."

Tom raised an eyebrow but didn't comment. Instead, his focus shifted, his gaze narrowing as he scanned the paper in front of him. "What about Nirvana? Any new leads on her?"

Mark hesitated for a moment, then gave a soft sigh. "Not much... unfortunately." His eyes lingered on a faded article, and for a brief second, his expression softened, lost in the memory of something from his past. "Except—well, there's this one mention in the County Post. Just a tiny mention, really." He paused, his fingers brushing against the paper as if the words held some deeper meaning. "Funny enough, I remember reading this exact article while training at the academy. Weird how things come full circle, huh?"

Tom, his curiosity piqued, didn't wait for further explanation. He grabbed the paper, his eyes scanning the words quickly, the dim light of the library catching on the yellowed edges of the print. Mark continued to sit back, watching him with a detached interest.

13-Year-Old Girl Rescued from Backyard After Alleged Abuse and Dog Attack, Mother Still Missing

A 13-year-old girl was rescued from the backyard of her home Sunday night, where she had been found tied to a tree, severely bruised, and suffering from bite wounds believed to be inflicted by the family dog. The dog, an underweight English Mastiff, was later found by the county's humane society and euthanized shortly after it was reported missing.

The neighbor who alerted authorities to the scene described a history of abuse at the hands of the victim's mother, Catherine Shor, who is now suspected of orchestrating the brutal attack. The neighbor stated that she saw from her bedroom window Catherine Shor fled the scene immediately after the incident, reportedly running into the nearby woods...

"And this one too," Mark added, and proceeded to read out a different article. "'A possible history of mental illness...' yada yada yada, 'her husband, renowned orchestral conductor Mitchell Shor, died in a car crash just six months before her disappearance...'" Mark paused dramatically, his eyes narrowing in recognition. "Ah, so they're one of those families. No wonder."

Tom shot him a look. "What families?"

"Musical families. You know the type." Mark's tone was dismissive as he leaned back in his chair, folding his arms behind his head. "Sensitive people. Too in touch with their feelings, not enough with reality. You'd be surprised how many end up—well, unhinged."

"Just because you don't understand them doesn't make them weird or crazy."

He shot Tom a sidelong glance. "Hey, leave my bias out of this. I'm just saying, things might not have been as black and white as they seemed."

Tom, undeterred, shifted his focus back to Nirvana. "Anything more recent?" he asked.

Mark rifled through the pile of papers in front of him. "Nothing solid. Mostly speculating stuff about her mother being—well, insane. A little about her dad, but nothing specifically about Nirvana." He paused for a moment to mentally consolidate his findings, then a flicker of excitement crossed his face. "Oh... wait a second..." His fingers froze mid-air as his eyes scanned the paper before he slapped it down on the table, nearly knocking over his coffee cup in his haste.

"Got something," he continued, leaning forward and reading aloud. "'Their daughter, who survived last year's backyard incident, is reported to be undergoing trauma rehabilitation at Heartstone for years of physical and emotional abuse...' Heartstone? Isn't that the insane asylum up in Oseding?"

Just then, the librarian, her patience clearly wearing thin, cleared her throat loudly, a pointed *AHEM* meant to warn them about the rising volume of their conversation.

Mark flashed her a grin, before turning back to Tom, his voice dropping to a lower register. "What do you say we go pay a visit to the doctors and nurses there?" he suggested.

Tom blinked, taken aback. "What for?"

"You want to find Nirvana, don't you?" Mark said, eyes locking onto Tom's with a playful glint. "You were the one who asked for this. I'm just following through."

"I'm not saying it's not important, but I also have a business to run. Responsibilities, you know? And it wasn't my idea to do your job for you. Besides, just because she was there once, it doesn't mean anything."

"Oh, come on. Don't tell me you're scared?"

"What? No," Tom said quickly, shaking his head. "It's *you* and your obsession with this case, and I don't get it."

Mark sat up straighter, his voice turning serious for a moment. "Hold on. Are you still believing that Jo chick was just trying to help? She lied to get to Ms. Shor, Thomas. She's not exactly an open book, is she?"

Tom hesitated, eyes flicking nervously as he tried to gather his thoughts. "I don't know... I don't think she's out to hurt anyone. I met her, remember? She seemed genuinely concerned about Nirvana. If they are, in fact, together right now, she won't hurt her."

Mark raised an eyebrow. "Wow... you and Dad never cease to amaze me. If you're so sure she's trustworthy, why do you still have doubt? Huh?" He leaned in closer, his voice sharp with challenge. "Why do you worry?"

Tom sighed, a reluctant admission in his eyes. "I guess... I suppose it's just that 'just in case' feeling. That *what if*," he said.

Mark's eyes lit up, triumphant. "Bingo!" he shouted, slapping the table so hard it rattled. Several people in the library turned to stare, but Mark didn't seem to care. "You're not stupid. You know something's off. Now, had you not exposed her location so willingly, we wouldn't have had to be here. And you are telling me you don't even feel remotely accountable?"

"Don't try to guilt me," Tom shot back, but his voice lacked conviction.

"I don't need to. You've already done that to yourself. I'm just reminding you." Mark watched his brother carefully, noticing the subtle shift in his demeanor—his defenses were lowering, even if just a fraction. He seized the moment, his tone turning more persuasive. "Here's the deal: give us the rest of the day. If by the end of it, we still don't have anything concrete on where Ms. Shor is, I'll take over the case myself."

Tom paused, rubbing his temples. He didn't respond right away, his mind clearly racing. "Isn't it more efficient to work with your colleagues than with me?"

Mark grinned, clapping him on the back with a force that nearly knocked Tom off balance. "More or less, but it's more fun doing it with my big brother. We're going to get answers. I've got a good feeling about this."

24

TRUSTING MARK'S INSTINCTS, the brothers set out northeast toward Oseding, a rural farm town infamous for the eerie collection of white concrete structures at its outskirts—Heartstone. The journey stretched on for hours, the landscape around them little more than dull fields and barren roads. But eventually, they crossed a weathered truss bridge, its rusting steel creaking as they drove over, and it led them directly to the hospital's entrance. Tom, ever the map-reader, guided them through a series of winding signs until they parked at the visitor center.

"If you take it easy with them, they'll take it easy with you," Mark warned, his eyes darting toward Tom as he flicked the car into park. It was a lecture Tom had heard many times, but one he wasn't quite sure how to execute. Mark's world of improvisation was lightyears away from Tom's need for structure.

"What exactly are we going to say to them?" Tom asked, his voice tinged with nervous uncertainty.

"Haven't you ever improvised before? Relax, just follow my lead," Mark assured him with a grin.

They walked into the sterile building together, Mark breezing past the receptionist's desk with an air of familiarity, while Tom followed in his wake, trying not to feel like a fish out of water. Behind the desk, a tall, cool-eyed receptionist greeted them with a smile of someone who'd seen it all.

"Hello, gentlemen. How may I assist you this afternoon?"

"We're here to see Nirvana Shor," Mark said, his voice smooth, like a practiced line.

"Is she a patient at our facility?" the receptionist asked, arching an eyebrow.

"Why don't you tell me?" Mark replied with a light, off-hand laugh. "Ha, yeah, you bet."

The receptionist's lips tightened, but she remained professional. "Do you have the visitation slip with you?"

Mark turned to Tom, who shook his head, unequipped for the script.

Mark sighed, a hint of faux frustration in his voice as he leaned toward the counter. "My brother has forgotten it at home. You see, miss, he's the type to forget his pants on his way out. A bit absentminded, if you catch my drift."

The receptionist's expression remained unchanged, ignoring Mark's clumsy attempt at humor. She glanced at Tom with a sharper gaze. "Do you have an account with us, sir?"

Tom blinked. "An account?"

"Yes. All visitors are required to have a pre-registered account linked to the patient they're visiting, or at least access to it."

"Oh... uh, no. I don't have one," Tom said, his tone a little lost.

The receptionist didn't miss the cue. "Are you a relative of the patient?"

Tom hesitated. The word "relative" suddenly felt heavy, like an expectation he wasn't prepared to carry.

"Eh..." He stumbled.

"He's her boyfriend," Mark cut in, sensing the opening. "And she's been dying to see him. There's gotta be something you can do to help us out."

The receptionist froze, her eyes flicking back and forth between them. She considered, then leaned toward a manager, who was standing by, and whispered to him. After a brief conversation, the manager approached with a polite but wary expression.

"I apologize, but could you please repeat the name of the patient you want to visit?"

"Nirvana Shor," Tom repeated, trying to mask his growing unease.

The manager typed something into his computer, glancing at the screen, then returned his gaze to them. "I regret to inform you that Ms. Shor is no longer under our care. She was discharged in October."

Mark's eyes narrowed, and he stepped forward. "That can't be. Didn't you just get a call from her doctor last week, huh? Johnny? That's what I heard."

Tom jumped in, playing along. "Yes, that's right. The doctor called me. He said it would do Nirvana some good to see me today."

"Did you say 'he'?" the manager asked, his gaze sharpening.

Tom's throat tightened, but he could not afford to flinch. "Ah, I meant 'she,' of course. What's her last name again?" He shot a quick, uncertain glance at Mark, who gave him a barely perceptible nod.

The manager was still suspicious but didn't push further. "Dr. Rimer is a very busy physician. She wouldn't normally contact patients' families directly. There's a department for that. If she did call you, I'm sure it was important, but I don't have any information on that."

Mark nodded, pretending to acquiesce. "I see. Well, Johnny, looks like we'll have to head back and wait for another call, huh?" He slapped Tom on the shoulder, already steering him away from the desk.

"Is it possible to see Dr. Rimer today?" Tom asked, pushing forward despite Mark's efforts to retreat. "I'd like to speak to her in person. We did drive many hours just to get here."

The manager's face stiffened, his patience running out. "We can't allow that. Our counseling services are by appointment only, and Dr. Rimer is booked until February. I'm afraid there's nothing we can do for you here."

Mark gave a quick, exaggerated sigh, pulling Tom away by the arm. "Alright, Johnny. Let's get out of here before we become a bigger nuisance."

It was never in Mark's nature to quit halfway. Once his mind was made up, nothing could shake his resolve. Tom knew that and so he followed his little brother—just as he always did—as he walked away. With a shared, unspoken understanding, they slipped out of the main area through a side door, their footsteps muffled against the polished floor. They walked across the center's courtyard, the cool air a contrast to the tension building inside them. The courtyard was nearly empty, save for a few scattered visitors who barely glanced at them as they passed. Mark kept his eyes scanning the surroundings, every inch of the place feeling like it might hold a clue—or a threat.

The directory they found pointed them toward the staff building. They walked quickly, yet with the practiced ease of those who'd been trained to blend into unfamiliar spaces. The building was quiet, nearly deserted, and the few staff members they did see were distracted, lost in their own thoughts or paperwork. The atmosphere felt different from the more formal reception area they'd just left—a more relaxed, almost clinical indifference.

A long corridor stretched before them, each door closed and unmarked—until they came across one with a silver placard that caught Mark's attention.

"Dr. Faith H. Rimer."

Mark's hand reached out to knock lightly, his motion confident despite the nervousness that thrummed beneath his unflustered exterior. When there was no immediate response, he didn't hesitate—he turned the doorknob and gently pushed the door open, stepping inside with Tom close behind him. The office was sparse, clinical, and eerily calm, the only sign of life the faint hum of a fluorescent light overhead. Mark's eyes scanned the room quickly, noting the file cabinet, the desk with a few papers scattered across it, and a chair pushed back from the desk as though someone had just stepped away.

Mark barely waited for Tom to close the door behind them before he went straight to the file cabinet, his movements purposeful. Tom, however, lingered by the door for a moment, their intrusion quietly pressing on his conscience.

"I can't believe I let you talk me into this," Tom muttered, a mix of anxiety and regret in his voice. "We're going to be in so much trouble."

Mark didn't even glance at him as he began to pull open drawers. "Chill out," he said calmly. "I know exactly what I'm doing."

But Tom wasn't so sure. "What's your plan here? How do we get out of this without getting caught?"

Mark turned to face him, his eyes calm, even amused. "Relax. We're not exactly at DEFCON 1 here. We're just having a little chat."

"A chat?" Tom's brow furrowed. "You think Dr. Rimer's just gonna walk in here and... what? Have a friendly conversation? What makes you think she wouldn't call the cops on us for breaking and entering?"

Mark let out a chortle. "Breaking and entering a room through an unlocked door? Ha. You're funny. We haven't broken anything yet, perhaps entering. Plus, have you forgotten that your brother is a cop?"

"If you are considering exposing your identity, you could have done so at the reception. It would have saved us the trouble creeping around."

If I'd told them who I was, they'd have dragged us into the chief's office before we could blink. Here, we get the direct line to someone who might actually know something."

Tom sighed, shaking his head, but before he could argue further, the sound of high heels echoed down the hallway. Mark froze, his gaze flicking toward the door. Tom did the same. The footsteps grew louder, closer, until they stopped just outside the door.

The door swung open with a soft creak, and in walked Dr. Rimer, her expression a mixture of confusion and irritation as her eyes quickly scanned the room.

"What is this?" Her voice was demanding, but also tinged with a hint of disbelief. "Who are you?"

Mark straightened, smoothing his expression into something more official. He stepped forward, his voice steady and authoritative as he introduced himself. "Detective Marcus Ager. This is my assistant, Thomas."

"Detective?" A slight frown appeared on Dr. Rimer's face as she regarded them both with new suspicion. "What is this about?"

"We're here to ask you some questions about Nirvana Shor," Mark said, his tone more serious. "I believe she's one of your patients."

Dr. Rimer's face hardened at the mention of the name. "Was," she corrected quickly. "She's been discharged."

Mark didn't flinch. "We know that," he said. "We're here for more than that."

Dr. Rimer eyed them both, her gaze cold. "What else do you need from me?" she asked, her posture straightening.

Mark took a step closer, his eyes locking with hers. "I think you know exactly what we're looking for."

For a moment, Dr. Rimer said nothing. She stared at them, her face betraying only the faintest hint of uncertainty. Then, with a quiet sigh, she closed the door behind her and moved toward her desk.

"Did you come from the chief?" she asked after settling into her chair, her tone now more measured, as though she were deciding how much to reveal. "I take it this is about the incident? I was the one who suggested calling the police, but my recommendation was... overturned. However, from what I know, they've already located her."

Tom's heart skipped at the mention of an incident. "She was missing once before?" he asked, his voice edging with concern.

Dr. Rimer nodded slowly. "The day she was released. Instead of following the discharge procedure, she left in her guardian's car."

"Who is her guardian?"

The doctor didn't respond right away. When she did, her voice was guarded. "I'm afraid I can't provide you with that information."

Mark leaned in just slightly, his voice lowering but gaining in strength. "You can, but the real question is—will you?"

"What makes you think I'd tell you?" Dr. Rimer's voice was flat, but there was an underlying edge—an attempt to mask the uncertainty creeping into her professional demeanor.

Mark's lips twitched into a half-smirk. "Surely it depends," he hinted, his tone casual but laced with something dangerous.

"On?" she asked, narrowing her eyes slightly, already sensing the shift in the conversation.

"What kind of a doctor you are," Mark pressed on.

Dr. Rimer's posture stiffened, and she shot him a look. Her lips pressed into a thin line, her eyes flashing with irritation. "What is that supposed to mean?"

"It depends if you want to go down in history as the doctor who selfishly withheld key information to protect her own stature... which ultimately led to her patient's death."

"You can't threaten me."

"This is not a threat," Mark responded calmly, but with quiet intensity. "I'm dead serious."

Dr. Rimer leaned back in her chair, her hands instinctively folding across her chest as if trying to create distance—physical, mental, emotional. "Then am I being interrogated here?" she asked, her voice hardening. "Because I will not continue this conversation until I have my lawyer."

"Why? What do you have to hide?"

"*What?* I don't care who you are, but I will not abide blind accusations. You boys have invaded my personal space without permission. If you don't leave now, I'll call security."

Mark shot her a cool glance, one that had become a well-worn mask over the years of doing whatever was necessary to get the job done.

Meanwhile, Tom stepped forward, his face gentle but insistent. "We just want your cooperation, doctor. Nirvana is missing."

"And possibly being held against her will," Mark added.

Dr. Rimer said nothing at first, her gaze flicking between the two men as if trying to gauge their seriousness. "Is this true?" she asked.

Tom nodded slowly. "We need your help to find her," he said, his voice soft and earnest, laced with the same genuine worry he had felt when he first discovered Nirvana was missing.

Dr. Rimer shook her head slightly as she processed Tom's words. After a while, she sighed, rubbing her temple as if trying to clear away the fog of confusion and frustration.

"Still," she began, her voice more resigned now, "patient information is by law confidential. I'm legally bound to share it only with her close relatives, if that."

"I'm Nirvana's boss. I own a plumbing shop in Grand Prairie. She's one of my employees. We're not just employer and employee—she's become a friend. A close one."

For a brief moment, something glinted in Dr. Rimer's expression—a softness, a vulnerability that broke through the cold professionalism. It was almost imperceptible, but it was there. "She was working?" she asked Tom, her tone unexpectedly gentle.

"Yes," Tom replied. "She fit right in. The whole shop liked having her around."

There was a brief pause before Dr. Rimer allowed a small, sincere smile to tug at her lips. "I'm glad to hear that," she said quietly, almost to herself, her voice taking on an uncharacteristic warmth that softened the edges of her previous stiffness.

Before the moment could stretch too long, the intercom buzzed to life, slicing through the fragile pause.

"Dr. Rimer?"

She pressed a button on the machine, her professional mask snapping back into place. "Yes, Sue?"

"6345 is here. I have her waiting in the treatment room."

"I'll be right there." The intercom clicked off, and Dr. Rimer glanced back at the two men, her expression once again set in a neutral, guarded expression.

"You call your patient by a number?" Mark scoffed, unable to resist. "How barbaric."

"It's one of our many efforts to protect our patients' privacy," Dr. Rimer responded dryly. "We don't want people like you barging in here during daylight hours, snooping around and stealing private information."

Mark raised an eyebrow, his voice laced with mockery. "Then you should think about investing in some locks for your cabinets—"

"Those bite marks on her arms," Tom cut in before the tension could escalate again, his tone polite but serious. "They were her mother's doing, weren't they?"

Dr. Rimer's face faltered for a moment. She paused, as if lost in memory, before exhaling a quiet breath. "She's always insisted that what happened that night was inadvertent," she said slowly, choosing her words with care. "That the leash came loose, and the dog just... lost control. Having not been fed for days. Whether that's the truth or not, it doesn't change the years of torment her mother put her through. And her father..."

"What about the father?" Tom probed.

Dr. Rimer's expression tightened once again. "He might not have been physically abusive," she said, her voice hardening, "but his actions were just as damaging, just as toxic. In my opinion, his contribution to Nirvana's childhood trauma was even worse... I've said too much already."

Tom's concern deepened, but he didn't press further. "I'm worried about her," he said quietly, the words carrying a sincerity that finally seemed to crack Dr. Rimer's professional exterior.

She gave him a long, careful look, her eyes searching for the truth in his. It was a look that seemed to measure him, to test his resolve. And after what felt like an eternity, she relented.

"Is the guardian's name Michael?" Mark pressed, his voice steady but impatient.

"No," Dr. Rimer replied, shaking her head slowly. "But there is a Joanna Nickson. She's been Nirvana's only contact from the beginning. If you'd like her number..."

Without a word, she opened her desk drawer, rifling through papers until she pulled out a laminated list. She picked up a pen and scribbled something on a blank space, then handed the slip of paper to Mark.

The men glanced at it, their eyes widening in surprise. The number—Nirvana's emergency contact—was a duplicate. They were looking at the same number that had appeared on her file, the one that had seemed so important.

"This is as far as I can help you," Dr. Rimer said, her voice now final, her earlier warmth gone.

Mark nodded, slipping the paper into his pocket. "Thanks, doc. This is exactly what we came for. We won't keep you any longer." Shortly, he turned to leave.

Tom followed Mark, but before he could step out of the room, Dr. Rimer rose from her chair and called after him.

"Mr. Thomas... Tom!"

He stopped at the door, turning back. "Yes, doctor?"

She paused, her eyes softening just a little. "My number's on the back of the paper. If you find her, please don't hesitate to call me. I want to personally check on her. See how she's doing."

Tom smiled at her, the earnestness in his expression reflected in hers. "You can count on it," he promised, before slipping out the door and following Mark down the hall.

25

*B*LAM! BLAM!
THE sharp crack of a gunshot shattered the tension in the air, sending shockwaves through the ground beneath Nirvana. She flinched, every muscle locking in place as the deafening noise reverberated through her. And then—silence. Absolute stillness. The world seemed to hold its breath, waiting for the aftermath.

Nirvana's pulse thundered in her ears, but as the silence grew longer, hope flickered within her, like a fragile candle against the wind. Aid had come. She wasn't sure how she knew, but the feeling was unmistakable. Her heart pounded in anticipation, and then, the blindfold was ripped away.

Michael.

She blinked in the dim light, disoriented, as he worked quickly to untie her. But her gaze darted down. The bloodstains marred the floor beneath her, a path leading to the lifeless body of Sadie, her beloved dog. The sight hit her like a physical blow, the pang of grief colliding with the fog in her mind. She swayed, dizzy, struggling to process it all.

"How did you find me?" Her voice was raw, trembling.

"What do you think?" Michael's tone was calm but taut with urgency.

"I don't know... how?"

"I was acting on a hunch," he said, barely pausing as he untied the last knot. "Call it my sixth sense, but save the chitchat. We need to get out of here."

Nirvana felt herself lifted, her body heavy with exhaustion and fear as Michael helped her to her feet. The ladder loomed ahead, a rickety escape from the suffocating hole she'd been trapped in. As they clambered out, Nirvana sucked in the fresh air. Wild summer weeds and earth— distinct, earthy, unmistakable. She knew this place.

But as they ran across the overgrown lawn, a chill crawled up her spine. Her feet faltered for just a moment before she tugged back, slowing their pace. Michael stopped, his eyes darting to the house in the distance.

"We have to go," he insisted, but Nirvana's gaze remained fixed.

"She's in there," Nirvana murmured, her voice tight with a strange mix of fear and determination.

"So? We can't afford this," Michael replied, a note of exasperation creeping into his voice.

Nirvana hesitated for only a second, before dragging her feet. "Give me ten minutes. Wait for me out front. I'll be right back."

Michael gripped her arm, his fingers digging into her skin. "This is a bad idea."

"I need to do this," Nirvana shot back, the fire in her voice undeniable. "I've wanted to do this for so long. I'm not leaving without it."

Michael sighed, frustration clouding his face. "What are you going to say to her? What if it doesn't change anything? Have you thought about that?"

Nirvana's jaw clenched. She didn't need to explain herself, but she would anyway. "I have to try. I'll feel better. I know I will. I have to... hope."

Michael's expression softened, and he finally released her arm. "Do me a favor," he said, "let this be the last time."

Nirvana nodded, her resolve steady. She was already moving before he'd finished speaking.

With Michael gone, Nirvana crept toward the deck of the house, every step a calculated risk. She barely reached the stairs when a floorboard beneath her creaked with a loud protest. It betrayed her, and the silence that followed felt suffocating

"Nirvana! Get in here!"

Her mother's voice cut through her doubt, cold and commanding. Nirvana didn't think—she just acted. The door, old and stubborn, slid open with a scrape, and the smell of cooking meat hit her immediately. Thick, savory, almost sickening.

The kitchen was dimly lit by candlelight, steam swirling through the air, and there she stood: her mother, poised like a predator, her hands gripping a cleaver as she hacked mercilessly at the pork roast before her. Blood and juices splattered onto the wooden board with each brutal strike. Nirvana's stomach twisted.

Her eyes locked with her mother's for a moment, and the world seemed to stop.

"What are you doing?" her mother snapped. "Are you still standing there? Set the table. We're having pigs for dinner."

Nirvana's hand trembled as she moved to set the table. She tried to mask the revulsion that surged inside her as she picked up the plates. Once done, she approached her mother. "Let me take over for you, Mommy."

Her mother's gaze faltered for just a heartbeat, and she lowered the cleaver. Reluctantly, she pulled her hand away, watching with acute fascination as Nirvana took her place, slicing and dicing up the meat. The words spilled from her mother's mouth like a foul song, each syllable laced with venom.

"It was a young one," she continued, her voice almost detached. "The butcher told me. Barely two weeks old when he slaughtered it. Active little thing. Took two shots to kill it. 'You raise them to eat them,' he bragged, 'that's life for most of these caged bastards.'"

Nirvana's stomach twisted again. She was mentally repressing her urge to hurl. Her hand went still, knife poised in mid-air as her eyes flicked up to meet her mother's gaze. The intensity in her eyes was unsettling, but she couldn't look away.

She swallowed hard.

It could be anything—or nothing at all, she told herself, grasping at whatever fleeting comfort she could find.

But even that small solace couldn't mask the truth. When it came to her mother, it wasn't just the uncertainty that terrified her; it was the unpredictable, explosive fury that could snap at any moment. But she wasn't here to keep the peace. She wasn't here to cower or to appease the lioness in her den. No, Nirvana had come with a purpose—one that she couldn't ignore, even if it meant facing the very thing that made her blood run cold.

With a steadying breath, she stood straighter, squaring her shoulders, trying to project the confidence she wished she could feel. "What is it?" she asked, her voice edged with a quiet defiance, though her heart raced in her chest.

"Why are your lips red?" Her mother's voice dropped, a dangerous calm taking over. Her cold glare locked onto Nirvana with the force of a thousand stones.

"My lips?" Nirvana's breath caught in her throat, her hand fluttering up to her mouth, trying to play it off. "That's their natural color, Mommy. Just like yours. Just like everybody else's."

Her mother didn't buy it. "No. That's from lipstick."

"I'm not wearing any makeup, Mommy." Nirvana's hand grasped a napkin, wiping her lips vigorously. "See?"

Her mother had an exhaustive scan of her proof, narrowing her eyes, her lip curling with displeasure. Then, her gaze dropped lower.

"And your breasts... they've sure grown. You haven't been wearing the bras I bought you, have you?"

Nirvana felt the blood drain from her face. "They're too tight. They hurt," she protested.

"Stunting their growth is the whole point," her mother explained as if she made perfect sense, "Pain's expected. Unless you want to walk the streets like a whore, then go ahead. But I won't have you doing that under my roof."

The insult stung. Nirvana swallowed her indignation but she was done shrinking.

"No one turns out to be a prostitute just because they have breasts," she said, the words slipping out before she could stop them.

Her mother's eyes snapped toward her, pupils dilating, fury replacing her earlier calm. "What did you say?" she asked.

"I said," Nirvana continued, her voice rising ever so slightly, "*not all women turn out to be prostitutes*—large-breasted or otherwise."

"And where did you learn that? From that rebellious boy you've been hanging out with?"

"No one taught me, Mommy. I've always known we're not normal. I've known for years. We are as isolated as we can be now, and it's been common sense keeping me whole."

Just then, her mother's fingers tightened into claws, her voice dripping with scorn. "You think common sense can fix this? How about you listen for once. Be a good daughter and fix yourself before I lose my patience."

Nirvana stood her ground: "No."

"No?" Her mother's face twisted with anger. "Go to your room. Now."

"I didn't come in here to argue about how I should cover myself, Mommy. And if it weren't my lips or my breasts, it would have been something else you are displeased with. I know everything's different since Daddy died, but the truth is, things have been broken long before that."

"Don't you drag your father into this... don't you dare."

"I have to, Mommy," Nirvana said, her voice cracking with the weight of her plea. "I have something important to tell you. Please, don't turn me away again... not this time—"

Before she could finish her sentence, her mother's fury erupted. In a flash, she was on her feet, and the slap came so fast and hard that Nirvana barely had time to brace herself. The impact sent a searing wave of heat through her cheek, and her head snapped to the side with a sickening jolt. The world around her spun, and she tasted the salt of tears she hadn't realized were welling up in her eyes. In that instant, she understood: she had hit a nerve, one that was buried so deep in her mother's soul that it was bound to cause this kind of eruption.

She figured if she didn't speak up now—if she didn't face this demon *now*—it would consume her forever. So she steadied herself and met her mother's furious stare with a strength she didn't know she had, despite the lingering fear gnawing at her gut.

Now or never.

"Do not cross me, young lady," her mother hissed. She jabbed a finger in the direction of the stairs. "Go to your room, and don't you dare come out until I say so."

"NO!" Nirvana shouted, her voice raw, a desperate demand for attention.

"Have you gone deaf?"

"I heard you, Mommy, and I understand perfectly. But this—this isn't the time for games, to see who's got the upper hand. You can try to insult me, hurt me, tear me down—*but I won't stop*. Not until you hear me out. I *need* you to listen."

Her mother clenched her teeth, hands trembling with barely contained wrath. But then, in an instant, everything changed. Her face softened, her shoulders slumping, as if the spleen had been sucked out of her.

"Fine," she said, her voice suddenly flat, distant. "Do what you want. I don't care anymore."

Without another word, her mother seized the tray of diced pork from the table. She shoved her chair back with a harsh scrape, the sound of it like nails on a chalkboard. Then, with an animalistic ferocity, she tore into the rare meat, shoveling pieces into her mouth with her bare hands, chewing them down hungrily, almost violently. It was as if she were devouring not just the food, but some dark, primal need that could never be sated.

Her eyes—once a striking jade, full of life and sharp intellect—had turned into something monstrous. They were wild, feral, void of all human warmth. There was no soul behind them, only the raw hunger of a lioness, of a beast.

"Mommy... I have to tell you something..." Nirvana's voice wavered, thick with dread. Despite the calmness she tried to muster, every syllable trembled in the air, weighed down by the fear that lurked beneath.

Without warning, her mother's hand shot out, slamming the table aside with a violent force. Nirvana flinched, her heart pounded against her ribs, the rhythm frantic and erratic, as her mother surged to her feet. There was nothing restrained about the movement—her mother was all fire, like a beast who had lost control of her senses.

Her mother didn't look back as she stormed into the kitchen. Nirvana's body froze. She knew this wasn't over. She knew this was only the beginning. She knew, deep down, that this wouldn't end well. She barely had time to catch her breath when she saw her mother return, a gleam in her hand.

Scissors.

The cold metal flashed in the dim light. Its opening and closing echoed through the room, making her skin crawl. It was like a switch had been flipped. Her mother's movements were fast, too fast for Nirvana to comprehend. Before she could even react, she was thrown to the ground. The air was knocked out of her lungs with a sickening thud. Her mother was on top of her in the next instant, pinning her down with brutal force.

Her counters were clumsy, unfocused. She couldn't gain any ground, couldn't break free. Every motion was more constraining than the last, as if her body was being held down by invisible chains, each one tightening around her. In a flurry of motion, her mother's hands moved to her shirt. The scissors snipped and tore through the fabric with a vicious eagerness, slicing through the material as though it were paper. Nirvana gasped for air, helpless beneath the assault. Her back arched against the floor as her mother continued, indifferent to the suffering she caused. There was no mercy in her mother's eyes, only the dark satisfaction of a violent release.

Eventually, with one last cruel tug, her mother rose off her. She lay there in stunned silence, breathless and broken, her heart still racing. The room felt unbearably cold now, and the silence that followed was ever smothering—thick with unspoken words, with the grasp of everything that had just happened.

"You brought this on yourself," her mother snarled, her voice ragged, still raw from the violent outburst that had consumed her. She stood above Nirvana, chest heaving with the aftermath of her fury, eyes burning with something dark—something unforgiving. "Now you've got what you deserved. Go put something decent on, like I told you. Go! You look hideous..."

Despite the wave of shame threatening to drown her, something inside Nirvana snapped. Tears—hot, relentless—slid down her cheeks, each drop an undeniable surrender to the overwhelming pain. Then, with a strangled cry, she burst out, her voice filled with frustration and fury, the hurt within her finally spilling over. "Why... why do you hate me? I'm your daughter, am I not? I'M YOUR DAUGHTER!"

Her mother's expression hardened. "Yes, you are my daughter," she spat, her voice low, venomous. "My precious little baby who disgusts me."

"I'm sorry about you and Daddy. But you can't blame me for the failure of your marriage... and especially not for his infidelity. It wasn't *my* fault!"

"It wasn't your fault!" she roared back. "So it wasn't *you* who stripped yourself in front of him? It wasn't you who *offered* yourself to him!"

"It was *he* who lured me into his den. It was *he* who stripped me and forced himself onto me. I was scared, Mommy! *Scared!*" Nirvana spoke, each word a raw scream from deep within. Her hands trembled, the accuracy of her confession nearly too much to bear. She continued bravely, "I was a wimp when it came to Daddy's demanding ways... I didn't know how to fight him! I didn't know how to say no! *I wanted to come to you so many times!* But you *never listened!* You never even tried to hear me! You never wanted to listen to *me*, to what I had to say, to what I've been living with! If only you would just stop... just *feel* for a moment! Feel for *me*, Mommy! For what I've just poured out here, the truth, the *hurt*... Maybe, just maybe, you would begin to *understand*. You'd see *me*—the real me! And you'd *believe* me."

Her eyes locked onto her mother's, wide and desperate, as if searching for any sign that her words might finally reach her.

They did not. The lengths her mother was willing to go to avoid confronting the truth were sadly staggering. It had built an unbreakable wall between them—one she could never tear down, no matter what.

"You filthy... little... whore. You useless... piece of... shit! I should have ripped you out of me when you were still a fetus... I should have killed you before you could come into this life and ruin mine... you... you have ruined everything!"

After her brutal honesty was met with disdain, Nirvana caught her mother swinging her arm again with ferocious intent. With a burst of instinct, she threw herself backward, but not fast enough to avoid a fierce slash across her chin from the killer scissors. She stared dumbfounded at her mother slurping the droplets of blood off the blade, as if watching a demon get resurrected from hell by its longing to feast on human flesh. It craved their sickly smell, their metallic taste. This *thing* was no longer her mother as far as she knew, for it would not quit there, not when it was this mad, not when it had completely lost its sanity. Not now, not anymore.

With the last reserves of strength she could muster, Nirvana pushed herself off the cold, unforgiving floor. Another slash was coming, she could feel it, and if she didn't move now, she would be sliced open again.

Her gaze shot toward the front door, and without a second's hesitation, she lunged for it. Her fingers fumbled briefly with the handle before she threw it open with an aggressive jerk. The door screamed on its hinges, but it didn't matter. The world outside, shrouded in the cool embrace of night, beckoned her like a lifeline.

She didn't look back.

26

MICHAEL's EYES LOCKED onto Nirvana as she dashed past him, her figure a blur of panic. He acted without hesitation, sprinting after her, his hand clamping down on her shoulder just as she neared the tree line. She yelped in surprise, but the moment she turned and saw him standing there, her body collapsed into his. Her breath hitched in quick gasps as she buried her face in his shirt, trembling uncontrollably.

His arms enveloped her, strong and steady, as he allowed her the space to unravel. His fingers brushed through her hair, the rhythm of his touch slow and gentle, soothing the terror that gripped her. He didn't rush her. He let her cry, let her pour out the disjointed explanations she could hardly find the words for. He murmured soft reassurances, his voice a steady anchor in the storm of her panic.

When the tremors began to subside, he led her deeper into the woods, guiding her with his hand firmly placed on her back. The trees stretched tall and imposing, their boughs swaying in the wind, creating a low hum in the quiet. Eventually, they came to a secluded clearing, where a dilapidated shack sat abandoned among the towering pines, its edges weathered and cracked by time.

Nirvana sank onto a worn stump, her posture slumped. Michael sat beside her, his presence stilling the air. He didn't speak for a while, just sat there, watching her with a patience that seemed both comforting and unsettling.

Finally, he broke the silence with a question, his voice laced with just enough sarcasm to cut through the thick atmosphere.

"So... you've confronted your mother. Was it worth the trouble?"

Nirvana didn't answer right away. She stared at the ground, her fingers absentmindedly pulling at the frayed threads of her shirt. "I don't know," she said softly, her voice still raw. "It's too soon to tell."

"You still think she'll come around?"

She lifted her head slowly, meeting his gaze with a hollow look in her eyes. "I mean for myself," she murmured. "All these years... countless therapy sessions later... I don't think I've actually forgotten anything. I don't think I've ever really been able to let go. I think I've always felt the way I do now."

"And what's that?" Michael asked, his voice gentle, yet probing.

"A little restless," she answered, the words tasting bitter as they left her lips. "A little broken. If anything, I've only learned to better self-preserve."

Michael didn't speak for a moment, just looked at her with unspoken understanding. Then, without a word, he gently cupped her chin and tilted her face up so he could examine the cut on her cheek. It was a jagged line, red and still oozing a little, but it wasn't too deep. His thumb brushed over the wound with the gentlest touch.

"Does it hurt?" he asked.

"Sure," she said, her lips twitching in a humorless smile. "But it's a numbing kind of hurt."

Her gaze dropped again, her hands clasping tightly in her lap as she continued. "Rimer constantly tells me not to run from my problems. 'Face up to them,' she'd say.'" She shook her head. "But I've spent my entire life running from them. Running from my mother. I was always in such a hurry to move on. I thought... I thought that's what I had to do."

"Who can blame you? You've been away for so long." Michael's voice was low, almost absent, as if he were speaking to himself as much as to Nirvana. He leaned back slightly. "Hell, if I could have, I would've taken you out of there from day one."

Nirvana turned to look at him, her eyes widening slightly. "You would?"

"Of course," he answered, his tone firm, his eyes unblinking. "You've always been you to me.

"A sad smile flickered on Nirvana's lips, but it didn't reach her eyes. "You only say that because there are things about me that you can't see. Things that are hidden underneath the surface."

Michael shifted closer, his hand finding hers and giving it a gentle squeeze. "No, I meant what I said. I accept you for who you are. Everyone's a little strange, a little broken. Wouldn't you agree?" His gaze softened, though there was an underlying edge to his words. "So don't be so hard on yourself. We're all just living this crazy life in the best way we can. I say we live it to the fullest—enjoy it, however we please..."

She caught the shift in his tone, the subtle change in his expression. Her stomach tightened, a feeling she couldn't quite name. As he spoke, his eyes lingered on her more than he probably should, tracing the curve of her neck, the rise and fall of her chest with a kind of hunger that made her skin crawl.

But she smiled, the motion fleeting, unsure of what else to do. She didn't trust his smile. She didn't trust his words either, no matter how sweet they sounded.

Michael's voice dropped lower, a soft murmur that slid into her ears like a whispered promise. "You know, you've been through a lot. But you're strong. You've made it this far. All these scars, inside and out—they don't make you weak. They make you... beautiful."

Despite the softness of his tone, there was something inherently possessive about the way he looked at her. Nirvana's stomach tightened some more, and her smile faltered. She knew him too well. She knew the games he played.

Before she could respond, his hand reached out, fingertips grazing the edge of her shirt where it clung to her collarbone. She stiffened, instinctively pulling away, but he didn't let go, his fingers catching the fabric as he gently tugged it, his eyes never leaving hers.

Her heart pounded as she met his gaze, feeling the unease curl in her gut.

Then, his voice broke the silence again. "She seemed to have messed you up pretty bad. Why don't you take that shirt off, let me have a look?"

His words felt like an order, not a suggestion. Nirvana stared at him for a beat, her mind racing, searching for the right response. She could feel the potency of his stare, like something heavy that she could barely bear.

"No," she replied, her voice firm, but there was a doubt in her eyes.

Just then, Michael's lips curled into a slow, almost ravening grin. "You can still trust me, right? No matter what happens, you'll always be my sweet angel, my little piglet..."

That nickname sliced right through Nirvana, a cold shiver racing down her spine. *Piglet*, a word that seemed to come from some deep, twisted place, and in that moment, she could see the darker side of him—the side he often kept hidden, wrapped in the guise of tenderness.

Before she could stop him, he leaned in, his lips brushing against the side of her face, his hand slipping down the curve of her leg. Nirvana froze, every instinct screaming at her to pull away, but her body remained frozen in place, caught between fight and flight.

She inhaled sharply, breaking free from his touch, eyes wide with sudden clarity. "Wait," she said, her voice trembling slightly. "This place... I know this place. Haven't you brought me here before?"

"Took you long enough," Michael murmured, his voice transpiring into something evil. "This is where we first... you know."

Nirvana's heart skipped a beat. The memories—fragmented, twisted—flashed in front of her eyes like a distorted mirror, everything familiar and yet unbearably wrong. The old shack, the isolation, the sudden sense of déjà vu. The realization hit her like a freight train, sending a wave of nausea through her.

She hadn't come here by accident.

And then, just as the world seemed to close in around her, Michael pulled out a small plastic bag from his pocket. Inside, two pink pills lay in the palm of his hand. His voice was whispery, almost seductive as he offered them to her.

"Let's chase our nirvana together," he said, the words a promise of something wicked, something more than just sex in the wilderness, something far more dangerous than just escaping pain.

Suddenly, a second recognition struck Nirvana like a thunderclap. It was as if a long-buried piece of memory, deep within the recesses of her subconscious, had been unearthed and now surged to the surface with overwhelming force. An intense, suffocating terror overcame her that she couldn't shake. Her eyes widened in horror as the truth settled in.

Her eyes locked onto the pistol tucked behind Michael's belt. In a swift, almost instinctual movement, her hand shot out, seizing the weapon with urgency. She yanked it free, the cold metal pressing against her palm as she leveled the barrel directly at Michael, her breath quick and shallow, her finger poised on the trigger.

"Stay back!" she yelled as she sprang to her feet.

Michael's gaze remained steady, unshaken, as if her sudden aggression were nothing more than an amusing diversion. He tilted his head slightly, a wisp of a smile playing at the corners of his lips. "Where did this hostility come from?" he asked, his voice almost too calm, a stark contrast to the storm raging inside Nirvana.

He took a step toward her.

"*I said stay back!* I will shoot you, I swear."

"What kind of gratitude is this? After everything I've done for you—pulled you from the jaws of hell, dragged you out of the lion's mouth—and this is how you repay me?"

"Shut up and let me think!" Nirvana's voice broke with raw frustration, her mind spinning in a chaotic whirl. Her fingers tightened around the gun as she tried to steady her racing thoughts. "I need to think..."

"Not a fan of breaking the laws of nature, huh? Fine. But don't kid yourself. This—this doesn't change who I am. You can't wish that away."

"I never asked for you, and I've never wanted any part of you," she declared, her eyes intense and unwavering.

Michael smirked, his gaze never faltering. "Ha! Big talk, huh? You want me to act scared? Is that what you need from me? You may have the power right now, but it doesn't scare me. I know you, Nirvana. I know you better than anyone ever could."

"Yeah? Well, did you know I was going to do this?" Nirvana's words went razor-sharp, and before Michael could respond, she had fired a shot.

The bullet struck the earth near his foot, sending a cloud of dirt into the air. He reacted instinctively, his body jerking in a panicked hop as he sidestepped the shot. He regained his balance, but the carefully constructed mask of carefree bravado slipped from his face, leaving only shock.

"Give me the gun," he demanded.

"No!"

"Give me the gun, Nirvana! I will not tolerate this any longer than you want to tolerate me."

"Big talk for someone panicking like a sitting duck," she shot back, her voice cold, her finger still tight on the trigger.

Michael's eyes looked briefly to the weapon, then back to her, his composure teetering. "Just hand it over, Nirvana. Alright? I'll go. I'll never bother you again, if that's what you really want."

Nirvana's lips tightened into a thin line, and she muttered almost to herself, "There is no end to this mess, is there? Unless I end it myself." Her free hand slid over the grip, her fingers wrapping around the trigger guard, tightening in preparation.

"You're not doing this..."

She paused, a flash of contempt crossing her face before she spoke again. "No? Well, I happen to have a different opinion. The truth is... I should've gotten rid of you years ago."

Michael's expression darkened, his tone dropping to a low growl. "Rid of me? ME? Your mother's right. You are just a dumb little swine. A swine I happen to love fucking."

Right then, Nirvana went off half-cocked and shot him in the arm. He screamed, and he groaned in deep anguish, one hand over his wound oozing blood, while the other hand clenched into a fist at his side, knuckles white, the muscles in his arms twitching as though ready to unleash something brutal.

"Don't mock me," Nirvana cautioned him, undeterred as ever.

Outraged, Michael cranked up his intimidation, his eyes narrowing to slits as if he could slice through Nirvana with just a glare. "You... you think you can become a killer overnight, huh? I made you! *I* molded you into what you are today. Have you *forgotten* that? Remember that time, huh? When your mother murdered your damn cat? Made you watch her cut its throat and pulled out its guts—*slowly*—before she tossed its body into the lake like it was nothing more than garbage?"

Nirvana's breath hitched, and he saw a memory flash across her eyes. He saw her shoulders tense, the small tremble in her fingers as if she were physically trying to push the memory back down, but he wasn't done yet. Not nearly.

"You cried for days," he continued, his voice softening but laced with cruelty. "How long did you weep over it? How many nights did you toss and turn, staring at the ceiling, wishing you could forget that feeling? Let me make this clear, Nirvana. You don't have it in you. You wouldn't be able to live with the guilt. The weight of it would crush you. You're too soft. Too broken."

"Try me," Nirvana snapped back with suppressed rage. She stood taller, her back straightening, the flare of defiance in her gaze igniting into something far fiercer than Michael had ever seen. "I'm not that innocent little girl anymore. She's long gone. She died the first time you looked at her differently. She died when you first touched her with the most disgusting idea in mind. You made her die, Michael. And now... there's nothing left but what I've become."

"You are right. Now you're just a pathetic little brat who craves attention," Michael pressed on. "Go ahead, *I* dare you. Do it. Fire away. I'm waiting."

The third shot rang out with a loud crack that echoed across the silent woods. The bullet found its mark—

Michael's leg—and the force of the impact sent him crashing to the ground. A sickening, jagged scream tore from his lung as he buckled, his hands instinctively clutching at the bleeding wound, the pain twisting his face into a grotesque veil of agony. He collapsed onto his knees, his body writhing and shaking, the dirt beneath him already stained with blood.

"I warned you," she said coldly, as if speaking to a stranger, a ghost, someone long past saving. "I think you have better luck begging."

Michael's breath came in sharp, ragged gasps as he tried to push himself upright, but his leg wouldn't hold him. "Beg?" His voice cracked, a bitter laugh escaping him. "You want me to beg! Fine, I'll beg. I'll beg for anything you want. You want me to admit I've wronged you? To say I'm sorry? Is that what you want to hear!"

Nirvana couldn't afford to be moved, not by his pleading, not by his rage. She'd seen it all before. The lies. The manipulation. The desperation. She was past all of it now.

"I don't need you to say anything," she replied softly, her voice now a whisper of ice. "I want you quiet. Silenced. Zipped... Eternally."

"You want me out of your life? Is that it?" Michael spat, getting increasingly desperate. "Okay... okay. Fine. I'm *out*. You've won, haven't you? *Happy now*?"

"That's not good enough..." Just then, Nirvana adjusted her aim to align with the center of Michael's forehead. The tension in her body was taut, focused, as if the world had narrowed down to this single moment—this single decision.

Despite being distinctively unwell, Michael shot back bitterly, "You are your mother at the end of the day. You are heartless, just like her. Crazy, just like her. You are *cursed*, don't you see? Cursed forever! You can't ever escape that. Plus, you don't have the fucking guts— "

"Watch me."

214

The words fell from her lips like a verdict. She didn't blink. Didn't flinch. Her finger pressed firmly against the trigger, and shot after shot, they rang out with a deafening crack.

BLAMMM!

"DIE..."

BLAMMM!

"JUST DIE..."

BLAMMM!

Michael's head snapped back as the bullets tore through his skull. His body jerked violently, his arms flailing for a moment before collapsing limply onto the old dirt path, his eyes wide, staring at nothing.

"Begone now," Nirvana whispered to herself, her voice flat and void of emotion, as though the words had lost all meaning. She paused, standing over Michael's lifeless body.

She had nothing more to say. Nothing more to feel.

The end had come. And it was over.

27

BY NIGHTFALL, TOM and Mark pulled into the long, winding driveway of the Shors' last known address, their car crunching over the gravel road. The country cottage loomed in front of them—a two-story building, half-ensconced by a tangle of spruces and bare birches, the kind of place that had once been picturesque but now stood quietly derelict. The weeds had overrun the yard, and the wooden siding was faded and peeling. The windows were dark, their glass cracked or missing altogether, and the roof sagged with neglect. It was clear no one had cared for this place in years.

Mark killed the engine, and the silence that followed felt somehow unnatural—too heavy for such an isolated spot. Both of them sat for a moment, staring at the house as if it might suddenly come to life and reveal its secrets.

"Remind me again, why are we here?" Tom asked, his voice breaking the stillness.

Mark shrugged, his posture slumping slightly as he leaned back in his seat. "Has it ever occurred to you that Joanna Nickson might have been an aunt or cousin of Ms. Shor? A blood relation of some sort?"

Tom looked out the window, studying the broken-down cottage. "I suppose. You think whoever it was moved in after the backyard incident?"

"I thought it was worth a shot—until I saw the state of this place," Mark said, shaking his head as he looked at the house. "I mean, who would want to live here? And to say that I was expecting to see a mansion. A million-dollar house, something that matched the name."

"Mr. Tilly did mention it was a country house," Tom said casually.

Mark turned to him sharply. "What does that dirty old fox have anything to do with this?"

Tom exhaled, leaning back in his seat. "It's a long story, but regardless, this place... is a little underwhelming."

"Underwhelming?" Mark echoed, his voice tinged with sarcasm. "This place is de-pressing. A ghost house, no matter which angle you look at it... Come on, let's get this over with."

With flashlights in hand, they stepped out of the car and approached the porch. A feeling of foreboding crept up their spines as they ascended the weathered steps, but they pushed that aside. Mark knocked on the door. The silence that greeted him seemed more unsettling than a response would have been. After a moment, he turned the doorknob. It creaked open with alarming ease.

Inside, the air was thick with dust, the kind of dust that clung to everything—a grim testament to years of neglect. The walls, once bright and inviting, now appeared lifeless, their colors muted by time. Furniture was left in disarray, each piece covered in a layer of grime. The atmosphere was so heavy, it seemed to suffocate any semblance of life that might have once lived here.

Tom stepped in behind Mark, eyes scanning the room.

"Careful where you step," Mark warned after nearly tripping on a mound of wax at his feet. "These people sure are obsessed with candles."

Tom noticed it too—wax drips scattered across the floor, leaving behind bizarre little formations.

"Imagine they were all lit," Mark mused. "It would have been a hell of an illumination show in here."

Just as he finished speaking, a sudden noise came from above them—something scrambling across the ceiling, followed by a series of hurried thuds. The men glanced up.

"It's probably some wild squirrels or a raccoon, reacting to our intrusion. I highly doubt squatters would settle in a place this far from the town center," Mark presumed.

Tom's gaze narrowed. "I'm going to check it out anyway."

"By all means. I'll poke around down here. Holler if you need me."

With that, Tom ascended the stairs, the creaking of the old wood beneath his feet echoing in the stillness. At the top of the staircase, he barely had time to react before a panicked raccoon darted past him, its claws skittering across the floor. He stumbled back into the hallway, heart racing, but his eyes caught a glimpse of something else—a door slightly ajar at the far end of the hall.

Curiosity gnawed at him as he approached it and gave it a tentative push. The door creaked open, revealing a room that seemed as forgotten as the house itself. Sheet music was scattered across the floor, but it was the sight of a ruined pianoforte near the bay window that drew his attention first—a broken heap of mahogany, its keys missing, the remnants of an expensive instrument now reduced to junk. Shards of ivory were scattered across the floor, catching the weak light that filtered in from the window.

"Must all musicians destroy their instruments?" Mark's voice echoed in the doorway behind him. "I never get the purpose of that."

Tom, crouching beside the mangled piano, studied it closely. "I don't think this was for show."

Mark stepped closer, inspecting the scattered pieces. "For one thing, this room tells me whatever happened here wasn't 'fun and games.'"

The two of them moved deeper into the room, and Mark's eyes darted to a corner, where streaks of dark red marred the baseboards. He knelt down, examining the paint-like streaks before looking up at Tom. "Come look at this."

Tom moved closer and got down on his knees, studying the stains. "That's paint," he said, his voice tinged with a glimmer of hope.

"Red paint on a blue wall? I don't think so." Mark ran his hand over the wall where small, almost imperceptible dents marked the surface. "And how do you explain these?"

Tom pushed himself up and placed his fingers along the indents. "Probably just normal wear and tear," he offered, trying to dismiss the rising unease in his chest.

"Wear and tear?" Mark scoffed, incredulous. "Oh, no. These—these little ivory blocks? They didn't just end up like this by accident. They were used as weapons. Trust me."

Tom froze, his mind racing. "What are you saying?"

Mark met his gaze squarely, his expression hardening. "Given the mother's history... it wouldn't surprise me if she ran a torture chamber right here."

Tom opened his mouth to protest, but the words caught in his throat as he slowly processed the possibility of unspeakable violence that might have once occurred in this house—things that could have happened to Nirvana in this cold, forgotten place. He tried to shake that thought, but it clung to him.

Mark continued. "You think famous musicians make a lot of money, that they live in big mansions, with pools and butlers. But this place? This is a hole. And the only other house around here is half-demolished. This place is a far cry from anything I imagined."

Tom frowned, a creeping suspicion settling in his gut. "Did you go down to the basement?" he asked suddenly.

Mark looked at him, utterly confused. "What basement? There's no basement."

"No basement? Are you sure?" Tom pressed.

"Is that supposed to be important?"

"Well... Mr. Tilly mentioned there was one."

Mark's eyebrows shot up. "Now, what's the deal with this conversation you had with Tilly? I sure as hell want to know," he said, his voice edged with curiosity and irritation. Then, he shifted, his eyes narrowing as he scanned the house once more. "As far as I can tell, this building has only two floors. But I did find something in that one bedroom downstairs that might be useful to us."

He pulled out two photos from his jacket pocket, the edges worn from being handled. Without waiting for a response, he handed them to Tom, his fingers brushing briefly against his brother's. "Here, take a look. Does this girl look like Ms. Nirvana Shor?"

Tom studied the images for a moment, recognizing the familiar features. "I think so. She looks younger here, but it's her."

Mark smirked. "And who's this guy? Her boyfriend? Cousin?"

Tom squinted at the photo of a boy kissing a middle-school-aged Nirvana on the cheek. Something about it felt off, and then it clicked. He pointed to the photo. "This isn't a boy," he said firmly. "This is a girl."

Mark's jaw dropped. "What? No way. Look again and look carefully this time."

"I don't need to. I know this woman. She's the one who came into the shop three days ago, called herself Jo."

"That woman?"

"I'm telling you, yes!"

Before Mark could respond, the distant sound of an engine caught their attention. They both turned to look out the bay window, holding their breaths. A car had just pulled up into the driveway, its engine humming to a stop. They watched, tense, waiting for the driver's door to open—but nothing happened. Instead, the brake light flickered out.

"Shit," Mark hissed, and without a word, he darted for the stairs, bolting out the door.

Tom followed him, but by the time they reached the driveway, the car was already speeding down the gravel road, disappearing.

"Damn it!" Mark shouted, his fists clenched in frustration.

Tom arrived beside him, breathing heavily. "Why do you think they left?"

"Our damn car, that's why," Mark growled, eyes scanning the road. "At least, that's what I'm assuming. I'm moving it behind those trees."

Tom's brow furrowed. "You think they'll come back?"

"I don't know," Mark said, moving toward the car. "But I'm not giving up just yet. I saw an axe by the base of the deck earlier. Let's gather some wood, make a fire. I don't know about you, but I'm freezing."

Tom hesitated, then nodded. His fingers tightened around the flashlight as he followed Mark toward the trees, his heart still pounding. Something about this place felt wrong in ways he couldn't yet explain, and he had a sinking feeling that the night was far from over.

28

K NOCK! KNOCK! KNOCK!...
        The distinct, insistent sound shattered the quiet of the house. Mrs. Ward's eyes snapped open, her pulse quickening as she sat up abruptly in bed. She glanced at her husband, who was already out of the sheets, his face hardening with concern.

"Someone's at the door," she whispered, her voice tight with unease. She threw back the covers, her feet hitting the floor with a soft thud. "Who could it be at this hour?"

"I don't know, but it doesn't sound like a social call," Reverend Ward replied, his hands quickly working to fasten the last button on his shirt. He was already moving toward the door.

He took a step toward the stairs, his wife close behind, their children trailing cautiously after them. Mrs. Ward muttered under her breath, her eyes darting between the darkened windows as they moved through the hall. "Who in their right mind comes knocking at ten o'clock at night?"

By the time they reached the front door, the knocking had grown louder, more urgent—each rap on the wood like a demand. The reverend glanced through the peephole, his expression flicking from confusion to recognition.

"It's her," he murmured, barely above a whisper.

"Who?" Mrs. Ward asked.

Their fifteen-year-old daughter, Liz, peered over her mother's shoulder, her eyes squinting as she took her turn at the peephole. Her lips curled into a mischievous smirk as she straightened up. "It's that dyke," she said, her voice filled with fascination. "Her name's Jo. I've seen her at church a few times."

Mrs. Ward's face reddened in shock. "Hush, child!" she scolded, her hand slapping Liz's arm in reprimand. "We don't use that kind of language. She's... just confused, that's all."

Liz rolled her eyes but said nothing more.

Turning to her husband, Mrs. Ward's voice took on a note of desperation. "What are you going to do about it?"

The door was still being assaulted with loud, impatient knocks. Then, without warning, they heard Jo's voice on the other side, forceful and demanding.

"Reverend Ward! I need to speak to you! Open the door!"

Mrs. Ward huffed in exasperation. "What a troublesome child," she said under her breath.

Liz, her chin resting in her hand, smirked again. "'Troublesome?' I think she's quite... interesting." She absentmindedly twirled a lock of her hair, clearly more intrigued by Jo's audacity than upset by her behavior.

"Children, to bed," The reverend ordered, his voice gentle, carrying a tone of finality. "Leave your mother and me to handle this."

"Oh, come on," Liz whined, crossing her arms. "I want to see how this goes down. I can't imagine her being as uptight as the rest of us."

"Liz, go to your room. Now. And take your sister with you," Mrs. Ward commanded.

With a dramatic sigh, Liz grabbed her younger sister by the wrist, pulling her along as she sulked up the stairs. Mrs. Ward watched them go with an almost imperceptible shake of her head.

Reverend Ward turned back to the door, his hand on the handle, the weight of what was to come settling heavily on his shoulders. With a deep breath, he swung the door open, his face pulling into a polite, if strained, smile.

"Good evening, Jo," he greeted.

Jo's posture was almost brash, her shoulders squared as if she wasn't just standing at the door of the reverend's house—she was staking her claim.

"I need to talk to you," she said, her tone flat, devoid of pleasantries. Without waiting for permission, she strode forward, brushing past the reverend and into the hallway.

Reverend Ward's voice remained steady as he offered, "You can come to church tomorrow any time before 5 p.m. I'll be there. We can talk through your problems then."

"I can't wait that long," Jo replied. "You have a nice house—humble, yet lovely."

Mrs. Ward closed the door behind them with a soft click. She stood in the doorway, a faint frown creasing her brow. "Jo, is it? You're always welcome to join us ladies for Bible study this Saturday," she began, her voice laced with a forced sweetness.

Jo didn't even glance her way. "I work that day," she said bluntly.

Mrs. Ward's mouth tightened into a thin line. She swallowed the indignation that rose in her throat, but it was clear she was struggling to keep her composure. "Well, we hold one every Saturday—"

"I came here to talk to the reverend," Jo interrupted dismissively. "Not you."

The rejection stung, sharper than Mrs. Ward had expected. She had been raised to be gracious, to offer kindness, especially in her own home—but this woman had cut her off without so much as a second glance. Her cheeks flushed with a mixture of anger and disbelief. She opened her mouth to retort, but the reverend's calm voice stopped her.

"Why don't we step outside, Jo?" he said, his tone firm but gentle, as though he'd already anticipated this moment. He looked at his wife, his hand brushing against her cheek in a tender gesture. "Darling, go on to bed. Don't wait up for me. I'll be back shortly."

Mrs. Ward blinked, her heart thudding. She was caught between irritation and worry, but she held herself together. "Fine," she muttered.

With that, the reverend turned, leading Jo toward the back door. The evening air was cool against his skin as they stepped outside. He wasted no time.

"What is it, Jo? What's so urgent?"

Jo hesitated, settling herself into a nearby garden chair. She shifted uncomfortably, staring at the ground for a moment as if the words she needed to say were tangled up with the roots beneath her feet. Her fingers nervously played with the hem of her sleeve, and she finally spoke.

"I apologize if I've disturbed your sleep. I just... I had to talk to someone," she said, her tone wavering slightly with her confession.

Reverend Ward, though tired, gave her a kind, understanding smile. "It's okay," he reassured her. "I'm used to staying up late managing the church finances anyway. It's my wife and children who are more difficult. They tend to get cranky the next day when they don't get enough rest."

Jo managed a small, tight-lipped smile at that. She looked away, biting her lip, wrestling with how to begin.

"I did something crazy today... care to know what it was?" she asked, a nervous chuckle escaping her lips.

"Sure," the reverend replied, his voice soft and inviting. "Will you tell me?"

Jo hesitated again, as if she were still weighing whether or not she should reveal the truth to him. When she started to speak again, this time, it was more intentional, more calculated.

"Remember that Sunday a few months back, after your sermon? I approached you—remember?"

Reverend Ward nodded, his mind immediately going back to that afternoon. "Oh yes," he said, "I remember distinctly. How is your lady friend?"

"She... she's fine. You don't need to worry. I was just going to see her, but..." Jo trailed off, the sentence unfinished, as if her thoughts had gone elsewhere.

Meanwhile, the reverend continued. "Is she still at the hospital?"

Jo looked up at him then. "She's been out for a while," she answered about Nirvana, her gaze lingering with something that might have been pain or, worse, guilt.

The reverend, noticing, replied with a small but positive smile. "That's good news. God bless her. I take it she finally agreed to go home with you in the end?"

Jo didn't correct him. Instead, she changed the subject, her voice heavy with something else—something darker. "You're a wise man, Reverend Ward. Let me ask you—what does the Bible tell us about love and hate?"

The reverend's posture straightened, his heart lifting slightly. He was confident in matters of scripture, and he had often found comfort in the clear-cut lessons of the Gospel. He answered without hesitation.

"Well, love is patient, love is kind," he said, the words rolling off his tongue like a well-worn prayer. "Jesus indeed spoke similarly about hate. He said: 'Love your enemies, bless those who curse you, and do good to those who hate you.'"

Jo nodded slowly, absorbing his words. Her expression was contemplative, yet filled with a strange urgency.

"But what if—what if I've been patient and kind to someone, yet they still insist on hating me?" she asked, her voice trembling slightly. "Wouldn't it be justifiable for me to do something about it?"

The question hung between them, thick with the unsaid. Reverend Ward took a moment, a thoughtful furrow between his brows, before he responded. "By 'doing something,' I suppose you mean correcting them," he said slowly, carefully. "If you care to know what Jesus would have done in that circumstance... well, I believe He would have let things be. He would have allowed His love to conquer all hate, and He would have inspired those eager to change, rather than forcing them to."

Jo stared at him for a long moment, her lips slightly parted as if his words had struck a chord deep inside her. Then, with a quick breath, she spoke again, her voice low and intense.

"That might be what He would do," she said, her eyes narrowing as though testing him. "But that's not what you would do, is it?"

Reverend Ward blinked, taken aback by the directness of her question. "I would be prompted to do what I preach," he said firmly. "So yes, I would."

Jo looked away, her jaw clenching. Her fingers curled tightly around the edges of the chair, her knuckles pale against the darkness of the night. For a while, she was silent. Then, she looked back at him.

"What about... what about when that person hurts you so badly?" she asked, her eyes red, her voice cracking with raw emotion. "What if they hurt you so much that you feel like your heart could just... give out?"

The reverend froze, the gravity of her words sinking in like a stone. He saw the way her face twisted in pain, the deep lines of sadness carving into her features. For a moment, he thought she might break, that she might crumble right there in front of him.

He stepped closer, instinctively reaching out, though he didn't touch her. His gaze softening as he shared a more personal side of himself. "I know what that's like," he said, his voice quieter now, as if inviting Jo into a space of trust. "My eldest daughter can also be a real trial."

Jo's curiosity piqued, and she leaned in just a little. "How?"

Reverend Ward exhaled a small, knowing breath, his eyes briefly distant as he recalled the frustrations of fatherhood. "Well, I can see past the poor report cards, but the constant back-talking... that's the hardest part. Trying to reason with her, and she just shuts you down. She goes out with her friends without telling me and ignores the curfew we set for her. My wife especially, she's at her wit's end with that child."

Jo blinked, genuinely surprised. She hadn't expected the reverend to reveal so much of his own struggles, and a blink of something—perhaps empathy, perhaps admiration—crossed her face.

"Then what?" she asked. "What do you do to fix it? To fix her?"

Reverend Ward's smile was calm, almost serene, as if his response were an answer passed down through generations. He spoke slowly, but his words were firm, full of the quiet strength that seemed to radiate from him. "Nothing, except that I wait and have faith. I choose to forgive her every time she steps out of line. I try to let my love and acceptance inspire her, and I hope and pray to God every day that she will grow up to be a valuable member of the society."

"And if she doesn't? What if she becomes a thief, a liar, a cheat? Would you forsake her then?"

Just then, his gaze softened further, and he looked at Jo as if this were the most natural thing in the world. "I would still love her. As a parent, I could never hold my love for my children hostage. Otherwise, what kind of example am I setting for them?"

The sincerity in his response hung in the air like a tender prayer, and Jo felt something inside her shift. She'd never had a father figure like this in her life. Her own father had never been around, and the idea of unconditional love—of a father's unwavering support despite his children's mistakes—was something she could only imagine. She almost envied Reverend Ward's daughter.

"You're a good father," she blurted before she could stop herself, her thought slipping out like a secret she hadn't meant to share. She blinked, and for a brief moment, she considered reaching out to hug him, but she quickly held herself back.

The reverend, humbled by her praise, felt a surge of warmth. It was a subtle thing, but he couldn't deny the satisfaction of knowing his words had made some impact. Jo's internal agony seemed to have lightened, even if only by a fraction.

He leaned forward slightly, his words coming now with the quiet confidence of a man convinced of his righteousness. "Look, Jo. I don't plan to tell you how to run your life. But if you were my daughter, I'd advise you to stop, take a step back, and reflect on what you've done— before someone gets seriously hurt. Sometimes, it's only human to commit sins. But it's important to recognize them, to come around and seek salvation."

Jo's brow furrowed in confusion, and her gaze sharpened. "What kind of trouble do you think I'm in?" she asked, her voice cautious, fully alert to his implication.

The reverend took a breath and articulated his thoughts more clearly, as though he were delivering a lesson he'd taught a hundred times before. "God created Adam and Eve for a reason. That's how life has always been intended."

Upon his assertion, Jo's mouth fell open. At first, she wasn't sure whether to laugh or to get angry. Then, a bitter laugh escaped her—loud and cutting. "You know what's so funny?" she said between breaths, her chest tightening with incredulity. "I came here looking for guidance, but all you ended up worrying about is my sexuality."

The reverend's face remained composed, though an undeniable discomfort passed through his eyes. He'd expected some resistance, of course, but the intensity of her reaction still stung.

"That's not all I'm saying," he replied, his voice firm. "But you can't deny that's the root of your problem."

Jo shook her head, her anger rising like a tide. "I love her, Reverend," she said, her eyes blazing with conviction. "I love her like you love your wife. And if that bugs you, so be it."

"I'm sure you do. But does she love you in return? You needn't get defensive with me. I'm not attacking you, Jo. I'm simply trying to help you see things from a different perspective. If only you would step back, you'd see that the world has always worked the way it does. You can't change that. And you can't *make* someone want what you want. I pray that you learn to accept the inevitable... and let her go."

"Let her go? Humph, never," Jo snapped. She stood up tall, her face a mixture of defiance and pain. "You don't know her, nor do you know me."

"I'm not saying I do either—"

"Then you should know, you have no right to come between us. She loved me. She *has* to love me still. She just needs a little time. A reminder. That's all."

Though still calm, Reverend Ward couldn't hide the frustration in his eyes. His mind raced with the question that gnawed at him. *What drives a woman like Jo to fixate on another woman like she does? What is this... this unyielding fixation?*

"Why does she have to? Why must she not move on? Why must she stay with you?" His probing held an undercurrent of something almost selfish—an urge to understand, perhaps even control, a mindset that both baffled and fascinated him.

"Tsk, forget it—"

"I don't want to forget it. Is it because of desperation? Or is there something deeper, Jo? Some... evil energy that tempted you to choose your own sex? To commit the sin you've committed? It isn't a conscious choice, is it? Please, do enlighten me."

Jo's lips curled in disdain, her jaw tightening. "You may always be right in your flock's eyes, but you're so wrong when you're looking at me."

"Why are you so angry?"

"Because!" she exclaimed, her breathing quickened, her eyes flashed with a hurt that ran deeper than mere irritation. "Everybody has somebody. Why must I be alone? I've been by myself *forever*, Reverend. And then, when I finally find someone to spend my life with, you— *you*—tell me to let her go? It's not fair! It's not fair..." Her voice trailed off, shaking with emotion, and for a moment, it was as if the walls around her heart cracked just enough to show the vulnerable person underneath.

Unable to look away from the raw pain in her eyes, Reverend Ward felt something twist in his gut. He took a slow breath, but before he could respond, Jo cut him off, her words sharp like a whip.

"If only you knew how we were, how we *used* to be together. If you understood *that*, you wouldn't have said what you did."

"That's not true—"

"I refuse... I refuse to listen to anyone who disapproves of Nina and me being together, especially not some closed-minded pastor from a remote town who just decided to play God."

The reverend took a step back. He felt the rare trust Jo had shown him slipping through his fingers like sand. He looked at her for a moment, searching for a way to reach her, but there was nothing—only that cold, resentful stare.

"I didn't mean to make you feel rejected," he said regretfully. "But you are sinking, Jo. Can't you see that about yourself? You're a good young woman underneath all this—beneath all the anger. But you're letting something dark and hateful control you. Why do you really think you came here? If you were so certain about your actions, about your life, you wouldn't need anyone's reassurance. Especially not mine."

Jo crossed her arms over her chest, taking in his words with a scoff. "I wanted someone to agree with me," she said, "For once, I wanted someone to tell me I was doing something *right*. To tell me there's nothing wrong with loving someone so deeply. But you—clearly, you're not the person I thought you were."

"If that's your opinion, I don't intend to change it."

"But you intend to change me!" she shouted. "Every Sunday, you preach about God's love, how He accepts all things, and then here you are—calling me wrong, calling me evil. I'd rather not know Him at all if He's anything like you."

Reverend Ward's face hardened. His heart ached for Jo. His voice remained calm but tinged with sorrow. "Wake up, child," he said, "I pray for you."

Jo shook her head. "Is that all you have left to say? You can learn to be someone's friend for a change," she spat bitterly, turning away from him.

The reverend stood still, watching her retreat. "I don't think anything else I say will make a difference now," he murmured, almost to himself.

Jo didn't respond. Instead, she nodded—slowly, almost resigned. It was a movement that was equal parts mad and sad. "I think I'll let you get back to sleep, Reverend," she said, her voice barely above a whisper. "Thank you for your time. And I'm very sorry I stopped by."

29

THE BOYS SAT in a rough circle around the fire they'd kindled in the backyard, the crackling flames casting fluttering shadows on their faces. The sky above was thick with clouds, a faint moon barely visible, as fate tested their patience.

"... He left you the shop. That's something," Mark said, his voice muffled by the cigarette dangling between his lips. He blew out a cloud of smoke, the ember glowing brighter in the dim light as he recalled their father's will.

Tom snorted, his hands tucked tightly under his armpits as if trying to trap the warmth that seemed to be fleeing him with each gust of the cold night air. "He only did that so you could continue to run wild, do what you love to do. On the other hand, he never bothered asking me what I wanted to do with my life," he said, ever so slightly jealously.

Mark raised an eyebrow, his face a flicker of surprise, though he hid it quickly behind a smirk. "What *did* you want to do?"

Tom paused for a long moment, his gaze distant. "I wanted to teach... become a college professor."

"A professor?" Mark's laughter was loud, a bit spiteful even. He shook his head, almost choking on his own amusement. "You stink at public speaking. Remember the poop-in-your-pants incident back in high school?"

Tom's jaw tightened at the old wound, but he pushed it aside. "A man can dream."

"That's a dull dream, though, isn't it?" Mark scoffed, leaning back against the log he was sitting on, puffing out more smoke as he fixed Tom with an incredulous look.

"Not to me," Tom replied evenly, though a glimmer of frustration sparked behind his eyes. "I don't see how educating the young and helping them succeed could ever be dull." He paused, steadying his voice. "When I started working for Dad in the summer of my freshman year, he already had it all planned. He wanted me to take over the shop someday."

Mark smirked again, a half-chuckle escaping his lips. "He probably thought you had a flair for this business stuff. And let's not forget, you could've walked away from it at any time."

Tom's face darkened, and he rubbed the back of his neck, uncomfortable with the reminder. "I didn't want to disappoint him."

Mark flicked his cigarette into the fire with a lazy motion. "Well, you're free now. You can close the shop down or sell it to Sam if you really want to. I don't get why you're so tied to it."

Tom stiffened at his brother's nonchalance. "How can you say that so lightly? You know how important the shop was to Dad."

Mark didn't flinch. "If the shop's holding you back—"

"I didn't say it was," Tom snapped, his eyes flashing.

Mark tilted his head and sighed. "Then I guess Dad wasn't so wrong about you after all, huh? You've always been the responsible one—the goodie-goodie, like him. If only I were more like you guys..." He trailed off, a rare glimmer of self-doubt creeping into his voice.

Tom blinked. He was taken aback by the unexpected sincerity. "Since when have you thought that?"

Mark shrugged, his gaze wandering to the fire. "Since about two weeks ago," he said quietly, as though it pained him to admit it.

This was new. Tom watched his brother, bewildered by the shift in tone. "What's going on, Mark? You... never talk like this."

Mark exhaled sharply, running a hand through his hair. "Alright, fine. The truth is, I've been placed on administrative leave." He paused, letting his own admission settle in.

Tom stared at him, his brow furrowed. "What?"

"I've been suspended," Mark said, rubbing his face as if exhausted from carrying the secret. "Temporarily. It's no big deal."

Tom let out a slow breath, already forming an assumption. "Let me guess. You punched a colleague?"

Mark smirked bitterly. "I wish I did. No, I just cussed them out. Walked off. They're pissed because I called the shots when it wasn't my place."

"Great," Tom said dryly. "So now the whole department's under scrutiny because of you."

Mark waved a hand dismissively. "It's not that bad. I've made some enemies in the past, yeah, but this is just a few higher-ups making noise. It'll blow over." He looked over at his brother, trying to lighten the mood. "But hey, at least this screw-up let me spend the whole day—and now this fine night—with my big brother by a campfire, having a smoke and freezing my ass off. Only things missing are beer and marshmallows..."

Tom shook his head, his expression turning serious. Somehow, Mark's attempt at levity felt flat, like the words were just that—words—hollow and disconnected from what really happened. Tom could sense his little brother was trying to cover up something.

He leaned forward, searching Mark's face for any hint of the truth, the slightest shift in his eyes, a crack in his usual deflective demeanor.

"You've been acting different," he said, his voice low, not accusing but filled with an undercurrent of suspicion. As the words left his mouth, something clicked in his mind, and his eyes narrowed. "That's why you've been so enthusiastic about finding Nirvana. After all, this is no charity case. What's in it for you?"

Mark's face froze, and for a moment, Tom thought he might not answer at all. The usual smirk was gone, replaced by a guarded look that Tom knew all too well. Mark shifted slightly, his gaze dropping for a split second before he met Tom's eyes again, a little too quickly.

"It's not like that," he protested, though the defensive edge in his voice betrayed him.

"You're not in this to look good in front of your colleagues?" Tom's tone was cutting now, each word coming out like a bite.

Mark's eyes narrowed, and he shot back, "You're the one who brought it to my attention, remember? Not the other way around. You're as much in this as I am."

Tom's jaw clenched. "Yeah, but I'm not betting on some tragedy to make headlines. I don't get off on that."

Upon the sting of the insinuation, Mark instantly fell silent. It landed like a slap, forcing the air right out of his lungs. He hadn't expected it. Not from Tom. The cool night breeze grazed his flushed skin, biting and cold, but it couldn't erase the heat rising from the sudden ache in his chest. He kept his face impassive, forcing his features into that familiar, practiced mask of detachment. But his eyes, the only traitor of his emotions, flickered briefly with something raw—a flash of hurt, before he willed it all back down. He wasn't going to show it. Not to his big brother.

But Tom, watching Mark's every move, saw it anyway. The shift. The unease in his brother's stiff posture, the way his lips had tightened as if holding back a retort that would never come. For a moment, his heart clenched.

"I'm sorry," he muttered, his voice barely above a whisper, a soft, reluctant, but sincere admission that seemed too small for the space between them.

Mark merely shrugged. "Don't say sorry if that's the way you feel," he said candidly. "Look, I'm a cop. I'm doing what I'd do on the job. This is real. I'm not playing some game. I swear." He shifted, pulling a folder from his jacket and tossing it into Tom's lap. "Here. I snatched this from the doctor's office. It's Nirvana's medical history."

Tom's heart sunk at the sight of the folder. He was disinclined to touch it but did anyway, opening it with hesitation.

"Don't be a saint," Mark chided. "Read it. You're the one who cares."

Tom paused and let out a frustrated sigh. "I don't want to read it," he said, but Mark ignored him.

"If you won't, I will," Mark said, already flipping through the pages.

"Listen to this," he read aloud, voice dropping an octave. "'Preliminary Assessment. July 12th, 1996. Ms. Shor is categorized as a severe case of child maltreatment. Upon her arrival, she displayed clear symptoms of post-traumatic stress, evident in her aggressive behavior toward hospital staff. She was combative, explosive, and paranoid. It is believed these traits are a direct result of prolonged physical, emotional, and sexual abuse perpetrated by both of her biological parents...' Yikes... That's... brutal." He continued reading, oblivious to Tom's tightening grip on the folder. "'Record. January 10th, 1997. Ms. Shor is struggling with intense anxiety attacks. Night terrors have been reported, recurring nightmares in which she's attacked and mauled by dogs...'" Mark shook his head in disbelief. "Jesus, that's messed up."

Tom remained quiet, his expression hardening as the implications of what he was hearing sunk in. His mind raced as he considered the kind of trauma that could have happened to Nirvana. It was hard to imagine. Too hard.

Mark skimmed ahead. "'Cognitive behavioral therapy has been initiated to help mitigate her symptoms...' Blah, blah, blah, therapy, therapy... 'Record. June 30th, 1998. Ms. Shor continues to suffer from hallucinations. Three separate incidents have been documented in the past week. Notably, there are multiple reports detailing interactions between the patient and someone named *Michael*. These communications are of particular concern...' Michael... who the hell is this guy?"

That name. Tom's eyes shot to that last line. His breath caught in his throat. *Michael.* The name felt wrong, like an unwelcome shadow lingering in the corner of his mind, but there it was, underlined in black ink.

"Could it be that guy from Wisconsin?" he suggested.

Mark shrugged. "At this point, I'm not sure that guy exists at all."

"That name must get mentioned elsewhere... let me take a closer look."

So Mark moved away and let Tom take over the skimming. His fingers trembled slightly as he came across that name again. It was from a snippet of a transcript highlighting Nirvana's hypnotic account that Tom first learned of the man in question—Michael—and his precise, unsettling origin. As he disgusted the details, each more disturbing than the last, his stomach churned.

"... he made me call him Michael. The first time, we were in the darkroom in a tub. We were stark naked, sitting and facing one another. I was scared, terrified, not knowing what horrible things were to come. I tried my best to hide my true feelings, fearing to let him down should I refuse to engage in the playacting he had meticulously planned. I was naïve for trusting that he wouldn't hurt me—that he loved me. It was very difficult... The second time onwards, Daddy would tranquilize me with these colorful pills to stop me from crying. Thank God for those pills. With them, it was easier to perform, easier to forget about the pain and nausea, and that I was there, doing what we did. He would watch me bathe, have me masturbate in front of him, and on occasions—for him. This toxic thing went on for three years till his death, happening as frequently as twice a week, or at the very least every time he came home from a job out of town..."

"Find anything?" Mark interrupted, noticing Tom's attentiveness to the page.

Tom gulped. "Nothing," he said firmly, his voice leaving no room for further questions. He wasn't about to share what he had learned—not even with his own brother. It was information meant to stay buried for Nirvana's protection. With that, he slammed the folder shut and tossed it into the fire.

Mark watched the folder curl and blacken in the flames, his eyebrows arching. "Good riddance, I guess. But what's really going on between you and this girl? You in love with her?"

"It's complicated," Tom answered.

That answer hardly satisfied Mark, who had never been one to let his brother's "complicated" love life slide without probing. Undeterred, he fired off a barrage of follow-up questions.

"One-sided, huh? I can tell." His lips curled into a sly smile.

"It's not like that."

"Why? No spark? Or is she playing hard to get?"

Tom flushed with annoyance. "What? No."

Mark chuckled. "You're scared of rejection, that's it. Although, going by what I've read, she does sound kinda messed up if you ask me."

"I didn't ask for your opinion, nor am I bothered by her past because she's a great girl regardless."

"Then what's the problem if you like her and she likes you?"

Tom's gaze dropped to the ground as he spoke quietly. "She wouldn't want to be with a guy like me."

"What? Mr. Nice Guy doesn't suit her exquisite taste?"

"What I meant was she should be with someone who understands what she's been through, someone who knows how to take good care of her, help her, not a guy who's as clueless as a fence post. And that is, if she's even looking for someone at all."

Mark studied Tom, his expression shifting slightly as he leaned forward, his hands clasped together. "Don't sell yourself short. You do tend to rise to the occasion. Besides, you really shouldn't compare yourself to me."

"I'm being serious."

"So am I," he said, his voice mellowing for a moment, as though offering a rare glimpse of sentiment. "What is she to do anyway? It's fate that brought you two together, not logic. And quite honestly, maybe she doesn't need help. The hospital wouldn't have discharged her unless she's recuperated from all her old scars and traumas. Or are you saying she seemed off?"

"No," Tom said quickly, shaking his head. "She adjusted just fine. I never would have guessed she came from an abusive home."

"It sounds like she's doing her best to regain her life. That's a pretty brave girl you have there. You tend to second-guess yourself too much."

Tom's face softened, but he looked away, as though ashamed. "I've just been taking things slow."

Mark chuckled lightly, his voice laced with teasing."Slow is good. Slow is great. You know what you're doing. How long did it take you to finally tell Dominique that you had the hots for her again?"

"I knew telling you that would eventually come back to bite me."

"I just want you to keep it real this time, big brother, for your own good. I've never seen you more worked up over someone. You didn't even shed a tear at Dad's funeral, but I can imagine you crying over this girl."

"Don't exaggerate," Tom said, a blush creeping up his neck, but there was something affectionate in his eyes. "If we find her..."

30

AS THE BROTHERS chatted, the same car from hours ago suddenly reappeared, rolling quietly up the driveway. The engine cut, and the brakes squealed as it came to a halt, alerting them. Mark, with a sharp instinct, reached for his phone and redialed the number he'd been trying to reach all day. This time, it rang—faintly, but unmistakably—from somewhere near the front of the property.

"It's her," he murmured, informing Tom. "Joanna Nickson."

Mark didn't need any more information. Without a second thought, he was already on the move, his stride purposeful and quick, heading for the driveway. His hand shot to his sidearm as he sprinted, adrenaline surging.

"Hey! Police! Get out of the car! Now!" he shouted, his badge gleaming in the harsh light of the headlights as he drew closer. But the driver merely shifted the car into reverse, tires screeching on the asphalt as they peeled away, leaving the driveway in a cloud of smoke.

"Oh no, you don't!" Mark snarled, his teeth gritted. In one fluid motion, he pivoted on his heel to run toward their car. Tom didn't need to look to know what was coming. Mark wasn't about to let her get away—not this time. Meanwhile, his focus had already turned elsewhere.

As the sound of Mark's engine faded into the distance, the atmosphere around Tom began to shift. The air had turned crisp with a fresh layer of snow falling heavily from the sky. The first snowfall in days. Tom stomped the last of the fire into the dirt, its embers flickering out in a cloud of ash. He walked toward the roofed deck, the wind stilling for a moment as the world seemed to hold its breath.

The wind had stilled, leaving the trees eerily calm. In the near silence, a strange noise cut through the air—a low, muffled growl, repetitive and indistinct, as if something was snarling underground. Tom froze, his breath catching in his throat. He scanned the quarter-acre backyard, now rapidly turning white under the blanket of snow. His eyes narrowed. There—twenty yards away—an unusual bump in the terrain caught his attention.

His heart quickened, a gut feeling gnawing at him. He couldn't shake the sensation that something wasn't right. Without a word, he started toward the spot, his shoes making a trail behind him as he approached. He crouched by it, brushing aside the snow, and soon his suspicion was confirmed. A concrete septic tank riser lay half-buried beneath the fresh layer of snow. He ran his hands over the sturdy lid and the seam between the tank and the ground. The hooks that would normally help remove it had been broken off, leaving it sealed shut.

Just then, Mark's frustrated voice echoed in the distance as he returned from a failed pursuit. "I lost her at the intersection. Those damn tires of yours are garbage in the snow. I skidded out of control—almost wrecked in a ditch."

Tom didn't respond right away. His eyes remained fixed on the septic tank riser as his mind worked quickly. Finally, he looked up at Mark. "I need that axe you used earlier. Where is it?"

Mark raised an eyebrow, clearly curious. "The axe? You gonna chop down a tree or something?"

"No," Tom replied, his tone direct. "I need it to pry this thing open."

Mark stared at the septic tank riser. "Why?" he questioned. "I'm not sure what you expect to find down there besides shit."

"Let's just say I have an inkling."

"An inkling of what? Don't tell me you think Ms. Shor is down there."

Tom's lips curled into a hard, determined line. "And who's to say she isn't?"

"Whoa—now who's thinking the worst? If you want to make a point, then make a point with facts. If you found something while I was gone, now would be a good time to clue me in before you go off on some wild tangent."

"I didn't find anything, but instead of wasting time playing twenty questions, you could help get this done faster."

Mark didn't move at first. He stood frozen, watching his big brother with growing suspicion. Seeing Tom's unwavering gaze, he gave in. Soon, he headed back to retrieve the axe from under the deck. When he returned, he handed it to Tom with a slight toss.

Tom caught the axe with a firm hold, his fingers curling around the handle with quick, practiced ease. Immediately, he worked to position the blade into the seam where the lid met the body of the septic tank, and with a deep breath, he motioned for Mark to help. "On three," he said quietly. "One... two... three."

With a combined grunt, they pushed the axe down with all their weight. The lid shifted, the concrete groaning in protest, and after a few more heaves, it finally gave way, lifting with a horrible screech.

The stench hit them both at once—rank, sour, and thick with the unmistakable odor of decay. Mark's nose wrinkled in disgust as he recoiled, his eyes watering. He clapped a hand over his face, doing his best not to gag.

"Ugh! God, that smell!" he groaned. "And here I thought my nose had stopped working under this awful weather! Whatever you need to do, Thomas, do it quickly. It stinks to high heaven."

Tom didn't flinch. He simply dropped to one knee and shone his flashlight down into the darkness below. The light flashed across something that shouldn't have been there. A shadow, unmoving, at the bottom of the tank.

"Oh my God..."

"Oh my God, what?" Mark asked, still fighting the urge to gag. He leaned forward, his eyes narrowing as he peered into the hole.

Tom's flashlight beam settled on the grim sight at the bottom—*a human skeleton*. The flesh long gone, only the stark white bones remained, contorted in a strange, unnatural position, like they had been thrown into the tank and left to rot.

"Holy Moses..." Mark whispered, his voice thick with disbelief.

Tom took a steadying breath, his expression grim as he crouched down, studying the remains in the dark. "Are you thinking that is—"

"Catherine Shor." Mark didn't need him to finish the sentence. He knew. "You bet I am."

Tom's gaze flicked back to the hole, a chill running down his spine. The mystery was unraveling faster than he could process it. But something else nagged at him. Something still wasn't right.

"*Hush*," he said sharply. "Do you hear that?"

Mark blinked, confused. "Hear what?"

Tom's eyes darted around, his body rigid. He could feel the hair on the back of his neck stand on end. "A dog. Barking."

Mark's brow furrowed. "I don't hear anything—"

Tom pointed, his finger trembling slightly. "There! Again."

Mark stood up, his expression perplexed. He shook his head, the cold air biting at his skin. "I don't know what you're talking about. But... I'm calling my superintendent. He's not going to believe this. This is huge."

Tom didn't respond. He was already moving, instinctively following the sound of the growls. His eyes scanned the yard, scanning every shadow, every movement. He needed to find the source of that noise. It felt too important, too urgent to ignore.

As he moved farther into the snow-covered yard, he came upon a section of stockade fence. His eyes locked onto a series of boulders scattered along the edge, one of them slightly out of place. His instincts kicked in. Something was hidden here.

He crouched low, brushing the snow away from the base of the boulder. His heart raced as his fingers found the cold metal handle of a trapdoor. He pushed the boulder aside with a grunt, and then, without hesitation, he yanked open the trapdoor.

The hinges screamed as they gave way, and immediately, a loud, frantic bark echoed from below. Without thinking, he grabbed the steel ladder mounted against the wall of the trapdoor and started descending, his flashlight barely cutting through the thick darkness. With each step, the barking grew louder, more desperate.

Tom reached the bottom of the ladder, his breath quick and shallow. He expected to find some kind of animal—maybe a dog locked up in a kennel. What he found, however, made his blood run cold.

There was no animal—just an old tub and a table. A battered tape recorder sitting on top, playing the same growling, snarling noise over and over. The source of the barking had been artificial all along.

He moved quickly, his hand shaking as he turned off the tape recorder. The sound stopped abruptly, leaving an eerie silence in its wake. As the silence settled in, Tom's attention was drawn to a movement in the corner of the room. Something—or someone—was moving.

A faint, weak voice drifted from the shadows.

"*Jo...*"

Tom's heart lurched. He turned, his eyes widening as he saw Nirvana, blindfolded and bound to a chair, her skin pale and bruised, her body slumped in exhaustion, curled up on the cold concrete floor.

Without a second thought, he rushed to her side to remove her blindfold, untangling the ropes that had cut into her wrists and ankles, blood staining the thick nylon. He gently cradled her head in his lap, his hands trembling as he whispered her name.

"Nirvana... it's me, Tom. Are you with me?"

Nirvana's eyes fluttered open. She was barely conscious, but her shallow breath was a faint comfort.

Mark, having followed Tom down, stood frozen at the bottom of the ladder. He watched in shock as he took in the sight of Nirvana. "What the hell..."

"Call an ambulance!" Tom barked, his voice a raw edge of command. "*Do it! Now!*" Then, he returned his attention to Nirvana, his voice soft, soothing as he brushed the hair from her face. "You'll be okay. You'll be fine now..."

PART FOUR

31

*B*REAKING NEWS: FIVE *days have passed since Nirvana Shor, 21, was rescued from her childhood home, where she had been confined in an abandoned bomb shelter in the backyard for over 48 hours. Authorities confirm that Shor is in stable condition, but have withheld further comment on the ongoing investigation.*

A human skeleton discovered at the scene has been identified as the remains of Catherine Shor, Nirvana's mother, who had been missing for nearly a decade following a tragic dog attack that led to her daughter's institutionalization.

This morning, we spoke with Detective Marcus Ager, the lead investigator on the case, who described the discovery as a "travesty of justice." Detective Ager emphasized that his team is committed to thoroughly addressing the case and correcting any previous investigative oversights.

Authorities have urged the public to remain patient as the investigation continues. We will keep you updated with any new developments...

"How do I look on TV?" Mark's voice sliced through the quiet of the room. Tom's eyes flicked from the screen to the doorway, where his brother was standing with an air of insufferable self-satisfaction. He immediately felt his irritation stir, the presence of Mark—uninvited, unannounced—almost a physical strain on his shoulders.

Mark, unabashed, continued, his tone smooth and smug. "I mean, you've always been the better-looking one between us, but with this new badge and rank, I'm starting to have my doubts."

Tom's eyes narrowed, a frown tugging at the corners of his lips. "Don't you ever knock?"

Mark smirked, stepping into the room. "Your door was open. And hey, they're still talking about me. Looks like I'm kind of a big deal now." He threw a glance at the television screen, where an image of him flashed across the news.

Tom switched off the screen, his voice carried a blend of annoyance and and disbelief. "What are you doing here? I thought you were busy, you know, actually investigating something."

"Oh, I have been," Mark said with a chuckle, his eyes dancing with a mix of mockery and sincerity. "They don't just promote anyone, you know. But even Sherlock Holmes needs to eat. I was on my way to grab lunch. Thought I'd drop by, see if my big brother wants to join. With this weather, we could even eat al fresco." He motioned toward the window, the sun streaming in as if trying to emphasize the point.

Tom glanced out at the glaring sun. "It's twenty degrees outside."

Mark shrugged with feigned innocence. "Yeah, but it's sunny. That counts for something."

"Ha, ha, ha," Tom responded dryly, didn't even try to hide his disdain. "Thanks for the invite, but no thanks. I've learned my lesson."

Mark was taken aback, but for only a moment. "What are you talking about?"

Tom leaned back in his chair, his expression unamused. "The last time we went out for lunch, I spent the whole afternoon running errands with you."

Mark's face twisted slightly, as if trying to process this as an insult. "And what's wrong with that? Besides, I'm really hungry this time, like, for real." His grin returned, wider now.

Tom shot him a pointed look. "'For real?' You're not going to pull some stunt and make me do your job for you in the middle of our meal? Or drag me out to some crime scene while I'm trying to eat?"

Realizing his usual charm wasn't working, Mark rolled his eyes and let out a dramatic sigh. "Alright. Fine. You want me to be straight with you? I need your help." His voice, though casual, was suddenly serious.

Tom's lips quirked into a small, incredulous smile. "Here we go..."

"Look, we had a good run before, right? So I thought, why not keep the pot boiling—"

"That's exactly your problem."

"If you'd let me finish," Mark said, momentarily irritated by the interruption, but he pressed on. "This is about *your lady*, Ms. Nirvana Shor."

The moment her name left his lips, Tom's chest tightened involuntarily. His heart stuttered for a beat, a feeling he didn't want to acknowledge coursing through him. *Nir-*

vana—the name had been on his mind more often than he cared to admit.

He clenched his jaw, trying to steady himself. "If I remember correctly, I'm not a detective. You are."

Mark didn't flinch, but there was a tightness in his voice now. "She won't talk to me, okay? Not to anyone else on my team either. I need someone who can get through to her."

Tom's lips curled into a dull, disinterested smile. "Maybe you need a new team, then."

Mark's face darkened, the mask slipping for a brief moment. He stepped closer to the desk, leaning in as if his next words mattered more than anything. "Come on, Thomas. If I weren't so desperate, I wouldn't be here."

"Thanks. That's just what I needed to hear," Tom replied dryly, though a wink of empathy sparked behind his eyes.

Mark ignored the sarcasm, his expression earnest. "You made me say it."

Tom stared at him, his mind whirling. He hated when Mark got serious like this. It made him feel cornered. And just as he opened his mouth to respond, Gabe stepped into the office, the ever-present smirk on his face.

"Sorry to interrupt, but can I just say something?" he said to Tom, "It would be best if you go talk to her before one of us has to smack you upside the head for being a total dumbbell."

Tom shot Gabe a glare, though it lacked its usual bite. "What? I don't know what you mean."

"You *know* what I mean. You and I both know you care. You've been avoiding it, but it's obvious." Gabe glanced at Mark, who was trying to hide a smile. "I've been telling him to visit Nirvana. He's been putting it off."

Tom's stomach churned, but he stood his ground. "I'm not putting anything off."

Gabe raised an eyebrow, unbothered by Tom's defensiveness. "No? Then why are you watching every news segment about the kidnapping like clockwork? How many times have you replayed that footage? You look like you haven't eaten or slept in days."

Mark joined in with the mockery. "Oh really? That would explain the pale face. For a minute there, I thought you were *actually* starving yourself. What's it been? A couple of days?"

"You wouldn't believe how many tapes he's gone through," Gabe added, trying not to laugh. "It's like when he was in love with Dominique. Same deal. Photos, tapes... hell, even agates."

Tom's face flushed.

Mark burst out laughing. "The agates! I don't even want to know how many jugs of those rocks he went out and collected for her."

Gabe grinned. "Who knows? He spent so much time on the beach, he practically lived there."

Mark was beside himself. "Hahaha! And she was so damn picky about them, too. It's like there was some grading system for ornamental rocks!"

Embarrassed, Tom felt his face growing hotter. His voice finally rang out, cutting through their laughter. "Hey, hey, *Enough!*" He slammed his hand down on the desk. "I'm a *hopeless romantic*, okay? Unlike you two nimrods. Can we *please* get back to the point?"

Mark, still chuckling, wiped a tear from his eye. "Alright, alright. The point is—" He straightened himself up, businesslike. "You're coming with me to the hospital. Ms. Shor's got no one else. No family. No support. And if you're really her friend, the least you can do is show up and *be there* for her."

Tom couldn't deny the pull in his gut—the one that told him it wasn't just a favor anymore. It was something more. Something he couldn't avoid whether he was ready for it or not. "I can't guarantee I'll be any help."

Mark's voice softened, but the intensity remained. "Don't jump to conclusions. You might just be the missing piece I've been looking for."

32

WHEN TOM ARRIVED at the hospital, nervous would be a severe understatement—terrified seemed closer to the truth. His heart pounded as they neared Nirvana's room, his breath coming short as if each step carried a weight he wasn't sure he could bear. Every inch closer felt like an eternity, and his body was taut, ready to flee, yet rooted in place by the deep, quiet pull of his own unresolved feelings.

But as soon as the door opened and their eyes met, all that fear seemed to dissipate. In those first few seconds, Nirvana's face lit up with a joy that took him by surprise—so much so that he almost forgot how to breathe. Before he could register her movements, she leaped from her bed with an exuberance that was almost childlike, and in one swift motion, she threw her arms around him. Tom stood frozen for a moment, his hands unsure, but then instinctively wrapped his arms around her. Her warmth hit him like a burst of sunlight on a cold winter's day, and the sensation—so foreign and unexpected—was like nothing he had ever known.

The embrace lasted longer than he expected, and as her fingers tightened around him, it felt less like an act of reunion and more like a quiet, profound moment. The awkward tension of the past weeks—of worry, guilt, and uncertainty—melted away in the space between them. Their connection was palpable, even in the silent room, and it didn't escape Mark, who stood off to the side, watching them with a growing sense of purpose. His eyes narrowed, his lips twisting into something close to a grin. He couldn't wait to leverage this moment to his advantage.

"I'll take over from here. You boys can leave us. Grab lunch, take a walk, or do whatever. Go now," Mark said, his voice a little too smooth. His eyes flicked to Tom, and there was a brief but unmistakable challenge in his gaze. With a quick nod to his associates, Mark ushered them out of the room and closed the door behind him with a soft click, leaving Tom and Nirvana alone in the quiet.

Tom took a deep breath, his body still tingling from the contact, but he shook it off as he made his way to Nirvana's bedside. "How are you?" he asked, his voice betraying a hint of concern, though he tried to keep it steady.

"I'm doing fine, much better than a couple of days ago," Nirvana replied with a soft smile, her voice surprisingly calm. She gestured for him to sit down as she slowly eased herself back onto the bed.

Tom sat down beside her. "What happened?" he asked quietly.

"Panic attacks, mostly," she answered, her eyes meeting his, not with the fear Tom had expected, but with an unsettling poise. "My doctor said it's normal to have them after everything I've been through. Nothing I haven't heard before. Ever since I started this new medication, things have been looking up."

"Your doctor, you mean Dr. Rimer?"

"Yes. She mentioned that you met..." Nirvana trailed off, her words delicate but laden with meaning.

Before Tom could respond, Mark's voice cut through the silence. "Ahem," he interrupted, his tone commanding. Tom exchanged a brief glance with him, a quiet understanding passing between them before he turned back to Nirvana. He continued, his voice hardening slightly.

"The reason we're here... well, we need your help to catch this person."

"Which person?" Nirvana asked dully, though there was something in her eyes that spoke to a deeper pain.

"The person who was trying to kill you," Mark clarified, his tone laced with impatience as he leaned forward, trying to exert control over the conversation.

Nirvana's expression didn't falter. "You mean Jo..." She paused, her voice oddly distant. "She wasn't trying to kill me. She was just... teaching me a lesson in her own way."

"In her own *messed-up* way, yes," Mark added, clearly agitated. "Tell me this—*is she the woman in this picture?* A.k.a. Jo Shor and Joanna Nickson?"

Nirvana's gaze flicked to the old photograph Mark was holding out for her to see. She studied it for a moment, her brow knitting slightly. When she spoke again, her voice was clear, almost too matter-of-fact. "No, that's not Jo."

"It isn't?" Mark's eyes narrowed, his skepticism hardening like steel.

"No." Nirvana's response was firm, and her eyes met his with a directness that suggested she wasn't afraid of his interrogation.

Mark didn't let up. "Then who the hell is it?"

"She was a dear friend of mine," Nirvana explained, her voice quieter now, tinged with an emotion that Tom couldn't quite place. "She died a long time ago."

Mark scoffed, a bitter laugh escaping him. "Oh, did she?" he said mockingly, eyes flicking to Tom. "You heard that, Thomas? You must have seen a ghost that morning."

"What are you talking about?" Nirvana asked, her face a mask of confusion.

"He said the woman in this picture came into his office last week looking for you," Mark shot back with a smug look, enjoying the discomfort he was creating.

Tom opened his mouth to speak but hesitated, as Nirvana's gaze locked onto his. Her eyes were cold—*too* cold. She had no interest in playing the part of the victim or answering questions she didn't want to.

"I could've been wrong, I suppose," Tom said finally.

"Don't go back on your words, Thomas." Mark's voice dropped to a low growl, but Nirvana wasn't intimidated. Her eyes stayed fixed on him as she turned to Mark, un-flinching.

"If you're so sure of yourself, you wouldn't have to come to me for answers," she said, her tone unwavering.

Mark paused, taken aback for a moment by her steady composure.

Tom pushed forward, changing the subject. "You said before that Jo was trying to teach you a lesson. Why would she do that?"

Nirvana's expression softened briefly, but the sad-ness in her eyes never fully dissipated. "It's a long story. But in the end, I guess... she felt rejected. She wanted us to get back together, but I refused."

"Get back together?" Tom repeated, trying to under-stand.

"We had a period of experimentation when we were younger," Nirvana explained. "We dated for a few months, though looking back now... I'm not so sure 'dated' is the right word. We never went out anywhere. I was home-schooled the whole time, and neither of us had a car. The farthest we had ever gone was Mrs. Jones' backyard."

"Who is Mrs. Jones?"

"She was an old woman who lived next door. Jo's fos-ter parent at the time."

"So... did your relationship ever turn into something serious?" Tom asked curiously.

"To her, it was serious," Nirvana replied, her voice cold, as if recalling memories that no longer held any warmth. "But I was thirteen. It was more of a self-exploration thing for me. She was the only real friend I had. I remember, sometimes she'd sneak in through my bedroom window at night... stay with me, protect me." She paused, her lips tightening. "She used to say it was to protect me from my parents."

"Protect you from your parents?"

She nodded, her gaze dropping. "Mostly from my mother. Jo hated her. With everything she had."

"I'm sorry about what happened to her," Tom murmured, his voice soft, but Nirvana's face remained relaxed.

"That's okay," she replied, did not seem to mourn in the least. "To be honest, I felt a sense of calm when she died."

Tom's brow furrowed in surprise. "You knew she was dead all this time?"

Nirvana nodded slowly. "I was there when it happened." The words tumbled out before she could catch them, and immediately, she realized her mistake. Her eyes shot up, meeting both men's stunned gazes.

"Who killed her?" Mark's voice was harsh and direct.

Nirvana looked at him with steady eyes. "You're asking me?"

"You said you were there," he pressed. "You must've seen the person who did it."

Nirvana's gaze remained cold.

"Marcus, I think we should—"

"Shh! Let's give the lady a chance to speak for herself, Thomas. Yes? Ms. Shor. What do you have to comment?"

"I never said it was murder," Nirvana responded, her voice controlled.

Mark wasn't convinced. "Then what was it?" He leaned in, his posture aggressive, as if daring her to deny the truth. "I hope you're not planning to convince me it was an accident. Your mother didn't just *accidentally* fall into that hole. And if she did, the fall wouldn't have been enough to kill her. She would have cried out, and you would have helped her."

"Are you sure?" Nirvana countered.

"About what?"

"Are you sure I would have helped her?" she shot back, her voice biting, filled with an icy bitterness that shocked even Tom. Her eyes locked onto Mark's, unwavering and relentless. "You may have an unerring talent for reading people, Mr. Ager, but don't pretend to know me."

Mark stilled for a moment, taken aback by the rawness in her voice. Tom watched the exchange, feeling the intensity of the moment in the air like static before a storm.

Then Nirvana continued, her voice calmer now but just as firm. "I don't remember how it happened. It's been so long. All I know is that she's gone. And I'm free. I don't intend to dig up what's been buried for good."

Before Mark could respond, the door opened. Dr. Rimer entered, her presence temporarily alleviating the edginess like a welcome relief.

"Am I interrupting?" she asked, though her eyes settled on Nirvana with concern.

"Oh, no, please, come in," Tom said quickly, grateful for the distraction as the doctor moved to examine Nirvana.

The men were then ushered out of the room by the nurse. Mark's frustration was palpable, his voice rising as soon as the door clicked shut behind them.

"She doesn't know, my ass. She's a *terrible* liar," he grumbled, crossing his arms in disbelief. "For all I know, she probably offed her own mother—"

"Hey, watch it," Tom warned.

"Did you hear the way her voice suddenly quieted? What does she take me for? An amateur cop?"

He sighed deeply, feeling the tension between him and Mark start to crack open once again. "Where's your sensitivity? Her mother died."

"Yeah? What's your point?"

"Nothing... I'm going back to work."

But Mark wasn't finished, not nearly. He stepped in front of him, blocking his path with an assertive tone. "Whoa, whoa, hold it. Who said we're done?" he demanded. "We haven't figured out who this Jo is yet."

Tom shook his head, feeling the force of Mark's relentless drive. "You are telling me you have no leads whatsoever?" he asked incredulously. "Why do they even bother giving you a team to work with? What about that Joanna Nickson? Ever think about starting there?"

"I'm way ahead of you. There's no Joanna Nickson in the entire state of Minnesota or Wisconsin," Mark said, his voice growing sharper, though he tried to keep it level. "The few in the system live down south, and they're either in their late forties or dead. I've checked."

"So?"

"For what I can tell, Joanna Nickson is just another alias."

"Why are you telling me this?"

Mark's mouth tightened into a thin line as if the answer was obvious. His gaze dropped briefly before locking back onto Tom. "Don't make me beg. I told you. I need your help. So do your little bending-over-backward thing for your little brother, like you always do. Make an exception, stay, and help me out. What do you say?"

Tom froze, the words hitting him harder than he had expected. He stared at Mark, stirring a mix of resentment and old hurt. "You don't need my help. You need help getting ahead," he snapped. "Maybe take a look in the mirror sometime and stop pretending it's all about 'doing your job.' I'm sick of it."

"Excuse me?" Mark's voice shot up, his eyes narrowed, offended by the harsh scoff. "I was only joking about the 'bending-over-backward' comment."

Tom's gaze hardened, his posture shifting to something colder, more defensive. "No, you weren't," he said flatly.

"I don't believe this. I get interviewed by a few PR flacks, and suddenly you think I'm trying to be a damn celebrity? Are you *seriously* that jealous of me?"

"Jealous? Ha. Nice job, Marcus. Way to make *this* all about you."

Mark's face reddened, a touch of bitterness creeping into his tone. "Oh, I get it now. It's because I didn't say 'thanks' all this time and took all the credit, huh? Come on, Thomas, you can admit that. That's it, isn't it?"

Tom's fingers flexed at his sides, his jaw locking as he met Mark's gaze with quiet fury. "No," he replied, "I don't care about who gets what. I'm just... disgusted. That's all."

"Disgusted? Wow. You better explain that one, *big brother*."

He waved a dismissive hand, his eyes flicking away for a moment as if he couldn't be bothered to explain. "Tsk. Forget it—"

But Mark was having none of it. His hand shot out, grabbing Tom's arm with surprising force, pulling him back. His grip was unyielding. "Nah-uh. You don't get to walk away from this. You better finish what you started, or so help me, God." He leaned in, pushing Tom to face him. "You always do this. When things get too hot, you bail out. Just like Dad."

"I'm just trying to avoid a conflict."

"So was he! And look where it got him." He took a step forward, his eyes locking with Tom's. "If you've got something else to say, then say it. Don't make me drag it out of you. It's not every day you learn your brother hates your guts, and I wanna know *why*."

Tom paused, a knot of frustration and guilt tightening in his stomach. He took a long, steadying breath, his eyes fixing on the ground for a moment before he raised them to meet Mark's. His voice softened, quieter but with a painful sincerity. "I don't hate you," he said slowly. "I just... I can't play with someone else's life for personal gain. That's not how I help people."

Mark's nostrils flared, his anger still simmering beneath the surface. "You think what I'm doing is for personal gain? You think I'm just out here for the glory?"

"Mostly, yes," Tom shot back, his eyes unwavering. "I'm just trying to get through this, Marcus. But sometimes, I can't handle the games you play."

"You can't handle it? That's funny, because it seems to me, *I* have to handle it all, every damn day."

A long pause followed as the air between them thickened with unsaid words. While Tom stood there facing his little brother, suddenly, he felt something shift—an understanding, perhaps.

Finally, Mark spoke again, his tone unexpectedly sincere. "I'm not as bad as you think I am. I've just been through a lot. Just because I'm not a softie like you doesn't mean I don't have a heart." His words came out fast, almost too quickly, a rush of candid emotion he wasn't used to expressing. "I'm not perfect, Thomas, but you think about this—how many crackheads and assholes do you deal with in a day? How many dead bodies have you seen? How many goddamn murder mysteries do people rely on you to solve every single day? If I stopped to piss and moan about every case, I'd lose my damn mind. What I'm saying is, after enough time, you go numb. It's the only way to survive."

Tom was struck silent by the rare vulnerability that Mark had just bared. It was as if the walls his little brother had so carefully built had cracked open for a split second. A fleeting moment of truth. He moved slowly to a nearby bench, sitting down with a heavy sigh. He stared ahead, his mind racing as he tried to make sense of what Mark had just said. After a moment, Mark joined him, sitting beside him without a word.

"Do you think she went numb after everything that's happened to her?" Tom asked eventually, his voice tinged with a raw empathy for Nirvana, for everything she had endured.

Mark leaned back, staring into the distance. "You'd have to ask her yourself," he replied quietly. "But my guess? Yeah. Deep down, I think she still feels like shit. You just hope it's not every single day."

"I can't imagine anyone torturing another human being, let alone a parent doing that to their own child." Tom's face twisted in sorrow, his heart aching as he thought about Nirvana's pain.

Mark's face darkened, a shadow passing over him. "I know. I tell myself that every time a damn domestic violence case lands on my desk. You wouldn't believe how many monsters there are out there. They walk around in sheep's clothing, hiding in plain sight."

Tom's shoulders slumped, and he exhaled deeply. "I don't know what's gotten into me lately. I'm usually so calm. So... collected. Now, I barely recognize myself anymore."

Mark glanced at him, his tone softening. "You don't know, but I do," he said quietly. "You care a hell of a lot about this girl. You've always had trouble coping when someone you love gets hurt."

"But this isn't like Dominique losing her job or Mom having a fall. This is... different." Tom's gaze dropped to his hands, the burden of his own helplessness pushing down on him. "This is something I can't even wrap my head around. Something that no matter what I do, no matter what I say—"

"That you can't take away her pain?"

Tom nodded slowly, the lump in his throat growing. "Yeah."

Mark turned to him, his expression softening even further. "Have you tried?" he asked, his voice surprisingly gentle.

"What? You think a hug will suddenly fix everything?"

"No. But it's a start. Did you see the way she hugged you back there? She's opening up to you."

Tom's brow furrowed as he processed the words, the meaning slowly sinking in. "You think so?"

"No doubt," Mark affirmed. "You should be thankful that she's as strong as she is. No matter what she's been through, she's still here. She's still fighting. That's incredible. And you... you've been a part of that. She needs your support more than anything right now."

"Positive reinforcement, I can do. But good luck?" Tom shook his head, his voice carrying a trace of sadness. "Sadly, that's not in my control."

Mark chuckled lightly, the sound strangely warm. "No one's asking you to promise she'll never get hurt again. Honestly, I don't think anyone can guarantee anyone's happiness. But as for her luck? Are you kidding? You are *it*," he said firmly. "You've been her lucky star, her lifeline this whole time. Without you, who knows if she would've ever made it out of that dark place alive."

Tom blinked, struck by the unexpected lucidity of Mark's words. For a moment, everything else faded, and a spark of hope sparkled within him. It was like a shift in the clouds, a sudden clarity.

He looked at Mark with a rare sense of gratitude. "I don't think I've heard more sense come out of your mouth since Mom's wedding."

Mark grinned, shrugging with a hint of awkwardness. "I don't do the whole 'gooey' thing, but I have my moments. Now, would you stop moping and make up your mind? Are you in, or are you out?"

Tom sat up straighter, his thoughts now settled in a new determination. "Count me in," he said, his voice certain with new resolve.

33

"**Y**OU KNEW THIS entire time?" Nirvana said, her breath catching in her throat. She looked away, heat rising in her cheeks as the realization of being uncovered settled over her like a heavy cloak. She had her worries, but she had never imagined Dr. Rimer would find out.

Dr. Rimer sat back in her chair, the corners of her lips lifting slightly. "It wasn't just yesterday that I became your therapist," she said, her tone gentle but firm. "Being able to properly observe and interpret your behaviors and emotions *is* part of my job description."

Nirvana stiffened, pressing her palms against her thighs as if trying to steady herself against the rushing tide of embarrassment. "So why did you approve of my discharge then?"

Dr. Rimer's expression went distant for a moment, as though revisiting the decision in her mind. "I waited for a certain spark, Nirvana. A fire in you that would tell me you were ready to fight. I thought, finally. But I'll admit—" She paused, her fingers tapping against the notepad. "—I've second-guessed my leap of faith since."

Nirvana folded her arms across her chest, a defensive gesture, and shook her head slightly. "You're not responsible for what happened to me. I'm not your patient anymore, Dr. Rimer. I'm not your problem."

"I wasn't speaking from a professional standpoint," Dr. Rimer replied, her gaze meeting Nirvana's personal and real. "I take my responsibilities seriously, but this? This isn't just about therapy. It's about you. Your future."

A long, uncomfortable silence stretched between them before the doctor continued, her voice lighter now, almost coaxing. "You seem to be doing much better today. Would you finish telling me about that candlelit house dream? How did it end?"

Nirvana's gaze flickered toward the floor, a knot of unease tightening in her. She hesitated, knowing she was about to bare a raw part of herself, but Dr. Rimer's soft insistence made her want to try. Slowly, she spoke.

"As I mentioned earlier, in the dream, I confronted my mother. We fought, just like we always do, and she hurt me. Our relationship felt unchanged—her attitude toward me stayed the same, no matter how hard I tried to make things better. But as the dream neared its end, something was different. There was a change I can't quite understand."

Dr. Rimer leaned forward slightly, an encouraging gesture. "What was it? Tell me everything. Don't hold back."

Nirvana swallowed hard. The memory still clung to her like cold water. "Michael didn't rape me... I ended up killing him with a handgun before he could get to that."

Dr. Rimer's brow furrowed for a moment, but then her lips curved into a slow nod. There was something approving in the way she looked at Nirvana, like a teacher witnessing a breakthrough. She scribbled something on her notepad, then motioned for Nirvana to continue.

"I aimed for his head. I emptied the entire clip. And then, in that pause... it was like I connected with something inside myself, something I hadn't felt in a long time. For a split second, everything felt so... vivid, so real. But when I came to... I got hit with this brutal sense of reality." Nirvana's voice faltered as she spoke, her revelation sinking in.

Dr. Rimer's eyes remained fixed on her, intently listening, absorbing every word. "What reality?" she prompted.

"That... Michael is my father," Nirvana said, her voice trembling ever so slightly. "I've always known, but I... I chose to deny it. I didn't want to admit it, not to myself."

Dr. Rimer's expression softened with understanding. "Maybe you weren't ready to face the truth until now. He hasn't come around since, has he?"

Nirvana's response was faint, almost too soft to hear. "No... he hasn't."

Dr. Rimer's gaze sharpened with quiet concern. "What were you thinking just now?"

Nirvana hesitated, her hands twisting in her lap. When she spoke, her voice came to be thick with sorrow. "I was just remembering the times I was lonely, down... and he was there. Like some kind of imaginary friend we all have as children. You talk to it when no one else is around, you rely on it... it becomes part of you."

There was a long pause before Dr. Rimer spoke again, her voice soft but probing. "And you miss that?"

Nirvana looked to the window, where the light outside was beginning to dim. "I fear I'll miss it. Now that I'm out of the fog... I don't want to go back there. I was so lost for so long. But there's part of me that... that wants to hold on to it. Maybe because, in some twisted way, it was the only thing that made me feel safe."

Dr. Rimer nodded, her hands folded neatly on her lap. "There's nothing wrong with that, Nirvana. In fact, I'd encourage you to revisit that place sometimes, if you need to. It's important not to bury those memories, because they'll come back, whether you want them to or not."

A brittle smile tugged at Nirvana's lips, but it was fleeting, quickly replaced by doubt. "I always thought I had to forget everything. If I don't remember the bad stuff, it won't affect me, right?"

"You do remember, though," Dr. Rimer said. "And you're not letting yourself truly process it. When those memories rise up, if all you do is try to bury them, they'll only cause you pain."

"Then how do I break this cycle for good?" Nirvana asked, a hint of desperation in her voice.

Dr. Rimer paused for a moment, her gaze steady as she began again. "Think of your past experiences as your childhood home. You always have the key, but you no longer live there. You visit occasionally, but you don't stay. The present is where you live now. And it's only by revisiting those old places that you can develop a sense of who you are, how much you've grown."

Nirvana shook her head slowly, a bitter laugh escaping her lips. "That sounds like a nice fantasy. But what happens when a mirage feels so real that I simply mistake it for reality? Michael was part of my life for eight years. He was my creation, my monster. And I let him stay, let him consume me. What if I relapse? What if—"

Dr. Rimer's voice cut through her spiraling thoughts, smart and grounded. "What if he comes back and takes everything from you again? What if, what if, what if. We can't live in the what-ifs, Nirvana. They're useless. Worries are distractions. If you fall, let yourself fall. But know you have the strength and resilience to rise again."

A heavy silence filled the room. Nirvana closed her eyes briefly, absorbing Dr. Rimer's words like it was the first time she had heard them, taking them to heart. When she reopened her eyes, the weight of her concerns still somewhat lingered, and she blurted out, "You must know, my grandmother also went to Heartstone. Maybe this 'crazy' gene is in my blood, no matter how much I try to outrun it."

Dr. Rimer tilted her head, a subtle smile playing at her lips as she reassured Nirvana with an unexpected, unwavering certainty. "I'll take miracles over probabilities any day," she said. "Your past doesn't define you, Nirvana. Just because your family struggled doesn't mean you're bound to that same fate. You have the power to change your life, to move past this darkness. You can still find your place in this world and be happy."

Nirvana sat back, her shoulders relaxing. But the uncertainty still gnawed at her edges. It was as though the future was a fog, both inviting and terrifying. She said nothing further.

Dr. Rimer seemed to sense her doubt and gently extended her hands toward her to have her grab on. "Trust me on this. Close your eyes and focus on the sensation in your palms."

Nirvana blinked, her hesitation palpable, but she complied. Her fingers brushed Dr. Rimer's, the faintest spark of warmth between them. She inhaled deeply, shutting her eyes tight and exhaling slowly. Gradually, the remaining tension in her shoulders began to ease.

"Now, tell me, what do you feel?" Dr. Rimer asked softly.

Nirvana's voice was quiet but steady. "I feel... our hands. I feel the tips of our fingers touching, the way they rest together."

"Good." Dr. Rimer withdrew her hands, leaving Nirvana to sit in the silence. "Now?"

Nirvana frowned, concentrating. "I... don't feel anything. Not in my hands."

"That's it," Dr. Rimer said, her voice warm with satisfaction. "What's real is what you can feel when you touch. Everything else is—"

"Illusion," Nirvana said as she slowly opened her eyes. The word fell from her lips like a confession, and in the same breath, Dr. Rimer's usual, tightly controlled expression shifted, crumbling ever so slightly. It was a subtle change, but enough to let a small grin bloom across her face—a grin of quiet triumph.

"On that note, I should be going," Dr. Rimer said, the casual tone carrying a faint hint of self-assurance. She was ready to leave, to close the door on this chapter of their professional relationship, and she did so with the same confidence that had defined every one of their sessions.

As she began to gather her things, the soft rustle of paper and clicks of her pen against the desk filled the silence between them. She spoke again, her voice now carrying an almost playful edge. "Suppose I have my mother to thank for teaching me that little trick."

Nirvana, curious despite herself, lifted her head, her brow furrowing in question. "Your mother?" she asked. "Is she a doctor also?"

Dr. Rimer paused mid-motion, her hand hovering over her bag. "The opposite, actually. She was one of my patients—one of my first."

Nirvana's eyes widened in surprise. *A patient?* The idea of Dr. Rimer—so composed, so controlled—being shaped by a patient, let alone a mother, was a jarring image. Nirvana opened her mouth, but no words came, as she processed the unexpected revelation.

Dr. Rimer's gaze softened for the briefest of moments, and then she turned her attention back to the task at hand, as though the momentary vulnerability had been a passing cloud. "You, Ms. Nirvana Shor," she continued, her voice regaining its usual steadiness, "take good care of yourself from now on. My offer still stands, however. When you've made a final decision, give me a call, and I'll make any arrangements ahead of time if needed."

Nirvana felt both lighter and heavier at once. She nodded slowly, her mind swirling with the awareness that this might truly be their last meeting. "I will," she answered quietly.

For a moment, she stood watching Dr. Rimer finish packing, and a strange sense of loss crept into her chest. She felt an odd disappointment surge inside her, like parting with an old friend. As Dr. Rimer turned toward the door, her voice called out, soft but insistent. "Hold on a second, Doc. I have a favor to ask."

Dr. Rimer paused, her hand on the door handle. She turned back toward Nirvana, her brow lifting slightly, the faintest glimmer of curiosity in her eyes. "Yes?"

Nirvana moved toward her bedside table, her fingers brushing over the surface before she grasped the note she'd placed there earlier. It was a lengthy note, and a special one at that. It felt heavier now, more significant. She returned to Dr. Rimer. "Could you give this to Mia for me?" Nirvana asked, her voice quiet, as though speaking too loudly might shatter the moment. "I promised her I'd write before I left Heartstone. The past few nights, when I couldn't sleep, I finally got around to it."

Dr. Rimer took the folded-up paper from Nirvana. She glanced down at the name written across the front: *Mia Jaco*. Her face immediately stiffened, frowning even, her voice almost too calm. "I'm afraid I can't do that."

Those words hit Nirvana like a physical blow. Her heart stuttered, and she felt an odd coldness creep up her spine. *Can't?* A lump formed in her throat, but she fought to keep her composure.

"Why?" she asked. Her voice trembled, betraying the panic she tried to keep in check. She knew, *she knew*, what was coming. But hearing it aloud was a different thing entirely.

Dr. Rimer's expression faltered for just a moment— her face softened, her eyes deepening with a trace of sorrow that she couldn't quite conceal. She straightened before answering. "Mia Jaco has passed away. I'm sorry you had to find out this way."

For a moment, Nirvana couldn't breathe. Her mind raced, as if trying to run from the reality that had just collided with her. *Mia was gone?* The thought seemed almost impossible to comprehend. She had known Mia for years, laughed with her, cried with her, and through it all, there had been an unspoken promise that no matter what, they'd always have each other. And now—now Mia was gone.

The room felt smaller, suffocating in its silence. Nirvana's gaze fell to the floor, her eyes unfocused, as though the world around her had suddenly become distant, unreal. "How did she?" The question barely escaped her lips, raw and broken.

"She completed suicide," Dr. Rimer replied regretfully. "She went missing one morning. By the afternoon, a nurse found her body in a tunnel, hanging by the neck from a noose."

Nirvana's entire body went numb. The room spun as the image flashed in her mind—Mia, alone, in the "dungeon," her body lifeless. She fought to swallow her tears, but it felt impossible. She had known that Mia was struggling—had known it so well, in fact, that she had convinced herself that *she* would be enough to save her. But now... Now there was nothing left but the cold, hard truth.

"I knew... I knew all about her struggle..." Her words faltered, the burden of her own self-reproach too much to bear. "I should've been there for her. I should've done more."

"You *were* there," Dr. Rimer said gently, her tone firm yet kind. She took a step closer, her eyes meeting Nirvana's with a quiet intensity. "For what it's worth, she always mentioned you. She always spoke of you, even in her darkest moments. You were the one constant in her life—her saving grace."

But it hadn't been enough. It hadn't saved her. Nirvana thought and she swallowed hard. "Did she leave me a note? Something?" she asked, hoping, even though she knew the answer.

Dr. Rimer shook her head.

Nirvana felt a rush of inner turmoil wash over her. She closed her eyes, trying to hold it together, but the grief threatened to pull her under. "I'd like to be alone now," she murmured, her voice small and fragile, as if speaking any louder would break her entirely. She didn't look at Dr. Rimer as she spoke, turning instead to face the window, her gaze lost somewhere beyond it. "I need to be by myself for a while."

Dr. Rimer gave her a long, quiet look—no judgment, no pity, just understanding. She nodded slowly, and without another word, she turned the doorknob, opened the door and stepped out. The door clicked shut behind her, and Nirvana was left alone.

34

LATER THAT EVENING, Tom came back to visit Nirvana at the hospital, eager to see her. His steps were quick, almost skipping, as he clutched a bouquet of flowers in his hands. But when he reached her room, he found it empty. His heart dropped for a moment, but he wasn't about to give up easily. He asked the nurse at the desk, who directed him to a shared ward on a different floor. When he arrived, her ward mate said, "She's outside," pointing him toward the courtyard.

Tom nodded, his gaze already shifting in that direction. All of this distraction temporarily toned down his excitement, the kind that made him feel like a boy again—nervous yet hopeful. The courtyard was quiet, bathed in soft moonlight. When he stepped outside, he found Nirvana lying on a bench, wrapped in a thin hospital blanket, her cigarette glowing against the night like a tiny star. She exhaled a plume of smoke into the air, her eyes fixed on the distant horizon. There was something serene about movements, even in this small act of rebellion.

As soon as she saw Tom, she sat up quickly, the blanket shifting around her shoulders as she stubbed out the cigarette with swift, almost guilty motions.

"The woman in the next bed offered me a cigarette. I didn't want to say no," she explained, her voice tentative, as if she expected judgment.

Tom smiled gently, coming closer toward her. "It's okay, I don't mind." He paused for a beat, then added with a quiet politeness, "May I sit?"

She shifted over without hesitation, creating enough room on the bench for him. "They moved me down to the second floor," she said, settling back into the cold metal, her fingers curling around the edges of the blanket.

"Yeah, it took me a while to find you," Tom said, offering her the bouquet. "These are for you."

Nirvana's eyes softened as she took the flowers from him, a tender smile spreading across her face. "You didn't have to," she said quietly, but the sincerity in her voice made it clear that she appreciated the gesture.

Tom leaned back on the bench, feeling the chill of the night air seep through his clothes as Nirvana continued. "Dr. Rimer offered to admit me back to Heartstone as a voluntary patient," she said, her gaze wandering to the stars above them. "Since I've already been discharged, they can't make me go back, but it's an option."

"And?" Tom asked, his voice gentle but insistent, his eyes watching her closely.

Nirvana paused, her shoulders rising and falling with a deep breath. "I haven't quite decided yet. It's easier to say yes, I guess... considering my situation. I don't have anywhere else to go."

Tom hesitated, choosing his words carefully. "I know it's not my place to tell you what to do, but I would be really happy if you stayed."

Nirvana's lips curled into a soft, grateful smile. "I'd like to stay too."

A brief silence settled between them, comfortable but thick with unspoken thoughts. Tom's voice broke the quiet, soft but earnest. "You may not remember this very well, but I was with you when the ambulance took you here."

Nirvana's eyes met his, and something shone in them, a moment of recognition. "I know. They told me you held my hand the whole way here." She lowered her gaze, looking down at the bouquet in her lap. "Sorry that I lied to you. I shouldn't have. I wanted to tell you the truth, but I couldn't."

"You mean about your name?"

"That and... other things. I tried to be this 'good girl' in front of you all, pretending I wasn't as messed up as I am."

"That's a bit harsh," Tom replied, aiming to comfort her. "We've all enjoyed having you around, you know. Besides, everyone deserves a clean slate now and again. Life's complicated. It's messy for everyone."

Nirvana bit her lip, wrestling with thoughts she hadn't shared with anyone before. "Sometimes, I wonder why bad things keep happening to me. It's like either my luck is cursed, or I've got a terrible judge of character... maybe both."

"I hope meeting me and the others doesn't count as bad luck," Tom said with a teasing smile, but his voice held a deeper sincerity beneath it.

"Oh, no," Nirvana said quickly, shaking her head. "But I've learned a lot over the years. People don't often do things for free. They always want something in return. The more I ask for help, the less I have left for myself." Her voice wavered with bitterness before she softened again, "I didn't mean to sound so cynical."

"I don't think everyone's like that," Tom said, his expression thoughtful. "But I get where you're coming from. I understand why you'd feel that way. Life's a lot harder when you've been burned before."

Nirvana sighed, her shoulders slumping, her fingers playing nervously with the edge of her blanket. "Sometimes I wish I was someone else. Someone with a simpler upbringing and background."

Just then, Tom's voice turned a little firmer. "Can I say something bold?" His eyes locked onto Nirvana's. "What your parents did to you? It was wrong. On every level."

Nirvana stiffened, her gaze hardening briefly before she exhaled through her nose, like she was trying to dismiss it. "Yeah, you know musicians... they're temperamental. When things go wrong, they find a way to channel their anger, and I happened to be their channel." She shrugged, a hollow gesture that didn't quite cover the pain in her eyes. "My mom... she did it because she loved him. If my father hadn't been so... doting on me, maybe she wouldn't have acted the way she did."

"There's no excuse for that." Tom's words were blunt, cutting through her rationalization.

"No?" Nirvana said softly, glancing at him in surprise.

Tom shook his head, his jaw tight. "None," he replied firmly.

Nirvana might not say it, but inwardly, she felt at ease confiding in Tom, and was every bit appreciative of his support. As she continued, she looked away, her eyes unfocused, seeing something far away. "I used to be a daddy's girl. And when he died... I cried so much. But part of me felt relieved too. I didn't know how to feel, honestly. Everything changed the summer I turned ten, when I found his secret underground room." She paused, swallowing hard, the memory darkening her face. "I shouldn't have gone in there. Everything after that was different."

Tom could see the depth of the hurt in her eyes. He gently placed his hand on hers, squeezing it lightly.

Nirvana took a deep breath, her eyes closing briefly. "I should hate him. But I don't. I don't think I can. There were two versions of him, Tom. One who hurt me, and the other who loved me. As for my mom... I used to think she was crazy. She was always punishing me, always finding something wrong. When I look back, it's hard to believe we were ever happy."

"It wasn't your fault. You didn't ruin your family. They did. They should be the ones regretting, not you."

Nirvana's eyes welled up slightly. "I know. I did learn something from the eight years I spent at Heartstone. I could have done a whole lot worse. You wouldn't begin to understand what it was like in there. Some of the girls I knew haven't even thought about making it out, some unfortunately never will..."

Tom shook his head again, and his words were heavy with conviction. "What your parents did to you... what you had to go through because of them... they make everything I've ever complained about feel so small."

Nirvana smiled softly, but it was bittersweet. "I'm glad I can somehow make you feel better. I haven't done much to help anyone, might as well let my misery be good for something."

As soon as Tom realized how his words might have been misconstrued, a flash of discomfort crossed his face. His hand lifted, almost as if he were trying to push the awkwardness away. "I didn't mean it like that," he hurried to clarify, his voice more solemn than he intended. "I apologize. I never meant to come off as a condescending jerk." He met her eyes, hoping she could see the sincerity in his apology.

Surprised by the genuine regret in his tone, Nirvana shook her head slowly, a faint smile tugging at her lips. "If anything, you definitely aren't that," she said quietly. But then, her smile faded, replaced by a brief shadow of guilt. "I feel terrible, though. I dragged you into this mess. I was so caught up in trying to find my way out of it that I was so careless."

"I'm happy to be involved, really," Tom reassured her.

Her gaze softened at his earnestness. "Thank you, Tom," she said, a faint blush creeping into her cheeks. "But please, don't feel bad for me. That's the last thing I want."

"What is it that you do want?" he asked, his tone gentle but insistence.

"I just want... to be normal," Nirvana replied. "Like you and Gabe. I want to be treated normally, live a normal life—just... normal."

"I see. Well, we might not the 'normal' you think we are, I'm afraid."

She blinked, her brow knitting in confusion. "What do you mean?"

Tom clasped his hands loosely in his lap. He seemed to hesitate for a brief moment before speaking, as if he were choosing the right words, unwilling to risk making Nirvana feel more out of place. "Well, Gabe's parents divorced when he was in middle school. Before that, his dad was... well, a deadbeat. An alcoholic who drained the family finances. His mom had to work three jobs for a while just to catch up, and Gabe—he practically raised himself. You know what happens when kids are forced to grow up too fast? They fall in with the wrong crowd. Gabe, well... he struggled with addiction for a while. I think most people would never guess, but he was still running the streets when he came to my dad for the apprenticeship."

Nirvana's eyes widened. "Really? I never knew that, and I never would've guessed," she murmured.

"Yeah, but he's been clean for a few years now. Thankfully."

"And you?"

"Huh? Me?" Tom shifted uneasily, rubbing the back of his neck, his voice trailing off. "Well... I'm a wimp. My father was, and I guess I just... inherited it. My parents divorced a couple years back, and I don't think I've really gotten over it."

Nirvana leaned in, her brow furrowing with genuine curiosity. "How so?"

He shifted in his seat, his eyes drifting to the floor as if searching for the right words. "It's not that my mom leaving bugs me. It's how my father handled it... or, I should say, *didn't* handle it."

Nirvana's gaze softened, urging him to continue.

Tom swallowed hard, his voice suddenly brittle, as if each word cost him something. "He didn't react. He was... cold. Emotionless. Like it was just another thing that happened. I don't know, I almost wish he *did* something. I almost wish he *lashed out*, screamed, hit something... Hell, grabbed my uncle by the neck and just... *tore him apart.*" His fists clenched, his jaw tight as if the anger he hadn't fully allowed himself to express was now clawing at the surface. "I was angry—*so angry*—but I couldn't process it. I couldn't let myself. I just... couldn't. Like I said, I'm a wimp."

Her expression tender, Nirvana said to him resolutely, "You are not a wimp. Not to me." Her gaze lingered for a moment, feeling the tension in his face begin to ease. "Sometimes, we just don't know how to react. Things happen so fast, it's like we don't even have time to *think*, let alone feel what we're supposed to. Trust me, I know that feeling all too well."

Tom gave her a look then, one that spoke volumes. "I guess... As I was saying, everyone has their public face, their way of fitting in. If I were you, especially, I wouldn't stress too much about trying to meet some 'normal' standard."

Nirvana turned that over in her mind. "Why not?"

"Because—if someone as interesting as you tries to be like everyone else, what's left of the mystery, the excitement? Being 'normal' is overrated, anyway. I'll take being special any day."

Right then, a touch of amazement flashed in Nirvana's eyes before she said, almost absentmindedly, "Jo told me something like that once." She let out a soft laugh. "Most people judge her, think she's tough, cold. But like you—deep down, she's one of the most softhearted, kind people I know. I just... I wish things hadn't turned out the way they did."

Tom's eyes narrowed, a mix of understanding and something else behind them. "Do you feel obligated to protect her?" he probed gently, suspecting she'd been carrying this burden for far too long.

"In a big way, yes," Nirvana admitted, her voice thick with emotion. "She was my one confidante during one of the worst times of my life. She was a blessing, a friend."

"I understand that. But if you let it go this time, do you think she would just walk away?" His voice was quiet, but there was a certainty in his words. "I only asked because, on the one hand, you say you want to start fresh, but on the other, you seem to have a hard time letting go."

Nirvana swallowed hard. The question bore a weight she couldn't escape. She let out a slow breath, almost as if to release the pressure inside her. "Jo won't stop coming after me, even if I'm dead. But even so—how can I betray my friend after everything she's done for me? I get what Detective Ager wants, but... I can't give him what he's asking for."

Tom exhaled a deep breath that seemed to anchor him to the moment. "You have to know, I didn't come here because my brother asked me to," he said softly, his voice purposeful, and he turned toward her. "He's not asking you to blindly accuse your friend, either. What she did to you? It was wrong, criminal. You could have been seriously hurt even if it was unintentional." He paused, his gaze steady on her, full of concerns. "I know it's easier said than done, but I thought maybe you might want a chance to really live your life. To have a future that's not defined by the past. And this could be a good place to start."

For a moment, Nirvana just stared at him. The words settled over her like a warm, heavy blanket, and for the first time in a long time, she let herself *really* imagine a different life. Slowly, almost imperceptibly, the tightness in her chest began to ease. She let out a shaky breath. "So... I can just ... let go? Just like that?"

Tom gave her a small, understanding smile. "I'm no expert. But I believe that's the first step. Yes."

Her eyes wandered to the floor, the thought of it all stirring something deep inside her. Her chest tightened again, but not from anxiety. From something else—

something blooming within her, threatening to make her believe that maybe, just maybe, she could let go of everything.

Tom's voice cut through her thoughts as he continued, "Everyone deserves to be a little greedy with their own life. If you don't take control, you'll end up giving in every time. Take me, for example."

She looked at him, her voice catching. "You saved my life, Tom. If it weren't for your selflessness... I wouldn't be sitting here."

Tom's lips curved into a smile, his voice softer, but somehow more intense. "I try to help everyone. But... I wouldn't have done what I did for just anyone. Not the way I did it. *You*... you matter to me, Nirvana."

There was a brief silence before she leaned in, closing the gap between them. Their foreheads locked gently. The kiss that followed was quick, but velvety, unexpected, and full of something she hadn't allowed herself to feel in far too long. Passion. Connection. And something else—a recognition that she didn't have to feel so alone anymore.

When she pulled back, her breath was shallow. Tom blushed, his eyes wide. Like a little boy falling in love for the first time, he was clearly a little stunned by the intensity of the moment. She smiled, a soft, mischievous grin, her eyes meeting his. "Your cheeks are cold," she murmured, her fingers gently grazing the side of his face.

Tom smiled faintly, his voice a little shaky. "Really? I thought they were flushed."

She laughed quietly, then he reached for her hand, intertwining his fingers with hers. "Listen... I can't undo your past, no matter how much I wish I could. But I want you as you are, and I'm not going anywhere," he promised her. "I want you to trust me, Nirvana. No matter what comes, I'll be here."

Her fingers unintentionally traced the back of his hand, as if she was afraid that giving too much attention to his heartfelt vow would make it poof and disappear. It would be just her luck, Nirvana thought, but it was the lack of faith that kept her from fully trusting anyone.

She didn't trust easily, but with Tom, she was willing to try.

"You don't have to promise me anything," she whispered softly, almost a plea. "I wasn't expecting."

"I know. But I want to," Tom said, his voice unwavering, no longer holding anything back. He leaned in, his forehead touching hers once again. "Can you trust that I mean it?"

She met his gaze, and then, with a small smile, she nodded. "I already do."

35

WITH TOM'S HELP, Mark secured Nirvana's cooperation and in the process, uncovered crucial details that had long eluded him. The early morning sky hung low with gray clouds as he, alongside his partner, arrived at the auto repair shop in New Town where Jo allegedly worked. They stepped out of their car, radiating the usual cool confidence that came with their job. The atmosphere around them felt tense, charged with the promise of something worthwhile. Together, they moved toward the front door, their gait deliberate, like two predators on the prowl.

Inside, the shop was bustling with the clank of tools and the hum of machinery. The lone sales clerk behind the counter was engaged with a customer, his back turned to the men. Mark hung back for a moment, but his presence was immediately noticeable, as if something about his stance—too still, too watchful—was enough to draw attention.

The clerk finally broke away, walking over with an air of mild annoyance. "Sir," he said, a hand raised toward the staff door, "you can't go through there. That's for technicians only. See the sign?"

Mark's eyes flicked to the laminated paper tacked to the wooden door. He smirked, a quiet chuckle escaping his lips. "You call that a sign?" he drawled, flashing his police badge with the casual ease of someone who knew he could break any rule on a whim. "I need to speak to your manager."

"I'm the manager." A man's voice cut through the air, thick with authority, as a burly figure emerged from behind the counter. He was wearing a stained mechanic's apron, his expression hard as stone. "And I'm also the owner. That," he gestured to Mark's badge dismissively, "doesn't mean jack here. The rules are the rules. And if you think you can just barge in, you're sorely mistaken."

Mark leaned forward, studying the man's features with an almost clinical interest. "Paul's Auto Shop... I take it you're Paul then?" he said smoothly, offering his hand, but the gesture was met with a firm refusal. Not missing a thing, Mark dropped his hand back to his side and shrugged. "No handshakes. That's cool. I'm not big on them either."

Paul snorted, clearly irritated. "Phony act, huh? What's this all about? Last I checked, state troopers don't just storm into private property like this. You think you're above the law?"

Mark held up a hand, his tone softening just enough to be disarming. "We've gotten off on the wrong foot here, Paul. For the record, we're not state troopers. I'm Detective Ager, and this is my associate." He motioned toward his partner, who remained silent but alert, watching the exchange closely.

Paul narrowed his eyes, still skeptical. "And what do you want from me?"

"I'm afraid we've got some bad news," Mark said, his voice low, steady. "May we chat in your office?"

Paul hesitated, his instincts telling him to refuse, but after a moment, he relented, nodding toward a door at the back of the shop. Once inside the cramped office, he lit a cigar, the pungent smoke filling the space as he leaned back in his chair, clearly more at ease in private. Mark and his partner took seats across from him, and after some brief explanations, Paul sent someone to fetch Jo.

While they waited, Mark studied the man in front of him. "How long has Ms. Walz worked for you?" he asked, keeping his tone conversational, but there was an underlying tension in his words.

Paul exhaled smoke, his eyes flicking to the side. "She came on just before Christmas. I didn't use to hire women—especially not as mechanics. Call me old-fashioned, but I still think some jobs are better done by men." He shifted uncomfortably in his chair. "Jo's the exception, I suppose. My only other female mechanic who quit before her had the whole bodybuilding vibe going, masculine and everything. Jo, on the contrary, is a butch but not exactly butchy. Ironically, when she first came in for the job interview, I swear on my dead mother's eyes, she could have fooled me had she said she was a man."

"I believe you. So you think she's a good mechanic?"

"I do," Paul replied, tapping ash from his cigar. "She's quiet, keeps to herself, but she works hard. I don't think I've ever seen anyone more eager to learn than she is. But... there's something off about her, too. Something you can't quite put your finger on." His voice lowered, as though hesitant to speak more. "She's not like the others. Hell, she's not like anyone I've ever met."

Mark leaned in slightly, intrigued. "What's she like, as a person?"

"Isolated. A hermit, really. Doesn't socialize much. Always has a journal with her, writes down God knows what. If you ask me, she's got no friends. None that matter, anyway." Paul's voice grew quieter, his eyes darting toward the door. "A little over five minutes ago, I would've said she's alright. But after everything you've told me... who knows?"

Mark nodded, absorbing the information. "You know the old saying. You can't always judge a book by its cover."

Paul shrugged, glancing around as if the walls themselves might hold answers. "Guess not..."

Just then, a knock on the door broke the uneasy silence. Paul looked up, his brow furrowing. A young man entered, his face pale with worry.

"I can't find her," the man said, looking to Paul, and then to Mark.

"What do you mean you can't find her?" Paul's voice rose, full of panic. "This place isn't that big. Where the hell did she go?"

"She... she went out for a smoke, but the guys haven't seen her since," the man stammered.

"When did she leave?" Mark asked, trying to keep his voice neutral.

"About ten minutes ago," the man replied.

Mark's eyes narrowed. "Did you check outside?"

"I did. Should I check her car in the lot?"

Paul's eyes snapped to the man. "Yes. Do it now."

Mark cut in before the man could move, however. "I don't need you to do that. If she's going to run, she'll do it when she sees me. What I need to know is, can you confirm the kind of car she drives? Is it a red sedan?"

The man hesitated for a moment before speaking. "It's blue now. She just had it detailed and put on a fresh coat of paint. Looks all shiny and new. Can't miss it."

Mark nodded curtly. "Thanks. I think we've got it from here." He gave his partner a quick glance. "Stay here in case she comes back," he told him, and then without waiting for a response, he turned and briskly made his way to the parking lot. His eyes scanned the surroundings, and within seconds, he was behind the wheel, the engine roaring to life as he sped down the road, his focus sharp as a razor.

As luck would have it, a blue sedan was parked at a gas station just down the street. Jo was standing beside it, pumping gasoline. Mark's pulse quickened as he recognized her for the first time, a knot tightening in his stomach.

He approached, his steps heavy and determined. "Jo-lie Walz!" he shouted, his voice cutting through the morning haze.

Jo glanced up, her face unreadable, but she didn't stop her task, didn't acknowledge him at all.

Mark slammed the door of his car and strode toward her. "You're a hard person to track down," he said, his voice colder now. "Any last words before I make you famous with these?" He motioned toward his handcuffs.

Jo's lips quirked into a wry smile, and she pulled the cigarette from her mouth with obvious slowness, her eyes locking with his. "Who are you? What do you want?"

Mark's expression hardened. "You can drop the act. You know exactly who I am and why I'm here. Otherwise, why the hell would you slip away like that?"

She raised an eyebrow, defiance showing in her eyes. "Did Nirvana send you?" she asked with an edge of bitterness. "I presumed that is how you found me. You roaches can't possibly be that smart with your pea-sized brains and minuscule intellects."

Mark's jaw tightened. "Watch your mouth—"

"Oh, sure. Sorry," Jo shot back, her tone dripping with sarcasm. "So, what am I in for? The kidnapping? Or the murder?"

Mark's stomach twisted at the mention of murder. He hadn't heard anything about that from Nirvana. *Homicide?*

His mind raced, but he kept his cool. "She trusted you," he said.

Jo's gaze flicked away, a shadow crossing her face. "Did she tell you that? Doesn't matter now, does it?"

Mark decided to press on. "Why did you do it?"

Jo let out a hollow laugh, her eyes narrowing. "Why did I kill her mother? You want to know about that monster?" She leaned in, her voice dropping to a low hiss. "You have no idea what kind of woman Nirvana's mother was. She was pure poison."

Mark's pulse quickened at the unexpected confession, but he didn't let it show. "You're under arrest," he said, his tone steely. "Now, you can either make this easy, or we can make a scene right here in the middle of the gas station."

Jo's lips curled into a smile that didn't reach her eyes. "Oh? What's it gonna be? Ten? Fifteen years? Life?" She smirked, as if the burden of her fate no longer mattered.

"I'm not used to man-handling women, so I suggest that you—"

"What if I refuse?"

"Refusing arrest?"

Jo nodded, looking unreservedly at him.

Some nerve on this one. Mark thought, and then persevered in essence, "Look. I'm taking you in whether you put up a fight or not."

"Then, mind if I ask, what gave you the impression that I would *ever* consider following your lead? You are only *one* person," Jo said with a sneer, emphasizing his limitations.

"You really don't make this easy, do you?"

"No. Sorry to have your job cut out for you, Agent Whatever. But if you want to arrest me, you'll have to work a lot harder..."

As soon as Jo finished speaking, she flicked her cigarette butt to the ground, the glowing tip landing in a pool of spilled gasoline. In an instant, a burst of flame shot up, igniting the fuel dispenser in a violent explosion of chaos. Mark instinctively recoiled, his heart pounding as the fire spread rapidly. During the havoc, he lost sight of Jo amid the thick smoke and the panicked screams of bystanders.

With his mind racing, he sprinted back to his car, shouting into his phone as the flames roared in the background.

"Damn it! Pick up... pick up!"

"Yes, sergeant?" Calton's voice crackled through the receiver.

"What's your location?" Mark demanded, his words clipped.

"We're at the apartment building, just got to the elevator. It's out of order, so we're climbing up."

"Fantastic," Mark said under his breath. "Listen, the suspect's on the run, possibly heading your way. She's dangerous—completely unpredictable. Keep your guard up. I'll be en route to you as soon as the firemen arrive."

"Firemen?"

"Long story. I'll explain later."

"Copy that."

He hesitated before adding, "By the way, my brother... he's not there, is he?"

"Yes, sir. He's with us."

Mark let out a long sigh of frustration. "Goddamn it... I knew it. Why even bother briefing him? He's going to do what he wants anyway."

"You want to talk to him? I can put him on."

"Do I—"

A moment later, Tom's voice came through, casual, as if nothing were wrong. *"Hello, Marcus."*

"You son of a gun! What the hell are you doing there? I told you to stay back and let the guys do their job."

"I'm not getting in anyone's way," Tom replied breezily. *"I don't want to wait in the car for who knows how long this's gonna take."*

"I warned you not to come. I said I would make time for you to meet after we apprehended her."

"We've been through this."

Mark clenched his jaw, annoyed by his big brother's obliviousness. He took a deep breath to calm down before continuing. "Look. I know you are carrying out some special mission for your lady, but at the end of the day, you are still my brother. I don't want you to get hurt."

"What lovely sentiment, Marcus. But honestly, how dangerous can a search warrant operation be?"

"I've already met her, Thomas. Things got *hostile*. A bit of a hotspur, that tomboyish punk. Now I'm left to deal with the fire she started... This is no joke. I only wish for once you wouldn't get on my nerves."

"Fine–fine. You want me to go back to the car?"

"Forget it. You're already here. Just stick close to Calton and Brown, alright? They've been trained for this. You haven't."

"Are you serious?"

"As a heart attack," Mark bit back.

"Remember I've met this woman too. When she shows up, can't we just talk things out? There's no reason to resort to violence..."

Tom's suggestion sparked laughs as the two agents overheard it, and both found it ridiculously absurd. Mark heard the laughter in the background, thus adding to the mockery. "Yeah, sure. We'll sit down and share a drink with her," he said, rolling his eyes. "Come on, Thomas. You can't possibly be this naïve."

"What's naïve about peace?"

"Ha! Don't toss that big word at me. Peace doesn't come without a fight. You make peace through battle, not talk. That's my motto. I'm not explaining war tactics to you. I'll be there soon, so keep your head down. Calton, I'm counting on you to babysit my brother. Got it?"

"You bet, sir. I won't let him out of my sight."

36

MARK'S TWO ASSOCIATES, whom he had entrusted with the search and seizure, couldn't have been more different in terms of their work ethic. Calton, the wiry, short man, had a peculiar sense of responsibility when it came to the apartment. He moved with the careful precision of someone who didn't want to leave a trace, a faint impression, or worse, a mess. For him, it was about the job, yes, but it was also about respecting the sanctity of the place they were tearing apart. Meanwhile, Brown—an absolute mountain of a man—seemed to take a perverse pleasure in leaving destruction in his wake. His massive muscles, a testament to years of narcissistic pride, made the tiniest space feel like an arena where he was the only one allowed to win.

"... Takeout... takeout... takeout," Brown drawled, his voice an exaggerated enthusiasm as he flung open the refrigerator door. "Anyone want a slice of this moldy cheesecake?" He held up a lump of ruined dessert on a plate like it was the rarest delicacy, his grin wide and mocking. He gave the thing a theatrical sniff, then dropped it back into the fridge with a careless toss, the plastic wrap ripping as it hit the shelf.

Calton glanced over from where he was digging through a pile of books, his nose wrinkling in disgust. "Is that where that offensive stench is coming from?" he asked dryly, as though he couldn't believe he had to even ask.

"Probably," Brown replied, his voice too casual, "and a fine mix of other festering garbage." He shoved the fridge door closed with a thud that echoed in the small room. With a grunt, he turned and immediately began to wreak havoc elsewhere—rifling through drawers, tossing aside anything that didn't fit his idea of 'useful.' His arms were a blur of movement as he went through everything, his posture nearly predatory, as though he were some kind of beast on a rampage.

Calton, on the other hand, barely stirred as he sifted through some papers on a nearby table. He gave a quiet, almost dismissive chuckle. "Looks like someone's not much of a gardener. These poor bastards were left to die in their vase." His finger traced the wilting petals of the flowers—what little was left of them.

At that moment, Tom, who had been silently watching the chaos unfold, spoke up in a soft voice. "Dahlias," he said.

Calton paused, his head turning slightly toward Tom, who was standing awkwardly near the kitchen counter, his hands folded in front of him as if he were trying to avoid drawing attention. "Excuse me?"

"Those flowers," Tom clarified, a hint of pride in his voice as though he was finally contributing something to the conversation. "Those are dahlias. I learned that last summer, in a... class."

Brown, who had been mid-search, froze. His eyes narrowed, a look of annoyance creeping across his face as he shifted his gaze toward Tom. "Oh, pardon us. We didn't know Ager's sister was in the house," he shot back sarcastically, his words aimed like daggers at Tom's quiet demeanor.

Tom blinked, caught off guard by the hostility in Brown's voice, but he stood his ground, lifting his chin slightly. "I was just stating a fact."

Calton, now mildly intrigued, glanced between the two men. The tension in the room shifted. Brown's expression darkened further, his massive frame blocking most of the light as he took a step closer to Tom, looming over him like a shadow. "Stating a fact? It sounded more like mocking our intelligence." Brown's voice was low, laced with something harsh—threatening, almost. He towered above Tom, his fists clenched at his sides.

Tom could feel the heat of Brown's anger radiating from him like a furnace, but he refused to back down. He pressed on, his voice trembling only slightly. "I wasn't mocking anyone," he said, though the words felt small against Brown's oppressive gaze. "This has nothing to do with intelligence. It's only a matter of memorizing names—"

"You're still talking?" Brown, clearly enjoying the discomfort he was causing, leaned in closer. His breath was heavy, his eyes practically glowing with a mixture of contempt and amusement. "You sure about that?" he growled, his body tense, ready to escalate at the slightest provocation.

Tom looked up at the hulking figure of Brown, who stood just inches away, his knuckles cracking and his biceps bulging with menacing intensity. A wave of intimidation washed over him. Desperate for some kind of reassurance, he glanced at Calton, hoping for a sign— maybe a casual grin, or at least a subtle shake of the head to defuse the sudden tension. But Calton offered nothing. His face was as deadpan as ever. He simply watched, arms crossed, with an almost eerie calm, as if he were savoring the moment, waiting to see how Tom would handle it.

For a moment, Tom thought Brown might actually go too far. But then, to his relief, Brown's tense posture relaxed. The monstrous frown he wore melted into a wide, almost too-cheerful grin. "Ha! Hahaha!" Brown laughed suddenly, the sound booming and jarring, as if the tension had never existed. "I was just fucking with you!" He slapped Tom on the back, the force of it nearly sending him stumbling forward. "I swear, I scared the shit out of you, didn't I? You were holding it together better than most people, though. Better than I expected."

Tom stood there with a mix of ease and disbelief. "Yeah... I guess."

Calton, who had been watching the entire exchange with a slightly bored expression, finally rolled his eyes. He sighed audibly, his patience worn thin. "Would you just cut it out, Brown? We're here to finish the job, not act like we're on a sitcom. I've got better things to do, you know."

Brown looked unbothered. He shrugged, flashing a grin that was pure mischief. "Better than this? You've got to be kidding me. This is way more exciting than sitting at a desk all day, filing reports. Trust me, this? This is the kind of chaos I thrive on."

Without further warning, Brown grabbed the nearest wooden chair and, with a swift, effortless motion, swung it over his head. The chair splintered as it slammed against the floor.

Calton looked over, unimpressed, his face blank. "Very classy," he muttered, the sarcasm dripping from his words.

Brown only smiled wider. "Wasn't meant to be classy. Just meant to have a little fun."

"We're meant to be serious," Calton snapped.

"Who said I wasn't?" Brown retorted, as he bent down to examine the wreckage of the chair. "I thought there might be something hidden in this thing, alright? Gotta destroy it to find out. There. Serious enough for you now?"

"You're beyond help," Calton grumbled, shaking his head as he returned to his search. "Just get off your high horse and keep looking. We don't have all day."

Brown, unfazed, went right back to his rampage, turning the room upside down with his usual lack of concern for anything other than his own amusement.

Meanwhile, Calton's keen eyes spotted something of interest. "Well, well," he said, a slight smirk playing at his lips as he retrieved a shoebox from under the couch. "Found something." He pulled it out, tossing aside some old magazines and dust to reveal the contents: a spool of thick nylon rope, a utility knife, and some childhood photos of Nirvana.

"Hey," he called to Tom. "Find what you came for yet? I'm about ready to wrap this up."

"Not yet," Tom replied.

Calton raised an eyebrow. "What exactly are you looking for?"

"A small purse," Tom said, glancing toward the bedroom.

"Don't bother with that pile of junk," Calton said, waving a hand dismissively toward a corner Brown had already trashed. "I did see a black fanny pack in the bedroom closet. It was hanging on the inside of the door. Go check it out. That's probably what you're after."

Tom nodded quickly. "That's it. I'll grab it."

"Hold on." Calton's voice sharpened, his tone suddenly authoritative.

Tom stopped, looking back at him, confused. "Yeah?"

"You want Brown to come with you?" Calton asked, a sly smile creeping onto his face. "I did promise your brother I'd keep an eye on you. He can be your bodyguard for the day."

Tom ignored the jab, more concerned with getting the job done than dealing with Calton's teasing. Without another word, he walked down the narrow hallway and into the bedroom.

The room was neat, almost unnervingly so. He moved toward the closet and opened the door gingerly, letting it creak on its hinges. His eyes scanned the rack of clothes for the fanny pack Calton had mentioned. As he found it, his head knocked into a floating wire shelf, sending an old, weathered journal tumbling to the floor.

The journal landed with a soft thud, its pages flapping open as it fell. Tom reached down to retrieve it, his fingers brushing against the worn leather cover. He gazed at the open pages, his eyes catching on the hastily scrawled paragraphs, the ink smudged in places. He studied the words for a moment, feeling a strange pull to read on. Something about the disarray of the writing intrigued him, as though the journal held a fragment of something important, something unfinished.

He leaned in, the dim light casting shadows over the text as he read, the weight of the words heavy in the quietness of the room.

06/25/04

Another day drags on. Suffocating. Dull. There's this gnawing ache in my chest, growing sharper with every passing hour. Why does it have to hurt so much just to think of Nina? This emptiness is real. Unbearable. I feel like I'm falling apart when she's not around. When she doesn't acknowledge my existence. I'm nothing. A ghost. A shell. How do I fill this void? How do I keep going when it feels like part of me is already gone?

7/16/04

A blonde walked into the workshop today, all smiles and laughter, moving with a kind of effortless charm. I watched her for a while, a quiet observer, as she flirted and joked with the others. Our eyes met for a split second. Something passed between us—something that struck me with a sudden jolt. A look. A glance that echoed Nina. That same electric spark I've never been able to forget... Who am I kidding? Every woman I see, in some way, reminds me of her. I can't escape it.

8/3/04

It makes me mad how Nina still refuses to let me see her. I drove all this way, pouring myself into this futile hope, and what did I get in return? All I wanted was to say hello. I just wanted to see her, to hear her voice again. She's constantly in my thoughts, and this brain of mine—this rotten, twisted thing—won't shut off. God, if you're really out there, please... show me a sign. Show her that we belong together. That this endless pain, this endless separation, doesn't have to be the way of it. Stop her from hurting me anymore.

10/1/04

Saw Nina today. Finally she let me visit. I had one shot—one chance—and I blew it. Completely. I can't even begin to imagine how much she must hate me right now. HATE me. How do I make her see? How do I make her want the same thing I do? She's right. She deserves more than I can give. She deserves someone who isn't so broken. But still... we're perfect together. If only she can see that. If only she can understand we are meant to be.

Tom's eyes skimmed over the entries, each word sinking deeper into his consciousness. His focus was absolute, as if the ink on the paper had a pulse, a rhythm of its own. Jo's words—a raw, unapologetic confession—spoke to something buried within her, something far beyond the reckless, cold-blooded criminal she'd been painted to be. There was desperation in her tone, a desperate yearning that bled through every line. A devotion that spiraled into obsession, pushing her toward something that sounded more like a plea for salvation than anything else. *Nirvana*. She was reaching for it, clawing her way through her own wreckage.

Tom couldn't help but feel it—a pull of empathy, faint but undeniable. He saw her words not as mere ink on paper but the frantic cry of someone lost, someone who longed to escape the chaos they'd created. He felt the cold mass of her suffering. His heart softened, less burdened than it had been in hours.

But it was fleeting.

A sound—the scrape of a chair against the floor, followed by the hurried shuffle of feet—pierced the silence of the room. It was jarring, a sudden disruption that snapped him out of his trance. His body stiffened, instinct kicking in. The fanny pack, still in his hands, was quickly shoved into his coat pocket. The tension in his muscles coiling as his feet carried him toward the door. His movement was deliberate, quiet—every step calculated to keep him from being noticed. His hand touched lightly the doorframe as he lifted crept toward the hallway, lifting his head just enough to peer into the living room.

What he saw stopped him dead in his tracks.

Calton. Held hostage. The gun at his temple was unyielding, its cold muzzle pressing against his skin, a silent promise of death. The knife pressed to his throat gleamed dangerously, the edge threatening to slice open the tender flesh at any moment. Jo's grip was tight, merciless, her eyes cold and unwavering. Calton was frozen, his breath shallow, his body trembling ever so slightly.

"Easy... take it easy..." Calton's voice was shaky, a strained whisper that barely carried across the room. The words were more of a plea than a command, his eyes wide with fear, searching for any sign of pity.

Tom felt a knot twist in his stomach. He could see the terror on Calton's face, feel the raw intensity of the moment press against him like a vice. But he knew better than to move—his body went perfectly still, blending into the shadows, hoping beyond hope that he wouldn't be noticed.

But Jo's eyes were sharp. Too sharp. They cut through the dim light, locking onto him with pinpoint precision.

"You!" Her voice rang out like a crack of thunder, searing and dangerous. "Hiding back there. Don't think I don't see you. Come on out from the bedroom, now!"

Her words were a demand, not a request. The stern certainty in her voice brooked no hesitation. Tom froze, his pulse hammering in his ears. He had no choice.

Slowly, carefully, he stepped out from behind the doorframe, his arms raised in a gesture of surrender. He made his way across the room to the kitchen counter. His eyes fixed on Jo as he reached a safe distance.

"Stop right where you are! Don't come any closer or I will slash him up right here and now." Jo stood tall, every muscle tight with warning, a storm barely held at bay in her eyes. Her body was a steel trap, coiled, ready to snap.

Tom stood where he was. He didn't flinch, a mask of forced calm on his face. "Hi, Jo. Do you remember me?"

Jo studied him. Her eyes flickered, distant at first, then recognition. It took her a moment—longer than it should have—but then she spoke, her tone almost disbelieving. "It's you... that plumber guy." She chuckled dryly, but there was no humor in it. "Guess I've underestimated you."

Tom's heart skipped a beat, but before he could respond, a howl erupted from the far corner of the room. *"Drop your weapons!"* Brown's silhouette loomed there, a menacing figure holding his gun and targeting Jo's head like it was an extension of his own rage. "If you know what's good for you, you'll let him go," his voice was low and guttural, vibrating with tension.

Jo didn't even blink. She stood her ground, the embodiment of granite resolve. Her lips parted, but there was no fear, no hesitation—only pure, cutting defiance. "Will you take his place, then?" she spat, her words laced with venom.

Brown's eyes narrowed, his finger twitching on the trigger. "This isn't a negotiation," he snarled, each word coated in cold contempt.

"You are going to kill me either way, so why should I care what you say?"

His jaw tightened, his face a mask of barely re-strained violence. "You will lose, kid. Big time. Let me tell you that now," he warned, his words slow, like he was sa-voring every moment of his power.

In turn, Jo smirked. "Oh, is that your idea of a threat?" Her tone was almost mockingly sweet. "Too bad I don't scare easily, especially not by you, roach head. I'm not afraid to die, unlike you, roaches. But if anything were to happen to me, one thing I know for certain is that I'm tak-ing this one with me."

A slight flex of her elbow further secured her lock around Calton, a conscious reminder of who held the power in this little game. Calton's breath hitched as the blade grazed his wafer-thin skin, the faintest few seconds of touch but enough to send his heart into overdrive. His pulse pounded in his neck as fear surged through his veins like fire. He could feel the force of her control, a con-stant, suffocating pressure. He could barely breathe, bare-ly speak. "Easy... take it easy..."

"Tell that to your minion," Jo shot back. "I don't mind being the bad guy. But it's your head that's in jeopardy."

Calton swallowed hard, his mouth dry, his legs shak-ing. "Why don't we all just cool it, huh?" He tried, his voice a pathetic attempt at defusing the escalating tension.

Jo scoffed, "Cool it?" Her voice dropped, mocking him. "I came home and saw my apartment trashed—*you* want me to relax? If I blew your head off by accident, I could argue breaking and entering. Self-defense."

"You are under arrest, big shot. We don't need a war-rant to search your apartment," Brown informed her, his smug sneer back in full force. "Try and argue that."

"Yeah, well, do you see me in handcuffs?"

"If you think you can bicker your way out of this, you're talking to the wrong person."

Jo's gaze met Brown's head-on, unyielding. "And if you think you'll get me by putting your partner's life on the line, you should seriously rethink your occupation, roach head," she retorted, her tone razor-sharp.

All that constant belittling had been building inside Brown like a slow-burning fuse, each word from Jo a spark, each sneer a provocation he couldn't ignore. His blood simmered with rage, thick and boiling, and his hackles stood on end as if his very body was preparing to lash out. He could barely hold his tongue. Playing meek and puny wasn't in his DNA, though there was nothing he could do about the sting in his chest—the bruised ego and the tiny heart that couldn't take one more insult. He had to do something.

His index finger hovered over the trigger, tense with possibility. For a long time, it wavered there, each pulse tempting him to pull it, to end the entire farce with one clean shot. *It's all about the aim*, he reminded himself. *Precision. Just cause.* But each time he thought he was ready, a different part of him pulled back. *Culpable negligence.* The word played in his head like a warning bell. The line between doing the job and being totally reckless.

If only he could toss aside all that moral baggage, all those rules, and act purely on instinct. If he could forget about the consequences for just a second, he would have made his shot already. Instead he needed something first—something solid, a guarantee. One slip. Just a momentary distraction, one lapse in Jo's concentration, something—anything—that would give him the green light to pull the trigger without paying for it later.

Suddenly, the shrill buzz of a phone pierced the tension in the room. It was Calton's. It rang for far too long before finally cutting off. The seconds stretched painfully until Brown's own phone rang. Both agents knew what it meant. Mark was checking in, covertly keeping tabs. They shared a brief, reassuring glance.

Jo's voice broke out "Nobody moves, or I will end him," she spat, her gaze darting between the men, her every movement controlled. She backed away toward an open window, dragging Calton with her, her arm like iron around his neck.

Brown's eyes narrowed, a smirk twisting his lips. "Eleven floors is a long way down. I wouldn't jump if I were you... too messy for us to clean up afterward."

His words were a calculated jab, trying to provoke, trying to hold onto some semblance of dominance. But Jo was not threatened in the least. In turn, she erupted in a fit of hysterical laughter, her breath coming in gasps between peals of chaotic sound.

"Ha! Hahahaha!" she howled, as if the words he'd just spoken were the punchline to some dark joke only she understood.

Brown was momentarily stunned, his confidence faltering. "What's so funny, huh?"

Jo gasped between breaths, still fighting to compose herself. She paused for dramatic effect, her eyes gleaming, a wicked glint that made Brown's skin prickle. "I've had plenty of ultimatums thrown at me. But yours... yours has got to be the lamest I've ever heard. Ha... haha... haha!" She doubled over with another fit of laughter, as though the absurdity of his words was too much to bear.

Brown's face flushed a deep shade of crimson. Nobody—*nobody*—had ever dared ridicule him like this. Not even his closest colleagues had made a joke at his expense and got away with it. And here Jo was, *laughing*. Laughing at him.

The insult clearly stung, a searing pain through his pride. His vision tunneled. His heart raced, each beat a drum of pure, unfiltered rage. "I will get you eventually... I swear to God, I will!"

His voice was raw, desperate. He wasn't just threatening her anymore; it was personal. All he could think about now was retaliation.

Jo's lips curled into a sly, half-smile. "Go on. Swear away," she said coolly, "If only God would stop His ambivalence and hear you out. He's already failed me plenty of times, but feel free to try. I'd love to see Him deliver on *someone's* wishes. Maybe even a miracle or two..."

The standoff had escalated into a fragile stalemate, the kind that stretched long enough to suffocate the hope of resolution. Just when it seemed like any possibility of peace was too far out of reach, Tom, who had been quietly watching the situation unfold, decided to give it a shot.

"God hasn't failed you," he said, his voice steady with quiet resolve. "He's trying to guide you back to the right path. You've just been too stubborn to see it."

Jo's eyes flicked to him, like a hawk locking onto its prey. "Well, well, well. Mr. Plumber has something to say, does he? I almost forgot you were here. You really think that's what this is? You think *that's* why He sent you here—to tear down everything I've fought for, everything I've built with my own two hands, and then preach His laws at me?"

"We've come to talk."

"Talk? Ha... you've got some nerve. You think I'm gonna sit here and listen to you, an undercover cockroach pretending to be some kind of savior, telling me who I am and what I should do?"

"I'm not a cop, Jo. If that makes any difference."

She narrowed her eyes. "If you're not one of them, then what the hell are you doing here?"

Tom hesitated, choosing his words wisely. "I've come in place of Nirvana."

At the mention of Nirvana's name, something shifted in Jo. For a fraction of a second, her face softened—just the briefest flicker—before it hardened again, her features bolting into that familiar mask of resistance. She straightened, a practiced coldness flooding her expression, as though she was trying to will herself into emotional numbness. Her posture shifted subtly, but Tom caught it—a crack in her armor, however fleeting.

"She would've come herself, but this is all too much for her right now," Tom continued, watching her carefully, weighing the impact of his words.

Jo's gaze flashed with something like hope, quickly smothered by doubt. "You've talked to her... Is that what she coached you to say? You can't take me down by force, so now you're trying to tame me with the gospel? Well, you can tell her that won't work. God's dead... he's dead! So save your sermon for someone who still believes in that crap."

Tom's expression remained genuine, calm. "She didn't coach me to say anything. I want to help you."

Jo paused, her breath catching in her throat. Then her voice came, quieter now, but brittle, raw. "Tell me this, Tom... How is she?"

"She's doing fine. Still in recovery."

A shadow of concern passed over her features, before she masked it again with the practiced indifference of someone used to hiding vulnerability. She continued, "Where is she? Did they send her back to Heartstone?"

"No. She's staying with me for now. She'll want her own place later."

"You don't want to pamper her too much. She'll end up hating you if you do," she said, as though speaking from bitter experience.

Tom responded with a quiet firmness. "She's a strong, independent woman. I've come to learn that. Jo, listen—she still thinks of you. Despite everything that's happened, she still cares."

"That's a horseshit lie."

"It's the truth, and you know it," he insisted, "Deep down, you know it."

Jo's eyes spoke something unspoken, a well of self-loathing that seemed to pull her down deeper with every word. "She hates me. There's no doubt about it. Just like she hated her mother, she wants me gone."

"She does not—"

"Shut up! You don't know anything about us. Nina and I—we have history you'll never understand. She deserves better than me. She always has."

"You're right that I don't understand your relationship, and it honestly baffles me how she can still protect someone who's put her through so much. But she does. And she needs you, Jo." Tom paused, eyes locking onto Jo's with a mix of concern and perseverance. "She needs you to be alive and well. What do you think she'd say if she were here, seeing you like this?"

Jo swallowed hard. Her expression was pained, but it was no longer quite so hardened. She seemed to shrink back, as though Tom's effort was beginning to reach the fragile parts of her she had worked so hard to shield. "She would've scolded me. Told me to stop being stubborn," she said, her voice faltering. "She would've told me to let go of my anger, before it could destroy everything."

"She would be torn apart if anything were to happen to you. She can't lose you, Jo. She needs all the support she can get right now. She really can't afford to lose a dear friend."

"You still think I can support her when I can't even save myself?"

"That's why I wanted to help," Tom pressed on. "I still do. But you need to let me. Let us."

Jo pondered his heartfelt words, very much tempted to take up his offer. Her somber demeanor began to alter, coming out of its shadow of gloom. "You think she'd want to see me? Not now, but maybe in the future? When she feels ready to reconcile?"

"I'm sure she would," Tom replied gently, his tone sincere. "She just needs some time to heal."

Jo nodded slowly, her posture shifting ever so slightly, as if she were finally starting to breathe again. She seemed less tense, less rigid, but there was still a heaviness in her eyes.

The dark presence of Brown lingered in the corner of the room, his simmering rage still palpable. His eyes never left Jo, the coldness in them a silent warning.

"I didn't mean for things to get so out of hand," Jo said, her words a childlike remorse, as if she were apologizing for something far larger than herself. It was a tone that, for all its softness, could not undo the damage already done.

"I understand. We can all learn to be a little more forgiving," Tom said, his voice attempting to keep steady, though it wavered as he spoke for the others. He cast a quick glance toward Brown, silently hoping for some form of acknowledgment—a sign of mutual understanding. But Brown remained unmoving, his gaze fixed ahead, unyielding. The absence of any response, not even a slight glance his way, sent a chill through Tom. This had him worried, but not that he could do anything about it.

"I'm going to let go of him at a count of three," Jo said, each word heavy with the realness of her own fear. "I promise I will go with you quietly. I won't resist. If you can, in turn, promise me safety."

Tom nodded, his eyes tight with resolve. "Of course. Calton?"

"Safety first... of course," Calton replied, didn't hesitate for a second.

"Brown?"

Brown's finger twitched on the trigger. He had been looking for an opening to fire. Tom saw the unrelenting, dark hunger in his eyes—the kind that only came when vengeance had consumed a man's soul.

"What do you say, Brown? Do you agree?" he prompted with the slightest edge of desperation. The words felt too light, too hollow against the looming storm.

"Sure," Brown spat out eventually, his lips curling into something that might have been a grin, but wasn't. He lowered the gun just slightly. "Whatever you say, buddy."

Following Brown's acknowledgment, all eyes snapped to Jo. The room was still, the air thick with anticipation."All right... a deal's a deal..." Her voice was a fragile thread that barely held her together. With a deep, shaky breath, she counted, each number a slow, reluctant surrender to fate. "One... two... three."

As Jo let go, Calton sprang forward. His body seemed to ignite with motion. In roughly the same instant, a sudden explosion of noise—a gunshot—ripped through the room. Tom heard the click of Brown's gun, the sound unmistakable, final.

His heart sank as he saw Jo's head snap back violently, her body jerking in agony, then—two more shots in quick succession. Her chest took the blows, each one puncturing deep into her flesh. "NO!" he cried out, but it was too late. It was too late in terms of salvation, in terms of saving Jo. The damage had been done. She was already slipping away, the light fading from her eyes, and all he could do was watch in horrified helplessness.

Jo's eyes widened, a mix of confusion and pain—until the life drained from them. Her body collapsed backward, pulled as if by gravity itself, and in that last, tragic moment, she was swallowed by the open window, her limp form falling into the void.

Tom rushed to the window, frantic, his hands gripping the sill as he stared down into the abyss. His chest felt as though it might explode, rage, grief, and guilt all twisting together into something lethal. His fists clenched, nails digging into the wood, the anguish inside him so intense it made him sick.

Brown and Calton were already moving on, discussing cleanup procedures in the cold, indifferent way that only those who had long since buried their humanity could manage. Tom, trembling, his hands shaking with fury, stepped into Brown's path, blocking his way.

"Why did you do that?" he growled, his voice thick with frustration. "She surrendered! She *surrendered!*"

"Did she?" Brown said sarcastically, a cruel grin stretching across his face as he shrugged. "I didn't get the memo."

Tom felt his blood boil. "You agreed—*goddammit!*"

"I don't negotiate with lowlifes," Brown replied flatly, "especially not a loudmouth who thinks she can talk her way out of everything."

"You were upset she had crossed you. So you went as far as killing her," Tom spat with cold clarity.

"Wrong. I was following a plan of action," Brown countered smoothly, dismissing the accusation. "And if I'm being honest, *you* owe me your life now, flower boy."

"You heartless son of a—" Tom began, but his words were cut short as he surged forward, grabbing Brown by the collar and yanking him off balance. His knuckles burned with the intensity of his grip, his fury blazing through him like wildfire. Brown's teeth ground together, his eyes flaring with irritation, but before anything could escalate, Calton was there, stepping between them.

"Come on, guys, break it up," Calton said in a low, firm voice. "We're all adults here. Let's act like it."

Reluctantly, Tom released his grip, though his hands trembled, fingers still itching for something to crush. Brown straightened his shirt, taking a moment to collect himself before speaking again.

"Not that I need to justify anything to you, but I'll explain so you get your closure. Ultimately, I felt threatened, so I took the precaution of taking her down before she could cause us real harm. You know, life-saving stuff."

"You cold-blooded bastard... Say something wise, would you, Calton? You were there. You saw."

Calton, standing a little apart from the scene, sighed deeply. "What do you want me to say?" he said, his voice almost resigned. "It is what it is. And if I were to pass judgment, I'm with Brown. There's a principle we live by as officers: 'Never trust a criminal.' No one could predict what she might've done next. Who are you to say she wouldn't have turned on us in a second and caused a bloodbath? It's never worth the risk."

Brown's smirk deepened. "There are some things you won't understand unless you're one of us. Just because you *play* a cop doesn't make you one. Now, go ahead with your whiny little ways and let us real cops finish the job..."

The sound of approaching sirens broke the air. The ambulance arrived, lights flashing, but Tom was already gone, slipping out the back before the crowd of onlookers could start to gather, drawn by the commotion. He couldn't bear it. He wouldn't.

Inside his car, the door slammed shut with a finality that almost felt like a death knell. It was as if the metal of the vehicle could somehow shield him from the chaos outside. He buried his face in his hands, pressing hard against his eyes as the loss crushed him. His body shook, wracked with sobs.

A sharp chime from his phone broke the turmoil inside him. It was a call from Nirvana. He fought to steady himself, forcing his tears back, swallowing the flood of his emotions. With a deep breath, he wiped his eyes and pulled himself together. He took one last look at the rearview mirror, gathering every scrap of strength he had left, and then turned the ignition. He was heading home—home to her. She was waiting, unaware of the nightmare he carried with him, expecting him to bring news.

But Tom knew, as he drove, that nothing would ever be the same again.

37

ARE YOU A religious person?" Lloyd, the cab driver, asked, his gaze fluttered briefly to the rearview mirror, studying Nirvana with a casual curiosity.

Nirvana stiffened slightly, her fingers absentmindedly twiddling the crucifix around her neck. The pendant caught the light, glinting.

"No," she answered. "Why?"

Lloyd chuckled softly, his tone warm but probing. "I see you've been messing with that thing around your neck."

"Oh... this." Nirvana hesitated, her fingers faltering in their movement. She paused, contemplating whether to say more. "A dear friend of mine gave it to me," she added and left it at that.

"Ah," Lloyd replied, a soft hum of understanding in his voice. He didn't push further.

The car slowed as they approached their destination.

"Here we are. 15 Park Street," he announced.

Nirvana gazed out of the cab window at the barren intersection, where the frosted streets met a scattering of run-down houses. A chill crept into her bones, but it wasn't just from the cold. There was something unsettling about the area—an unspoken heaviness that made her wary.

"Can you wait here? I won't be too long," she asked Lloyd.

Lloyd was eyeing the neighborhood with equal trepidation, his hands gripping the wheel a little too tightly. "No can do," he replied with blunt honesty, his gaze darting warily to the cracked pavement outside. "I usually avoid coming here. Too many bad memories, if you catch my drift."

"But you agreed to take me this far..." Nirvana persisted, her voice pleading now, eyes flicking nervously to the empty street. "I can pay you more if that helps. Fifty now, fifty later—just wait, please."

He hesitated, his jaw tightening. "Look, ma'am, I'm not saying I don't want your money. I'm saying I'd rather not risk my life for it. Last time I waited around here, I got held up at gunpoint—broad daylight, just like today. Cold, just like today. Not worth it."

Despite Nirvana's continued attempts to persuade, Lloyd remained firm. So she paid him, reluctantly gathering her things. As she was stepping out of the cab, she caught a glimpse of Lloyd's eyes softened by a flicker of pity.

"Fine—fine. You've got me," he said, finally relenting. "I could use a lunch break anyway. I'll come back in... twenty minutes. How does that sound?"

Nirvana managed a faint smile, relief washing over her. "Thank you, Lloyd," she said, her voice lighter. She waved him off as he drove away, the sound of his engine fading into the distance.

"15 Park Street, #63... 63..." she said the address to herself, checking the street sign again, then the mailbox. A deep breath, then she walked up to the weathered front door and rang the doorbell.

A moment passed before the door creaked open, revealing a man who seemed to have just woken from a long nap. His hair was unkempt, and his ripped undershirt hung loosely over his bulging belly. He blinked at her, squinting against the daylight.

"Good afternoon, sir," Nirvana said, her voice steady but polite. "My name is Nirvana Shor. I'm an acquaintance of Jean."

He yawned, scratching his chest. "Jean... who?"

"Jean Malloy. I'm told her son lives here. Elijah?"

The man's expression flushed with irritation, but he didn't move to shut the door. "You've got to be kidding me..." He yelled into the house, "Barbara! Some lady's here asking about your daughter!"

"Whose daughter?" a voice barked back from inside.

"YOURS!"

"Tell them I'm not here!" The voice was sharp, dismissive.

"Too late for that. I'm already talking to her!" he hollered back.

The man grumbled as he staggered inside. A woman appeared a moment later. She stood in the doorway, arms crossed, her face drawn with suspicion.

"Who the hell are you?" she demanded, her tone hostile, glaring at Nirvana.

"I'm Nirvana Shor. I was sent here by your daughter, Jean," Nirvana explained, her voice careful but firm.

"I don't know any Jean," the woman spat, rolling her eyes. "What is this, some kind of joke? Do you people have no shame? Look at this place!" She motioned behind her, as if to dismiss the very existence of the cluttered home. "Whatever problems you had with her, I'm not your therapist. Jean doesn't live here anymore. So unless you're here to do something useful, get lost. SHOO!"

"I'm not looking for her," Nirvana said, her voice cool now, despite the rudeness. "I'm here to speak with her son. Elijah."

At the mention of his name, the woman's demeanor shifted, just slightly. A hint of wariness crossed her face, but it was gone before Nirvana could register it. "Elijah?" she said, her voice suddenly lowering, cautious. "What do you know about him? You're not with the IRS, are you?"

Nirvana shook her head, puzzled. "I don't know anything about him. I'm just here to deliver something *to* him."

"Deliver something? Which is? I don't see you holding anything."

"I've been advised to give it to him personally."

"Personally, huh? I've heard that one before." She let out a humorless chuckle. "The day a daughter hides things from her mother, that's the day that family falls apart."

"Thought you said you didn't know Jean?" Nirvana challenged, eyebrows raised.

"Oh, give me a break! I don't have time for this," the woman snapped. "You want to see Elijah, fine. He usually gets home from school at this hour."

"I'll wait," Nirvana said, her voice steady.

"Suit yourself." The woman scowled, then her voice muffled, "By the way, you don't happen to have any cash on you, do you?"

Nirvana stiffened. When she shook her head, the woman's face twisted in irritation before she slammed the door shut.

Before Nirvana could collect her thoughts, a voice called down from above.

"It's useless reasoning with a couple of sponges who just suck the life out of everything. Trust me, I've tried. You'll have better luck bribing them with booze."

Nirvana tilted her head, looking up in surprise. A small boy, his legs dangling over the edge of the roof, looked down at her. His face was scruffy, his eyes bright but cautious.

"Who are they to you?" Nirvana asked him.

The boy jumped down, landing in a snow pile with surprising agility for someone so small. He brushed off the snow and stood, his posture a curious mix of confidence and vulnerability. "He's nobody. She's my grandmother," he said, voice flat, as if it didn't matter. "She tells people she's my mother. Tax benefits, you see? At least she believes there's a difference. She's just looking for ways to fund her drinking." He looked up at Nirvana, studying her. "So you're a friend of my real mom?"

Nirvana took a deep breath, looking him over. "You're Elijah," she said. "I've known your mom for a long time, that's all. We're not exactly close, barely on a first-name basis."

Elijah's eyes narrowed, and a sardonic grin tugged at his lips. "What? You too fancy to be friends with her? You came all this way for her, and you're the first friend of hers who's ever dropped by." His tone was a mix of mockery and curiosity.

Nirvana paused, considering her words carefully. "I'm not any fancier than the next person you see."

For a brief moment, Elijah fell silent, taken aback.

She took the opportunity to change the conversation. "What happened to your face?" she asked, noticing the bruise on his cheek.

"I fell," Elijah mumbled, his gaze shifting uneasily. "But that's not important." He shrugged it off, visibly trying to avoid the topic. "Wanna hear how I figured out my grandma's little scheme?"

Nirvana's eyebrows arched. "Sure."

"Well, people are more honest when they're drunk. And my grandma's drunk a lot. She's said stuff, and I've been listening. One day, I found my birth certificate. And right there, in black and white, it says 'Jean Malloy,' not Barbara Malloy."

"You're a smart little person," Nirvana said, surprised. "You are seven?"

"Eight," Elijah corrected her, a touch of pride in his voice. "Had my own little birthday party last month. A cupcake Mrs. Goodman gave me in math class and a half-candle I found by the side of the road."

"So, the usual," Nirvana smiled, a small but genuine warmth spreading in her chest as she was reminded of a similar occurrence in her own childhood.

Elijah giggled. "Hey, I can't complain. At least I'm not stuck working in a sweatshop like some orphans in Asia. They barely survive. I've got it good."

Nirvana's smile softened at his unexpected maturity. She pulled out the letter from Jean, still clutched in her fanny pack, and handed it to Elijah. His fingers hesitated before taking it. He studied the envelope with careful scrutiny before tearing it open. Inside were two hundred-dollar bills and a handwritten note:

I love you always and with all my heart.
— From Mom

Instead of the warmth Nirvana had expected, Elijah shoved the money into his pocket and crumpled the note into a ball.

"You have a lighter?" he asked, voice flat.

"Why?" Nirvana asked, confused.

"I want to burn this," he muttered, his face twisting with frustration and somewhere in there—anger.

When she shook her head, he tossed the note to the ground, as if it were nothing more than trash. He turned and started walking away, not waiting for a response.

Nirvana bent down to pick up the note, smoothing it out. She looked at the message, her heart aching. "You think she lied to you," she said, quietly, but firmly. "But if she was going to lie, why would she go through all this trouble?"

Elijah spun around, his anger flaring. "So you think my love is for sale? She thinks she can buy me with money."

"I don't think she's trying to buy your love," Nirvana replied gently. "I think she's just doing the best she can. Two hundred dollars may not be much to some people, but for her, it's a lot to give."

"How do you know that?"

"Because I was in a place like that once," she said, her voice soft, almost distant.

Elijah stopped in his tracks, his posture softening as he absorbed her words. After a long pause, he asked, "Where was that?"

"Heartstone," Nirvana said simply.

"The madhouse?" Elijah said, his voice thick with disbelief. For a moment, his tough exterior faltered, and a flicker of raw hurt flashed across his face. "I always thought she just left me for some rich guy... that she'd be living the high life, getting spoiled, showered with gifts every day. What am I to her..." He trailed off, and his gaze wandered, as if he was retreating into a place where those thoughts made sense.

"What made you think that?"

He looked at Nirvana. "The mind is a curious thing. When you're left with gaps, you fill them however you can. Plus, my grandma... I should have known better than to believe a word she said," he said, his voice quieter now, less defiant.

"Now you don't have to guess anymore," Nirvana reassured him. "The truth is right in front of you."

He nodded slowly, a glimmer of relief mingling with the sadness in his eyes.

"Looks like my job here is done," she said softly. "I should go now."

But as Nirvana turned to leave, Elijah rushed to stop her. "Wait... I don't really hate her. It's just... I get picked on because of my size. I'm the smallest in my class. All the other kids have their parents to back them up, but my grandma? She doesn't care. She makes it worse."

"If they want to tease you, they will find any reason," Nirvana said.

"But listen to this," he continued, his tone bitter. "Just yesterday, a new kid's dad marched into the principal's office after his whiny son got a bloody nose from Billy the Bully. And now? The kid's untouchable. Golden. It wasn't even that bad of a punch, not compared to the crap I have to deal with. You get what I'm saying?"

"I know. It's not fair."

"And I can't fight them all," he muttered, his shoulders slumping as the burden of his words settled between them. He let out a heavy sigh, his voice softer now, more vulnerable. "Is life always this hard?"

"No, it gets harder," Nirvana told him candidly. "The bullies never go away. And you're right, you can't fight them all. But the truth is, you're only as weak as you believe yourself to be. Instead of wasting your energy on people who couldn't care less about you, shift your focus to those who do. Because, no matter how tough life gets, you know you always have someone who loves you unconditionally. Even if they're not there physically, they're with you—in here." She placed her hand over her heart. "Love like that is rarer than you think, and it's something worth holding on to."

Elijah paused, taking in her words. A slow, reluctant smile spread across his face. "Can I see her? Can I visit my mom?" His voice wavered with longing, as though this could be the thing that could heal his emotional wound.

"You'll need approval from the hospital," Nirvana said, "and an adult to accompany you."

He groaned. "Grandma? Pff. Like that's going to happen."

Nirvana's gaze softened. She wasn't about to shatter a child's fragile hope of reconnecting with his mother, so she thought on her feet. After a brief moment of silence, she spoke gently, as if the idea had just occurred to her. "Well, I suppose I can pay my old doctor a visit. It's been a while," she said, offering the suggestion with a slight smile.

"When?" Elijah asked eagerly, his eyes lighting up. "I can go with you. I'm free anytime." He flashed her a wide, hopeful grin.

Nirvana raised an eyebrow. "Don't you have school?"

Elijah waved her off dismissively. "Nah, school can wait. This is way more important. But..." He hesitated. "Do you think she'd want to see me?"

Nirvana met his gaze with a calm assurance. "I don't see why not. You've turned out to be one fine young man."

At her words, Elijah stood up a little straighter, as if her approval somehow lightened the load on his shoulders. Nirvana continued, "But first, I need to make some arrangements. It'll take me a bit of time. Can you wait?"

"I'm gonna have to."

Before she left, Nirvana scribbled her number on the inside cover of one of his school books, promising to return soon. His eyes sparkled with gratitude as he retrieved the book. Despite his sharp wit and maturity beyond his years, there was still an innocent boy in there, one who believed—just for a moment—that something good might actually come from this.

Back at the intersection, Nirvana's cab was waiting. She slid into the seat with a lighter heart than when she'd gotten out. Lloyd looked at her curiously.

"So, everything went okay?" he asked, the concern in his voice genuine.

"Oh, yes," Nirvana replied, her tone full of quiet satisfaction.

As the cab pulled away, she caught sight of Elijah running after it in the rearview mirror.

"That kid knows you?" Lloyd asked.

"That's Elijah," Nirvana said. "Quick—stop the car!"

The cab screeched to a halt. Elijah caught up, breathless but determined.

"What are you doing here?" she asked Elijah.

"I followed you," he replied, still panting.

"I know, but why?"

Elijah held out a folded-up drawing to her. "I want you to mail this to my mom," he said, his face serious.

Nirvana took the paper from him, feeling his sincerity. "What's this?"

"It's my Valentine's Day project. We don't have stamps or envelopes, but here's five dollars. It should cover the cost. Next time you come, I will have something much nicer ready for her."

"Don't worry about the money," Nirvana assured him. "I will take care of it."

"You sure?"

She affirmed him.

"You are a very generous lady."

"Not always, but I don't mind being one for a good cause."

He smiled. "Thanks. You've done more than anyone else. You've kind of fixed some of the stuff my grandma messed up."

"What's that?"

"My respect for adults," he said with a wry smile. "Have a good trip home. Toodle-oo!"

As the cab pulled away again, Nirvana felt something in her stir. Lloyd was quiet for a moment before speaking. "That was one cheeky kid. A relative of yours?"

"No," Nirvana replied softly. "He's the son of... one of my old friends."

"Ah," Lloyd said with an understanding nod, glancing at her in the mirror. "I wouldn't get too excited though."

"Why's that?" Nirvana asked, curious.

"Well, time changes everything," Lloyd said cynically, "and people change with it. Humans are fickle, it's in our nature. It's inevitable. I just don't want you to get your hopes up too high and set yourself up for disappointment."

"I see," Nirvana responded, her voice steady, "I think I will take my chances."

As they drove off, Nirvana unfolded Elijah's drawing. The picture showed two hands—one small and one slightly larger—joined together in the shape of a heart. On the back, in childlike scrawl:

I love you all the same, Mom.
— From your boy, Elijah

J.Y. Barris is an independent author, artist, mental health advocate, and the founding editor of *Moody Melon Magazine*. She brings creativity and compassion to everything she does, weaving themes of healing and hope through her work. She lives in Minnesota with her husband, Sam, and their son, Maxwell.

Visit her at www.jybarris.com

Follow her at www.instagram.com/jybarris

Subscribe at www.MoodyMelon.com